IT STARTED WITH THE HIJACKING OF FOUR ATOMIC BOMBS . . .

In nine days space shuttle *Antares*, first of the new-generation orbiters, would lift off from Cape Canaveral with an international crew of American, Russian, and European astronauts.

Nine days . . . all the time there was for NASA, the CIA, and Interpol to find four atomic bombs, any *one* of which would be enough to completely destroy *Antares*, a mass of world dignitaries, and most of the surrounding area.

The enemy: a group of vicious killers who refused to bargain, whose members were as willing to die as they were to vaporize millions of innocents. But Zoboa's leader was faceless and invisible, a man whose real identity had never been established . . . and time was running out.

MARTIN CAIDIN

ZOBOA

BAEN
SCIENCE FICTION
BOOKS

ZOBOA

A Baen Books Original

Baen Publishing Enterprises
260 Fifth Avenue
New York, N.Y. 10001

First printing, September 1986

ISBN: 0-671-65588-4

Cover art by David Mattingly

Printed in the United States of America

Distributed by
SIMON & SCHUSTER
TRADE PUBLISHING GROUP
1230 Avenue of the Americas
New York, N.Y. 10020

NOVELS BY MARTIN CAIDIN

Zoboa!★
Killer Station
The Messiah Stone
Marooned★
No Man's World★
The Cape
Four Came Back
Starbright
ManFac★
Jericho 52

Aquarius Mission★   The Mendelov Conspiracy★
Cyborg★   Almost Midnight★
Operation Nuke   Maryjane Tonight At Angels 12★
High Crystal   Wingborn
Devil Take All★   The Final Countdown★
The Last Dogfight★   Three Corners To Nowhere
The God Machine   Deathmate
Anytime, Anywhere   The Long Night
Whip   Cyborg IV
The Last Fathom

★Sold as a major motion picture or TV series

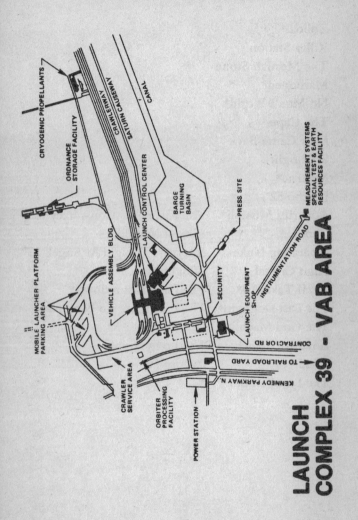

LAUNCH
COMPLEX 39 - VAB AREA

CRYOGENIC PROPELLANTS

ORDNANCE
STORAGE FACILITY

CRAWLERWAY

SATURN CAUSEWAY

CANAL

MOBILE LAUNCHER PLATFORM
PARKING AREA

VEHICLE ASSEMBLY BLDG

LAUNCH CONTROL CENTER

BARGE
TURNING
BASIN

PRESS SITE

SECURITY

CRAWLER
SERVICE AREA

ORBITER
PROCESSING
FACILITY

LAUNCH EQUIPMENT
SHOP

INSTRUMENTATION ROAD

MEASUREMENT SYSTEMS
SPECIAL TEST & EARTH
RESOURCES FACILITY

CONTRACTOR RD

POWER STATION

TO RAILROAD YARD

KENNEDY PARKWAY N.

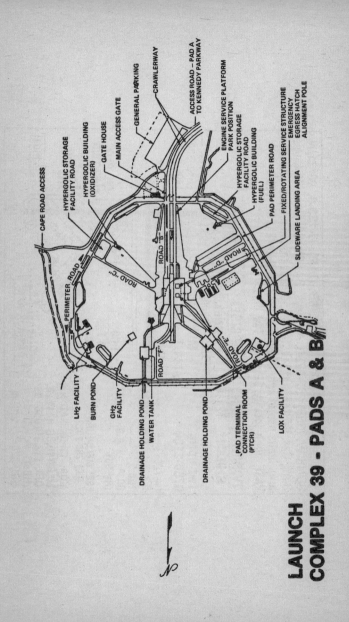

CAPE ROAD ACCESS

HYPERGOLIC STORAGE
FACILITY ROAD

HYPERGOLIC BUILDING
(OXIDIZER)

GATE HOUSE

MAIN ACCESS GATE

GENERAL PARKING

CRAWLERWAY

ACCESS ROAD – PAD A
TO KENNEDY PARKWAY

ENGINE SERVICE PLATFORM
PARK POSITION

HYPERGOLIC STORAGE
FACILITY ROAD

HYPERGOLIC BUILDING
(FUEL)

PAD PERIMETER ROAD

FIXED/ROTATING SERVICE STRUCTURE

EMERGENCY
EGRESS HATCH
ALIGNMENT POLE

SLIDEWARE LANDING AREA

PERIMETER ROAD

ROAD "B"

ROAD "C"

ROAD "D"

ROAD "E"

ROAD "F"

LH₂ FACILITY

BURN POND

GH₂
FACILITY

DRAINAGE HOLDING POND

WATER TANK

DRAINAGE HOLDING POND

PAD TERMINAL
CONNECTION ROOM
(PTCR)

LOX FACILITY

LAUNCH
COMPLEX 39 - PADS A & B

N

SHILOH AIRFIELD. TIX. 35'. 6S. (IAP). U-123.0. 28°31'N 80°48'W. (305) 267-8780. Att days. F-100J. S5. Bcn. H/Motels 3 mi, Car. WRMF 1060 D, 164°/4. Ctm: Overhead p-lns in T-hangar area limits use to acft 12,500 GWT & less. P-lns E. PCL: 118.9 - Rys, VASI, apch lgts ry 36 when Twr clsd.

TWR/CTAF	GRND 121.4	APC/DEP
SHILOH		Patrick
118.9		119.25—0700-2300
Twr oprts		MIA Cntr
0700-2100		124.1—2300-0700

I—TIX• •– • • • – • •		
ILS	OM	MM
108.7	––	––
001°	6.0	0.4
(Ry 36)		

RCO
MLB FSS
123.6

FSS: MELBOURNE
(LC) 269-2022

VOR	FREQ	RAD	NM
MLB	110.0D	341°	26
ORL	112.2D	096°	28
(RBn):			
GGL 375		170°	4

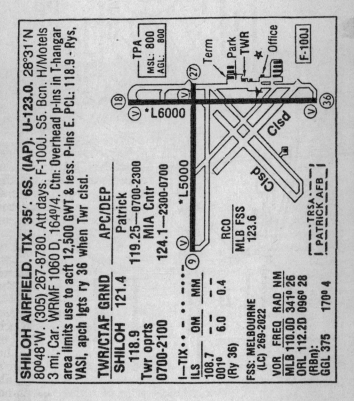

TPA
MSL: 800
AGL: 800

27 — Term — Park — TWR — Office

18 — *L6000

*L5000

Clsd

Clsd

36

F-100J

TRSA
PATRICK AFB

✛ 1 ✛

OPENING MOVES

The little red car rocked steadily from side to side, trembling on its shocks, its polished hood and fenders gleaming under the condominium floodlights along the beach. At regular intervals the ghostly beam of Canaveral Lighthouse hushed over its surface. The MG became more frenetic as it began to bounce on its front and rear springs.

"The fucking thing's alive," Officer John McCabe of the Cocoa Beach police force said in reverent tones. McCabe sat with Sergeant Tom Unster in their patrol car, wreathed in shadows but with a clear view of the shaking MG.

"It ain't alive and it ain't what's fucking," grunted the leathery sergeant. Unster had worked the beach better than twenty years and he'd seen a hell of a lot of animated cars in his time. "You know something?" he said in the casual tone of the grizzled veteran who's seen everything, "Right now, on this beach, counting all the condos, of course, there's more than three thousand apartments where those kids could be screwing. Three thousand! And that ain't counting all them motels. That's another thousand rooms. You walk in, pay for the room, and have at it. Clean sheets, shower, nice and comfortable. *And private*," he added for emphasis. He glanced at the rookie with him and gestured. "You'd think *these* people," he cast a contemptuous look through the windshield, "would have someplace better than that little shit of a car to get it off. They could even hump themselves silly on the sand."

"No, they couldn't," McCabe rebuked his superior, earning a nasty look from Unster. "I mean," he said hastily, "every time you catch them humping on the beach you bust their balls, remember?"

Unster nodded slowly and spit a glob of tobacco juice into a styrofoam cup. Unster wasn't neat. Some of the sticky glob splashed on McCabe's trousers and shoe. He kept his face frozen and his mouth shut. Unster became a real loonie when you complained about his juice spit.

"Yeah, I guess so," Unster said amiably. He hitched up his belt, took another bite from his wad, and motioned impatiently to McCabe. "Ease up on them. No lights and no noise. Not a sound. Just start this thing and let it roll dark behind them. I'll tell you when to hit the blues."

McCabe grinned, started the car, and eased it into gear. Silent except for tires crunching on sand, the police car eased up to the front of the MG until the bumpers of both cars were almost touching. "Stop," Unster said in a whisper. He licked dry lips. This was the best part. He didn't give a rat's ass if these kids wanted to fuck their brains into jelly. He enjoyed the hell out of their reactions to the law coming down on them like the wrath of an outraged god. He motioned with a forefinger. McCabe hit the switches.

Dazzling blue light burst into the MG, turned into blinding white as the police cruiser headlights flashed on. The lights were like an explosion within the small car, which shook even more frantically as the couple within separated in panic. A cry of pain and a shrill scream preceded the doors flying open, and a naked girl sprawled from the passenger side onto the gritty ramp. From the driver's side a naked man flew in a mad scramble of arms and legs. He lit on all fours, turned with a look of hatred at the police car, and was off in a wild dash for thick croppings of sea oats.

2

"Holy shit," McCabe swore in disbelief.

"Damn!" Unster said.

"Is that who I think it was?" McCabe asked. He didn't wait for an answer. "Should I go after him?"

Unster opened his door, turned to the stunned McCabe. "Don't bother. You'd never catch him. He's not only the pilot of the shuttle, he's also a track star. And forget you ever saw him."

Unster walked up to the girl, shivering with fright, hands covering her pubis in an awkward clasp of crossed wrists. The policeman ignored her, reached into the MG, and withdrew her clothes. He held them out to her. "In the police car, miss. Get dressed." She snatched the clothes, gave Unster a helpless animal look of gratitude, and ran to the cruiser.

Unster leaned against the MG and spat tobacco juice onto the sand, shaking his head in disbelief. The fucking commander of *Antares*, for Christ's sake! NASA's primo space cat, screwing himself silly in a fucking MG on the fucking beach in front of the whole fucking world! He turned as the girl appeared before him, clothes hastily donned, hands fluttering.

"Miss, we're going to drive away from here," he told her. He gestured to McCabe to kill the dazzling lights. In the sudden gloom he turned and pointed. "Your hero's up in those bushes, there," he went on, "shivering his precious balls to a fare-thee-well. When we leave, you tell him to come on down and get dressed, and then you drive this piece of tin out of here and don't *ever* let me catch you, *or him*, on this beach again like this. You read me, little sister?"

She gulped, nodded her head furiously, and glanced at the rustling sea oats. When she turned, the police car was backing away. It drove around the MG, the lights came on, and it left up the ramp onto A1A. Chris Johnson stifled a giggle, put two fingers in her mouth, and whistled. "All clear!" she shouted.

Blacky Moran, Commander, USN, Shuttle commander, *Antares*, hotshot NASA astronaut, genuine American hero, stumbled down the sandy slope, flaccid penis covered

3

with brambles and sea oats. Chris Johnson fell back against the MG, laughing hysterically.

They weren't laughing at the Kennedy Space Center eighteen miles north of the hysterical oceanside scene on Cocoa Beach. None of the engineers and flight support team leaders of the National Aeronautics and Space Administration knew of Chris Johnson or her splendid body or her sexual agility in the elbow-bashing confines of her MG. But clearly they knew the commander of the most critical shuttle mission ever scheduled, and mission director Al Manfredini was steaming as he kept glaring at the large digital time readout in the headquarters mission conference room. "Where the hell is that son of a bitch!" he shouted to the assembled astronauts, engineers, and NASA officials.

Susan York tapped a pencil against the polished desk. York weighed 110 pounds, was built tight and sinewy and sexy as hell in her Olympic-athlete body, and was the leading brain for the upcoming *Antares* mission. She was also shuttle First Officer, which meant she rode right seat in the flight deck and was second pilot to fly the huge spacebird. She wasn't at this moment thinking of the mission. She had a clear vision of ramming her knee into the balls of one Blacky Moran for screwing up like this—failing to make a damned important flight readiness meeting. Strange, she mused, how you sometimes needed to wallop a man's gonads to reach his brain. She gestured to Manfredini. "A nickle gets you a buck it's rutting season on the beach," she offered.

"At five thirty in the goddamned morning?" he shouted back.

Susan York offered him the All-American sweet smile. "Gee, sir, I never knew an erection could tell time."

Manfredini crushed a cigarette into an overflowing ashtray. "Damn son of a bitch," he grated. "For two cents I'd kick that perfumed flyboy's ass right off this mission! If he doesn't start keeping his zipper closed from now on, I'll—"

"You won't do shit." The man at the end of the table spoke with quiet power. "I don't even want to *hear* any

4

more of that talk. Moran's the best pilot in this business. You live with it."

They all studied the speaker, as they'd done many times before. Coke Stevens had come into the conference room in his usual dark suit and dark tie and dark briefcase and very dark history and, as always, taken the seat at the far end of the polished table, stuck a slender cigar in his mouth, and blew strong smoke in defiance of the signs forbidding that very action. Often he never said a word. But he was always there and he was here *now*, and because verbalizing seemed almost to go against his religion, whatever it might be, when he did speak Coke Stevens got instant attention. All that Manfredini or anyone else knew about Stevens was that he was plugged straight in to the Oval Room at the White House with no in-betweens.

"The problem isn't Moran," Stevens went on after an appropriate pause. "It's management. You don't recognize the problem. Politically the United States is taking the greatest step into space in our history. Blacky Moran is mission commander. Zipper open or closed, he is *the* man. Only death or crippling illness can remove him from this flight. Your problem, Manfredini, is hardly new. There have been cocksmiths all the way back to the Roman Legions and beyond. If you can't handle our flyboy, he stays, you go and we get a new mission director. Do you read me?"

Manfredini didn't back down an inch, but he also recognized what he had before him. "Oh, I read you loud and clear. But so as to keep the record straight, you're telling me that political considerations transcend everything else on this flight?"

Coke Stevens showed him the barest trace of a smile and no small measure of lofty contempt. "In the lexicon of the modern fable, you bet your sweet ass."

Stevens tapped an ash onto the thickly carpeted floor: another move calculated to be noticed, to irritate and to keep attention on himself. "In the meantime, sir," Stevens added, "we need to discuss that matter of security I mentioned earlier."

Susan York groaned audibly. "Oh, shit, here we go again."

It begins with deep orange light streaking the highest clouds of a Saturday morning. The horizon hugs the remaining stars in a final gasp of night. Many critical events begin to stir. Some involve huge installations and thousands of people, others are deeply human and so subtle they are invisible. One way or the other they are all related, and they will all play their vital roles in the nine days to come.

Among other possibilities, one hundred thousand human beings may live or die. Fate will not deal the last hand until the final moments . . .

It is T Minus 9 Days and counting . . . On the ninth day following this predawn morning the huge shuttle spaceship, Antares, *is to blast off from Pad 39A of the Kennedy Space Center on the east coast of Florida. This is no ordinary mission. It commands the attention of all the world and the compelling attendance of its most influential leaders.*

The world could go to war over its consequences.

Twenty-two miles north and slightly west of the beach where Command Astronaut Blacky Moran struggled into his clothes, a group of pilots, engineers, and mechanics, men and women both, had met through the long night . . .

The bearded man in the grimy flight suit crawled on his hands and knees beneath the table. He moved through a thicket of male and female legs and feet, tapping time to a devastatingly loud rock beat pouring from huge speakers at the far end of the room. His hands and knees banged painfully on beer and whiskey bottles strewn about the floor but he paid them no heed, as oblivious to debris as he was to the occasional boot that whacked into his head or ribs. Above and about him pounded a painful din of shouting, yelling, singing and cursing. Glasses clinked or shattered from being hurled against any convenient wall. Continuing his perilous path beneath the table, Lars Anderson paused a moment to bare stained yellow teeth before a creamy thigh, readied a massive overbite, then remembered his preferred goal. No creamy thigh or full breast, that. Lars paused a moment, blinking at the lights suddenly brighter by a casual coincidental movement of legs and knees the length of the table. He stared at the banner strung across an entire wall.

<u>WELCOME! STRASSER AIR CIRCUS!</u>

"Fuggin' A," Lars grumbled emphatically, and resumed his journey. Finally he reached his goal. Lars balanced himself carefully, reached out with both hands, hauled the furry mass closer to him, and sank his teeth down as hard as he could onto the tail of a huge dog.

One hundred and forty pounds of agonized animal howled piercingly above the party uproar. The huge beast, a thick-haired Bernese Mountain Dog, jerked his tail free to leave Anderson with a mouthful of canine fur, turned with a bellow, and lunged with bared fangs at Anderson. That worthy, having been this same route before, was already clear of the animal's lunge and had shoved the nearest person in the dog's path. Magnum didn't care whose flesh was available for his revenge. Powerful jaws closed on the fat ass of a rotund Arab pilot. Yusuf Hamza leaped into the air in a buttery streak of screaming pain, arms awhirl and feet flailing on empty whiskey bottles. His feet went out from under him, and as he went down for the count his wildly waving arms, grabbing for support, backhanded a beefy German pilot seated at the nearest table.

Major Karl von Strasser blinked several times, the side of his face red from the blow. He turned to impale Hamza with a look of beatific joy that someone could really be that stupid. "Schwein! Better yet, *slimebag!* Even better—*raghead! Wog! Dune monkey!*"

"Fucking Nazi! I'll kill you!" Hamza screamed.

"*Ja!* You try," Strasser invited.

Hamza's foot lashed out into Strasser's groin. It almost made it. *Almost* counts only in pitching horseshoes, not in a barroom brawl. A thick fist snatched at the Arab ankle, squeezed. Hamza screamed in renewed pain and then gasped as his world swung crazily. The powerful German had yanked his foot back and then

7

upwards to dump Hamza onto his back. A very old pro at party time, von Strasser stepped heavily on Hamza's left ankle to pin him to the floor, shoved hard against his straightened right leg, and then with a flourish stepped slowly but very heavily onto Hamza's groin. He remained there with smiles and waves to the others, until the tall, rugged Israeli pilot, Abe Lansky, launched himself through the air to land a tremendous forearm blow alongside von Strasser's head.

That was the signal long delayed the entire night. Tables erupted as Jay Martin, Bill Santiago, Mad Marty Morgan joined the others in a fierce pummeling mob. The huge dog, Magnum, remained in the thick of the scrimmage, protecting his master, Mad Marty, by snapping at anyone who approached him from the sides or rear. The loose assemblage of battlers rolled toward a large plate glass window, seemed to pause a moment, then from sheer inertia and continued punching and kicking and strangle holds crashed through the window with an explosive roar of shattering glass, shouts, barking and screaming. By now there was as much laughing as cursing, and a single voice pierced the uproar. *"Time!"*

The signal was recognized and accepted. Fists relaxed, strangle holds eased, boots rose from groins and teeth unclenched from ears. The bleeding and battered mob began the grisly task of picking themselves up to collapse in more relaxed positions and to sweep away shards of glass. Jay Martin lurched to his feet, stumbled into the main party room where festivities went on unabated, and returned with a bottle of Jack Daniels. He slid to the ground, took a long swallow, and passed the bottle around. *Peace.*

A bright red light flashed on the scene, accompanied by intermittent buzzing. Several men looked up. Above and to one side flashed the sputtering neon letters of *Paradise Motel*. Nearby loomed a large and brightly lit sign reading: *GOOD LUCK, SHUTTLE ANTARES—9 DAYS TO LIFTOFF.*

Von Strasser climbed heavily to his feet, a look of sobriety coming unexpectedly to his face. He leaned against a tree, staring across the waters of the Indian

River to the east. Glowing lights and warning beacons flashed just over the trees, except where he knew he would find the massive cubical bulk of the world's greatest building. There in the monstrous volume of the Vehicle Assembly Building men carried out their ministrations to leave the world behind. Von Strasser was grateful that at this moment no one recognized the emotions striding so heavily through his mind. Many, many years before this moment he had stood on another slope at the edge of water and looked across to where men prepared the flaming giants for the rush upward toward vacuum. But that launch complex was called Peenemunde, and no lights were *ever* visible at night, for a single light would bring down the wrath of thousands of tons of British bombs.

Almost as if history and the present together could share his thoughts, von Strasser saw an intense pencil of light snap into being and spear upward at a sharp angle from the surface. Then another, and yet another, until dozens of the powerful searchlights formed a wide circle, their beams joining in a central area to make day of night where the launch complex held the enormous *Antares*.

Major Karl von Strasser, former fighter pilot ace of the Luftwaffe, veteran of uncounted battles in the skies and destroyer of more than a hundred American and British aircraft in those battles, permitted himself the luxury of a brief smile. *Ah, there is the difference between then and now. We hid ourselves in the dark. Now these people go forth boldly. They are not afraid of the light.*

Engrossed in the then and now, von Strasser failed to see two forms move furtively from a side door of the motel. Nor did he see the car without headlights drive slowly, silently from the parking lot.

He saw and rejoiced silently in the lights and all they stood for.

Across the waters the lights were the signal for hundreds of technicians and engineers to gather at the altar of the space gods, the swarm of worker ants who would attend to the needs of the thick-bodied giant standing tall in its service platforms and awaiting its baptism of flame. Shuttle *Antares* was very much like a god-creature: to be attended, ministered to, afforded millions of tasks large and small before it would swell with volatile liquids and embrace its human crew nine days hence.

There was more than the shuttle itself. Surrounding every such venture to reject a planet is a vast orchestration of supporting motions. There is security along the surface in all directions and a careful watch for offending and potentially dangerous weather. And there is the need to keep the skies clear of intrusion from piloted machines. The systems to support *Antares* performed other tasks as well, for man does not live or work by spacecraft alone.

Beyond the sprawling launch pad complex, surrounded by high metal fencing and under constant surveillance of electronic monitoring systems and remote television cameras closer to the beach, one of those systems was beginning its own ascent from the earth. Infinitely slower, infinitely lighter, the helium-filled gasbag blimp known all along the coast as Fat Albert rose above the tree line, swaying in the offshore breeze as its restraining cable played out slowly. Trucks and vans with CHARTER ELECTRONICS painted on their sides, the technicians wearing the same identifying lettering on their jumpsuits, monitored the ascent of the 157-foot-long silvery shape. As it rose above tree level, Fat Albert was struck by a silent explosion of light from a brilliant searchlight. In the light, trailing beneath the blimp and glistening like festooned tinsel, stretched hundreds of pounds of radar equipment that would be carried as high as twelve thousand feet above the shoreline of the Kennedy Space Center and the Cape Canaveral Launch Center. At the control room of the cable, warning signs rose above the ground in a metallic thicket. KENNEDY SPACE CENTER SURVEILLANCE RADAR. WARNING! HIGH VOLTAGE! WARNING! LETHAL RADIATION.

Once the blimp and its electronic systems were airborne, the radar systems beamed out their signals safely and for long distances, sniffing and hunting for unauthorized aircraft. "Unauthorized" along the platinum coast of Florida meant drug runners, gun smugglers, transporters of illegal aliens, and anything else violating the laws of the land.

Cocaine, deposed dictators, and a giant poised to rip away the shackles of gravity. It made an interesting comment on the human race.

Karl von Strasser saw the blimp clear the trees, watched the flashing strobes strung along the cable snap into life. He sighed. In a few short hours he and these drunken happy fools sprawled on the motel lawn before him would turn back the clock. The former Luftwaffe pilot smiled. The war was more than forty years behind him and he was still flying the old warbirds. Life was good!

On the shores of the Indian River in Florida, Major Karl von Strasser smiled. Far to the southeast, near the waters of the Windward Passage, along the flight line of Guantanamo Air Base on the southern coastline of Cuba, not a smile was to be seen. There is little to smile about in the midst of signs that warn of DANGER! NUCLEAR RADIATION and MAXIMUM SECURITY AREA! and where the guards have both automatic weapons and trembling fingers on triggers. The senior officer on duty checked the time, made a notation on his clipboard, and lifted his head as a buzzer affixed to his ear rattled his skull. He turned. They were right on time. Captain Jeff Baumbach moved his hand more by reflex than directed thought to check the .357 Magnum on his hip. He gestured at the armored vehicle slowing at the gate, its every movement covered by heavy automatic cannon.

"Check 'em *all* out!" Baumbach called. Military Police motioned the truck in between heavy barricades until it was secured. They checked the identity passes of every man, went through, atop and beneath the vehicle, finally sent it through the final barricade to the flight line where two machine gun-armed jeeps rolled alongside as escort. The armored truck stopped by an old Convair 440 twin-engined transport with bright lettering on each side of its fuselage. The cargo doors of the

11

transport of ST. THOMAS ORCHARD FARMS opened wide. The crew wore Air Force fatigues and all carried sidearms.

A master sergeant studied the truck and the men. "Move it, move it," he said impatiently. "Load 'em up. We're behind schedule."

Four cases moved with exquisite care from the truck to the loading conveyor to the aircraft. Each case carried the same identifying line but differing serial numbers. It didn't really matter. NUCLEAR WEAPON MARK 62 is enough of a grabber without any silly serial number.

The bombs were loaded and secured with steel cabling and heavy webbing tiedowns, men signed their names and exchanged papers, doors slammed closed, and the right engine of the Convair whined as the pilots brought power to the metal bird.

Machines for flight were coming to life all throughout the southeastern United States and as far beyond as Guantanamo. But not all the activity took place on huge airfields or vast and complex engineering bastions. In central Florida, horses moved through the tall morning-wet grass of a remote field. It is an ordinary scene of an ordinary Florida ranch . . . until the trees and the fences begin to move.

Tractors pulled the trees, tugging with steel cables to move the wheeled dollies from the soft ground. Pickup trucks and jeeps latched on to fence ends and moved slowly to swing the fences at enormous hinges. Within minutes a clear path seven thousand feet from north to south had been created, and the whine of machinery sounded over the staccato beating of equine hooves. Men kept the animals clear of field center, where high grass moved as if by magic to reveal an asphalted airstrip beneath. Still invisible to any eye, powerful jet engines rose from a deep-throated whine to ear-twisting shrieks and the cry of acetylene torches. Shouting male voices diminish to feeble cries in the rising crescendo of power, and workers move hastily aside as the front of a hill disappears into the ground and two jet fighters roll forward slowly, bobbing on their nose gear.

In the cockpit of each jet fighter, laden with g-suits,

helmets, and survival gear, are the same two men who eased away so quietly from the uproarious brawl at the Paradise Motel on the shore of the Indian River. Both men stay on the brakes, engines at idle, listening to the voice of their controller, who is monitoring dozens of communications bands—each of which is unaware that every word they transmit is stolen.

"Sir, they're loading now," the controller tells the lead pilot, knowing the second man also listens. "Are you ready to copy? I have their time hack for takeoff and the stages for their route."

The man in the lead jet fighter responds in flawless Arabic. "Quickly; I copy. And do not speak English again."

"Orchard One, you're clear to the active and clear for takeoff. Over."

Captain Jim Mattson pressed his yoke transmit button. "Ah, roger Gitmo Control. Orchard One clear for the active and rolling takeoff. Over."

"Orchard One, it's all yours. Over."

"Roger that, Gitmo. Orchard One is rolling." Mattson advanced the throttles steadily, his copilot, John Latimer, placing his left hand securely atop the knuckles of his pilot. The Convair sped toward the ocean, lifted smoothly and began its long climbing turn over open water.

The horses shied nervously with the relentless howl of the jet fighter engines. Everyone on the field waited for the right words to pass between the controller in his underground bunker on the side of the runway and the two men in the fighter cockpits. A headset in the lead fighter hummed.

"Control here."

"Go ahead."

"Your quarry is in the air. Confirm ready."

The pilots glanced at one another. "Allah One ready."

"Allah Two waits."

"Very good, sirs. Three minutes, sirs."

*　　*　　*

13

Charley Morgan, the pilots often said to one another, could churn the nuts of a brass monkey. It was more than her high, firm, full breasts or the perfectly proportioned legs or the golden hair or the flat tummy, or even the dazzling smile and the devastating *look* she could give a man. More than anything else about this beautiful woman-child you noticed her eyes, piercing right through a man, laughing at you and with you. Charley was the whole package of woman sensuality. She was also as sharp as a whip between the ears. Her eyes could keep you fascinated for hours: pale green and icy or shining, as her mood dictated. Hair that shone in the sun. And the way she moved! Catlike, always balanced. She was too strong and muscular, in the way a man loves, to be a fashion model or beach beauty. Her muscles had hardened beneath smooth golden skin from flying since she was a little girl in her Daddy's lap, then taking the controls herself and wrestling with airplanes large and small, fighters or great lumbering bombers, it made no difference; Charley found a fierce joy in throwing all her strength into mastering a slab-sided iron jangler that had been a roaring combat machine in wars fought before she was born.

Charley Morgan was all these things. She was also the owner, manager, and chief pilot for Morgan Aviation on Shiloh Field, an expansive hunk of real estate with long hard-surfaced runways and big hangars and a hell of a lot of airplanes, all a short twelve miles due west of the Kennedy Space Center. Straight west from the huge cube of the VAB and across Merritt Island to the Indian River and then the mainland, across U.S. 1 and upslope and you were on Shiloh Field. There you'd find, among the usual complement of spamcan aircraft and small airliners and old military transports used for cargo hauling, plus mosquito sprayers and crop dusters, some machines you might never expect. Fighter planes. Hugh bombers and transports. Liaison aircraft, trainers, reconnaissance ships, jet fighters. All from a half-dozen wars and a dozen different nations. Most of the old warbirds rested on the long flight line before the hangars of the Strasser Air Circus, from where the old

14

German ace carried on the tattered and fading tradition of the barnstormer and airshow performer. Charley Morgan and Karl von Strasser were unlikely but hugely successful partners in this line. Every weekend they put on a razzle-dazzle thunderer of a show complete with scares, frights, thrills, exploding ersatz bombs and maching gun fire and—

Charley forced from her mind those thoughts of the airshow she was scheduled to fly tomorrow. That was Saturday. *This* was Friday morning. Barely Friday morning, in fact; still pitch-black dark to the west where Charley trained her binoculars. She stood in her darkened bedroom in the apartment over the Morgan Aviation hangar, staring across the airfield to the Brevard County Mosquito Control hangar. She wasn't interested in mosquitos or their control, but in the two men standing together, their faces flashing in and out of shadow from the rotating beacon and strobes of the helicopter behind them.

The helicopter bore a large NASA SECURITY sign and a badge on the cabin door. Charley allowed herself a moment of introspection. The scene was surrealistic, the lights transforming the slowly turning rotor blades into fluttering mothlike wings. No question who was there. Mitch Bannon was; well, she knew that powerful body from better than this long-range view. Mitch lived in his own apartment within the hangar, a jarring note to the expected picture of the professional pilot. Mitch belonged to the beach. Tall, muscular, athletic, a shock of hair bleached platinum by the sun, body bronzed, a champion surfer and, if the stories circulating through the teenage subculture carried only a smidgin of truth, setting new records in conducting racial procreation. Charley didn't care a whit about *that*. What she found unsettling about this man about whom she cared so much was his sideline of running grass by the bale. He had the iron bird for it: a huge single-engined torpedo bomber from the second world war. She could see it now in the binoculars, but like everything else at this moment she pushed it aside in her mind.

That other man. She recognized the security chief

15

from the space center. What the hell was Bernie Hudoff doing *here*, with Mitch, at this ungodly hour? It was hardly a social call; by the forceful gestures that went along with their conversation there was some real heat being generated. Charley glanced at her watch. After five. Time was slipping away. She lowered the binoculars and finished getting into her jumpsuit and boots. She felt frustrated, snatching at coffee, chewing her lip. She turned back to the window at the deep whumping sound of the helicopter churning up to takeoff power. The flashing beacons and strobes rose swiftly and the chopper turned its nose toward her window, and for a moment the world was all dazzling glare from the landing light. Then it thundered low overhead and was gone. Charley walked back through her bedroom into her office studio, surrounded by framed pictures and models and a lifetime of flying memorabilia. She grabbed the phone, punched in the first number on the automatic dialer, and smiled.

Mitch had had just enough time to get back into his quarters and drop onto his couch. Charley smiled. Lover boy would *just* have fallen asleep again.

Mitch Bannon rose groggily against the tide of overpowering sleep. Holy Jesus, he'd just put his head down on the pillow! First Hudoff and his triple-damned security shit and now— Bannon struggled through the molasses of gummy eyes, groped with toes on the floor, stood up and kicked the coffee table. He yowled like a cat on fire and hopped his way through the debris of his office-studio-living room-bedroom to the phone. He almost made it without further grievous damage to his body, but in the minefield of parachutes, jackets, coffee mugs, cigar boxes, ashtrays, flight manuals and only God in dim memory knew what else, he managed to skin an elbow and whack his shin. He reached the phone at a precarious angle, clutching the end of a filing cabinet for support.

"My God!" he gasped into the phone, "you know what crazy fucking time it is?"

He heard the crystal sound of laughter. It had to be—

"It's time to fly, lover," she said. "Does that feeble brain of yours remember your promise of last night?

Bannon's voice reflected exquisite dismay. *"Already?"*

"Bannon, these pilots have a dawn patrol to fly, remember? Advertise the show to the county? Fly about with agility and verve? *They're not here, Bannon.* I need you to fly with me."

"Guck," Bannon croaked. "Uh, sure, yeah."

"Now, mister!" The crystal tones were gone. "I'll start her up. Get your ass over here."

Charley kept her hand on the phone. She could do one more thing. Just to be sure. She called the Paradise Motel, expecting a maelstrom of noise in the background when the clerk answered. To her surprise all was quiet. "Jack?" She knew the clerk. "Charley Morgan here."

Jack's voice sounded close to despair or death; it was hard to tell.

"Are my pilots there, Jack? I though they were having a party at the motel tonight."

"They're here, Miss Morgan. They've *had* the party. They are not drunk. They are smashed, bombed, utterly paralyzed." His voice ran on. "All the lawn furniture is in the pool. Six bedroom suites are on the lawn. We are missing three plate glass windows. *All* the other guests are gone. They have *fled* for their lives. That, that *dog,* or whatever the beast is, has the bartender and two waitresses trapped in the rest room, and—"

"You know I'll take care of the damages, Jack," she broke in.

"Yes. Of course, Miss Morgan. But please? Be nice to someone else? Next time have your party at the Holiday or the Ramada? *In Miami.* Good night, Miss Morgan. If I talk with you any more I shall kill myself." The line went dead.

Charley replaced the phone quietly. She picked up a headset and microphone from her desk as she left her apartment. On the flight line she walked resolutely to a hulking twin-engined B-25 bomber. She lowered the crew access hatch, pulled down the ladder, and climbed into the airplane, leaving the ladder down for Bannon.

17

*   *   *

"You are cleared for takeoff. Remain this frequency. Go!"

"Allah One to full power."

"Allah Two to full power. Ready to follow."

"We go!" The exultation burst from the radio of the lead jet fighter as the pilot released the brakes. The second fighter started its own roll in tight formation. The two fighters sped faster and faster, following the racing spots of brightness from their landing lights. On each side of the runway men stood proudly, holding aloft their clenched fists, all of them shouting over and over the war cry of their holy crusade.

"Zoboa! Zoboa! Zoboa!"

The two jet fighters tore into the black fabric of night.

"Colonel?"

Colonel Zack Stetson looked up from his command desk and nodded to the sergeant technician before him. "Go ahead."

"Sir, we have confirmation that Alamos Twelve is off Guantanamo en route for Los Alamos."

"Very good. Call sign?"

"Orchard One."

Stetson made sharp notations on his clipboard. "Radar confirmation?"

"Full contact, sir."

"In the computer?"

"As soon as I leave you, Colonel."

"Very good, Sergeant. Let me know when Fat Albert picks up the bird and confirms their squawk ID."

"Yes, sir."

Colonel Stetson relaxed. A calm, ordinary night. Buried deep within the steel-reinforced concrete walls of the master radar control center of Patrick Air Force Base, eighteen miles south of the great space center, he might as well have been on the moon for all the excitement they ever had down here.

Charley's hands moved with her usual brisk efficiency amidst the forest of switches and controls of the B-25

18

cockpit. She brought in battery power, primed the right engine, double-checked the brakes and control movement, leaned close to the open window to her left and shouted. "Clear!" She waited several seconds, worked starter, booster, fuel pumps, listened to and watched the great propeller grinding around, then catching, hurling back a blast of smoke as the engine caught. The B-25 shook itself to life like a dog shaking sleep from its brain and body. She felt the hatch down below close with a muffled thump, and moments later Bannon climbed into the right seat. He watched Charley fire up the second engine and he switched on radios and electronics and lights. Charley monitored the engine gauges, nodded with satisfaction, and released the brakes to ease the powerful bomber forward.

Bannon looked ahead and to both sides as they taxied slowly between a long row of winged history. To each side of their own bomber stood a parade of rare surviving machines of past wars. Those with folded wings became great humped dinosaurs with etched silhouettes against the night. Charley stopped short of the active runway and began the pre-takeoff runup.

The two jet fighters arced steeply into the first hints of dawn. Above them waited the tendrils of the distant sun. Both pilots listened to their control. "Your heading one seven zero. Allah be with you."

The lead pilot did not talk. The less said on open radio channels, the better. He clicked his mike button three times in their prearranged acknowledgement signal.

"Man, it is a beautiful morning up here." The copilot of Orchard One looked out at huge towering cumulus, their tops beginning to glow from the first moments of day. Well ahead of the Convair the clouds fell away and disappeared. The copilot pointed.

"It looks just like a map. We'll be able to see the whole Florida peninsula pretty soon. Hey, see there? I think that's Lake Okeechobee."

The pilot nodded. "Keep talking, mister. It makes me forget what we're carrying behind us."

His copilot punched him gently on the shoulder. "Piece of cake, buddy. Piece of cake."

"I've got the throttles, babe. Let 'er rip." Mitch Bannon placed his hands on the power levers of the B-25, also checking mixture and prop controls, scanning the engine gauges by reflex. He saw Charley nod, both hands on the yoke, and Bannon went forward on the throttles. From each side demons thundered and howled at them and huge scythes screamed as the props wound up to full power. The B-25 threw itself forward. Charley kept her eyes outside where they belonged. She and Bannon were an experienced and smooth team and she waited for his callouts in her headset. "You've got sixty, sixty-five, seventy-five, you're through eighty, coming up on ninety, and—"

Ninety was enough the way they were accelerating. She eased back on the yoke and the pounding from the runway fell away. She tapped the brakes. "Gear up," she said quietly, and from the corner of her eye saw Bannon's hand move, green lights wink out and red come on, and the gear *chunk* into the wells. The fury of sound eased as Bannon came back on the props and throttles, synched the props and set up a comfortable high-cruise power setting. The old warbird was honey smooth, and he held up both hands in the signal to Charley that everything was in the groove. She climbed to eight hundred feet and his brows went up slightly when she leveled off. Charley glanced at him.

"Was that Hudoff I saw?"

He nodded and thumbed his talk button. "Yeah. He's hot and bothered."

"What did he want? And why you?"

"Wants me to keep alert for any strange planes or people. Asked me to pass the word to all the spray plane pilots. They got word someone may try to blow up the shuttle for the next launch."

Charley stared at Bannon. "That's crazy!"

He nodded again. "Sure."

✝ 2 ✝

FIRST DAWN

Dawn is the faint streak of orange slicing thinly upward from the eastern horizon off the Florida coast. In that first hint of the star yet to appear, when only silhouettes and shadows may be discerned in the thinnest of light, great battlements rise upward from the ocean. They are the cloudy marker of the Gulf Stream and its flowing warmth, the birther of storms. It is a most beautiful sight, this animated brushwork of nature and heaven. But it is impossible to see, let alone register a sense of wonder, when your brain is paralyzed, your eyes closed gummily, and your body showing all the strength and purpose of a rag doll flung onto a trash heap.

God in all His powers and Nature in all Her wonders brought forth the living canvas of the miracle of sunrise. About the poolside and lawns of the Paradise Motel set so carefully along the banks of the Indian River, the pilots, mechanics, crewmen, wives, and girlfriends of the Strasser Air Circus greeted this sweep of wonder with utter and devastating indifference. Their unconsciousness was complete, as if they had all been struck down by an epidemic of savage effect.

Human flotsam littered the lawns, lay twisted with the mangled lawn furniture, sprawled amidst beer cans

21

and whiskey bottles. Broken glass mixed with garbagy food remnants. Torn clothing, eyeglasses, shoes and hats, cigarette and cigar butts, and over all the stink of stale beer and dried vommitus, broadcasting its powerful call to bluebottle flies, mosquitos, palmetto bugs, beetles and as-yet-unidentified but disgusting insects that buzzed and crawled and danced across open snoring mouths and into nostrils and over eyelids.

Far to the south and east, unseen and unnoticed by the depraved but unconscious fliers, two of their own sped low over the Indian River in the menacing shape of their B-25 bomber. They were destined for a rendezvous in a future scant minutes away.

They came out of the sun, silvery streaks trailing the unsuspecting shape of Orchard One. Their presence remained unknown until the instant a powerful electronic jammer in the rear cockpit of the lead T-33 broadcast its signal to overpower any electronics aboard the Convair. The shriek pierced the eardrums of the Convair's radioman and he ripped off his headset. In the cockpit, Captain John Latimer, flying right seat, mirrored the reaction to the icepick scream in their ears. Instinct brought Captain Jim Mattson's hands to the yoke. But the automatic pilot held true, and the Convair did not wave or tremble. Only the radio and electronics systems had seemingly gone mad. The flight engineer rushed to the cockpit, squeezed Mattson's shoulder, and shouted to him. "Sir! To our left! There!"

They looked out to see the all-black fighter with Arabic lettering on the fuselage and tail. The pilot's face was concealed behind an oxygen mask and goldfilm visor. "Who the hell is that?" Mattson wondered aloud, and in the same breath turned to Latimer. "You all right?"

Latimer sat back, shaking his head to clear the battering echoes in his brain. He nodded. "Yeah, sure; fine. What the hell was that?"

The radioman wailed painfully into the flight deck with them, his face furrowed in pain. "Jamming ... somehow they're jamming us. They must have, God, I don't know ... but I can't get out on anything."

22

They exchanged glances. Not a single word was needed to confirm that they were in deep shit. Nobody shows up in a black T-33 jet fighter with Arabic markings and knocks out all radio frequencies unless they're a nasty crowd with killing on their minds. Mattson instantly became the professional military pilot.

"Emergency beacon?"

"No joy, sir. Blocked."

"Anybody see more than one fighter out—"

The answer came in a hammering vibration that blurred their sight. The Convair yawed sharply to the right as metal exploded far out on the right wing. "There's another one out there, all right!" Latimer shouted. "He just shot the hell out of the wing! He's coming alongside—"

They watched the black fighter slide into perfect formation to their right and just above their mangled wingtip. His dive brake extended. The pilot pointed down with his forefinger and then his landing gear extended.

"Jesus Christ!" Latimer exclaimed. "He's ordered us to land!"

"Screw that," Mattson snarled. "Sparks! Get Patrick Control and tell them we're under attack. We need—"

"Sir, goddamnit! I can't get out on any frequency!"

Glowing tracers lashed the air before the Convair. The T-33 on their left had eased back and above to give them another warning burst. They looked out at the fighter to their right. The pilot tapped his left wrist to signify his watch, then drew a finger across his throat.

Latimer looked at Mattson. "He means it. Either we follow him down or they shoot us down." He glanced again at the fighter. "Jim, we don't really have much choice."

Mattson nodded. "I can't believe this ... we're over the middle of Florida, for Christ's sake, and we're being hijacked by jet fighters with Arab markings and—"

He jerked his head violently as a burst of machine gun fire slammed into the left wing. "We'll get the next one in the cockpit or in the tanks," Latimer said quietly. "We won't be any good to anyone if we go down in a ball of flame."

Mattson came back at once on the power, flattened out the props. The Convair slowed dramatically. "Gear down," he snapped to latimer. "Give that asshole on your side the okay sign." Latimer made a circle of his thumb and forefinger and saw the fighter pilot nod.

"There comes the other one," Mattson called out. The second jet fighter appeared ahead of them, gear down, banking to the north as he dropped rapidly. "Sparks!" Mattson yelled. "Get one of those locators out the chute right away. And set it for delayed opening!"

The radioman raced back into the cabin. As the Convair dropped earthward under the guns of the black jet fighter above and behind them, the radioman tapped a computer panel on a long cylinder, hit the ACTIVATE switch, slammed it into a drop chute, closed the loading port, and fired the homing cylinder. It fell unseen from the descending, turning transport. A mile below a cover flew away and a parachute opened. Instantly a powerful emergency radio signal flashed out, to be heard over a distance of nearly one hundred and fifty miles.

The snores grew louder. Then a distant deep rumble of sound mixed with fluttering lips and buzzing flies and groans emanating from the bodies dropped uncaringly about the lawn and poolside of the Paradise Motel. The new sound remained deep and steady, unfluttering like the drunken snoring. It began to rise in volume, a sound strangely of power.

It was no snore. It came from the direction of the orange and pale violet of dawn to the east, across the Indian River. Had anyone of the human debris heard the sound, or looked to the east, they would have seen a tiny silhouette poised above the waters. The only response was the twitching ears of Magnum, and even that canine worthy suffered a beery hangover.

The sound grew louder, the silhouette larger.

The golden glowing edge of the sun touched low sky.

* * *

Captain Jim Mattson rolled the Convair steeply behind the landing jet fighter before them. "Let's have it all," he called to Latimer. "Full flaps, keep everything ready for immediate full power. Once we're on the ground those fighters will be breaking away and we'll have a chance to bust out of there and stay low."

"Got it," Latimer said, tight-lipped, his hands flying in the cockpit.

"Harry!" Mattson yelled to the flight engineer. "Weapons to everybody! Get two of them up here also. Anybody comes near this aircraft I want you to open fire immediately and *keep* shooting, got it?"

"Got it, sir!" Heavy-duty submachine guns appeared at once.

Mattson killed power in the flare, dropped the Convair heavily to the ground, rolling straight ahead. The first jet fighter was slower. "Good! That's one out of the way ... he won't be able to take off now!" Latimer pointed out his window. "There goes the other one. He's staying upstairs to cover us."

Ahead of them they saw heavily armed men running and jeeps tracking them down the runway. "Get ready!" Mattson yelled. "I'll slow down, you open the cabin door and start shooting and we'll go to full power soon as I hear your fire!" He glanced at Latimer. "I'll take the controls, John. You get your weapon out your window and give them everything you've got!"

The Convair bounced gently on the nose gear. Mattson kept his right hand on the throttle ready for immediate power and followed the jet fighter arcing overhead. He'd have to time their escape perfectly. He wanted to get into the air while the T-33 was hauling around in a hard turn. The Convair was light, and Mattson was an old fighter type. He figured to come around hard, stay just with the treetops and then turn into the fighter, forcing a break and giving them the chance to play hide-and-seek on the deck.

He glanced behind him, saw his engineer kick open the cabin door. A blast of machine-gun fire boomed through the transport. "Let's go!" Mattson yelled, and slammed the throttles forward. The radioman was shooting and now Latimer opened up with steady bursts. "Go! Go!" Latimer shouted over the uproar.

Mattson saw a jeep slew around ahead of them to block their takeoff. He kept full power on and just before they reached the jeep he crossed the controls, brought up the right wing and the gear and prop with it to clear the obstacle. He felt a slight thump and knew his gear had torn into men, but they were accelerating beautifully and he knew they'd make it, and then a long burst of machine-gun fire from a jeep on his other side tore his head from his shoulders and shattered the window to his left and blew away the top half of Latimer's skull. Reflex brought Mattson's hand full back on the throttles, the final act of a dead man. The Convair ran off onto the grass and heavy fire ripped into the bodies of the radioman and the engineer. Blood ran down the floor by the open hatch.

The sergeant stared at her control console in the radar room beneath the surface of Patrick Air Force Base. Her eyes widened with the flashing lights before her and instantly her hand shot forward to bang a large red button. Strobe lights flashed and alarms clamored through the radar room. Colonel Zack Stetson and several other officers were at her side immediately. She looked up, frightened and efficient, then pointed to her console.

"Sir! Colonel . . . Alamos Twelve . . . it's disappeared!"

Stetson took several moments to study the console. The tracking panel assigned to Alamos Twelve was blank.

"Give me last track," he snapped. Her fingers flew. The path of Alamos Twelve from takeoff to last radioed position flashed on the electronic board.

"Any warning?" Stetson demanded. "Distress call? Anything?"

"Sir . . . *nothing.*"

A lieutenant came up to Stetson. "Colonel, we picked up some very strong high-frequency jamming a few minutes ago. I don't know if that's a factor, but—"

"What *I* know is that there are four atomic bombs in that airplane and it's gone. I—" Stetson stopped short as a chime sounded from the console and a red blinker began flashing. He knew the signal. "That's their full emergency call. They've fired an automatic transmitter from the plane. Get me full tracking on it and *stay with it.* Lieutenant, get three choppers, fully armed, into the air and on their way to that beacon position. Major, scramble two fighters immediately and we'll vector them after they're up. Sergeant, hit full alert. Get *everybody* on this one. I want all search teams out. Get me NORAD. We'll see if they've picked up anything, and get me General Marcus in Pentagon Command. *Move!*"

Mitch Bannon opened his mouth to speak, swallowed, and flung his arm forward instead. The dark waters of the Indian River, tinged with the first wispy touches of orange from the sun rising behind them, flashed by with the whipping blur of high speed at perilously low altitude. Charley held the yoke in both hands, lips tightly pressed with her concentration. Their world was thunder and a sensation of speed so great they might as well have been hurtling through space in the B-25.

"You're too goddamned low, damnit," he snarled at her.

Charley smiled, never taking her eyes from straight ahead. "Not low enough," she told him. She eased forward a hair on the yoke, they saw the river inch closer, and Charley leveled out with the props almost slicing water.

"You'll fly *through* the blasted motel this way!"

She laughed at him. Even over the harsh intercom line and the furious thunder about them he marveled at the crystal sound of that laugh. "I want every mother's son down there *awake*, Bannon! We've got a dawn patrol to fly in two hours, the TV news teams are coming in for their flights, we've got a record crowd this weekend, and *I've* got a bunch of dead-drunk, puking pilots I'm going to *wake up!*"

Bannon groaned. "Charley, they'll *still* be drunk!"

"But they'll be *wide-awake drunk!*"

Bannon stared. He'd kicked up enough water with propellers in his own time, just as low as they were flying right now, but *not* in the fucking dark! Charley would—

"There it is," he heard her say, and he looked ahead of the glass nose. Lights gleamed along the shoreline where the Paradise Motel loomed from the water. They hurtled at the motel like a giant shell flung from a cannon.

They boosted the first men into the cabin on the Convair. Gunfire sounded from within the airplane, the commandos of the Zoboa force making certain the Americans were dead by pouring heavy gunfire at point-blank range into the bodies. A truck backed up to the cabin door. More men climbed inside. One pilot ran to the cockpit. He turned back to two men with assault rifles at the ready.

"You won't need these. Quickly, now, get them out of these seats. Dump the bodies in the cabin. Quickly, I say!"

Other men went directly to the crates containing the atomic bombs. They checked for booby traps, found the thermite charges an unsuspecting handler would detonate, disarmed them, and signaled for more men to unload the crates. Outside the Convair, a jet helicopter rolled forth from a stand of trees, its rotors turning over, armed men standing by its opened cabin doors. The truck rolled from the Convair to the helicopter, men transferred the bombs, closed and locked the doors. A tall figure in starched fatigues and thick moustache drove up in a jeep. He was obviously in command.

"The sun's coming up! Get that machine the hell out of here *now!*" A soldier banged on the side of the helicopter, ducked and ran back. Immediately the chopper went to full power, rolled forward as it lifted, and vanished beyond the treetops, its powerful rotors churning out broad swaths of condensation. The commander in the jeep spoke into a hand-held radio. "Allah Two, do you read?"

The voice answered in Arabic."Two here. Your orders?"

"You weren't supposed to land, you fool. Taxi back as

28

quickly as you can to the end of the runway and take off *at once*. Acknowledge."

"Allah Two, I read you, sir. Taxiing back."

"Allah One, this is Blue Fox. Come in."

The first black jet fighter was at six thousand feet in a wide circle over Lake Okeechobee. "One here. Go ahead."

"Remain in your holding position until Two joins you. Then proceed to your original destination. This is your last transmission. Acknowledge according to plan."

He heard three clicks on the radio. He turned his attention back to the Convair. He saw men in the cockpit. The cabin doors were closed. He held the radio close to him.

"Blue Fox to Roadrunner. Will it fly?"

"Yes."

"Are you ready? Can you roll out from where you are?"

"We can do, sir. We recommend we go at once."

"Roadrunner, *go*. Cease all transmissions from now on."

His answer was thunder pouring from the engines of the Convair. It rocked and bounced on the grass, moved slowly back to the runway, and went to full power for takeoff. They watched it climb away at a steep angle.

"Clear this field!" the commander ordered. "Bring up the animals!"

Five minutes later there was no airport. Horses ran along a distant fence, and a dairy herd stood dumbly in the center of the tree-filled meadow.

"Are those guns charged?"

Bannon leaned forward to check the gauges on the propane-fired machine guns mounted on each side of the B-25 fuselage, as well as the single heavy machine gun secured in the glass nose. "They're okay," he told Charley. "Full pressure. You want them hot?"

"You bet, lover. We're going to give them our best greetings."

Bannon sighed, flipped the switch to ON. When Charley squeezed the gun trigger on the yoke, the propane bottles would emit a blast of flame ahead of each of the five machine guns. And they sounded just like the real thing. Enough to scare the shit out of any hero.

"Let's have all the power!" she called to Bannon.

By now he'd given up. If Charley was going to kill them, so be it. He pushed the prop controls all the way forward and shoved the throttles against their stop. Thirty-four hundred horsepower screamed with volcanic thunder. He glanced at Charley, the tip of her tongue just showing through her lips, reflecting her intense concentration. A single wrong twitch here and it would be curtains for them. *And* whatever they hit . . .

Charley aimed for the space between the tall illuminated sign and the motel building itself. PARADISE MOTEL appeared to rush out of the night straight into the cockpit as she squeezed the trigger. Five machine guns roared and bucked. Flame spat ahead of the bomber. The noise of the engines and exhausts and propellers was explosive, mind-shattering, shaking air and ground and rattling windows and buildings. The B-25 tore above and almost through the motel with scant feet to spare. Bodies jerked convulsively and leaped upward. Men cursed and women screamed, Magnum howled, and a tremendous gale swept through the lawn and the pool and blew in riverside windows. A cloud of debris sucked upward in the wake of the speeding bomber and then tumbled with the sounds of clinking cans and bottles and breaking glass.

The B-25 fled to the west, Charley hauling the bomber into a steep climbing turn. She looked back, laughing at the sight of the motel receding behind them. Bannon grinned hugely with relief and his own imagination of the havoc behind them.

"They're awake *now!*" Charley shouted with glee.

"All right. We are eight thousand feet. More than enough. You are ready?"

The pilot in the right seat nodded. "The autopilot. I will do it. You go back."

The man to his left nodded. He released his harness and, clumsy in his slim backpack, climbed from the pilot's seat to move to the rear of the Convair. Moments later his friend joined him. "All is set!" he shouted. "The charge goes off in three minutes!"

"Very good! I get door!" The pilot opened a plastic cover, yanked down on a steel cable, then pulled down on a red handle. Air roared explosively about them as the cabin door flew away from the Convair. They leaned out. "There!" shouted the pilot, pointing. "There is boat!"

His friend clapped him on the back, grinning. "We go!"

They dove from the Convair, whipped back and away like rag dolls from the prop blast. It took only seconds for them to fall freely and snap out their arms and legs to stabilize. Both men turned to fix the waiting cabin cruiser in sight, and began tracking as they fell toward the ship. Fifteen hundred feet up they each opened their chutes, then rode the square canopies down to soft landings alongside the ship. They turned to look up, in the distance where the Convair was a silvery dot in the sky. The shining object appeared to expand with reddish silver, and a smoke trail followed the transport. Flames glowed in the air, the smoke trail bent downward, and they saw the Convair beginning its death dive into the Gulf of Mexico.

On the cruiser's deck they embraced their fellows. The lead pilot held aloft a fist in a final gesture of contempt.

"Now we have the Yankee Satan where we want him!"

The second pilot laughed. "By the balls!"

The main gear touched whisker-soft. Charley held the nose gear off the runway as the B-25 slowed, then brought down the nose and the third wheel painted itself without a tremble onto concrete. They rolled easily down the long runway, taking the first turnoff to the taxiway leading to Strasser's hangar. Charley and Bannon kept grinning like kids at one another. Every pilot likes a buzz job, and these two were still flying high on their smash run almost through the Paradise Motel.

Charley parked and they shut down. They sat for several minutes in the darkened airplane, their hands

31

reaching across the cockpit center to hold one another. "You're one hell of a woman, Charley," Bannon said after a mutual silence.

A smart-ass answer sprang unbidden to her lips. Just in time Charley bit her tongue. It was a rare moment when Bannon gave out compliments. She wasn't sure if he meant his to her skills as a pilot or as a woman, but she decided to settle for the offering. She squeezed his hand. "Thank you."

They climbed down the ladder, closed the hatch behind them. Bannon held her close, kissed her deeply. "We've got a whole hour before we fly again," he said huskily, nibbling on her ear. She loved it. But standing beneath a bomber, crackling and spangling as hot metal cooled, and with hundreds of pilots and crewmen about to descend upon them, well—

"You're a love, Bannon," she told him. "An hour, you said?"

"Yeah. Right. A whole hour for us to—"

"Take a cold shower, Bannon. And you might shave, also. I'll see you at the briefing."

She walked off, and his eyes followed her with agonizing longing. Of a sudden he lashed out with his foot to kick the tire nearest him. He howled with pain, dancing about like a madman. The same damned foot again!

✦ 3 ✦

FIRST MORNING

The body twisted slowly as it fell away, legs bent, left arm outstretched and right arm raised in a final salute, tumbling slowly and helplessly, falling down the gravity well toward the planet waiting below. A stark line of blue-white curved sharply and fell beneath the diminishing form. The visual effect was devastating. No one could look at such a scene and not feel as if they were also falling forever into that maw. The music didn't help, either. It rose and fell with its own dizzying impact. Enormous speakers on all sides of the futuristic theater thundered and rumbled and hammered at the guests staring in open-mouthed awe at the earth and its tumbling, rolling, helpless human on a screen three stories high. NASA had built a winner with its IMAX theater screen at the space center. For this performance only a handful of people clustered in the seats of theater center, watching the screen and listening to a tiny figure standing at its base.

Gene Woodbury wasn't tiny. At six feet four inches and 242 pounds, he carried himself with the same assurance with which he'd galloped through fragile defenses on many a gridiron. He'd replaced the football outfit and the pigskin for an Italian silk suit and a silk tie, and his voice was deep and clear and above all believable. He was the perfect briefing officer for NASA; just one exposure to his commanding voice and presence established that NASA knew how to pick winners.

Woodbury's performance early this morning wasn't for the public. Woodbury rarely moved his bare feet from bed to floor before ten o'clock in the morning, and today was a ghastly event in his well-ordered life. But the call had come through on his private line, and Ann Fleming, his secretary of long tenure with NASA, laid it out cold for him.

"It's Hudoff. Don't ask questions, Mr. Woodbury. I know when the grizzly is hungry, and Hudoff is bristling from cold nose to tail. He wants a briefing to begin in one hour flat. I have the idea that if you don't make this one you needn't bother ever to wave your magic wand again for the public."

Woodbury made it with twenty minutes to spare. He didn't mind the sudden rush. This was different, unplanned—*exciting*. If Bernie was on the warpath, then fireworks wouldn't be too far behind. So Woodbury stood at the speaker's rostrum on stage with an incredible changing scene behind him, and he ran through his briefing spiel for Hudoff and his select group.

It hadn't taken him more than a few moments to understand what this was all about: the *Antares* launch in nine days, the biggest event since *Columbia* first crashed upward to launch the entire shuttle program. As NASA Security Chief, Bernie Hudoff was going through every element of security well before the space center would be inundated with the super-sensitive, critical world leaders invited by the President to witness the great event.

"You get up on that stage, Gene, and you tell me what you are going to say to these people and how you're going to run your shifts," Hudoff told him with no room for nonsense. "Don't leave *anything* out."

So Woodbury took the stage and gave it his best shot, which was very good indeed. "During the three days prior to liftoff," he said via his concealed lapel mike, his voice caressing anyone within reach of the speakers, "which is scheduled for nine days from now, we will brief as many as four thousand honored guests in this IMAX theater. We will require at least eight to ten separate briefing sessions with world leaders and government heads. The time hack is not possible to pin down specifically because of the need for real-time translation. We'll be bringing in our best available translators from the United Nations, where what is a problem for us is an everyday event for them."

He paused, and Bernie Hudoff took the moment to groan inwardly. He held a small microphone to his lips and a tape recorder in his jacket took down his notes. *"There's a gaping hole in this translator shit. We can't get a dossier on all the people who may come down here. They're protected by this diplomatic crap with the UN. Talk to Woodbury after this is over about having his briefings printed in as many languages as are necessary to have the guests understand what's happening. Screw the kid gloves treatment; security comes first. Keep Washington on tap on this matter."*

He sat back, listening to Woodbury's spiel. The man was really good and the show they were putting on even better. It was impressive as hell. The effect of that giant screen couldn't be described. It absolutely overwhelmed the viewer. And whatever Woodbury chose as his subject came to life on the screen, leaping out to clobber the audience with its immense size and brilliant color.

"The space station, *Olympus*, is in high orbit. The last flight showed everything in excellent shape." *Olympus*, all steel girders and cylinders, huge antennas and enormous solar arrays, rolled slowly from the viewpoint of an inspecting shuttle crew. The camera turned into the blinding light of the sun and dissolved, coming out of the dissolve to brilliant floodlights at the launch pad and the shuttle looming upward into black. "The countdown for *Antares* continues on schedule—"

Two astronauts walked into focus. "Two American astronauts will command and fly the shuttle. Blacky Moran is *Antares* commander and this will be his fourth shuttle flight. His first officer and pilot is Susan York, veteran of two previous missions in orbit in *Antares* and *Atlantis*—"

Hudoff watched the scene dissolve to a training room and a second beautiful girl appeared. "Adrianne Cortez is the chief mission specialist. She will be our first Brazilian astronaut in the shuttle program." Behind the dark-haired beauty appeared a beefy astronaut, clearly confident of himself, with CCCP on his flight suit. "Cosmonaut Georgi Mikoyan from the Soviet Union will lead two other astronauts on EVA assignments and—"

The huge screen flashed in bright red light in a fast on-off sequence. The effect on Woodbury was that of a physical blow, freezing his voice in mid-sentence. A deep alarm chimed in unison with the flashing red light. Hudoff was on his feet immediately as an urgent computer page boomed above the alarm. A uniformed security officer was at his side in seconds, holding forth an attaché case. Hudoff leaned forward, studied glowing digital numbers atop the case. He tapped numbers quickly. The case sprang open and Hudoff reached within to extract a telephone.

"Security One here. Go ahead," he snapped.

He listened intently. His face wrinkled into a frown and he glared at his security officer. "Tell them to shut off that goddamned alarm!"

He concentrated again on the telephone. The alarm was gone but the red light kept blinking on and off with frightening, surrealistic effect.

"You're absolutely certain of all this?" The small group with Hudoff, joined by Woodbury, stood off to the side, listening, containing their own apprehensions. Except for Joe Horvath from Secret Service. He edged closer to Hudoff, trying to hear, and his impatience finally spilled over.

"What the hell's going on?" he demanded.

Hudoff raised a bushy eyebrow at Horvath. "Shut up, you idiot," he said with quiet force. He returned his attention to the phone. "*No!* Absolutely *not*. Not one word to the outside. Go to Level Three Security at once. *Now.* I'm on my way back."

He tossed the phone to the officer as the flashing red lights faded and the overhead theater lights came on.

They all seemed frozen in the blinding glare from the IMAX screen.

"Goddamnit, Bernie, I want to know what's coming down!" Horvath said with heat.

"Not so fast," Hudoff said. He turned to the others. "You're all under full security. No discussions of what's happened with anyone outside this group unless I clear it first. You bust this wrap and I'll throw your ass behind bars myself."

Brenda Lamb from NASA Protocol held her hand to her throat. Her world was diplomatic sweetness and light. A handkerchief fluttered perfume at them as she brought it to her lips. "What *can* it be, my dear Hudoff. You are *so* upset!"

His expression went from disbelief to gritted teeth and an exaggerated slowness in response. "Upset? Of course not, *dear* Lamb. It's just another pleasant morning here at oceanside, isn't it? However . . ." He turned to Horvath and it was another man speaking as Hudoff continued.

"About an hour or so ago an Air Force transport plane was forced down here in Florida." Hudoff took a deep breath. What he had heard was just sinking in, *really* sinking in.

"There were four atomic bombs on that plane." He sucked in air, controlling his voice. "There's no trace of those bombs. The blue-suiters believe they've been hijacked."

"Good God," Woodbury said hoarsely.

Brenda Lamb's hands fluttered about her throat and bosom. "But . . . but *why* would anyone want to do such a thing!" she wailed. She didn't understand everything that was going on, but she knew these people well enough to recognize *their* reactions. "I can't imagine—"

Horvath's hand shot out to grasp her shoulder and jerk her roughly about. "I'll tell you why!" he shouted into her face. "Because whoever it is they're going to blow up the whole fucking Cape!"

Brenda Lamb fainted. Hudoff looked down at her, said, "Oh, shit," and stepped across her body on his way out.

*   *   *

Three old school buses painted ghastly green and
yellow rolled up to the gate of Morgan Aviation on the
flight line of Shiloh Field. The drivers opened the doors.
No one moved within the buses. The drivers had been
this route before; they all leaned on their horns. Inside
each vehicle horror stories unfolded from seats, crawled
along the floors. Creatures barely resembling men and
women shuffled in obvious agony to the doors. From
the lead bus stepped a huge barrel-chested man with a
shaven skull. Karl von Strasser gripped the rail in a
massive fist and felt for the ground with his foot. A
black patch was fastened before his left eye. Dead center in the patch was a gleaming monocle. Somehow it
made sense. He managed both feet to the ground, turned
and held out his hand.

Mad Marty leaned heavily on his friend. He didn't
make it down the steps. His feet turned inward and he
began to crumple. The German pilot got him under one
armpit and his crotch. Mad Marty's mouth opened in a
wide O. No sound came out. Behind him Magnum slunk
low to the ground. He collapsed at Von Strasser's feet
and managed a long, low, and painful howl. Finally the
three of them managed to stumble toward the office.

By now a crowd of newsmen had drifted from the
flight line and the office to watch the painful ordeal.
They looked with utter disbelief at the torn and stained
clothing, listened to the groaning and farting as the
moving wreckage flowed and lurched slowly past them.
Charley and Bannon sat on the wing of a fighter, shaking their heads. Mad Marty paused once to look up at
his sister. He stared at Charley, tried to speak, and
belched wetly. Charley closed her eyes.

The flight crews somehow managed their way into
the cavernous hangar. Planes and equipment had been
pushed back into corners and the sides of the hangar. A
briefing platform occupied the deepest part of the building, and along one wall were long tables with waiting
tomato juice, doughnuts, and tanks of steaming coffee.
Added to the sounds of groans, gasps, farts, and belching
were smacking noises of chewing and slurping. A group

38

of pilots sat on the concrete floor, sucking desperately from oxygen masks. One youngster threw up. He was still wearing his mask. He began to choke and writhe on the floor until someone took pity and yanked away the mask. It was a mistake. The pilots nearest the choking youngster began to gag and choke themselves.

The heavy metal door leading from Charley's office banged open and then was slammed shut with a crash that brought cries of pain from about the hangar. Mixed with the clanging echo were hobnailed boots striking hard against the concrete floor. "Oh, *no!*" went up the quavering wail. No matter. Wendy Green was on the scene, short and sort of cute-dumpy.

Wendy Green, who ran Morgan Aviation for Charley Morgan, had a Shirley-Temple smile and dimpled cheeks stacked atop a body mashed too close from head to foot. Wendy had stuffed her bounty into a zippered flight suit two sizes too small. The suit pulled tight along her calves, thighs, and hips and made a joke out of concealing her huge breasts. Hard nipples threatened to puncture the fabric. But no one in that hangar could have cared less were those nipples fluorescent and blinking as Wendy Green stomped her way with drill-sergeant ferocity to the wooden stairs leading to the briefing rostrum. She stood wide-legged, fists locked to her hips, her eyes glaring and her face puffy-wrinkled into what she hoped was a scathing look.

"My heroes!" she screeched. Heads turned painfully. Some. Other heads were buried between knees or hidden beneath anything to block out the sound.

"You scumbags!" A hobnailed boot came down with a crash onto the wooden platform. It was hollow beneath and the impact of her boot sounded like a great kettle drum. Pilots winced and groaned.

"You're supposed to fly an hour from now! *One hour!*" Her eyes bored into every man jack and woman in the hangar. "And you sons of bitches are by God *going* to fly!"

Middle fingers rose in the air like a forest of digital

39

peckers, accompanied by boos and hisses and catcalls. To a stranger the scene was on the edge of being a psycho ward. To those who knew these pilots and the friendly-enemy exchange between their ranks and Wendy Green, it was a scene all too familiar.

"You listen to me!" Her voice continued to gain in volume. When she screeched, Wendy sounded like a giant piece of chalk on a giant blackboard. She could have used the public address system, but she enjoyed the zest of shouting too greatly to give it up for efficiency. She pointed her finger in a wide swinging motion and abruptly her arms flew out to regain her balance as the platform began to shake. Her mouth opened in astonishment as the platform rattled and thumped beneath her. Heads turned, real interest waxed with the new scene. Wendy dropped to hands and knees and reached down for the heavy curtain hanging from the platform. She jerked it aside. Two half-naked bodies stared in shock at her. Jay Martin and a red-haired beauty in the most compromising of positions. "Bitch!" screamed the redhead, snatching the curtain back.

A dozen pilots lunged forward to tear the curtain aside. But in those brief moments Jay had disengaged himself and he and his love partner clutched their clothes to their bodies. Now they took off at a dead run, Jay holding aloft one hand with his thumb erect. Whistles, applause, and laughter escorted them through the door leading to Charley's office.

"You assholes!" Wendy shouted. "Aren't you forgetting that you're going to be *flying* in less than an hour from now? Shape up, dummies!"

Mad Marty limped by, heading for the men's room, Magnum dragging slowly behind him. Marty stared with soulful eyes at Wendy. She went for it, her acid tongue abated for the moment. Mad Marty lifted his head, all innocence and boyishness.

"Wendy, baby . . . after we fly, why don't we have lunch today? Just you and me?"

Wendy blushed, her face beamed with a smile, and she nodded. "Y-yes, of course, I'd love to—"

Mad Marty's face transformed into a horrible grin

and he grabbed his crotch, thrusting forward with his pelvis. "And I got lunch for you right here, sweetheart!"

Guffaws and roars greeted his sudden performance. In a swift motion Wendy reached into her purse by her feet, snatched up an aerosol can with a horn blaster, pointed it at the pilots and squeezed the trigger. A terrible blast of sound ripped through the hangar, echoing and bounding back and forth. Again and again Wendy gave it to the pilots until they shouted in pain for her to quit. Eyeballs seemed to roll in sockets. The tearing sound of the horn faded, replaced with renewed groans and swearing.

At the main entrance to the hangar the newsmen had gathered protectively in a group, like a small bunch of animals shuffling together for protection in the midst of madness. A camerman pointed inside the hangar and turned to his associates. "Holy shit! We're supposed to *fly* with these pukeheads?"

Bernie Hudoff stood on the brake with his right foot, jerked the gearshift lever into first, left foot down to the floor-board, came off the brake and slammed down on the accelerator and popped the clutch. The scream of rubber as the Land Rover hauled ass from NASA Headquarter's parking lot was a fitting aural cry to the anger irritating his whole system. In the space of a few minutes he had all of the Kennedy Space Center on a Level Three Security, which was one step short of resisting armed invasion. But it didn't go that fast to the south, over the bridge to the Titan complex and still farther south to the military base of Cape Canaveral, where NASA was much more a tenant than a landowner. The blue-suiters had their own way of doing things, and the word hadn't passed to them with the same priorities that reached Hudoff. He understood that; the shuttle was on NASA territory and tight security could be exercised on the NASA side of the fence. Yet the delay in implementing the strictest measures possible flew in the face of all reason when you considered they were talking about four atomic bombs in the hands of what were obviously very well equipped, trained and functioning terrorists. No one took out an Air Force transport in broad daylight with jet fighters, for Christ's sake, unless they were a hell of a lot better than good! Hudoff still lacked more than a smattering of details, but he didn't need to be hit in the side of the head with a rock to judge the natives as unfriendly. He knew he wouldn't be satisfied with the emergency security level unless he personally went through the main avenues and systems of the whole spaceport where he could see and feel and *sense* the way things were going. Besides, it was time to show the flag, so to speak, and let the troops know that Bernie Hudoff was *personally* very much on top of things.

He hadn't intended to make it a show, but what the hell, fuck it. The more display of the chief of security on a one-on-one level, the more seriously his men would judge the situation. Besides, Hudoff concluded to himself, the first man or woman he found screwing off or exhibiting the wrong attitude, he'd bust their ass out of the spaceport so fast their eyeballs would roll. Civil service would scream and threaten him, but *this* time Bernie Hudoff had the biggest guns of all backing him. An atomic fireball brooks no shit from no one or nothing.

He raced north, feeling better for the physical release of doing things with his body as well as his mind. The wind howled past and into the open windows of the Land Rover, and on impulse Hudoff hit the flashing red and blue lights and kicked the siren to wailing. Again, that would have the effect on *everybody* he would encounter or who would see *him*. It's a lot more effective to come bursting onto the scene with lights flashing and siren screaming and tires burning rubber than to ease up on someone and have to holler, "Hey, you!" He pushed the Land Rover out of the access road from headquarters, raced through the forest of trailers jammed together to alleviate the desperate shortage of computer workspace, bounced over the railroad tracks, pushed his way through a red traffic light by screaming tires and horn blasting along with the siren, sped down a narrow service lane alongside the monstrous VAB, and hauled ass right through the main vehicle entrance without stopping. For a few moments the dying siren wailed like a fading banshee within the huge building that went straight up, open-spaced, from ground level to 550 feet above them. Gigantic rocket boosters and subassemblies loomed everywhere. Hudoff screeched to a stop and grinned as he heard feet pounding from behind him: the guards he'd ignored as he shot into the building. He'd been right. They were pumping shoe leather to get to him.

They ran up to the Land Rover, throwing hasty salutes to their top man, and Hudoff turned on them like a hungry wolf. "You assholes! I came right through you two dummies. *What the hell are those weapons doing in their holsters?*" He snapped out his badge and banged a hand against his ID badge pinned to his jacket. "The next time *anyone* gets through you into this building without your personally checking their ID you are fucking *fired.* Got it?"

"Yes, sir!" they chorused.

Hudoff jerked a thumb at the Land Rover, where Lieutenant Lou Elliott in full security uniform and Joe Horvath of Secret Service stared at the scene, wondering what the hell was going on. The two guards almost dragged them from the vehicle to check them out. Hudoff forced down a grin. The guards were armed, but so were Elliott and Horvath. If the guards got *too* enthusiastic, it could be a hell of a Mexican standoff.

Hudoff looked at one guard. "McGuire, get on your radio and notify all guard stations I'm coming through for inspection and a brief conference. Did you people get the word on Level Three?"

"Yes, sir, we did."

"Then how in the hell did we get through you!"

"Damnit, sir, the only thing we could have done was to . . . was to . . ."

"Spit it out!"

"Well, we'd have had to shoot you, Mr. Hudoff!"

Hudoff walked up to McGuire in a classic nose-to-nose meet. His voice went down instead of up. "Next time, you *better* shoot, McGuire, or I'm liable to shoot your balls off."

He turned and climbed back into the Land Rover, Elliott and Horvath hustling to get aboard as he started off with screeching tires again, drawing the attention of hundreds of workers within earshot. Just what he wanted. He hit every elevator door entrance and every personnel door, and by the time he tore through the last door away from the VAB he was supercharged with energy. They sped past the gigantic Saturn V moon rocket lying stretched out along the ground as a memento to past glories of the Apollo lunar landing program, raced around the huge shape of the shuttle *Enterprise* on public display, and headed for the last checkpoint before hitting the road paralleling the crawlway for the huge transporter that carried the monster spaceships from the VAB to the launch pads.

He had floored the accelerator when, almost of its own volition, his foot disobeying commands from his mind, he eased off the downward pressure on the pedal. Then he let the Land Rover coast ahead. He didn't even remember shifting into neutral as the vehicle slowed to a stop, tires crunching on sand and gravel.

Never before had the Space Chapel reached out and struck him with such enormous impact. To his right, along the banks of the turning basin where once huge barges had drifted in slowly with the building-sized booster stages to lift men to the moon, NASA had erected a chapel of stunning design. The chapel itself extended out over the water in seeming defiance of gravity, a design of counterbalance and swooping leverage. Gold gleamed in the morning sun in a massive arch toward the heavens, angled precisely along the same flight path followed by the great man-carrying vessels that sailed into the ocean through which swam the earth and other globes.

Hudoff rested his forearms on the steering wheel, looking, oblivious to the presence of the two men with him. His mind reached back in time. He hadn't been here when Apollo I savaged its interior in the pad fire that killed White, Chaffee, and Grissom. He didn't know the Russians who had died in Voskhods and Salyuts, but he'd seen their names engraved in pure Italian marble within the chapel. But he *had* been here on that shattering morning of January 28th, when just before noon on the first month of 1986, the magnificent *Challenger* tore itself apart in a shattering blast that snuffed out, instantly, the lives of five men and two women. Astronauts, specialists, engineers, and the school teacher, forever locked in the minds and memories of Americans.

And if that fireball appears again, it may engulf all of us and all of this . . .

He banged the Land Rover back into gear and took off with burning rubber, venting his tortured emotions in angry words to Elliott and Horvath. "As of right now, no more press tours! No more bus tours and cancel all VIP visits that don't have my personal okay!" He glanced at Elliott hanging on with one hand and scribbling with the other. "Don't just write it down, you dummy! Your fucking radio works. *Use it!*"

They cut right where the road forked, left to the launch pads for the shuttles, right southward to the beach road. Two buses packed with tourists sped in the opposite direction. "That's the last time I want to see *that* until this mission is over," Hudoff spat to Elliott. "When you get through with your first message, you pass the word on this one. No tours of *any* kind from now on, and that includes Air Force as well as NASA real estate."

They roared through the service and maintenance section of the spaceport, Hudoff screeching around corners, pointing as he drove, snapping out his orders. "All visitor's passes are cancelled! No one gets on this complex without a guard for an escort from the gate to where he's going, where he visits, and the guard stays with him or her until they're out of here. Make a note, Lou. Female guards with every group of women who come in here. They go to the potty and the guard goes with them. They don't buy the new rules, throw 'em out."

They flew along the road leading to the bridge crossing from NASA territory to the Air Force complex on Cape Canaveral. To their left stretched the futuristic facilities of the Titan complex; then they were in the midst of power terminals, missile and service hangars, and a forest of buildings built in the fledgling days of the '50s. "Notify the blue-suit security chief I want a meeting with him and his staff *today*," Hudoff said. "Have them come up by chopper to headquarters."

They slowed at the forest of missiles and rockets in the Cape Canaveral Museum. The giants of yesteryear were pitifully small compared to the Saturn V and the shuttle monoliths. "Have the Air Force close off this whole area! No visitors on the Cape from now on. The rules for us are the rules for them. Arrange for NASA guards to work with the Air Force people at all gates. If they don't have the manpower for an increased work-load, we'll provide it for them."

Despite his own urge for haste, Hudoff couldn't resist slowing his vehicle. The tug of history was simply too great to be ignored. *My God*, he thought, *here is where all those dreams began.* He felt what was almost an ache in his heart as he stared at the monuments. Redstone, Thor, Jupiter, Juno, Titan, Atlas, Navaho, X-17, Blue Scout, Shrike, Polaris . . . Christ, even the original German V-2 that had been captured on its launching pad in Belgium, aimed at the heart of London. He turned to drive along the perimeter road leading to Port Canaveral and at that instant they were struck with a devastating explosion. An incredible snarl hurtled from the sky to burst about them. Horvath yelled and Elliott ducked, but Hudoff had already slammed on the brakes and skidded wildly from the road onto sand, rooster-tailing as he half-spun about.

They leaped from the Land Rover and snapped their heads back to see three Mustang fighter planes howl by, barely above the tallest rocket, gleaming in the low morning sun. They banked steeply in formation and roared off to the south. Hudoff felt rage spilling from him. He shook his fist at the sky, bellowing. "Damn sons of bitches! Who the hell are they!"

Lou Elliott hastened to answer. "They're from the airshow group, sir. You know, the Strasser Air Circus from Shiloh Field. They're flying over the whole county this morning, what they call a dawn patrol, and—"

Hudoff's face was livid. "Who the hell gave them permission to fly through a restricted area!"

For a moment only the echo of the Mustangs came down to them. Then Joe Horvath, utterly grateful for the opportunity, smiled hugely. "*You* did, sir." Hudoff stared blankly at him, and Horvath hurried with explanation. "You said it was good for community relations and—"

They ducked as another blast of engines exploded about them. Two B-25 bombers thundered by, their shadows washing over the trio on the ground. Hudoff's temper spilled out of him in an almost visible wave. He grabbed the radio from Elliott and squeezed the transmit button. "Hello, Central!" No answer. "Goddamnit, answer the fucking phone!" he shouted.

By way of answer they heard another wave of engine thunder rolling down upon them. They looked up, this time to see a single blue-and-gold T-28 standing on its wing in a turn, barely missing a giant missle. Hudoff's jaw dropped not at the sight of the pilot in the front seat, but at the huge dog wearing goggles in the back seat, staring down at him.

✦ 4 ✦

SURPRISE!

The first wave of fighters took the beaches by storm. Three Mustangs in tight formation cut spray into the air a hundred yards off the surf of Cocoa Beach, racing south from their low pass over the giant spaceport complex to the north. They whipped by the breakwaters of Port Canaveral, frightening and thrilling the on-deck crew of a giant Trident submarine easing its way into the port. To the local shrimpers and fishing boats, the warbirds of the Strasser Air Circus were a familiar and welcome sight that added zest to local community life, and they were quick to wave and smile at the combat machines tearing overhead. The sight and sound of the Mustangs brought the locals quickly to their windows and balconies and out to the beaches, for they knew loose gaggles and formations would follow. They came in bunches, the B-25 bombers following the Mustangs, and then a mob of T-6 and SNJ trainers, engines blasting their distinctive thunder. Transports followed, along with trainers and liaison planes, and the T-6's and SNJ's circled wide to come back in fighter attacks on the transports. Propane machine guns and cannon yammered along the beaches, smoke poured from engines, and it was a high old time.

The Golden Girls always drew waves and shouts and

applause from the beach crowd. Sherri Taylor had built her own act with seven young beauties, all of them taught to fly under her tutelage. Sherri was one of the more experienced pilots flying the airshow; she had all the ratings in the book up to airline captain and helicopters, and was also an instructor in just about everything that had wings or flapping rotors. Competing with the Big Boys in their heavy iron, no matter how successful, would have made her just one more hotshot jock, and Sherri was too sharp for that. She was also rich enough to indulge her own whims.

She had bought the Beech T-34 trainers, swift and agile machines built originally for military training, but through the years used for a couple of dozen revolutions and small wars about the globe. She had them all painted a dazzling gold; eight were for showtime and two ships were kept for training and in reserve. Sherri taught her girls to fly tight formation. She also had their airplanes fitted with sheepskin seats and whorehouse lavender carpeting and sidewalls, and dressed all the girls in skintight hotpants and halters. Every one of them had golden hair and they were a smash hit, and when they came down the beach they hung in with wing-over-wing formation flying, all their lights on and strobes flashing and engines pouring out golden smoke.

Mad Marty Morgan flat-hatted the beach communities in the blue-and-gold T-28, the powerful ex-trainer that had been pressed into service the world over as a hotshot killer of ground forces. With fourteen hundred horsepower up front, Mad Marty had the oomph to hang the Trojan on its nose or stand it on its wing as he S-turned up and down the beaches, giving Magnum the flight of his life and bringing hundreds of people out to wave wildly at the big mountain dog strapped into the rear seat, including the people standing on their condo and apartment balconies as the T-28 raced well *below* them. Somehow there was something special about waving to a dog flying beneath your balcony.

Mad Marty eased the T-28 around several small planes droning like moths through the air, dragging long banners behind them to advertise the air show that afternoon at Shiloh Field. He slipped between two of the banner towers, careful not to dump the powerful vortex of air from behind his T-28 onto the small machines hanging painfully in the sky. Well ahead of him he saw dozens of planes fanning inland from the beaches to hit every community in Brevard County and farther south to the Vero Beach area. And all of them were in touch with Wendy Green back at the Shiloh tower. Wendy did a great job in shepherding her flock through the skies, but she took herself so seriously that the pilots found it impossible not to razz and irritate one of their favorite people.

Wendy's voice carried into every airplane and headset as she kept up her control chatter. "This is Shiloh, to all the heavy iron on the beach. Stay heads up, you people. We got at least eighteen birds along the surf and it's getting crowded. Watch for heavy traffic out of Patrick taking off to the south. They'll be breaking left and climbing out southeast." There was a brief pause and Wendy was back on the horn. "Patrick Control clears our aircraft due south along the beach through the Patrick area at fifteen hundred feet. When the B-25's clear Patrick, work the south county."

Tim Ryland sat comfortably in the lead B-25. White-haired, suave, attired in a tailored gabardine flight suit, wearing wings of solid gold, he was on a permanent busman's holiday after a lifetime of military and airline flying. He was also a master at tweaking. He removed the pipe from his teeth and squeezed his radio button.

"Ah, that's a roger, Pillsbury."

Pilots chuckling into their mikes could be heard all throughout the county and beyond. The radios began to resound with clicks as pilots pressed transmitter buttons to signify the size of their audience.

"I heard that, Ryland!" Wendy's voice was rising to the shrill cry that gave them so much delight. "I'll take care of you when you get back, I promise you that!"

Ryland grinned and returned her call. "Why, thank you kindly, Pillsbury. That's right nice of you. I'll, ah, take seconds right after the dawg."

The radio speakers and headsets degenerated into a chorus of pilots howling like wolves in heat. In the tower Wendy Green's face contorted into fury, and she stood shaking with helpless anger, fists clenched, breasts straining mightily at her flight suit.

"Shiloh Tower, Triple Deuce, the TBM on the taxiway. Over."

Wendy looked down and across the field. A powerful torpedo bomber taxied slowly. She recognized Mitch Bannon in the cockpit.

"Triple Deuce, this is Shiloh. What are your intentions, please? Over."

"Triple Deuce would like to proceed to hold short of the active for the runup and I'll call you when I'm ready."

"Triple Deuce, proceed to the active and hold short. No other traffic. Shiloh out."

"Got it, Shiloh." Bannon eased forward on the power and the thick-bodied TBM moved to the active runway. He held short and turned into the wind, running through his power check and pre-takeoff checklist. He was just about to call Shiloh Tower when a shrill beeping sound came to him over the subdued rumble of the idling engine.

Bannon's brows raised; immediately he removed a clip from his belt and brought it to his ear. He bent a wire-thin microphone to his lips. The belt contained a small battery pack and the extended wire became a highly effective antenna. Bannon cupped his hand about the mike to shield it from the rumbling engine.

"Shiloh One here. Go ahead."

"This is Big Time. How do you read?"

"Five by, Big Time."

"Okay. Code Three, Shiloh." Hudoff's voice hesitated. "Get with it. See you at home plate."

That was it. Bannon stared at the mike a moment, put everything back into his belt. He squeezed the TBM radio button. "Shiloh Tower from Triple Deuce. Got a bad mag here. Like to taxi back to my hangar."

Wendy Green nodded to herself as she responded.

"Roger, Triple Deuce. You're clear for a one-eighty and taxi back."

At his hangar Bannon folded the wings of the torpedo bomber, whipped the airplane around smartly in its parking slot, and shut down. He was out of the cockpit and through his door quickly, locking the door behind him. In his office he hauled open a metal file drawer, punched a code into a small electronic keyboard, and withdrew a security telephone. He pressed more buttons to activate the scrambler and ring into Hudoff's security system. A red light flashed and the words STAND BY glowed up at him.

Bernie Hudoff leaned against the hood of his Land Rover. Seagulls screeched nearby and a long string of pelicans in feathered line formation drifted overhead. The day was beautiful and warm and drenched with sunshine. Hudoff turned to watch a Coast Guard cutter sliding into its dock. To the left a Poseidon sub was taking on a load of powerful missiles for a test-firing mission. Port Canaveral bustled with shrimpers, huge radar ships bristling with domes and antennas, luxury cabin cruisers, even an enormous cruise liner.

Hudoff grunted to himself. All this made the thought of a terrorist group with four atomic bombs, right in his own front yard, seem impossibly remote. And impossible, he mused. How the hell could he equate the terrible, ultimate danger with this surrounding of friendly bustle and warmth? He rubbed his stubbled chin. Hell, he'd been in the danger thickets all his life. He loved those moments when the risks escalated to life-and-death situations.

Bernie Hudoff was a grizzly of a human with thick bushy eyebrows bristling over a thick neck and a great stomach as hard as a tree stump. No one about him knew for certain, but the word followed Hudoff that he'd been a hit man for the CIA in his earlier days. Hudoff thought about that. He'd done a lot more than eliminate individual targets; in his time he'd been responsible for a few revolutions and even one decent-sized war.

And all of it together couldn't hold even a feeble

candle flame against what he now faced. *Four atomic bombs!* He— Hudoff heard the insistent chime of his attaché case. He opened the top and saw the glowing letters CALL READY. Again he grunted to himself and motioned to Elliott and Horvath. "Get the hell away from me for a few minutes." He pointed toward the docks. "Go look at the ships, for Christ's sake. Piss off the pier. Anything. Just get out of here until I call you back."

As soon as they were out of earshot he yanked the phone from its cradle. "Shiloh? Confirm scrambler."

"Confirmed. Bernie, what the hell's going on?"

"I'll make it short and sweet," Hudoff replied. "First, if you hear strange background sounds, I'm on the coast guard dock at the Cape. I'm clear. No one can hear me. Now, listen carefully, Ace. We lost a blue-suit courier this morning with four nukes aboard. It—"

"Lost?"

"Hang in, damnit. You'll get more details later, but for right now this is all we've got."

"Where did the ship go down?"

"Just north of Lake Okeechobee," Hudoff detailed. "It was missing for twenty minutes. During that time, according to what little data we have, there was some severe electronic interference in the area. No direct contact with the crew. But we did confirm they released one of the emergency broadcast cylinders. Dropped by chute, and gives out a locator signal. It's supposed to be used only in the event of top emergency. Anyway, like I said, the Air Force told us the plane was missing for twenty minutes. The strange part of all this is that they got a skin track on it after the twenty minutes passed."

"What about transponder squawk?"

"You're getting what I've got, Bannon. Shut up and listen. Apparently it flew over the Gulf and then it went down. An airliner crew going to Tampa saw it trailing smoke; they were almost positive they saw flames. Whatever was going on, they said they saw it go into a steep dive and plow into the water."

"Any survivors?"

"No."

"It stinks, Bernie."

"That's how we look at it. Obviously, or as obviously as you can add it up, during the twenty minutes it was off scope it was forced down. We believe that whoever got them to land killed the crew, hauled off the bombs, then took the plane off again and when it was over the Gulf they set the autopilot and bailed out."

"Bernie, bear with me."

"You got ideas, Ace?"

Hudoff waited through a long pause. He figured it would be worth it for Bannon to make an omelet out of the broken eggs. Finally the other said, "Bernie, what about time hacks?"

"Shit man, we got the takeoff time from Gitmo, the real-time tracking records, full position reports until all the frequencies went haywire."

"Jamming. It's got to be full ECM jamming."

"Yeah. We see it that way, too."

"What was the time when the radios went out?"

"Damn close to six this morning."

"Anybody see anything else?"

"Yep. A fisherman reported hearing gunfire over Okeechobee. He said it was so crazy he almost didn't report it. But he's an old infantryman and he also said he'd never forget what machine guns sounded like when he was below them. We can't do any more with that but, Bannon, we got three sightings of parachutes. About seventy, eighty miles from impact."

"Of course! What the hell did you expect? Whoever pulled this off sent up a pilot or two who was also an experienced jumper. One gets you twenty a boat picked them up. Nothing to find even if you stopped the boat. Bunch of guys on a joyride." Another pause. "Uh, Bernie, what was the transport?"

"Convair. The regular shuttle."

"All military fighters accounted for?"

"*Whose* fighters, Bannon?"

"Don't give me shit. Air Force, Navy; whatever."

"*Mister* Bannon, *every* military aircraft is accounted for except those that are flown by that bunch of lunatics you fly with. What's that outfit called?"

"Strasser Air Circus. It's run by Major Karl von—"

Hudoff had lost any touch of humor. "Bannon, I don't want to know about any fucking Nazis right now." He took a deep breath. "But I'll tell you what I *do* want."

Bannon's voice dripped ice. "You do that."

Hudoff stared at his phone, shrugged, and went on. "This is for the record, Ace. I want to know where every goddamned airplane from your field has been at any time last night and this morning. Got that? I want the planes, and I want the names of the pilots, and I want a report on every last one of your crazy bastards!" He took a deep breath. "And I want it *right away!*"

"Are you crazy?" Bannon's voice had gone up a notch, Hudoff noticed. "We don't have any jet fighters in this crowd. It's all heavy iron from the second world war, for Christ's sake!"

Hudoff wasn't buying any of it. "Bannon, tell me the fighter planes you maniacs fly."

"What? Oh, well, Mustangs, a Thunderbolt, two Hellcats and a Bearcat, we've got a Wildcat, and, uh, a Warhawk, and there's John's P-38, and—"

"Hold it, Bannon, *hold it.* Can any one of those fighters outfly a Convair?"

"Well, yes, but—"

"But me no buts. Get that information. *Now.*"

Hudoff cut the connection.

Bannon sat for a long time at his desk. He lit up a cigar, walked outside, his brain in overdrive. That was the problem. He had to slow it down, put everything he'd learned and everything else he could figure into perspective. And there was one point that kept niggling around the back of his skull. It wouldn't go away. He jerked open the fridge and hauled out a tall Coors. It went down in a long, steady swallow. He crumpled the can and tossed it aside and opened a second. He took this one slowly and went back outside again with the beer and the cigar. He sat beneath the torpedo bomber, leaning back against the main gear, trying to sort it all out. They had some heavy shit on their hands. That was obvious. He needed more information. Hudoff needed a hell of a lot more information. And obviously they hadn't passed the word yet to the public that all hell might be hidden right next door. To anybody. Anywhere. At any moment.

Then he had it. That half-formed thought niggling about in the rear cavities of his brain. He went back inside and picked up his phone and tapped in a number.

"Sheriff's office."

Bannon knew them all. "Hillary? Bannon here."

"At this time of day? You sick or something, Bannon? You're supposed to sleep after servicing all those teeny-boppers on the beach, you know."

"Funny. Very funny, Hillary. Now give me the sheriff or I'll tell everybody you and I are making out."

"Make that come true and I'll *never* give you the sheriff. You need a full-grown *woman*, Bannon, not—"

"Damnit, Hillary!"

She put him through to Sheriff Bob Hughes. "What the hell do you want at *this* hour, Mitch? It's too damned early in the morning for problems and I've already got a bushel basket full of them." Hughes hesitated a moment. "Hey, wait one! Speaking of problems, I want to talk to you about some crazy bastard who just about blew the Paradise Motel apart not too long ago. With a plane. No doubt one of *your* planes, Bannon."

"What time, Bob?"

"As close to six o'clock straight up as you can get."

Bannon smiled. The smile broadened into a huge grin. He propped his feet up on the desk. "Sheriff, that's just what I wanted to talk to you about."

It was a scene straight out of the second world war. Or the Twilight Zone, considering that the war had ended with two huge mushroom clouds over Japan more than forty years before. Shiloh Field might have been snatched from history and brought to the present as engine thunder permeated the sky and rolled across the ground and rattled windows and walls and brought teeth to aching. From north and south and the west the warbirds began their return to Shiloh. Clouds of metal gathered in the sky, and other warbirds just arriving for the first airshow that afternoon began to slip into the formations and the long strings of heavy iron maneuvering to land, as if they were all massing about some enormous aircraft carrier.

The planes came down in a steady stream directed with crisp efficiency by Wendy Green and two other tower controllers. Gone was the hurrah bullshit of earlier that day between the pilots and Wendy. That was then, with plenty of room in which to screw up on the ground or with the planes spread across three counties. This was *now*, and into all the invisible funnels of airspace came the fast and the slow, the small and the large, the light and the heavy, the kind of air traffic mix that keeps the pucker factor at its max. The pilots were on their last legs, exhausted from the long horrible night, suffering from hangovers, desperate for sleep, in almost critical need of food and oxygen and coffee and last, but hardly least, hot showers to scrape away the grunge of the night and the sweats of early-morning flying. As quickly as they landed, the pilots swung to their parking places to shut down and switch off, then joined the bedraggled march to the closest vehicles for a fast run to nearby motels for their ablutions.

Not all the crews were so desperate for survival measures. Many of the pilots and their crew members had become inured to the effects of alcohol, lack of sleep, insufficient food and excessive coffee, and they thrived on a diet that should have left them tottering wrecks. They gathered in the ground-floor operations office of Morgan Aviation and in the pilot's lounge or sprawled on the floor of the offices, chain-smoking, sucking down coffee and vitamin B-1 and aspirin and lying to one another about how great they felt. Most of the men and women present were the flight leaders for the first airshow that afternoon, the Friday gathering they always flew as practice for the hard shows to be flown Saturday and Sunday.

It was normal, familiar weekend pandemonium and conversational uproar until a sheriff's car pulled up before the office door, its flashing lights visible through the picture windows facing the flight line. Moments later a hush fell heavily among the pilots and crewmen with two uniformed deputies coming through the door. The appearance of the law meant little, but the demeanor and grim faces of these two said volumes. They were here for business.

"We'd like to speak with Charlene Morgan, please," the lead deputy said at the counter. Doug Callahan, chief instructor for Morgan Aviation, pointed to his right and behind him. "That way."

They went to the entrance to Charley's office. Here they found neither indifference nor hostility. Charley knew both men. They'd been friends with her father. Deputy Harry Wilson shifted uncomfortably from one foot to the other. He fingered a paper nervously and then spoke in a thick, syrupy drawl.

"Miss Morgan . . . I mean, well, Charley, damn, I am truly sorry about this." The paper nearly crumpled in his nervous grasp.

"About what, Harry?" Charley had no idea why the deputies were in her office.

Wilson shoved the paper before him abruptly as if it were burning his hand. "Charley, I *do* rightly apologize." He swallowed hard. "This here is a warrant for your arrest, ma'am."

Charley took the paper in an automatic gesture. Her mouth opened and closed without sound. Behind the deputies the pilots had crowded into the office. Wendy Green bulled her way through the mob, grabbed Wilson's arm, and swung him around. She was all flint and sparks.

"Harry Wilson, what the hell *for?*" she shouted at him.

Wilson remained a gentle giant. "Miss Wendy," he paused to look sorrowfully at Charley, "this here ain't none of my doing. It's the manager of the Paradise Motel, you know, on the river? Well, Mr. Pardue, he filed a complaint with the sheriff. Swore out this here warrant. He said Miss Morgan just about tore his place apart. Wrecked it from one end t'other. Bunch of plate glass windows broken, dishes and glasses all busted, what few guests he had left after all the ruckus the night long hysterical and screaming-like. *That's* what for, Miss Wendy."

Deputy Enid Kovacs nodded dutifully. "Ma'am," that ain't all. There's the little matter of the other violations, you know? Like the sheriff says, Miss Morgan busted a noise statute and she endangered lives and property, and I hear tell the feds is mighty interested in the goings-on this morning."

Wendy Green was openly astonished. "How the hell did Miss Morgan manage all *that*?"

"Well, ma'am, she just about flew this here huge airyplane almost *through* the motel, she was so low."

Charley had gathered her wits about her. "Harry, *what* airplane? You haven't made an ounce of real sense yet."

"The big airplane, ma'am. The bomber you own and fly. A bunch of people saw it come over and—"

"Deputy, that is so much crap. You have witnesses who saw an airplane *in the dark*?"

"Uh huh. Yes, ma'am. Your airplane. The one you was flying, ma'am."

"It's impossible for anyone," Charley said slowly, "for anyone to know who was in that airplane, or whatever airplane it is you're talking about."

"Oh, they *know*, ma'am. Someone told this here Mr. Pardue, you know, the motel manager? They told him it was *you*, ma'am."

A pin striking the floor would have sounded like a gunshot. No matter how much they heaped abuse on one another, these pilots were tight to a fault with their own. *Nobody* finks on another pilot, never, *ever*, about anyone's low flying. More men pushed into the room to better hear what went on. Behind them the door from the flight line opened. Abe Lansky and Yusuf Hamza stepped in, puzzled by the crowd jammed into Charley's office. They had just landed from their part of the dawn patrol and, like the others on the outside edge of the crowd, they were confused.

Lansky pushed closer to Bill Santiago, their traffic controller for the airshows. "What the hell is going on in there?"

Santiago glared at the interruption. "Shut up so we can all hear."

Charley's voice came to them in the hush. She got hard eye contact with Deputy Harry Wilson. "Someone *told* the manager, you say?"

"Yes'm. They most surely did."

"Who?"

Wilson looked about him, more uncomfortable than ever. "I expect that's your own personal business, ma'am."

"*Who*, goddamnit!"

Wilson looked down at the paper in his hand and gestured helplessly. "The name in this here document, ma'am, is Mitchell Bannon."

Charley took her chair slowly, staring at Wilson. She didn't, she refused to believe, she couldn't believe this idiot. She saw her brother shove his way like a crazy man to the front of the group, stand as close as he could to Wilson. "That's a lot of shit, Deputy!"

Wilson wasn't as calm with Mad Marty. "Son, don't rile me. Step aside, now." He stepped closer to Charley's desk and he became stiff and formal. "Miss Morgan, you're under arrest, ma'am. The law requires that we *got* to take you in for booking."

He seemed to hear his own words for the first time and softened. "You know you'll be released immediately on your own cognizance, ma'am, but we have simply *got* to do the drill."

Charley's face reflected conflicting emotions. This didn't make any sense! Absolutely none at all. Yet, there was that big affable redneck in uniform and gun, more uncomfortable than anyone else in the room, and he was going to arrest her and *take her to jail*. Because . . . because *Bannon* had turned her in? It was crazy but—

Knock it off, lady, she told herself. *Go with the man. Like he says, you'll be out on your own cognizance. Don't make a fuss. Don't make waves. This outfit has an airshow to fly . . .*

She rose to her feet, looking at the pilots. "Karl?" The big German came through the crowd. He'd heard it all and his face was cast in stone.

60

"Karl, will you take over, please? The show?"

He stood before her as a bedrock of strength and she knew everything was in good hands. "*Ja.* I do it. I feel like maybe I could kill someone." The deputy gave him a hard look and got back the cold, uncaring stare of a man who's spent most of his life killing. Wilson quickly averted his eyes.

"Karl, do you believe this, I mean—"

"About Bannon?" Von Strasser shook his head. "No. I do *not* believe it. But that is not important this moment. Go with these oafs, do what you must do, and then come back. We sort it all out later. Go, Charley."

She walked around her desk, stopped for a quick hug from the German pilot. He patted her shoulder.

"Sis, you want me to go with you?"

She hugged her brother. Mad Marty's face was a mixture of anger and confusion. "No. Please work with Karl and Wendy."

She left for the outer office, the pilots melting away before her to clear a path. The door leading in from the ramp opened and Mitch Bannon walked briskly in. He was bright-eyed and bushy-tailed and bubblingly friendly.

"Hi, Charley," he sang out, "what's happening, babe?"

Charley never missed a beat in her determined walk to the door. She offered Bannon a dazzling smile and as she came up to him delivered a roundhouse right with all her strength flush on Bannon's jaw. Stunned and caught by surprise and off balance, Bannon tumbled over backwards to crash against the wall. Holding his jaw, he slid slowly to the floor, staring up at Charley.

She held her right hand in her left, grimacing with pain, all the way to the sheriff's car. Wilson looked like a giant puppy tripping over his own feet to get to the car ahead of her and open the door.

Behind her the pilots cheered and applauded.

✠ 5 ✠

THE PLAYERS

"Mister Hudoff?" Please?"

Bernie Hudoff was stomping down the long hallway to his office in spaceport headquarters, a stride that brought his heavy boots crashing to the floor. People in headquarters had learned to take the measure of Hudoff's temper by the measure of his march, and the indicators at this moment were all bad. At such moments no one bothered Hudoff. They did their best to be invisible to him. Now the elderly black woman stood before him in the hallway, her hand raised slightly, face lined with worry. She had nodded before to Hudoff. She had nodded to him for years when they passed in the hallways or in the elevators or the coffee shop. But aside from cursory greetings, they'd never spoken a word to one another. Now she stood before him, recognizing his position and yet, by her stance and demeanor, making it clear that he must recognize this moment as unusual and critical to her.

He stopped, as gentle with her as he was bearish with his own staff. He glanced at her ID badge but he didn't need it. He knew every employee in this building by memory. "You're Molly Johnson, aren't you?" He offered the recognition with courtesy.

"Yes, sir."

"You've been here a long time, Mrs. Johnson."

She nodded. "Yes, sir, since before even the big building was finished. Mr. Hudoff, I got something most important to ask you."

"Of course." His smile was brief but it was nonetheless a smile. "You've been here some years longer than I have, Mrs. Johnson. That gives you seniority. What can I do for you?"

"I got to ask you straight, Mr. Hudoff." She took a deep breath and the lines on her face seemed to stand out. "Should I move my family away from here until it's safe?"

Hudoff stared at the cleaning woman. *Cleaning woman*, by God! And already she knew more than his staff! But how—

"What do you mean, Mrs. Johnson?"

"Mr. Hudoff, time to play games is behind us. Never mind how I knows what I know. I don't talk about it to anyone but you, so you don't need to worry none. That bomb stuff, Mr. Hudoff. Them atoms, you know? Like what happened in Hiro— in, in Japan. It could happen here now, couldn't it?"

Hudoff checked the long hallway. No one else was there. "Yes, it could. But how in the name of God did you—"

A leathered hand gestured and he fell silent. "Nobody else I talk to," she said firmly. "Should I take my family away? That's all I want to knows from you, Mr. Hudoff."

He opted for straight honesty. People like Molly Johnson were often the best intelligence sources in any huge complex like the space center. Hudoff decided right then and there to leave it alone and play it above board. "There is a danger, Mrs. Johnson. I can't tell you whether to go or not. That must be up to you."

Her eyes held his with devastating effect. Hudoff felt as if he were faced suddenly with generations of dignity and truth. "You staying, Mr. Hudoff?"

"I'm staying, Molly Johnson."

A touch of a smile appeared. "You really goin' to stick it out?"

"Got to. It's my job. A lot of people count on me to do that job the best I can."

Her shoulders lifted. "Well, I 'spose that answers it all. Lordy, I feel better."

"What do you mean?"

"I can't very well walk out on you if you're going to stay here and do *your* job, can I?"

He started to speak and found his throat was choked. He reached out to squeeze her hand gently and walked quickly past her to his office. *There* he could shout at people.

"I don't know how you did it, Sarah," Hudoff told his secretary. "Getting these people here this fast—" He shook his head in appreciation. "Sure you're not Wonder Woman in disguise?"

Sarah Evans handed him a list of names. "I didn't get them all. I tried to but there simply wasn't enough time."

He studied the list, tapped the paper. "They're inside?"

"Yes, sir. Waiting for you. A few of them are, well, ticked off. They don't know what's come down yet."

"They'll know soon enough. Thank you, Sarah. Got the coffee and the rest of it?"

"All taken care of, Mr. Hudoff."

He nodded again and went into the conference room adjacent to his office. He knew Joe Horvath and Lou Elliott would be there, and he hoped they'd kept their mouths shut. One glance at them told him they'd done just that. He was surprised and pleased that they'd made contact so fast with Mario del Passo. That was a lucky break. The best man Interpol had in the field was working with drug enforcement teams in the Miami area, and they were able to get him into a private jet and bring him directly to the shuttle strip and then by helicopter to KSC headquarters. Hudoff was playing hardball where Mario del Passo was concerned. He knew the Interpol man from way, way back. If anything as big as hijacking a bunch of nukes was real, the former head of the Portuguese secret police would damned well have the angle on it. He nodded to del Passo. The small, slim man with the pencil-thin moustache and silver hair nodded back. They'd both save the small talk for later.

Roger Coats from the CIA shop sat quickly at the table. He had been easy to grab for this session. He'd been assigned to the local area for months, convinced his cover as a newsman was airtight. Hudoff knew of his presence within a day of his arrival, but they'd let Coats continue with his charade. He was on a constant witch hunt for Russian spies. Which was pretty dumb, because NASA held an open door invitation to Russian cosmonauts and scientists, and both the United States and the Soviet Union had been working for years on cooperative programs. Plus the fact, Hudoff concluded with sarcasm he kept to himself, that with the Russians sending one of their cosmonauts, Georgi Mikoyan, on the *Antares* mission, *not* to have Russians underfoot would have been the real mystery. But Coats was here because he might have something, anything, that would help Hudoff.

Hudoff looked about the table. He didn't recognize one face but he knew the stranger would be from the local FBI office working out of Melbourne. Arthur Low. Absolutely typical Bureau man. Dark suit, dark tie, dark hair, dark eyes. Hudoff wondered if he sang darky tunes. Unless he was losing his touch, Hudoff knew the FBI man didn't know beans about what had happened this same morning.

"Where's the blue-suit?" he asked Horvath.

"Colonel Lewis is flying," Horvath said simply. "I'll fill him in later."

Dumbshit, Hudoff muttered to himself. *Well, get to it.*

He laid it out as coldly and briskly as he could manage. He ignored the expected mixture of reaction except to study faces and take mental notes he could develop later.

"Let me review," he said to wrap it up. "If we hold to the present schedule, then nine days from now *Antares* will launch from Pad Thirty Nine Able. Eight astronauts will be aboard from seven different countries. If the flight proceeds as planned the shuttle will rendezvous with the *Olympus* station. Four of the astronauts will remain in orbit and four will return.

"This is the biggest show since the first landing on the moon. You all know what's involved. The VIP list includes four thousand of the world's top leaders. Presidents, premiers, kings, queens—the works. Also, of course, scientists, poets, philosophers; whoever each country considers important. We will keep these four thousand people in a separate area close to the VAB, isolated from the press and everyone else. We expect at least seven thousand news media people from about the world. Now, they'll be in the press site area and fully controlled as to their movement. We'll also have more than a hundred thousand guests in the viewing area, which is the usual repeat of what we've done before. Along selected roads, in lawn areas, atop buildings."

Mario del Passo raised his hand. "The different countries that will supply astronauts?"

Hudoff knew del Passo had the list. He was verbalizing for a reason he'd unfold later. "Besides the U.S., Brazil, Japan, Sweden, New Zealand, Israel, and Russia."

"None from the Arab lands?" A Portuguese eyebrow was raised.

"We've already flown three mission specialists from the Arab countries," Hudoff replied, "including a crown prince from Saudi Arabia. And if we hadn't, we didn't feel it was very smart to put an Israeli *and* an Arab aboard the same ship."

Del Passo smiled and acknowledged the answer with a nod.

"Now, there's another issue to be kept in mind," Hudoff swept on. "We've had a million people hit Brevard County in the past for the moon shots. We expect more for this launch."

"I don't see what all this has to do with us," Arthur Low said. "I mean, the Bureau is always happy to cooperate with the security needs of NASA and—"

"Why the hell don't you wait to find out what it has to do with you?" Hudoff snapped. "You have a hot lunch date or something?"

66

"Why, no, I don't, but—" He glared at Hudoff. "I'll wait."

"You said you expect more than a million people in the county?" Roger Coats broke in. "Why, you'd get that many people for a shuttle launch that's old hat—"

"I didn't say that," Hudoff broke in, brusque and open about his distaste for incompetence. "I said we had a million people hit Brevard County for past shots. That's a million people *above* the local population. And we won't get the mob this time because of the shuttle. We'll get the mob because of all the kings and queens, the Hollywood stars, the religious leaders, and that includes the Pope and *his* whole retinue—am I getting through?"

He waited until they nodded. "Now, imagine well over one and a quarter million people, locals and the visitors, invading the areas where they can best see the launch. There'll be a couple thousand boats along every river and canal and out in the ocean. There'll be people on every roadside, in every park, on every roof. We'll have them in every direction. But they're not the reason I had you in here for this visit."

Mario del Passo sipped coffee and lit a long black cigar. His eyes were gleaming. "Ah, now we come to the fun part," he said, and smiled at the hard stares he provoked from the others.

"Yeah, I guess you could say that," Hudoff answered.

"Why all this mystery?" Low demanded. "You're talking about guests and newsmen and mobs of people. That hasn't got a thing to do with *us*. Let the local police and the sheriff's department and the state police worry about it. What do you want from us?"

Hudoff bit his tongue. God, how he hated mealy-mouthing! Insufferable little shit who couldn't see beyond his own nose.

"I need your help," Hudoff said, almost having to force out the words.

"In heaven's name, *for what?*" Low said with unconcealed exasperation.

Hudoff leaned back in his chair and let the pregnant pause settle in the room like a layer of dust.

"Because," he said slowly, every word dropping heavily, "we have reason to believe a terrorist group will attempt to destroy the launch and viewing areas at liftoff."

"How could they possibly do that?" Roger Coats said acidly.

"You tell me," Hudoff said innocently.

"Why, to have an effect like that, in the area you're talking about," Coats said, "they'd need an atomic bomb. And I can tell you *we'd* know if they did."

"They don't?"

"Of course not!"

Hudoff sat wrapped in silence. The others began to fidget, to shift uncomfortably in their seats. They glanced at one another and back to Hudoff and their eyes began to widen.

Roger Coats sat up in his chair, eyes narrowed, staring at Hudoff. "Are you telling me . . ." His voice trailed off. He shook his head. "No, it can't be. The CIA would be the first to know. We . . ." Again his voice faded as he realized he was talking to himself more than he was to the others.

He was almost desperate now as he looked again at Hudoff. "My God, you mean . . . they have, I mean, someone has—"

"You bet your momma."

"A terrorist group," Arthur Low broke in, "*with an atomic bomb?*"

Hudoff shook his head. "No."

"Thank God for that," Low answered, smiling.

"Not an atomic bomb," Hudoff said in a flat voice. "*Four* atomic bombs."

The silence in the room was deafening.

Mario del Passo remained after the others had left. Hudoff wanted a one-on-one with the deceptive little man with the exquisite touch of the diplomat and the single-mindedness of Kublai Khan when he had been running his share of secret operations and small wars around the globe.

"You know a hell of a lot more than you let on," Hudoff told his old friend.

"Of course. Obviously, you didn't want me to speak when the others were here. If you had," del Passo said easily, "there would have been questions directed to me. Since there were none," he shrugged, stubbing out his cigar, "a short wait seemed in order."

"Thanks," Hudoff said. "Now—"

A perfectly manicured hand moved. "Wait. First, why did you leave Stevens out of this meeting?"

"Coke Stevens?"

"Yes."

Hudoff had a mental picture of the man who reported directly to the White House. Coke Stevens was cut from the same bolt of cloth as Arthur Low, right down to the same dark suit and tie. Probably the same damn tailor, Hudoff mused. "Because nothing really changes," he told del Passo. "If Stevens were here, he'd have contacted the White House before this meeting was even halfway done. Then when the other security agencies went to the White House, the President or his staff, or both, would have drawn all sorts of wrong conclusions. Stevens is an empire builder. He wouldn't have, he *doesn't* have, any idea of what the hell is involved here. So we'll brief him later today. I'll let Horvath handle that. Those two have been at each other's throats for a long time."

"Bernie, what you just said interests me. Do *you* have a real comprehension of what you're facing? It is so easy to talk about an atomic bomb!" The Interpol man seemed to sag in his chair. "Everything we have ever done, you, me, the whole crowd who went around the world plotting and killing and maneuvering, we are feathers in a cyclone compared to a nuclear explosion."

"You think I don't know that? Jesus, I wish I didn't. When I was a kid, Mario, I was part of the teams that volunteered to be under a couple of nukes we fired in the desert." Hudoff's face clouded. "We had full knowledge and protection, and thirty percent of our people bought the farm. A slight miscalculation, let's say. Yeah," he grunted, "I got a slight idea."

Mario del Passo offered a thin smile. "Tell me, Bernie. Tell *me*. As briefly as you can. Begin with the yield of the bombs that were lost."

He didn't get his answer immediately, but he didn't expect one. A man had to expand his thinking a million times to gain even an inkling of what was involved. Finally Hudoff spoke. "They're each four hundred kilotons," he began.

"No technical terms, please," del Passo said. He didn't open his eyes when he spoke.

Christ, but he's right, Hudoff told himself, and the quiet horror began to grow as he released his own imagination. Four hundred kilotons. A fancy catch-phrase. Each one of the hijacked bombs had the power of *twenty* bombs of the size that incinerated Hiroshima. Four hundred thousand tons of explosive force in a package the size of . . . of a bowling ball, for God's sake!

Think of the instant of detonation, he ordered himself. Think of that exact spot where the thing will implode when the trigger goes off. *Think!*

One hundred and eighty million degrees.

That's a bunch of fucking zeros, Hudoff! his mind shouted at him. *Even the belly of the sun is like the Arctic compared to that!*

He felt the perspiration begin on his face, beading on his upper lip as he fought to envision reality that could be, from the numbers they spoke of so easily, so glibly. He created a picture in his mind of *Antares* on its launch pad, all those visitors and press and the NASA people and . . .

A star will explode. You begin with *that*. A star will explode. The pressure will be more than a billion times greater than what had existed an instant before. All sanity is banished in the face of such insane force. The shock wave is so powerful it *burns* the air as it whips outward. But even before the shock wave moves a dozen feet there'll be the light, that God-awful light beyond all description. He built the scene in his mind of all the thousands and thousands of people before the altar that would hurl the giant spacecraft away from earth. People with their eyes wide and staring at the shuttle groaning its way upward.

The light pulse would burn out the eyes of everyone there looking at the shuttle.

Everyone in the VIP area, all four thousand of them. All seven thousand newsmen. All one hundred thousand visitors. Another fifty to sixty thousand employees and their families, and that was at the Kennedy Space Center *alone.* Everyone on Cape Canaveral, all the people in the boats ... Hudoff felt his stomach churning as he forced himself to think in terms of concurrent effects.

Del Passo measured Hudoff's thoughts. "You know that no one within three miles of where the thing goes off will even think about blindness," he said. Hudoff caught the oblique reference immediately.

"Yes," he replied simply. "They won't think about blindness because their eyes will *melt.*" *Good God* ... his voice went on, unbidden. "Just about everyone within direct line of sight, for two or three miles in every direction ... their eyes will melt and their skin will char and melt and their clothes and hair will burst almost instantly into flames ..." He conjured the awful vision of staying close to the blast as it began. No; *before* the blast, when the most elemental forces of nature were savaged loose. The fireball, pure blazing subnuclear energy, would loom above the earth's surface. That was the only way to imagine it. Even if the bomb exploded on the very surface, expending much of its energy in digging a center a few hundred yards wide and perhaps just as deep, the fireball would snap into existence as a dome of raging, pulsating, killing energy. A dome rearing more than a thousand feet above the surface, blinding, killing, pouring out heat and light beyond description and floods of lethal radiation. *A dome twice as high, and higher, than even that huge VAB!*

Hudoff opened his eyes to look at del Passo. "Mario, tell me something. Where did you learn so much about these things?"

The Portuguese smiled. "I went to the Pacific to watch the French test their hydrogen bombs. They used many test animals, as did your people. What happened to

71

those creatures is—well, at *our* worst, we are angels compared to that. The French, ah, those people of fine wine and love and music and art. Did you hear about the prisoners?"

Hudoff shook his head. "Nothing outwardly criminal, of course. But they offered amnesty to a select group of criminals. Idiots and mental patients mostly, who didn't understand what they would have to face. They all signed releases. Be tested and when the tests are over you are pardoned. All one hundred and thirty-two of them."

Hudoff made a steeple of his fingers and studied del Passo under the arc. "And?"

"Most of them died within twenty-four hours. The rest?" del Passo shrugged. "Crippled, burned, irradiated and absolutely stark, raving mad. They were too close to the bomb," he appended.

"You know," Hudoff said slowly, "until this moment I've been making a mistake."

"You are learning fast," del Passo said with a humorless smile.

"I had imagined what would happen to the shuttle if the bomb exploded at liftoff. I had this terrible picture in my mind of an invisible fly swatter smacking the shuttle right out of the sky. Very dramatic and—"

"And very real," del Passo added.

"But not realistic enough. Whoever has those bombs, if they're good enough to get one into position and fire it at liftoff, you know, close to the pad: holy shit, Mario, *the shuttle will be inside the fireball.*"

"The astronauts will never have to worry about crashing, will they?"

"No. They'll be dead right where they are. Dead a dozen different ways. Jesus."

He thought of the shock wave and huge blast that would follow, horribly *slow* to the hundreds of thousands of victims that would be writhing, shrieking, burning human grubs and—

The hammer of Thor. The phrase rose in his mind as he saw the VAB punctured like a flimsy toy, its thousands of panels and structural walls so much tissue paper. He tried a different and more everyday approach. *Shit, not so tough. A tornado about four miles wide at the ground base and with winds of over a thousand miles an hour.* That's a steel wall rushing through the air and— *Enough!* his inner voice cried.

A final thought gasped through his aching brain. *And those sons of bitches have four bombs . . .*

"I believe I may know who they are."

Hudoff's jaw fell. He forced it shut. "In the name of God, Mario—"

"Please." The raised hand moved with the word. "Spare me the blessings of your deity." He smiled with the discomfort of watching Hudoff realize he'd reverted to childhood imprinting in his phraseology. Del Passo leaned forward, elbows on the table. "There is one group, very smart, all the money they need, and technologically on a level equal with your own military."

"Who!"

"Zoboa."

"What the hell's ah, ah, say it again?"

"Zoboa. In a nutshell, a tight team, tremendously wealthy, absolutely fanatical. Long established in most of the western nations, lying under cover for many years until their moment arrives. Yours," del Passo commented unnecessarily, "appears to be at your doorstep."

"Okay, that's *what* they are. *Who* are they?"

"From everything we have gathered over the years, Arabic. You must be careful of clear conclusions drawn from insufficient data, my friend."

"Tell me something new," Hudoff murmured.

"Perhaps they are Arabic," the Portuguese went on. "The name could be a red herring. Not even the communist teams who work about the world know that much about them. I am welcome on both sides of the fence and I can vouch for that."

"What does Zoboa mean?"

"You understand the meaning of kamikaze?"

"Sure. Divine wind. The storms that sprang up to destroy the mongol invaders of Japan when they themselves were helpless against invasion."

73

"Ah, yes. Zoboa is the same to the Arab people. A fierce sandstorm that wipes out their enemies. Who were also from Asia, I might add."

"All right. To hell with the history lesson." Hudoff knew he was pressing hard, but he had no choice. "Mario, even if it means stretching your contacts, can you give me any names? Any real leads to go by?"

"Not yet. Remember, Bernie, all this began only this very morning. There's hardly been time—"

"Oh, for Christ's sake, Mario, we don't need to lie to each other. You couldn't give a shit about cocaine-running in the Miami area or South America or anywhere else. You're here for other reasons."

"And they are?"

"Mario, my friend, if I wanted to know I would have found out by now. *I don't care.* You were gracious enough to come here when you didn't need to. I don't want to know anything else. But I *am* asking you for help."

Del Passo stood up. He nodded slowly. "All right, you will have that help. I wish to use a secure telephone, please."

"You got it."

"And the moment I finish I wish to be on my way. Can you have me back in the Miami area two hours from now?"

"Where? What field?"

"Homestead. Either the private field or, preferably, my friend, the Air Force base."

"You got it. Use that yellow phone over there. You have my word it's a clean line. By the time you're finished a chopper will be here to take you to the strip."

"Thank you. One more thing."

Hudoff waited.

"It has been good to see one of the, ah, originals again, Bernie. I hope you get these people. It would grieve me to think that you were incinerated."

"Anyone ever tell you that you can be charming, Mario?"

✛ 6 ✛

HUDOFF

They were all gone. Bernie Hudoff gulped down four aspirin with three fingers of Jack Daniels. The private session with Mario del Passo had been a godsend. It had come barely in time, for the name Zoboa was no stranger to the higher security echelons of Washington. The top agencies, CIA and FBI all the way through NSA, all had the name locked into their computers. They also held to the theory that Zoboa was Arabic, supported by everything from Libya to the PLO to the Syrians, and they were terrorists whose targets were to be found in the United States. At that point all consensus of agreement evaporated in the usual steamy vapors that so effectively clouded judgment. If Hudoff had learned one thing above all others in dealing with the slick-suit, pointed-shoe types from Disneyworld North, it was that they all felt that to be less than absolutely certain of what they were saying was calamitous. They didn't think or believe or conclude or judge; they *knew*. They absolutely *knew*, even when they really didn't know piss from champagne.

Arthur Low was the proof positive. No sooner had del Passo departed Hudoff's office in one direction when, fortunately by coincidence, the FBI man was pounding down the hallways to meet privately with him. Low went through all the cockamamie furtive glances about him before he would say a word to Hudoff. He even set off a small transmitter in the conference room that would screw up radio bugs. He was paranoid to the point of flaming absurdity, but he *was* the official arm of the FBI, and Hudoff knew he must at least hear him out.

"Don't believe a word you hear about this being an Arabic operation," Low told him after double-locking the conference room doors. "It's not. I've confirmed this with Roger."

"Roger who?"

"Coats, man, Coats!"

"You mean the company office boy?"

"That's no way to talk about a fellow security agent, Hudoff. Coats is one of the best field agents in the CIA, and you of all people ought to keep that in mind."

"Top of the list. Now let me ask you what the hell you're doing back here," Hudoff said, making sure his impatience showed. "All you've got is to tell me things that are *not*."

Low leaned forward with his best conspiratorial air. "Roger's filed his report. The CIA position is that this is a KGB operation to destroy *Antares*."

"You're a lunatic. One of their greatest national heroes is going to be aboard that ship."

"I didn't say the CIA was right! They're *not*. The KGB doesn't care about the shuttle! We can always build more of those things." Low looked about him and his voice lowered. "I've been empowered—"

"You've been *what?*"

"Empowered, Hudoff. Surely you understand—"

Hudoff almost rolled his eyes to the back of his head. He waved a weary hand. "Forgive me. Go on."

"*We know* what's coming down. The KGB is involved, all right, but as a third party. They're financing this terrorist group. Their whole purpose is to make a surgical strike at President Markham while everybody is watching the goddamned spaceship."

"Get out."

"I don't understand—"

"Get out of here before I lose my last shred of sanity and throw your ass through that window. *Out!*" Hudoff rubbed his forehead. "My God," he said, as much to himself as to this idiot in the room with him. "A surgical strike with an atomic bomb. Good God."

"Hudoff, you can't—"

Hudoff lost it. He stood up and removed his jacket and pulled his tie free and advanced ominously around the table, his face contorted, massive hands balled into fists. Arthur Low took off. Hudoff went back to his seat, opened the drawer beneath the desk, and did the number again with aspirins and Jack Daniels.

They were all the bloody same, steeped in the same stupid thinking churned out by computer programs. Accountants and lawyers and shoe clerks. The *good* agents were out in the boondocks with their lives on the line and— *Nah, there're good agents here, too. God knows where they keep them. There's the rub. If they're really good you don't know who the hell they are.*

He needed people who wouldn't place their competitive bullshit over the danger at hand. He needed people who thought with their balls more than they worried over their reports. Hudoff didn't need a detailed dossier on this Zoboa group. He didn't need to know if they were for real or were just some Commie bullshit, and it didn't matter. Even an ape with half a brain could figure that when *Antares* went the spaceport would be the greatest target of its kind in history. Whatever came down would be directed against the whole works. The shuttle, the facilities, the news media, the visitors and, above all else, those four thousand guests from among the world's leaders.

He knew he'd have to work with the Russians. He grunted to himself. He'd done that before, even when he was pitted life-and-death against their toughest. With Cosmonaut Georgi Mikoyan holding one of the top seats aboard *Antares*, he didn't need a copy of the Communist Manifesto to know they'd have some of their best people around to keep a handle on things.

* * *

Mario del Passo had opened the door to lead him down a tunnel, dim and sketchy as it was. With four atomic bombs in the hands of a terrorist group—and nothing else would fit that scenario of the hijacking and probable murder of the crew—he would double, even triple all his security measures and systems at the Cape and here at the spaceport. *I'll seal this fucking place like a snare drum*, he told himself emphatically. *Sure, sure*, retorted his inner voice, *if you define letting over a hundred thousand guests from all over the world into NASA territory as sealing it off*.

Damn; he could easily hate himself for this infuriating murkiness of detail in which he was floundering. And he didn't have much time. He didn't know the *modus operandi* of this terrorist crowd, but it didn't take a genius to move an atomic bomb against so huge and inviting a target as launch day at the beach. The touch of sardonic humor in his own mind pissed him off. He forced himself back to that grimmest of visions before the light of lights savaged all sight from hundreds of thousands of helpless and unsuspecting human souls.

People dying or being killed didn't much bother Hudoff. He wasn't uncaring; far from it. His business had been cold-blooded killing, and all about him his closest friends had been killed. His survival had been due to a combination of brutal efficiency, keen intelligence, dedication, and inner voice that always gave him the right hunch at the right instant. All that, and no small dram of luck. The Lady was either on your side or she wasn't, and if the latter your life expectancy rarely went beyond one or two missions. Yet—and this kept his sanity safely between his ears more than anything else—he believed in what he did. He'd seen enough countries under the boot of repression. He'd seen everything from savage petty dictators to communism marching in massive rank and file. What he had done had saved more lives and kept more people free than he could ever count.

Yet Bernie Hudoff was pragmatic. He knew his country couldn't be the policeman for the incredibly mixed bag of cultures splashed about the planet. So he did his best, and he came to recognize that he *could* separate individuals from the faceless obelisk of government. Even if they *were* Russian agents.

Greed and the coveting of power had killed people: through repression, torture, mass murder and, above all, disease and starvation by the tens of millions. The bunch of scalps hanging from his own belt were due to his own rapier thrusts as a professional killer. Compared to the bleeding hearts and the power-hungry, neither of which had ever been his own failing, he was as clean as the driven snow.

So he'd retired, and because the powers-that-be knew that he was loyal, incredibly good at what he did, and still eager to serve in the best way he knew how, they threw him a damned big bone as security chief of the Kennedy Space Center. And now everything he had avoided—the spectre of mass killing and horror upon horror—was sitting with bared teeth right at his crotch. He hated the narrow corridor of choices forced on him through lack of information. If he did not find the way to turn, and if that goddamned bomb went off when he thought his unknown opponents would take their shot, then *he* would be right in the middle of that triple-damned crowd and *his* ass would fry along with the rest of them.

What a way to go. Fricassee Hudoff.

There was perhaps one thing worse in the security business than being short of help. That was having *too* much help. Arthur Low was his immediate prime example. Hudoff knew he'd soon be inundated with more of the FBI. There'd be the CIA and NSA and DEA and military intelligence and Scotland Yard and the Tokyo undercover police and local polices and sheriffs and highway patrol *and* the Coast Guard, and even the KGB, to protect their own astronaut aboard *Antares*. The moment his old opposite numbers felt that Mikoyan could be vaporized, they'd yank his heroic ass back to Mother Russia with near-orbital speed.

Drowning in secret agents, each of whom was convinced that only he—or she, for that matter—had the one true answer was a sure way to keep the terrorists free of his clutches. Trying to sneak up on a quarry you haven't yet identified, when your own people act like a herd of rampaging elephants, just ain't the way to go.

He needed a *secret* secret agent that nobody knew or could identify except Bernie Hudoff and a certain senator in Washington. The senator was very powerful and he also had a talent for keeping his mouth shut when that was necessary.

Well, I got him, Hudoff said with mixed emotions. His secret agent wasn't his idea of what a secret agent should be like. Maybe, he shrugged to himself, that's why his cover works so well. He was six feet two inches tall and a hunk of muscle and white teeth and golden hair, and women from teeny-boppers to grandmothers would gladly offer testimonials to his ability in the sack, or on the beach, or in a car or anywhere. Hudoff's secret agent did his best to maintain those standards by screwing himself half to death—when he wasn't flying or drunk, that is. Long ago, Hudoff had planted Mitch Bannon smack in the middle of the space coast. His cover was perfect. He hired out for crop dusting or mosquito control, and he had a big sagging old hangar at Shiloh Field, and inside the decrepit building he had a couple of spray planes and a huge old TBM single-engine torpedo bomber from World War Two. *And* a jet helicopter that cost a cool one point three million.

Everyone figured the chopper had been bought with the proceeds of running grass into the country. Hudoff and Bannon did nothing to dispel that belief.

When he wasn't dusting or screwing or drinking or whatever, Bannon flew the Turkey, as he affectionately called his TBM, in the weekend airshows at Shiloh Field. Airshows were big business along the Platinum Coast. A bunch of madmen gathered around the old German pilot, Strasser or whatever the hell his name was. He'd been a top ace in a couple of wars and he flew with men he'd once tried to kill, and they'd tried to kill him or men like him, but now all that was behind them and they flew and drank and whored together. To top off this deranged flying circus, they flew their airshows for a beautiful young woman who owned Morgan aviation at the field, and—

He forced a halt to his ramblings. Screw the peripheral data. The truth of the matter was that Bannon might well be his only ace in the hole. If del Passo had fingered this Zoboa group for real, then whatever they were going to try would have to be done not just with cunning but with speed and flexibility. That meant fast movement at any time of the day or night, and *that* meant machines that sped through the skies. Hell, that's how they'd nailed the bombs in the first place. They didn't send a telegram to the crew of that Convair to force it down. They needed heavy iron for that nasty little job and, obviously, that's what they'd used.

Complicating matters was the fact that Brevard County, with the space launch centers along its coastline, was almost an aircraft carrier. Airports were *everywhere*, big and small, along the major highways like I-95 and the Bee Line Expressway, and the county was a mecca for gun-running, smuggling, and moving staggering loads of illicit drugs. Which gave Bannon lots of brownie points by running his own loads of grass. That old Turkey of his was designed to haul a two-thousand-pound torpedo. He'd converted the space into a cargo hold, and he could haul a hell of a load and drop it from the air with no more difficulty than hitting the switch that opened the bomb bay doors.

Bannon was an untouchable. Hudoff had arranged for that. Hudoff never contacted the local or the federal authorities directly; that could have been a dead give-away; that's where his senator came in. The word came down through an appropriations subcommittee to the right people in Treasury that Bannon was really a drug enforcement agent and was *never* to be messed with. It made sense; it worked. No one knew the real story. Bannon was a bloodhound without a specific quarry in mind. He might never be used.

Now he was critical. Being a successful pot hauler meant that a lot of pilots trusted him and almost no one *dis*trusted him. He was a hell of a pilot, he was crazy enough to be real, and he was drinking buddies with von Strasser and Mad Marty Morgan and the "inner circle" of pilots and airplane drivers. He also had an inside track with the law that got a lot of his buddies off the hook for traffic violations and busting federal aviation regulations, and that opened more doors than anything else. So if anybody had his ear to the ground and could crack this egg of mystery about Zoboa, chances were it would be Mitch Bannon.

There was just this one problem, Hudoff admitted with a groan. There almost *had* to be a problem, and this one was familiar as far back in history as early biblical times. The dumb bastard was in love. He wasn't satisfied with more pussy than any cathouse could ever offer; he had to have heart pangs.

He was apeshit over Charley Morgan—Charlene Morgan, that is. She and her kid brother, Mad Marty, inherited Morgan Aviation from their father. The old man was killed, so the word went, by smugglers. He'd been flying a charter with a heavy cocaine load that he didn't know about, and when he discovered what he was carrying his clients snuffed him. Not even Bannon had cracked that case yet. Maybe it had a tie-in with Zoboa. And maybe the pope wears pink undies. The world was filled with maybes.

Hudoff didn't like the maybes and possibilities of a terrorist group infiltrating the crazies who flew old warbirds in crowd-petrifying maneuvers. The airborne loonies had more than a hundred and twenty machines, and every one of them could have gone off to war tomorrow morning. Everything a terrorist gang needed in the way of maneuvering room was ready-to-order for them, and they could pull it off without any of the straight pilots knowing what was going on under their noses. Or wings, Hudoff appended.

It was time to call in his private criminal element.

✦ 7 ✦

CRAZIES

Damn good thing he liked ghosts. Hudoff walked through the gloomy thickness of dense vegetation, following the old foot trail burrowing beneath carpeting overhang. To each side rose small clearings with boulders carved with strange markings. The trail wound back on itself and he stopped before a badly worn, ancient small pyramid. More heavy stones, chiseled into obelisk and rectangular shapes.

This was one of the Indian cemeteries that had been here on Merritt Island since before the first white men walked on land that would be known as Florida. *It's fitting*, Hudoff told himself. *Here on the same land from which our ships depart to ports of which these Indians never dreamed, we struggle into the future while we respect the past of others.* And that was part of NASA's deal on Merritt Island. Not only were the ancient burial grounds never to be desecrated, they were to be respected and protected.

He heard the sound from the air above him and hurried to the small house nearly buried beneath trees, but fronting on an open field. Mitch Bannon's turbine chopper sounded like a bloated steam shovel hissing in agony, the hollow torch of the turbine mixing with the *whomp-whomp-whomp* of rotor blades. Bannon set the big helicopter down with a feathery touch and killed the engine. He emerged from the cabin while the blades were still whapping over his head. He looked about him a moment before joining Hudoff. His chief couldn't have picked a better place for a secret meeting. When NASA took over more than eighty-three thousand acres of Merritt Island for its giant launch complex, it inherited several dozen private homes in the "fallback and security" areas far from the operational buildings and launch pads. Wisely, NASA neither destroyed these small homes nor let them go to seed, but kept them in excellent shape for private meetings and hideaways for engineers, government officials, and even the astronauts, when quiet and privacy were needed.

"I've got coffee, cold cuts, cheese, and fruit inside," Hudoff told Bannon by way of greeting. "What I don't have is a lot of time. Let's get to it."

In the kitchen, more comfortable with food and drink at hand and where he could slug down his Jack Daniels from a flask, Hudoff laid out everything he'd heard from Mario del Passo, the bizarre scene with Arthur Low, and his own consensus of everything that had taken place on this already incredible morning. "We got nine days to go before *Antares* is scheduled to fly," Hudoff wrapped it up. "*If* it flies. And that *if* is based on what the hell we do about getting those four nukes back in our hands. We got 'em, the bird soars. We don't get 'em, the shuttle's another lame duck chained to the ground." Hudoff stuffed a stack of salami and cheese into his face and took a huge swallow of cold beer. He wiped his mouth with the back of his hand.

"You've got your finger in every dirty pie in this whole state," he said without emotion to Bannon. "You're rotten through and through. You run drugs and you screw young girls *and* their grandmothers. You drink too much and you fly when you're drunk. Most of your friends are thieves and criminals. You're despicable."

"Thank you," Mitch Bannon said. He paused to light a grievously expensive cigar. "I do my job."

"Yeah, I can see that. You ought to try bathing once in a while."

"Think of it as aroma, Bernie."

Hudoff let the preliminaries slip by. "Okay, tough guy. By any miracle, you got any kind of handle on this Zoboa outfit?"

"I've heard of it."

Hudoff went rigid. Bannon wasn't playing games. "You *know* about it?" Hudoff hissed.

"Well, not quite. It's a yes and no answer. Hold it, boss-man," he said hurriedly as Hudoff started out of his seat. "I'm not playing with the words. Zoboa. I'm not the only one who's heard of it. That name's been used among the pilots. But we've also heard of the Green Hornets, the Cuban Avengers, the Sirocco Reapers, the Red Underground, the Black Angels, the Red Fighters for Freedom, and—" He stopped. "Want me to go on? I can give you a list of a hundred outfits armed to the teeth and ready for their own private wars, but I can't tell you if half of them are for real."

"Mario makes noises like it's for real. How good is your info?"

"From what I hear, from everything I can smell out, Bernie, it's for real."

"Think they've got the nukes?"

"Jesus Christ, how the hell do *I* know!"

"We've *got* to know!"

"Well, *I don't*," Bannon told him flatly. "Goddamnit, we hear stories all the time about those fanatics—"

"Ever hear anything about a hit on the next shuttle?"

Bannon leaned back in his chair and studied his boss. "Bernie, listen to me. I hear all the time what you likely never hear at all. We get the word before *every* shuttle flight about a hit."

"You know what's happened today. This isn't *any* other time. This is for real."

"You got that written in stone?"

"What the fuck do I look like? Moses coming down the mountain with the tablets? We get the best information we can and we work with the worst-case scenario. I've got to assume Zoboa is for real, that they got the bombs, that they're going to do whatever they can to use them when everybody's a sitting duck at launch time."

Hudoff emptied a beer into himself. He belched, grabbed for a sandwich wrapped in cellophane, waved it at Bannon. "And you, sweetheart, are to do the same. Now, dammit, assume this Zoboa is for real. Can you get me a handle on it that I can pump with?"

"I sure as hell can try." Bannon drew deeply on the cigar and blew away a cloud of blue smoke. His face grew serious. "You believe they can get through your security system to get a nuke on the Cape?"

Hudoff sighed. "Shit, I was afraid you might ask that. Look, Bannon, I'm the best in my business, okay? Now, if it was *your* job or your sworn vow to get a nuke onto the Cape, *through me*, could *you* do it?"

"I'd blow the fucking place to pieces." There was no hesitation in the response.

Hudoff nodded. "I got to agree with you. So you see what I mean, then?" He grunted in deep thought for a moment. "Think about where you'd start. To get the goods on Zoboa, I mean."

"You been to Shiloh Field, Bernie. You were there *this morning* rousting my ass out of the sack."

"Go on, go on."

"Remember what you saw there. We got the big three-day weekend airshow on tap. Starting later today, in fact. Okay? Now, there's *two hundred warbirds* on that field. I could start one hell of a war tomorrow with what we got at Shiloh. And it's all legal. We got historic machines. Lots of fighters and bombers and other stuff."

"I know about the fighters. We talked about them. I told you I want to know where every one of those things was this morning. *And* their pilots. And—"

"Boss, will you lay off a moment and just listen to me?"

Hudoff glared at Bannon and then nodded. "Keep it tight."

"They got millionaires on Shiloh. They own *big* companies. They deal all around the world. They got hardware like you wouldn't believe. They're export-import.

We got *real* drug runners. We got manufacturers. Honest people and crooked people. We got banana-brains who've inherited more bread than they'll ever spend. These people, most of 'em, anyway, also got *organization*. Contacts all over the world. They deal with governments. With private armies. They can get *anything they want*. You want jet fighters? You want jet *bombers?* You want missiles? I can get 'em." Bannon locked steely eyes with Hudoff. "And you're asking for a down-and-locked rundown on all these people," he paused and snapped his fingers, "just like *that?* You're crazy."

Hudoff was disarmingly relaxed. As Bannon was wrapping up his spiel, Hudoff brought a notebook out of his jacket and flipped through several pages. He held his finger on the last opened page and looked up at Bannon. "What about Ken Masters?"

Bannon smiled and shook his head. "I don't think you heard a thing I said."

"I heard. I asked you about Masters."

Bannon pointed at the notebook. "Private hit list?"

"Speak, damnit. Masters. He seems to be into everything."

"He is," Bannon confirmed. "He owns the Grotto Lounge in Cape Canaveral. Biggest seafood joint and lounge on the coast. *And* others in Tampa, Orlando, Palm Beach, St. Augustine, maybe a dozen more between here and Washington. Bernie, he takes in twenty mil a year from his restaurant chain *alone*. He has other things going for him. He's a nice guy. Old navy pilot. string of medals as long as your arm. He keeps his fighters in Charley's hangars."

"Fighters?"

"Uh-huh. Corsair, Hellcat, Bearcat. Even a F9F."

"Which is?"

"Panther jet."

"Jet fighter?"

"Yeah. Rest easy, man, will you? There's no engine in it. It would take three days just to install one. It didn't go anywhere."

"Think he might be part of this Zoboa bunch?"

"Only if you're my Aunt Matilda. What in the hell

for?" Bannon demanded. "He's true-blue American, worth a zillion bucks, owns the world and ain't mad at nobody, and every weekend he flies his ass off in a fake war and has the time of his life."

"Tim Ryland. What about Tim Ryland?"

"He moves hard and fast. He works the whole world. Don't get your hopes up," Bannon said quickly, as Hudoff's expression showed sudden interest. "You ever see Ryland? He's a suave, gentle, white-haired old man. A dyed-in-the-wool Jesus freak. The real gentle madman. He thinks God wants him to fly pieces and parts of human bodies all around the planet."

Hudoff chewed the end of his pen. "Talk about your banana-brains," he murmured.

"Shit, there you go again," Bannon snapped. "He's one of God's own. He keeps a couple of long-range Learjets here with cryogenic—"

"Deep-freeze stuff?"

"You got it. *He's* the man who delivers organs and hearts and livers and eyeballs and testicles and whatever for transplants. He's got contracts with hospitals all over the world. A hundred people work for him. Only God knows how wealthy he is. Bernie, you got any idea what millionaires *pay* for new body parts? We ain't talking chicken legs, man. These are people parts and—"

"Your good samaritan also a warbird lunatic?"

"He spent three quarters of a million rebuilding his B-25 bomber. Perfect restoration." Bannon chuckled. "He thinks none of us know his machine guns are for real."

"*Real* guns that shoot?"

"Fifty calibers, boss. You better believe it."

"What the hell for!"

"Because he can afford it, that's what for. And I can't turn him in. Even if I could, I wouldn't."

"Why *can't* you?" Hudoff sneered.

"I do that and some of your bastard friends might finger *me* and then where'd you be? No one to do your dirty work for—"

"Can it, hotshot." Another page flipped. "What about Jay Martin?"

"He ain't got a dime. But he has six helicopters and a flight school and lives like a king."

"How?"

"He's the best chopper pilot alive, for starters. He also looks more like Tom Selleck than Selleck does. The broads break their butts to get to him. That includes some very rich broads who own strings of condominiums along Cocoa Beach and Vero Beach and Lauderdale and—"

"They're crazy about him because he flies helicopters and has a moustache?"

"Not really."

"Get to it, Ace!"

"I hear tell he's got a fourteen-inch dick."

Hudoff groaned, then nodded. "It figures." He flipped another page. "*This* one's a lulu. Tell me about Bill Santiago."

Bannon smiled. "Now there's a *real* operator."

"Details."

"Escaped from a Castro prison when he was fourteen. He killed three men to do it. You know how he got out of Cuba? No? He busted into a munitions depot and hung hand grenades all over his body with all of them wired to a single pull. He marches into police headquarters, goes up to the big boy, and kisses him smack on the lips. They're gonna bust his head until he opens his jacket and everybody is very friendly. He pulls that wire, and tells them it's rigged with a dead man's grip so that if he eases *off* on the pressure, the whole thing goes off. It's goodbye Santiago *and* the top cop and anyone else within thirty feet. Next he wires himself to one wrist of the cop and they're instant buddies. They go to the nearest airport and they're on their way to Miami. The feds can hardly believe it, but they give the kid political asylum. Six months later he's running Little Havana."

Hudoff tapped the notebook. "They say he'll do anything for the buck. That puts him high on this list. So tell me, hotshot, why this Cuban angel wouldn't deal in nukes for the sandfleas?"

Bannon shook his head. "You don't understand, do

you, Bernie? The kid loves this country. Really. Sure, he runs guns and he fences stolen goods, he deals and he wheels, he handles prosties and he loan sharks and—"

"Terrific citizen. Anybody would send their sister home with him," Hudoff said scathingly.

"He won't do *anything* against the country," Bannon said coldly. "The U.S. took him in and gave him his chance. That's *everything* to him. Scratch him off the list."

"Would you put your ass on the line for him?"

Bannon's face was granite. "I have. He saved it."

Hudoff sighed and scribbled a notation. "Could he give us a lead?"

"I'll work on it. If he has it, we'll get it."

"I wonder about something, Ace. What the hell is Santiago doing *here* if the action's down in Miami?"

"You really don't know?"

"I told you I'm not Moses."

Bannon laughed. "You're closer than you think. He's got the hots for a Jewish broad. Wendy Green."

"Her?" Hudoff slapped his forehead in mock despair. "He could have any piece of meat he wants! Why a dumpy yuck? Wendy Green looks like my sister and *that* is Grade D ugly."

"He's in love. Maybe Wendy reminds him of his mother." Bannon laughed. "Santiago's a good pilot, but would you believe Wendy can fly his ass right into the ground?"

"Lemme see," Hudoff mused aloud. "This gets better. Wendy Green works for the Morgans, right?"

Bannon's face clouded. "Uh-huh."

Hudoff laughed. "Next page," he said, flipping paper. "Mitch Bannon. Hotshot beach bum. Got the hots for Charlene Morgan."

"You son of a bitch—"

Hudoff held up a blank sheet. "Easy, sweetheart. You're wearing your ass on your sleeve. Now, back to the Reverend Santiago. He's pure scum when it comes to the law. He has a hundred broads hanging on to his belt, his pecker, and his shoes, but he hotfoots it out of Miami because he's in love with Grossout Green, and he's trapped in this piss-ant neck of the woods. Wonder Wendy works for Charley Morgan, who along with her crazy kid brother, Marty, owns Morgan Aviation. And *you're* hanging by your tongue over Charley Morgan. So that leads me to believe that Santiago has good reason to stay asshole buddy with you in the hopes you'll put in a few good words with the fat Yid." He glanced at Bannon. "Okay so far?"

"You son of a bitch—"

"Admitted. Now, how does Dumbo feel about the spick Capone?"

"She'd like to do the scene with him but Bill scares the shit out of her."

Hudoff smiled. "I can't figure out why." He shifted his approach. "More important, maybe, how does this Morgan broad feel about *you*?"

"I'm working at it, you fat bastard."

"You ain't smiling, Bannon," Hudoff said in sing-song.

"It's none of your fucking business."

"Oh, *my*, but we are sensitive today." Hudoff flashed a smile and as quickly whipped it away. "*Everything* you do and everything about you *is* my fucking business! I don't care if you're humping the girl, Bannon. I want to know how strong you are with the Morgans. Both of them."

"Strong enough."

"Who keeps you on top of things?"

"The kid."

"The one they call Mad Marty?"

"Yeah."

"Where's the Mad part come in?"

"He lost a leg in a motorcycle wreck. Now there's nothing he won't do. He races speedboats, he's a sky-diver, he runs demolition derbies at the head of the pack, and he's one hell of a pilot: Flies a T-28 for the show—"

"I saw him, I think. With his fucking dog." Hudoff tapped his notes. "It fits. The kid's always got his ass in a sling and you and Sheriff Hughes pay off debts to each other, right? You keep the kid out of the slammer, and Charley Morgan's grateful to you for that. Not bad for a dumb cop, Bannon. It works and that's what counts."

"What else, Bernie? I got to get back for the airshow."

"Not yet. What about your competition with the Morgan girl?"

"Is *he* on your list?"

"Are you kidding?" Hudoff showed mock surprise. "Abe Lansky? the Haifa Hero? One of Israel's finest arms dealers, smugglers, *bon vivant* and all-around international prick? *Should* I suspect him, Bannon? He's a bona fide hero, m'boy. He has every license this government and the Israelis ever printed to buy and sell military equipment anywhere in the world. He has a dozen companies, and for the record they deal in printing presses, wheat harvesters, shit like that. But he's legal. He's clean. And you hate his olive oil ass, right?"

"Not really." Bannon cracked his knuckles. "But one day I'm going to tear his head off."

"Oho! I see lovelorn horns!"

"That's not all of it." Bannon fell silent for a moment and Hudoff didn't step in with any wiseass remarks. Something was bothering Bannon, and it wasn't personal. This one could be important, Hudoff judged. He waited it out silently.

"There's something greasy about him," Bannon finally picked up his words. "You know what I mean, Bernie. Something *doesn't fit.*" He showed his frustration. "I know he's whistle-stop clean on the books. But . . . look, half the people I know carry iron and you don't even think about it. Even if they don't have permits. They carry; they don't give a shit. But Lansky, well, he packs a thirty-eight and he *has* a permit, and it still stinks. Like he's the only one who needs to be justified in what he's doing with a Colt under his armpit. Do I make sense?"

Hudoff nodded. A cop's instinct is most often his best weapon, and Bannon had natural instinct coming out of his ears, even if Hudoff rode his ass mercilessly. Hudoff sighed. The problem lay in separating Bannon's yearn to bed Charley Morgan down in a bridal suite. Because he *did* get his hackles up over Lansky as competition for the Fair Morgan.

Hudoff was willing to go along with Bannon's instincts, but he couldn't ignore the permanent erection Bannon carried for Charley and—Hudoff hated to admit—he couldn't ignore the positive side of Lansky. He was easy to remember: a big bastard, rangy, with a definite hawkish, handsome cut to his features. Curly hair, a dazzling smile; right out of Hollywood. And Abe Lansky knew all the right moves. He was suave, charming, intelligent, and international, with a command of half a dozen languages. Even Bannon admitted Lansky was a sharp pilot. He flew, or had flown in the past, many of the most important arms runs for the Israeli Army. That took skill and it took guts. Lansky owned several big spreads in Florida with good cattle and he also had a prime ranch north of Ocala with fifty horses. He'd cut airstrips through every one of them, but that was no secret. Hell, they were on the government charts.

When Lansky didn't cotton to roughing it way down on his farms, he pitched tent in a sumptuous penthouse atop 2100 Tower above the shining sands of Cocoa Beach. Nothing but the best here. The best food and wine and gold necklaces and pearls and diamonds. A really tough act to beat. Especially for a surfer bum who had a rep as a pot smuggler and a cocksmith primo. Behind the scenes Bannon was a straight-arrow cop, but to most decent people he was a shit. Next to Lansky he was a gutter-rat in rags. If Charley Morgan's vision was gold in a bracelet rather than the stuff that makes a man, Hudoff grunted, Bannon was shit out of luck. But then, if he lost the broad he'd be winning. Time would tell.

Something else bothered Hudoff. He knew a lot more about the tubby target of Santiago's affections than Bannon realized. Wendy Green ran Morgan Aviation. She was Jewish, fat, and had an extraordinary, if limited, ethnic sex appeal. She was also the fastest, smartest, sharpest woman in all the county. Hudoff knew that. She ran the company with an iron hand, fiercely protective of Charley and her kid brother, despite being the butt of Mad Marty's constant ridicule. It was a love-hate relationship they'd both endured for a long time.

What nagged at Hudoff's constant reappraisals of all these people, especially now with *Antares* on the pad and Zoboa looming on the horizon as mass killers, was that there *wasn't* some kind of heartbeat between Wendy and Abe Lansky. Not sack-time stuff, but the "same people" sort of yardage. Lansky was a true-blue hero in Israel. Wendy Green should have felt damned strong toward him. Old Jewishness is thicker than holy water, or something like that.

It hadn't happened. Wendy Green despised Abe Lansky. His tall figure, shining curly hair, gleaming smile, and continental manners didn't mean diddly-shit to her. She didn't throw him out of the Morgan office only because one, Charley wouldn't stand for that, and two, Lansky was a very high-paying customer with cash on the line. Hudoff knew all these things because the sister of his secretary worked in the county commissioner's office, which just happened to be next door at the airport to Morgan Aviation, and Sandra was a natural-born spy.

For the moment, both Hudoff and Bannon remained immersed in their own thoughts. Not surprisingly, each mirrored the mental processes of the other, sharing the same uncomfortable feeling about Lansky. He spoke several languages fluently, for instance. Little touches arouse suspicions in a cop's mind, and Lansky was dotted with touches. What the hell was he doing in the United States? His base-of-operations routine made sense from an American point of view, but not from that of an Israeli. The Isreali fighters, especially the Sabra, can't wait to get into the thick of any fighting.

Lansky enjoyed where he was and what he was doing, and *that* was another rub. What was he doing in central Florida, when it hardly compared to the luxury digs, company, and professional contacts that Miami or Tampa had to offer? Sure, the traffic at Port Canaveral was less hectic and the air traffic much thinner, and Lansky maintained a running honeymoon with American military offices. Indeed, when he needed the strong arm of the government for cover, the Feds were always there to back him up. How much cleaner can you get than squeaky-clean Ivory?

Bannon's hackles raised well beyond Hudoff's when it came to Lansky because he had direct contact and an irritating interface with the big Israeli. Bannon didn't like Lansky. Okay. That was hardly enough to fire off warning flares. Bannon accepted that some people considered Lansky as tough competition for the hand of Charley Morgan. Well, maybe. If Bannon wasn't playing his undercover role and having to lie about it to Charley, he wouldn't have given Lansky a second thought. He'd have been just one more asshole in the crowd. But Bannon *was* involved professionally, and now this cold-blooded killing of the Air Force crew, the hijacking of the bombs, the shadowy presence of Zoboa, if it was real, brought his feelings about Lansky into sharper focus and examination.

"Bernie?" Hudoff snapped out of his own introspection. "If there's anyone I'd like to nail down," Bannon told him, "it's Yusuf Hamza."

"Sounds like a kind of shish kebob. Who or what is a yusufhamza?"

"Not what, who. Lansky's bodyguard." Bannon's eyes widened. "You've never heard of him?"

"I have," Hudoff said quickly. "Tell me what *you* know."

"He's no bodyguard," Bannon said with emphasis. "Right arm, gopher, toady; you name it all. I'm not saying it's out of the picture for Lansky to have some hired eyes guarding his back, but Hamza just isn't it. He's fat, greasy—you ever know somebody whose lips are *always* wet? He's got sheep oil, that's what I think it is, on his skin and hair and everything else. What the hell's a Jewish hero doing with this Arab slimebag?"

"According to his file, he's a Jordanian Christian." Hudoff kept his expression blank.

"Sure, just like I'm a Turkish princess," Bannon said, his expression one of obvious distaste. "All you got to do is drop a cigarette ash and Hamza will hang on to your neck weeping and crying all about his family getting beaten half to death by the PLO. He likes to shout at the top of his lungs that him and the rest of the Christian Jordanians are the Jews of the Arab world. But you never get any details, of course."

"Anybody make friends with this Hamza?"

Bannon thought on that one and then shook his head. "Now that you mention it, no. And you know something, boss-man? Despite everything else, that bloated son of a greasy pig is damned misleading."

"How?"

"For one, his fat throws you off. I've seen him working out in that gym we have behind the main hangar. Behind all that suet is some hard muscle. And he's a hell of a flier. Some men have a touch at the controls that's the mark of the born pilot. El Tubbo has it."

"What do you make of him?" Hudoff pressed gently.

"No self-respecting real Arab would have a thing to do with either Lansky or Hamza."

Hudoff chuckled. The notebook slipped back into his jacket pocket. "You got a show to fly, right?"

Bannon nodded. "Sure do. We figure to take advantage of the crowds coming into the county for the Antares flight. We ought to really pack 'em in. Bernie, why don't you take a look at the show? You'd see a hell of a lot better on the field than you can in that damn notebook of yours."

"I might just do that. You take off, Ace. I got a hot meeting with the enemy."

Bannon stared and Hudoff couldn't resist a laugh. "Don't sweat it, Ace. I'll introduce you."

✝ 8 ✝

FAIR MORGAN

Bannon lifted the clearing with a howl of power, booming almost straight up before swinging around to a fast run across the river back to Shiloh Field. He needed the open space about him and took the Long Ranger to four thousand feet for the sense of freedom, however short the flight to his hangar. Elbow room in the sky always helped clear the snot from his brain, and right now he felt as if his sinuses were pouring directly into whatever lay between his ears. He wanted to curse Hudoff for his eternal suspicions against people with whom Bannon had shared friendship and tough flying for years. He wanted to, but that was the source of his frustration. In all fairness not simply to Hudoff, but to the reality of the moment, he couldn't fault the man who'd backed him without question all this time.

Bannon had learned well under Hudoff's helm. *Always put yourself in the place of the man or woman you have reason, no matter how slight, to suspect. It's one hell of a different view, Hotshot . . .*

Damn, but he was so right! When he studied himself and his relationships, Bannon discovered he really didn't know that many people he absolutely *knew* were clean of any possible involvement with this Zoboa group—assuming, of course, that Zoboa itself was real, and they weren't blowing in the wind trying to identify the group that *had* hijacked the four atomic bombs. The more he thought of all the people he knew and their opportunities for working with a terrorist group, the greater became his dismay. How in the name of God Bernie Hudoff could separate all the wheat from the chaff, keep tabs on so many, compute what they might be thinking and what they could or would do, *and* run spaceport security, was a constant mystery to Bannon. Well, damnit, he'd play by the rules Hudoff gave him, and he knew when he made that decision that he was doing *exactly* what Hudoff had long before accepted he would do. The son of a bitch was moving him across a chess board.

There was, of course, the office staff and the flight line crew of Morgan Aviation. Forget the Morgans; he'd stake his life on them. Down the company ladder from Charley and her brother was Wendy Green, tubby and brilliant, but another person on whom Bannon would without hesitation bet his life. *That* was the formula with which Bannon must work. First, would he place his life on the person in question? Second, would he place the lives of a few hundred thousand people on the person in question? *Always make your judgment on the basis of the most helpless victims, Ace. Think of young children, pure and innocent and ready to be gutted like pigs in a slaughterhouse. Your decision determines what you'll do for them or to them.*

Shit. Now he built himself a fast mental picture of Doug Callahan, a big irish broth of a man who was Charley's top charter pilot. He has access to everything in Morgan Aviation, including the records, the planes, the helicopters ... the planes, the planes, the planes. The word repeated like a drumroll in Bannon's skull. What did he really know about Callahan?

Nothing, really. *You've got his records, he comes well recommended, and he could be one of the top agents for the Irish Republican Army, for all you know.* More and more Bannon came to comprehend Hudoff's method. He liked and respected Callahan and had not a single negative thought about the man, but he didn't know a single conclusive thing about his background. *Think of young children, pure and innocent* ... So that was the next step in playing God. You didn't accuse the man or even judge him as guilty of anything, but being incapable of completely exonerating the unknown, you kept him on the list of suspects. Christ, you could go paranoid real fast playing this game!

There were a few more pilots, plus the mechanics and flight service people, but Bannon found himself able to dismiss them from serious consideration. Another truth flopped by his feet. You didn't have to know that much about someone, positive or negative, to make that dismissal. They simply didn't move in the circles that mattered. They didn't fly, they didn't move with the aircraft; so whatever they did remained inconsequential. They were, therefore, under the threat they now faced from the (alleged) terrorist group known as (maybe) Zoboa, to be dismissed from the issue. *It didn't matter what they did or could do.*

Of course, sometimes reason was like a rubber band that you stretched out to wrap about other people and it snapped back to whack you right between the eyes. To any security agency diving into the intense hunt for the missing nukes, one of the prime suspects was Mitch Bannon. *Holy shit, and Bernie can't tell them otherwise.* That meant *he* could expect a lot of attention to whatever *he* did. *Face the truth, Bannon,* he told himself. The truth was effective but not pretty. Mitch Bannon, to most of the people who knew him, was a cocksmith surfer slob who made most of his money by running contraband drugs. Even his superb skills as a pilot and his friendship with the top people in the airshow business couldn't slake that reputation. How could it? His caricature to the public had been carefully nurtured. He was a beach bum, he stiffed teenage broads with hilarious if questionable prowess, he moved through a shadowy underworld held in contempt by the "good people" of the community. In sum, he was pretty much of a shit.

He grinned at his self-condemnation. Being a shit meant he could move easily in circles that would otherwise offer resistance. When you're a slob, most people melt out of your way. He laughed aloud as he neared Shiloh. Security had gone lopsided. Hudoff had personally selected Bannon as his private gumshoe in the midst of the crazies of the Platinum Coast, and not even Hudoff with his extraordinary talent for targeting people knew the full story of his chief agent.

Bannon's records showed a normal upbringing in a normal town in Indiana. Easy enough to show such records in a community wiped out by a train derailment. When the tank cars carrying propane blew up, they leveled the town. What sparse records survived were simple to alter, and now included the name of one Mitchell Bannon.

Because Bannon had a record, he preferred to keep within the complete obscurity of nothingness. When he was fifteen he ran off from a foster home. His name was Carruthers. But who gave a damn when his parents were dead and the Morrisons who had run the foster home were flattened along with the rest of the town? Mitch had been fishing a couple miles away when Doomsday replaced his community. He seized the opportunity to rid himself of a juvenile record, drifted through the emergency records centers with hints of his being a young survivor named Mitchell Bannon, and then he split.

The Foreign Legion was beyond his grasp, but the Freedom Brigade training Cubans deep in the Florida swamps for an invasion of their homeland was certainly within reach. Big for his age, willing to accept any severe training regime, he was welcomed by the ragtag bands who so desperately needed warm bodies to expand their ranks. Four months later Bannon was a young but tough and dangerous guerrilla fighter with a surprising command of Spanish learned in camp from his new friends. There was very little about his new skills that could be called fancy, but the newest kid in the swamps proved adept in tracking and killing. By the time the bravado began to fizzle and the expatriates were running out of steam and money, Bannon was an expert in every small-arms weapon that could be bought or stolen. He knew how to kill with knives, ropes, fire-hardened spears, snares, and traps, and how to *think* like a swamp rat. He had learned enough to know the Cubans weren't going anywhere; then he vanished from the swamps.

He wanted a *professional* killing outfit. The U.S. Army welcomed him with open arms and he volunteered for every dirty duty they could offer. Paratrooper, ranger, demolitions expert, saboteur, infiltrator; he did them all with highly commendable efficiency. When he had run through all their courses he went to Central America, where he killed selectively until too many survivors began to remember what he looked like. The Army yanked him from the jungles and kept their word. Mitch Bannon went into flight training in fixed wing and then rotary machines. He proved so adept and so natural a flier that after earning his wings with the smaller iron he went on temporary duty with the Air Force to fly the heavy iron with howling engines and razor-sharp swept wings.

That's when he was picked out of the crowd by one Bernie Hudoff. Their first meeting capped it for Hudoff; he knew what *he* wanted. He hit Bannon with a Mafia Special. An offer he couldn't resist. "You remain in the States. You play a double life. The *only* person who knows who or what you are is me. You get some specialized flight training. When you're through with that you live the life of Riley. You work for me for six years after training. You do not break the deal. You do not allow personal needs or desires ever to interfere with your assignment. And I want you to understand that if anyone steps out of the ranks—which means *you*—before you pull your full shift there ain't an insurance company in the world will cover your ass for a nickel. That's the deal. In or out?"

It *could* be a Trojan Horse, Bannon had considered for a full second or two. But then, he wasn't sure whether a Trojan Horse was the same as not looking a gift horse in the mouth—or whatever those phrases meant—and he didn't give a damn. He shoved his hand forward, they shook, and the deal was on. Bannon found himself in the Louisiana swamps days later, singing the old refrain of volunteers everywhere. "Where the hell am I and what am I doing in this sewer?"

But he didn't *ask*. He was shown a creaking old quonset hut full of mosquitos and roaches and leeches, and he didn't care about that either, because a rasp-voiced old man led him outside the quonset and showed him a row of powerful spray planes. "You gonna learn to fly 'em all, boy, and you gonna learn to fly 'em right. You know what right is, boy? Right is *my* way."

Bannon looked down at the old-timer. "I've been through full army flight school, old man," he said, a touch of the curled lip in his voice. "And jet fighter school. *And* helicopters."

"Now, ain't that jes' dandy," the old man chuckled. "You really think you can fly, huh, sonny?" He pointed to a stained and battered yellow biplane. "Put your ass in the front seat of that there flyin' machine, young pup, and we'll see."

When they came back an hour later the airplane was stained afresh with grass, weeds, birds, insects, and marsh water. Bannon felt like a helpless and incompetent idiot, slumped down in the front seat after flying beneath power lines, doing flat skidding turns below weed-top level, pulling straight up from mock dusting runs, patting wingtips on marsh canals and only God knew what else. The final contemptuous act was the old man climbing down from the steaming airplane, walking away, and jerking his thumb behind him. "Wash off the shit from that thing," he left in the wake of his departure.

The old man taught him. Bannon discovered one of the great truths about the old and true breed of pilots. Henry Potter—a.k.a. Old Hank—was determined to fly away the remainder of his life. He'd come here to the Lousiana swamps, under contract to the government for jobs such as teaching young pups, to end his life, hopefully with a lot of air between his wings and the ground when that time came. Bannon came to know the old man slowly but meaningfully in the next eight weeks. His last morning of training as a duster pilot started out no differently from any other morning. Then Hank handed him a cigar, gestured to a chair. "Get the coffee, boy. Light up that cigar. You done graduated."

Bannon knew he'd made it. The coffee, the cigar, the sharing. "You're good, son," Hank told him. "Now, when a pup graduates to a young spindly legged dog, which is what you are, we like to give him a present. Graduation, you know? I got something for you, Bannon. It's an hour."

Bannon looked blankly at his teacher. "An hour?"

"Uh huh. One hour. Finish your coffee and bring the cigar. The damn thing flies better with a cigar."

The "damn thing" almost knocked Bannon on his ass when Old Hank rolled back the doors to a padlocked hangar. Two men rolled out a gleaming, perfect Curtiss P-40E Kittyhawk. This was one of the fighters the Flying Tigers had flown against the Japanese in *1942*. "We spend two hours talking on the ground. You spend two hours crawling through the machine. You spend tonight reading the manual. Tomorrow morning you got two hours in which to answer my questions and prove how smart a spindly legged dog you are." Hank smiled and the flight line looked like the damned sun had come out.

"And then you got your present. You fly this thing, here, for an hour. Then, sonny, you are a pilot. A honest-to-God *aviator*." His eyes twinkled. "A little bit like me."

It wasn't until that next evening, his senses and spirits still soaring over the tidal lands as the Kittyhawk took him through sky and back through time, it wasn't until this last evening that Bannon realized how great a gift Bernie Hudoff had arranged for him. Old Hank was more than he seemed. "Yeah," he admitted finally, "I got me eighteen kills in Asia in one of these ships. Then I went into bombers because they didn't have many people to fly them."

Bannon stared at Henry Potter. "Hank," he asked quietly, "how old are you?"

There was that twinkle he'd concealed for so long. "Seventy-two, Bannon. I been flying for fifty-six years. It's nice to pass the baton down."

It was the first time in his life that Bannon went somewhere to be alone and found tears on his cheeks.

A week later, following telephone orders from Hudoff, he stepped off an airliner in Jacksonville. A nondescript car picked him up and delivered him to an out-of-the-way beach house in Crescent Beach down the coast. He went down to the beach and found Hudoff sprawled on a lounge chair, tall drink in one hand, cigar clenched in his teeth, and a two-way radio in the other hand. He was wearing the worst-looking Bermuda shorts Bannon had ever seen on a human being, and he'd added to the violently loud print ragged sandals and a battered straw hat. Bannon didn't need to ask. Tucked neatly within the band of those shorts was a compact handgun. He *always* had one somewhere on his person.

"You live here for two weeks," Hudoff told him without preamble. "You get a good suntan, hear? That's an order. We'll have someone bleach your hair. You'll find a complete wardrobe in the house. You know how to surf? *No?* You'll learn. You'll learn damn fast. Margo Eastman will teach you."

"Who the hell is Margo Eastman?"

"She's a dazzler, Bannon. A beauty. Built like a brick outhouse. Champion surfer. She works for me. She'll teach you. One bit of advice. Hands off or she'll bust a couple of your ribs. Among other things, she's an aikido black belt and she is being paid very well to teach you how to hang ten with verve and dash."

He surfed from sunup to sundown. He learned about the beach, the sand, the jellyfish and sharks and whatever else Margo taught him. She *was* built like a brick outhouse; she also had three kids and a husband with the Green Berets, all of whom looked just fine in their photographs on her bedroom dresser. At night Bannon studied. He was given books detailing the history of Brevard County, of Cape Canaveral and the Kennedy Space Center in particular. He learned the towns, the cops, the streets of Cocoa Beach and Merritt Island by heart. He had to identify every motel and bar and lounge from memory. He thought he knew drugs. He learned he had only a smattering of knowledge. He crammed on drugs. He studied flight charts of the area until he'd memorized everything pertinent. Then he spent a week flying up and down the county, again and again and again until he felt he'd lived there for years.

He was told to answer a newspaper ad for a duster and spray pilot at Shiloh Field, south of Titusville and due west of the great space center. "You'll get the job," Hudoff told him, "and you'll live in an apartment, sort of, in the old duster hangar. We got a present for you. It's yours to use just as if it was your own. A Turkey."

"A turkey?"

"No, damnit. With a capital T. Turkey. Also known as a Grumman TBF or a General Motors TBM. They used to call it the Avenger during the second world war. You, Bannon, are one of those weirdos who spends a fortune on an old warbird. Shiloh Field is a main center for warbird buffs and airshows. So you show up at Shiloh in this Turkey that you own. All the paperwork is taken care of. You apply for the job and you get the job and you've made the grandstand entrance and right away everybody knows you're there and they think they know who and what you are. A surfer bum, a duster pilot, a warbird buff. No one knows from where you get all your bread, but we'll arrange for some pot runs. Right away they'll love you, Bannon."

"Damnit, I've never flown a Turkey!"

"According to Hank Potter, you can fly anything. You'll find the airplane and its papers at St. Augustine Airport. Margo will give you the manual tonight. You leave in three days. Oh, yes; Margo will also have your Florida driver's license, your credit cards, whatever you'll need. Since you're keeping your own identity, we see no problems. Oh, yes, I got a present for you. I had my Bermuda shorts cut down to your size. You'll look terrific in them."

It was one hell of a transition from professional military killer to long-haired, sloppy surfing beach-bum pilot. He fell right into the role. He didn't know what the hell to do after a month. He did a few odd spraying jobs; a marijuana run was set up for him one night and the word passed along the beach that the new boy in town was the dude to know; and he mixed with the warbird pilots and their only judgment call was how he flew and how eager he was to fly with them.

Finally he called Hudoff with the question gnawing at him. "*What* am I doing here? What am I *supposed* to do?"

"Keep your eyes and ears open. Look for anomalies. Don't tell me about runners or dealers because I don't care. When something is *wrong*, Bannon, you'll know it, and then you tell me."

He did his six years under contract and they banked twenty thousand a year for him the whole time, over and above what it cost to play the role he found so natural that he made it his honest-to-God lifestyle. But they'd trapped him. By the time the six years were up, Bannon knew the space program as well as anybody in the business short of a top engineer or NASA official. He attended the launches from the press site with a pass from the local *Today* newspaper. And he came to understand, as the great shuttle program came on the line, that sooner or later some paranoid fanatic would make an attempt to swat a great shuttle from the sky during those terribly critical moments immediately after takeoff. Hudoff had pounded into his skull that because of distance, the size of the space complex, and a hundred other factors, the only way a terrorist group could succeed was through the use of aircraft. And who better than Mitch Bannon, now on the scene for six years and in the thick of *everything*, to spot people and activities who "didn't fit."

The trap? Again they made him an offer he absolutely couldn't refuse. Hudoff smiled at him like a spider with a hot meal in the web oven. "Just keep doing what you're doing. No more hard contract. We do it by handshake, Ace. Besides, you're screwing your brains out along the beach. You're the perfect pervert, Bannon. A natural at your job."

The bastard. Hudoff made yuks about humping teeny-boppers and flying the heavy iron in the Walter Mitty-dream-come-true, but the band played and the flags waved and they tweaked his patriotism and his moral conscience *just* right, and before he knew it Bannon was hooked for the duration because he *knew* just how badly people like him were needed. Yet, with all the amenities and the freedom to follow both his hunches and his erections, he didn't feel all that *right* about the deal. Bannon was, at heart, a loner. Now he was really part and parcel of a huge undercover security force. What salved his conscience was that he never finked or was asked to fink on anybody except where national security was concerned. "If it don't involve these people riding dragons into space I don't want to know about it," Hudoff told him.

And yet . . . there was this nagging burr in the back of his skull. He was the reluctant hero, but he was no fool. All the logic and moralizing in the world couldn't shake the feeling that he wasn't being true *to himself*. This Secret Agent G-9 shit just wasn't his bag. He wanted to fly, and Hudoff sure made his flying easier, but he preferred to make it on his own. He felt *kept*. Maybe it didn't make sense to anyone but himself, but then his was the only face in the mirror in the morning.

More than anything else he wanted to find Charley there with him every morning. Try as he might, he couldn't conceal completely his feelings toward her. Hudoff, the bastard, not only picked up on it but took every opportunity to insult his feelings and keep Charley on the same level as Bannon's private army of "spread-leg lulus" on the beach. That was a prime reason for keeping his thoughts to himself, but Hudoff could see through brick walls. Then again, Bannon sighed, he wasn't sure how many others had figured out his weakness long ago.

It *was* a weakness; and he knew that was why Hudoff came down so heavy on him. Few things can screw up an undercover man worse than feeling he's got to watch what he does and who he does it with. He starts to restrict his actions for fear his Only True Love will get hacked off and slide into cool sheets with some other dude.

But that's none of your business, Ace. . . .

Jesus, but he could hate his inner self! Homilies were a bunch of crap, and when they drifted out of his own skull they were a maddening itch he couldn't scratch. Worst of all, how could he not find pleasure in playing his role to the hilt? Hey, it's a real tough life to be on an unlimited expense account, drive a new Corvette, have your pick of airplanes, surf, and go bed-hopping like you're peaking from one wave crest to another. Real tough, man. Bannon had the idea he'd never find anyone to offer sympathy to him for his terrible burden of good food, good drink, and terrific love. He had to play his role to the hilt, because you might find the clues you sought anywhere. Even terrorists get hard-ons, and they'll go for the snatch that comes easiest and with the least visibility. So Bannon was always on the prowl for information; and he performed his sexual legerdemain through the invisible maze he'd come to detest and love at the same time.

What about the lady, Bannon? That stupid inner voice again. *You can't ignore it, Ace. How does she feel?*

First, he didn't need to question that Charley felt strongly toward and about him. That didn't mean it was all downhill, because a lot of what Charley thought about him was straight negative. Well, who could blame her? What was her picture of this guy Bannon? Were her feelings ever going to be strong enough to commit to a guy who would have to scratch for his livelihood? Running Morgan Aviation cost a lot of the long green. Charley worked hard and flew hard. Bannon made a sour face at himself. Who could blame her for responding to the attentions of someone like Abe Lansky? Why should a beautiful and talented woman be allergic to gifts of fine jewelry and dinners and continental manners and—

He could always drag Lansky behind the hangar and beat the shit out of him. *How old are you, Bannon? Twelve?* Deep inside him, he wished Lansky was tied in with this terrorist group. God, wouldn't that be the answer to it all! He could even kill the son of a bitch and then he'd be conscience-free and rid of his only real opposition with Charley and—

And you'd still be what she hates most of all in this world, hotshot. A drug runner . . :

No way out of that one. Again the thought of holding Charley's skin beneath his hands turned him inside out. He had all the nubile young bodies he could handle— and when he *did* handle them, he fantasized that it was Charley wrapped around his own body. Talk about your twists! It's usually those who are older who fantasize about the younger, and here he was going through his sexual life back asswards.

Knock off the shit. So long as you keep the word you gave the man, you're stuck with where you are and what you got. In that silent world of the teens, he had to admit, the kids had their own interface with the dopers and the dealers. Within the subculture of the beach you always got information that could tip you off to much bigger names and events. Skilled dope runners make skilled gun runners, and people in the gun-running business are only one step short of dealing with the operators who run heavy weapons. Finally you get big enough so that you're dealing in bombs and missiles. When did they get so big that the bombs became nuclear?

He was again going full circle. He began his descent into the time machine that was Shiloh field for the warbird airshow, and knew he must slip back into his role as a warbird pilot. And when that was over, back to the beach to hump his brains out, mixing with people both good and scummy, and prowling the shadows for any hint of this outfit they called Zoboa.

And when Charley showed even the first hint of distaste for what he was and what he visibly did, he couldn't tell her things really weren't the way they seemed.

It's hard to talk when you've got a beautiful fifteen-year-old body clawing and scratching and gasping beneath you.

Oh, yes, there was that other small problem he'd have to straighten out with Charley. He rubbed his jaw, and the memory of her roundhouse right brought a flash of remembered pain to him. Charley was most likely in jail right now. Because of *him*.

* * *

"Well, there's no problem far as I can see, little lady," Sheriff Bob Hughes said. He patted a sagging stomach and beamed expansively, then slapped his hand on his desk. "Bail money's right here, little—"

"Back off, Sheriff," Charley Morgan said coldly. Her eyes bored into his until Hughes shifted uncomfortably. "Just back it off and stay there. I'm not your little lady. The name is *Miss* Morgan and you use it, mister."

"Hey, hold on there—"

"No, damnit! You've been playing Little Hitler long enough here!" Charley pulled a fast rein on her emotions and voice. "I don't know where you got any bail money for me and I do not care. Your deputy said I would be—"

"The money's good, Charley! Damn, *Miss* Morgan. The money's *good*. What in tarnation are you so het up about, anyway? Western Union called and this here wire is a guarantee of *any* amount of bail you might need. Whole thing is set up by that Lansky feller and—"

"I told you I wasn't interested in who or what, but you have to make your point, don't you?" Charley said with telling effect. "Friends in high places. Bail money with a blank check. No deal, Sheriff. I told you that your deputy said I'd be released on my own cognizance *and that's the way it is.* You want to go back on your word, I've got over a hundred pilots *who heard the man.* So you stand behind your deputy and you release me or else you put me behind bars and I *promise* you one thing, Sheriff Robert Averill Hughes, you will hear the damnedest press conference you ever heard in your life!"

Hughes studied Charley. When he spoke, his voice was surprisingly calm. "You know something? Your daddy used to come in here, just like you, and he would stand where you're standing, *just like you*, and that goldarn fool would holler and shout and threaten me and I *swear*," Hughes shook his head, "ain't a damn thing really changed here at *all*."

Charley almost smiled. She'd known Bob Hughes since she was a little girl, when he'd fly with her father, and both she and Marty used to sit on Hughes's lap when he was a young deputy, and he'd sing raucous cowboy songs to them. So if Hughes was going through all this drill, and they both knew her word was absolutely as good as platinum, someone up higher than this man was putting on the squeeze.

"The feds on your case, Bob?" she asked, suddenly so warm and disarming that the big, bad sheriff smiled and patted her hand, jerking it back suddenly as if stung. He realized he'd let it all out and he sighed, nodding. "They sure are, Charley. Of course you're free on your own cognizance, *little lady*—" They burst into laughter together before he went on. "In fact, maybe *you* can tell *me* what's coming down. Big, big flap going on. The Feds have been crazy since earlier this morning. They want to know *everything* about an awful lot of people."

Charley shook her head. "Don't know a thing. Everything's the same crazy morning like every Friday showtime. Pilots drunk all night, tough to get them up—"

"Not so tough from what I hear you did to that motel. You *did* that number, didn't you, Charley?"

"No way," she said for the record, but nodding her head for Hughes. "Wait a moment, Bob. The only thing that is absolutely crazy this morning is Mitch Bannon. Your deputy said *he* told the motel manager that it was me flying that B-25."

"He surely did." Hughes frowned and rubbed his cheek in puzzlement. "I can't figure that. Not one bit. Bannon's real sweet on you, Charley—"

"For Christ's sake, Bob—"

"Now hold on, girl. He is more than sweet on you. Got his heart hanging out on a limb and—"

"I don't want to hear any more about—"

"And he must have his reasons for what he did," Hughes went right on, ignoring her interruption. "Although I can't figure what they might be." Hughes stood up. "All right, Charley, you go on back."

"Your boys brought me here, Sheriff, and they will take me back to Shiloh."

Hughes held up both hands to forestall any further hammering. "You got it." He pressed a call button on his desk and leaned forward to a microphone. "Bring a car up front immediately. Going to Shiloh with Miss Morgan."

They heard a chuckle as his secretary rang off with a "Yes, *sir*."

"How's Marty?"

Charley's shoulders slumped. "This off the record?"

"Like always, Charley."

The smile he'd seen, the spunky girl he knew, seemed to evaporate before his eyes as she thought of her brother. "He's hurting." She looked up, her own pain evident. "The more he hurts the more he uses, well, you know."

"I know," he said with understanding. "Charley, I'm hardly no fan of drugs. Not with my past and not with this tin star I wear. But, by God, I try to understand Marty. He's after some relief. Anything that will help . . ." He took a deep breath. "Is he getting much pain from his stump? Sometimes what's missing can seem to hurt more than what's left."

"I don't *know*," she said wearily. "But turning himself into stone, I mean, there's got to be a better way! He doesn't have to kill himself to get relief from the pain!"

"I don't know, either," Hughes said kindly. "But he's hurting, Charley, and we're only *talking*. Easy for us, tougher for him." He squeezed her arm. "Anything I can do?"

"You've been on his side from the beginning, Bob. You've kept the dogs off him. I thank you for that."

"No problems with his, uh, supply?"

Her faced showed twisted emotions. "Damnit, *no*. You know who takes care of *that*," she said acidly. She didn't need to say aloud the name of Mitch Bannon.

"He does it for a good reason, and— Charley, you want me to get him into the official program? I can get him signed into the rehab hospital in Gainesville and he can get this stuff legally until the doctors come up with something else."

"He won't go." She stood. "Thanks, Bob. But Marty would rather be dead than be in an institution."

"It's *not* an—"

"Can you picture Marty not flying?"

His smile was sad. "No. I can't."

"Goodbye, Bob."

"Take care, little lady."

She left behind her the ghost of a wan smile. The two deputies in the sheriff's car felt her need for silence. No one spoke as they drove south on U.S. 1 through Titusville. A deep roar echoing between buildings caught her attention, and she had a glimpse of a sleek fighter flashing sun from its cockpit.

Moments like this, resting in the back of a car driven by men so silent they might have been mutes, brought to her thoughts of her father. He'd been gone now for a long time, but everything they had ever done together remained clear and sharp in her mind. So many times they'd soared in the clear air high above the earth, and then she and Marty and their dad would go off to chase clouds, sister and brother taking turns in the lap of their father, little hands tight on the control yoke, plunging through the sharp edges of towering white columns. Rainbow chasing and rain splashing and emerging from even more tender years so that they had no fear of the skies and the machines they flew. They had respect, and appreciation, and even awe, but not fear when turbulence smacked the airplane hard or lightning turned everything into stroboscopic ghosts. There were too many marvels and miracles, Disneyworlds of the *real* world, the cities spread out for mile after mile like glowing pearls and in their midst the hard-burning red and yellow and blue and white and green diamonds that were lights they never knew individually, but which coalesced into oceans and rivers of burning gems.

There had never been a moment of instruction free of wonder and delight, and there had never been wonder and delight without its discipline as well. Charley's world—no one had called her Charlene since she was twelve—had always been one of utter honesty. Her father had left that legacy with her. "You can lie to a man, Charley. You can tell all the tall tales you want. But one of the things I love most about flying is that you can't lie to an airplane. Once you get upstairs, if you're lying, you're lying with your mind and your hands and your legs, and if you are, why, that airplane will flat kill you. So be honest with yourself and your machine and it'll never let you down. And neither will you let *yourself* down."

Their father fought and scraped and worked seven days a week from before sunup to deep into the nights to make Morgan Aviation a reality. He'd come home after the second world war with a burning desire for his own airfield. On Florida's east coast, just off the main artery of U.S. 1 between the small cities of Cocoa and Titusville, was a field the Navy had used during the war. The Navy yielded it and Cocoa didn't want the expense of running it, and when the city fathers put it on the auction block, Morgan grabbed for the brass ring. He went into debt over his ears, but slowly paid off his debts and created the winner that became known as Shiloh Field.

Charley and Marty were still kids at the airport when the Air Force started launching giant missiles from Cape Canaveral to the east. They saw the flame and the white smoke trails, and thunder boomed back to them from the high heavens, and the space frontier seemed to be just one more step beyond the high ascents from their own field. Then the new space agency came onto the scene and poured billions of dollars into Merritt Island to create a monster spaceport. Men going to the moon meant a huge increase in their own business as the local population soared and executive jets from the big aerospace companies came in by the dozens to base at Shiloh.

The space coast was *exciting* in a way that couldn't be found anywhere else in the world, and pilots who'd managed to survive the years of their own crazy flying settled in the area, drawn by great weather, terrific beaches, and some pretty nifty fishing. Most of them brought their favorite toys with them. Accompanying the surge of interest in walking on the moon was an unexpected quiet explosion in American history. The nation's pilots and flying buffs were on a nonstop tear with old military planes, most of them from the second

114

world war. A new mystique sprang into being and romanticism about the "last great good war" flourished, and all of a sudden airshows with the old military planes became the national rage. It was a new era of barnstorming revived. Shiloh Field, surrounded by a population nipple-fed on technology and things with wings, became a favored warbird bastion of the country.

Morgan played to the hilt the momentum of nostalgia. He gathered together on his field as many of the "crazies," as the locals considered them, and their warbirds as he could accommodate. While thunder rolled from Cape Canaveral and the NASA spaceport, Shiloh Field echoed to the deep-throated cries of Merlins and Allisons, Wasp Majors and Cyclones, and the skies gleamed with sunflashes off the flying museum pieces of the past combats. There were American, German, British, Italian, Japanese, and even Russian warbirds on the field, and as inevitably as the sun must shine at dawn was the natural inclination for these people to sally forth in mock battle with one another.

Charley developed the idea of turning flying fun and frolic into a hard-cash business. She and Marty talked the pilots into regular routines of simulated fighting before paying customers. Overnight they became a commercial success as the crowds discovered the thrills and excitement of being in the crashing midst and roar of past combat, all without risk or pain. Weather permitting, every weekend the old-timers and their sons and daughters, and the newcomers who could afford the high price of restoring the old, complicated, and often dangerous warbirds, clawed their way into the skies. The Morgan Airshow became justifiably famous.

Charley and her younger brother were superb pilots, but Charley without being aware of the fact had become a top attraction in her own right. Admirers from afar and would-be swains gnashed their teeth in frustration as Charley ignored flowers and gifts and entreaties for dinner dates, choosing instead to spend her evenings digging into the complexities of cylinders and connecting rods and carburetors. Few things could drive a pilot crazier than watching Charley in tight Levi shorts leaning into an engine. Greasy, stratched, hair a mess, she was beautiful. She broke hearts left and right. It didn't help matters for the admirers to have to run the gauntlet of Lars Anderson, top mechanic at Shiloh. A big Swedish bear of a man, Lars had worked for years with the elder Morgan and considered Charley a second daughter to his own and absolutely needing his protection.

Rarely, all too rarely, impelled by suitors and prodded by Wendy Green, she traveled to the restaurants and club lounges of Cocoa Beach or Melbourne to dine, wine, and party. Emerging from her evenings out was that Charley fairly equally divided her time and attentions between two men, the smooth and dapper Israeli war hero, Abe Lansky, and the bronzed and muscled surfer, Mitch Bannon. The strong money was on Lansky, who had just about everything a girl might find inviting. No one figured Bannon to have any chance of staying power. The beach bum and bedside companion of uncounted young females was regarded as interesting but uninviting for the long haul.

No one asked Charley. Lansky to her proved a delightful dinner companion, and she enjoyed the attentions of a man who knew how to delight and please the woman he coveted. He was gentlemanly to a fault. Bannon, on the other hand, quickened her pulse and brought a blush to her cheeks. She felt a oneness with Bannon that she wanted so desperately to complete, but—

Drug runners had killed her father. They were especially brutal. Anderson and Strasser, as well as Bannon, did everything they could to shield her from the grisly truth. She wanted to know. She wanted fuel to keep the fires burning in the years to come, when it would be easy to forget instead of always seeking out the men who'd torn her father apart at point-blank range with shotguns, threw his body back into his airplane like a slab of meat, and then set the plane afire. There isn't much to burying a charred log that was once your beloved parent. They'd never found the killers. Bannon and everyone else she knew never stopped searching. No success. That hurt.

Marty drowned his shattered feelings in alcohol and pot, and too often mixed his own devil's brews of strong drink and drugs. He never relented in his foot-to-the-floor racing in cars and his roaring motorcycles, and if he needed even greater speed he climbed into the cockpit of his powerful T-28 for a few hundred miles an hour more to soothe his battered psyche.

The howling airplane didn't get him. He skidded through a wild turn on a motorcycle and went clear through a wall, carrying huge pieces of jagged wood in his leg that ripped arteries and veins and bone. When he regained consciousness in the recovery room of Cape Canaveral Hospital, he'd lost more than twenty pounds. His leg below the knee.

The word was out that Marty was all washed up with the daredevil scene. Marty gritted his teeth, and after they stopped popping morphine, came to gladly welcome the pain-numbing haze from the finest Colombian money could buy. The haze carried him to a prosthetic limb and his own grit brought him over the top. Soon he was flying again and racing bikes and tornado-like cars and boats, and just to shove it up a lot of noses and prove he could stand even more pain, he took up skydiving. It proved a bitch. He didn't always land as neatly as he liked, and he busted himself up some more. He grinned through it all and sucked deeply on that top grade of maryjane and walked or lurched on his aluminum leg as his pain dictated, but he *walked*.

They called him Mad Marty. And they respected the hell out of him.

He grew a beard and souped up a Porsche and trained a huge dog he named Magnum. At a hundred and fifty pounds, the Swiss mountain dog commanded attention and covered Mad Marty's back at all times. He trained that dog to do exactly as he ordered, which was basically to scare the hell out of people. The Swiss dogs are basically powerful but gentle creatures. The dog would grin with all his teeth bared like a space creature, smiling the whole time ... but if Marty or Charlene were threatened he'd attack like a hound out of hell. Marty got around to wearing dark glasses and carrying a white

117

cane with Magnum at the end of a Seeing Eye halter. Magnum would help him up the wing of his T-28, from which Marty would fall with screams. He broke up crowds at the shows.

If he didn't fly, Marty went through his own act during an airshow. He'd taught the dog to skydive. Plenty of dogs jumped with firefighters and the military in the past, and Marty learned the details. For an airshow he'd hurl Magnum from an airplane and follow him down with his own blood-curdling scream. On the ground the crazy dog would lead his blind master away, cane tapping desperately along a runway filled with taxiing warbirds.

It was no secret that Marty was heavy into drugs. Sheriff Bob Hughes kept the narcs away from him. Anyone who used the stuff to drag himself up from the pit where cripples lay moaning was high on the hill, to Hughes. He also believed Marty would beat the drug rap and make it on his own.

Mitch Bannon was Mad Marty's savior as well. The kid couldn't stay out of trouble, and Bannon ran interference every way he could. The word had come down through private channels to the sheriff that Bannon was really a secret agent for the drug enforcement office out of Washington and that he was to be left strictly alone. That fitted Hughes's purposes perfectly. Whatever came into his office with Marty Morgan's name was altered; Morgan disappeared and Bannon went on the paper and *then* it could be stuck into the heavy safe in Hughes's back room.

Life has its strange moments. Bannon kept Marty out of prison. To do that, he needed to be over the line of the law in handling illicit drugs. Charley was grateful to Bannon for keeping her kid brother alive.

He also was a drug runner himself. And drug runners had killed her father. There were times when Charley felt she was going mad. She learned to bite her tongue rather than accuse or condemn Marty. Despite his free-wheeling reputation, she knew Marty never went a day without tearing pain from his stump. How do you fault your kid brother seeking surcease from agony!

Marty could kill himself in one of his madcap performances or races. No secret there. They'd both lost too many friends not to accept death as part of their flying or competition. Charley's greatest fear was that Marty would become involved so deeply in heavy drugs that not even Bannon's magic, nor the helping hand of Hughes, could keep Marty out of prison. And she knew he would make certain he died before he'd let that happen.

It tore her up. Marty broke her heart. She loved Bannon and knew gratitude as well as deep affection for him, and had to keep him at arm's length as much as she could because of his drug running. There had been that night when it all became too much and she said to hell with it and flew with Bannon to the Bahamas and spent a week of intense and emotion-wracked lovemaking with him.

He'd never been in bed with her since.

The sheriff's car took the last turn from the highway onto the entry road for Shiloh Field. More and more planes drifted above and about them. Shadows from the heavy iron landing at Shiloh more than once crossed the road before them. Charley ordered herself to put her personal turmoil aside. She *had* to, if she wanted to remain both sane and in charge of the big airshows. Business was business, and everything was coming to a boil. Hokey it might be, but the old rule still applied: The show must go on.

They had nine days to go before that shuttle, *Antares*, would fly. Ever since *Challenger* exploded and in a single shattering blast of flame killed seven astronauts and nearly broke the back of the space station program, the crowds had poured into Brevard County "just in case" it might happen again. That many people jostling into Brevard County meant that many people looking for excitement, and *that* meant a big airshow all this weekend, then the week in between, and another huge weekend when *Antares* would lift. They'd have a huge crowd this weekend—*my God; that's today and tomorrow and the day after*—that stood to be their biggest crowd ever

119

since they started the warbird shows. Over the three-day weekend they could net between eighty and a hundred and thirty thousand dollars. That could keep them in business the rest of the *year.*

They drove along the flight line, and she took the moment to thank her lucky stars that the German major was so solidly behind her. When the deputies took her away and she asked von Strasser to take over for her, she knew her business, as well as the airshow to be flown, were in the best hands possible. Major Karl von Strasser was a bull of a man, a close friend of her father years past, an incredible flier followed with almost slavish devotion by the other pilots. With good reason. He'd shot down over a hundred and thirty planes of all kinds when flying for Germany (when *we* were the enemy, she thought ruefully), and his gift for flight was touched by the angels. He taught the young pilots who lacked experience how to stay alive in their firebrand machines. He instructed all the pilots in formation flying, and he handled the flying business of her airshows with all the stiff-gaited efficiency of the steel-backed Prussian. With his shaved skull and bristling moustache, a beer in one hand and chewing an expensive cigar, he was as much a show himself on the ground as he was in the air.

More important to Charley than everything else was that Karl was Marty's best friend, his benefactor, *his protector.* They shared an expansive apartment on the beach. Karl was the primary reason her brother was still alive, Charley reasoned.

She was right.

Charley Morgan had company in her concentration on the chrome-headed, thick-necked, powerful Major Karl von Strasser.

Mitch Bannon had returned to his hangar office and was chewing over what he knew about the man he'd called friend a long time. And Hudoff and his security teams had run a hundred investigative drills on him. They'd never found a thing. Even if he *had* flown for the Luftwaffe over Europe during the second world war, no one could fault his performance *as a pilot.* And as a warrior. His nationality didn't mean beans. A man fights for his country; he's accepted on that basis. A killer in the skies, an ace among aces. Wounded a dozen times. Scars everywhere on that battered body; he almost clanked from all the steel and lead in him.

None of the investigators faulted him for shooting down seven American bombers in one day. Adolf Hitler had personally decorated Strasser for that incredible performance. Even *that* didn't raise a single eyebrow in security. What Strasser did *after* the war kept his file open.

"Would you believe the French Foreign Legion?" Hudoff dropped the file before Bannon one day.

"I'd believe just about anything about Karl," Bannon told Hudoff with a hint of irritation. Why the hell couldn't Bernie see the parts of a man that were all-important? Where honor was concerned, the handshake and the word of Karl von Strasser were absolutely unbreakable. "So he was a soldier in the Foreign Legion. So what? They had all kinds—"

"Nah, not a soldier. He *flew* for the French. They had quite a war going on in Indochina. We called it Vietnam. Strasser flew bombers for them against the Viet Minh."

"Give him a medal, then," Bannon offered.

"That's not important. Indochina, I mean."

"Then what's this all about?"

"He flew in a couple of wars in the Middle East . . ."

Now what he'd been told about Karl assumed sudden and dramatic importance. He flew for the Israelis and shot down a slew of Egyptian planes. Then he flew for the Egyptians in a few excursions into central Africa. He fought against the French for the Algerian rebels. *He had terrific contacts in the Arab world.*

Bannon couldn't believe that would mean much today. But he knew Hudoff's rules. *Everything means something.* Karl had moved to the United States and settled in Florida. A surprising number of ex-German pilots were to be found in that state. He brought a lot of money with him and opened an aerobatic training school. It kept him in gasoline, spare parts, beer, and cigars.

When the airshows started ringing cash registers like Christmas bells, Karl's savvy and teaching ability carried him along. He had four pilots working for him full time.

The airshow teams loved him. Hudoff's security people were suspicious of him. *A plant, Bannon, is someone who's put into place many years before he's ever needed. He fits in. He's a part of the local scenery. And until that moment when he gets his call you'll never know it. Never.*

So Karl would remain on the list of leading suspects. In Hudoff's office. Not by Bannon. He was betting on Karl, and he judged that the German would prove invaluable to them. He still had contacts throughout the world. More than a few Germans who knew they could never return to their Fatherland stayed in touch with Karl. They were an amazing sluice of information impossible to come by through any other source.

It was all starting to come together. More lives would be intertwined.

And Bernie Hudoff was taking a boat ride to meet with the enemy.

✦ 9 ✦

GALENKO

Hudoff stood by the bow of the Coast Guard cutter slicing easily through the waters of Port Canaveral. He breathed deeply of the bracing sea breeze and the smell of salt water about him. He appreciated the moment. It would be all too rare in the days ahead. An officer stood by his side, pointing. "There he is, sir."

Hudoff looked ahead of them along the channel. To their right, dark rocks formed the breakwater from which fishermen tossed their lines into the water. To their left, high sand banks and a channeled inlet to the Trident submarine base. Still to their left, but now behind them, were the missile loading docks for the Poseidon subs, wide open to public view. But Hudoff's attention was on a lone man in a fishing boat with an outboard motor, a boat drifting slowly with the current. Hudoff held out his hand and the officer placed binoculars in his grasp.

Hudoff focused on the boat. He saw a very large man in fishing gear, smoking a pipe, ignoring the tangled mass of his fishing lines—which, Hudoff could judge, had never held any bait. The large man sat with a 35-mm camera with a long lens held to his eye, clicking steadily. The lens was aimed in the direction of the nuclear sub facilities. Hudoff handed back the binoculars as they approached the fishing boat, and the cutter clanged bells to warn of its approach.

Hudoff went to the port side rail, leaned against the polished wood, and watched deckhands securing lines between the boat and the cutter. Hudoff smiled as the big man in the boat looked up and smiled. He waved at Hudoff.

"How's the fishing, Vladislov?" Hudoff called down.

He could see the other man's face crinkle in a huge smile. "It would seem, my friend, that I have become the bait!" The fisherman had a strong Russian accent. Not surprising, since his full name was Vladislov Galenko and he was as Russian as the Kremlin itself.

Hudoff laughed. "Vladislov, for the top KGB man in this country," he shouted, "you are a lousy fisherman!"

Galenko had tucked the camera in his coat and was climbing up the ladder lowered by the crew. He came over the rail to greet Hudoff with a two-handed grip. "Ah, my friend, let me tell you. The photography is not so good, either."

Hudoff shook his head. "What the hell are you doing out here, anyway? Damnit, man, you could buy better pictures in any tourist shop along the beach."

Galenko nodded. "To be sure, to be sure. But you must remember something." He offered a humored huffiness. "I am paid to *take* these pictures, not to *buy* them. Good pictures are not so important, do you see?"

"Who am I to argue?" Hudoff clapped Galenko on the shoulder and pointed to the boat. "Mind if we tow you in? I need some time with you."

"Much better up *here*, Hudoff." He turned to the officer standing by them. "Tell them to tow. But be careful! The man who rents me the boat is very worried about his property. He does not believe I am expert fisherman." Galenko chuckled, and walked with Hudoff to the bow where they would be alone. "Bernie, you have that flask with Jacques Danielle?"

"You mean Jack Daniels." He handed Galenko the flask and he drained half its contents in a long gulping swallow. He capped and returned the flask, kept his back to the wind to relight his pipe. His eyes held Hudoff as he turned back to face the wind.

"You are giving me a very special escort today, my friend," the Russian said, to hasten Hudoff's explanation for his unexpected presence in the middle of Port Canaveral.

Hudoff let his eyes drift over the ocean. A glint of reflected sunlight caught his attention. Fat Albert, riding high in the skies. "You might say the balloon's gone up."

Galenko made a face at him. "Spare me your Yankee slang. As your old and childish television shows put it, just facts, if you please."

"A condition."

"Of course! Is there not always a condition?"

"This one is necessary, Vladislov."

"You are so serious. You have my word."

Hudoff nodded slowly and turned to hold the eyes of his security counterpart. "We had four atomic bombs hijacked early this morning."

Galenko's expression was cast from granite. He spoke only after the most careful deliberation of what he'd heard. "I do not hear any accusations."

"There are none."

"All right, Hudoff, then—"

"The word we have is that whoever has the bombs is going after the shuttle when it flies nine days from now."

"And you are telling me this," Galenko said carefully, "because I am the security officer for the cosmonaut Russia has in your space machine?"

"That's part of it. One thing more."

"A hook, as you would say?"

"Not really." Hudoff held his conversation as people came closer. They watched the cutter easing to its dock. Then they were alone again.

"I need your help," Hudoff continued.

A smile began slowly on Galenko's face. Hudoff thought the Russians were the only people he'd ever known who could smile like the sunrise; slow and careful and beginning at one point on the face and spreading until all facial smile requirements were met. "I can hardly believe it," Galenko said quietly, and Hudoff couldn't detect any sarcasm in that voice. "American security is growing up. As you would say to your doctors, you want a second opinion?"

"Fuck you, Vladislov."

"You are upset by my comments?" Galenko slapped Hudoff on the shoulder. "No offense, but— What you said is taken with my understanding how serious it is. Of course you have my full cooperation!"

Again they held back their conversation. They left the cutter and walked briskly to the NASA security helicopter waiting down the dockside.

"Most of all, what I need is information," Hudoff said.

Galenko stopped in midstride. His sigh was an audible whoosh of air. "We have been expecting this," he said heavily.

Hudoff's expression told it all. He was amazed at the admission. It took only a moment for him to collect himself. "Then why the hell haven't you said something before *now!*" He gestured angrily. "Goddamnit, from the beginning we've worked this launch as a joint security project. Teamwork; remember? Our people are going up to that station and so is Georgi Mikoyan—"

Galenko was back to his poker face as he interrupted. "And so are cosmonauts from five countries besides ours."

Hudoff resumed his stride toward the helicopter. They climbed into the cabin, and Hudoff waved the pilot to get on with it. For several minutes they withheld their conversation, Galenko watching with unconcealed interest as they sped eastward over the sprawling solar research center and the Trident submarine base. Hudoff watched him closely. "Satisfied, Vladislov? Four Trident boats down there."

"Fascinating!" Galenko boomed. "I forgot to use the camera." He patted his coat and laughed. "Could I have your pilot take us around again? Hudoff, I could get a bonus for such pictures!"

"Some other time, Vladislov." He saw the Russian

peering down along the old missile row of Cape Canaveral, where Atlas and Titan boosters had speared into space. "That's the Delta pad, over there," Hudoff told him, pointing. "We're still using it for smaller payloads."

Galenko nodded. "And there is your museum." He frowned. "And the place where your smaller Saturns were launched. Where your three cosmonauts died twenty years ago."

"Never mind the Kremlin tour," Hudoff said, a bit harsher than he intended. "You know more than you've told me about what I'm certain is a very professional terrorist group. Level with me, for Christ's sake!"

Galenko was almost contemptuous of Hudoff's choice of words. "Not for *his* sake, if you please," he said sarcastically. "You of all people do not need emotional outbursts, Hudoff, and—"

Hudoff ground his teeth. "Goddamn you—"

Galenko had a thin smile on his face as he locked eyes with Hudoff. "*Zoboa*," he said.

This time Hudoff was ready. He showed no reaction. "I keep hearing that name more and more."

A Russian eyebrow lifted. "Oh? May I ask the source?"

"From one of my agents," he was told. "Among other sources. And from a mutual friend. Mario del Passo."

"Ah, yes." Galenko ran memories at high speed through his brain. "A very good man. He, specifically, discussed Zoboa with you?"

"He did. I'm being absolutely open with you, Vladislov. We have very little on this group. Who they are, even *what* they are. And what the hell is a Zoboa, or what does it mean?"

Galenko leaned back in his seat. He glanced out at the ocean and looked down on camera sites as the helicopter began its swing inland. "It is Arab, my friend. Zoboa is to the Arabs what kamikaze is to the Japanese. A wind of providence; the divine wind." Of a sudden Galenko became the KGB professional Hudoff knew so well. "Listen to me, Bernie Hudoff. You asked why I did not tell you before that we expect something very bad to happen. I did not speak because you would hear the words, but you would not have listened, really, and you

127

would not understand. Now that the danger is real, now that it chases after you, understanding will come with it."

Hudoff looked steadily at Galenko. He almost told him, *almost*, that he damned well knew that a zoboa was a desert whirlwind. But if a man is convinced he's both helping you and teaching you how smart he is at the same time, keep your damn mouth shut and listen. And, if you can, make it sound like you're awfully pissed off.

"You're a real fucking philospher, Vladislov . . ."

Galenko's hand shot up, then dropped in exasperation as he broke in. "See? Just what I mean! How impatient you are!" He gestured with both palms out toward Hudoff to calm him. "Let me tell you about Zoboa as the Arabs understand and *believe* in divine intervention."

Hudoff nodded, pleased with his own silence.

"More than two and a half thousand years ago the Persian king, Cambyses, invaded Egypt," Galenko resumed, letting Hudoff know that his recitation could only be the result of fairly recent study. Not even a top KGB man carried around this kind of detail from an obscure event five hundred years before the birth of Christ. "Cambyses had with him twenty thousand of the finest soldiers in the world. They swept all opposition before them. The Persians devastated everything. Typical for their day, looting and raping and wanton killing."

"That didn't change much where your country was concerned in 1941," Hudoff observed quietly.

Galenko flashed him a look of thanks for the American's understanding of the Nazi invasion, then continued. "On their last night before returning home, the Persian army quartered at the oasis of Sieva. They planned a final bloodbath as part of their departure. In the morning," Galenko said with a wan smile, "the sky was gone. Zoboa, the terrible desert cyclone, the sandstorm driven by winds of over a hundred miles an hour, struck at them. Almost to the last man the entire invading army was killed. The few who survived went mad."

Galenko watched the earth rising as the helicopter

128

swooped down smoothly. He kept his eyes on their descent as he continued. "The point is, my friend, that there is not and there can never be a compromise with Zoboa. It is all-destroying. That is the past and it is the present. Before, there was the wind of their gods. Today, they will control the wind. This time it will be a thousand miles an hour. Once released it cannot be controlled."

The fucking Russians love their parables, Hudoff thought with exasperation. Aloud he asked Galenko, "You're telling me that whoever, or whatever, this Zoboa group is, they won't be after a *deal*? I mean, no extortion, no blackmail?"

"No deals. No payoffs. They do not care about such things. *Zoboa does not make contracts. It destroys.* I told you, Hudoff, that you must understand the philosophy of these people before you can anticipate or understand what they do. Their whole purpose now is to explode one or more of those bombs. They will not even communicate with you, unless it is to further what they intend. The first you will know is that awful light—"

"You realize what the hell you're saying!"

Before the Russian replied, Hudoff motioned for him not to answer. The helicopter was touching down. They walked from the grassy heliport to a side entrance of the headquarters building, where Hudoff ran smack into the stringent security measures he'd instituted only hours before. The armed guard refused him entry with Galenko. "Sir, he has no pass," Hudoff was told by an unsmiling guard who a short while before had suffered Hudoff's wrath. "In fact, you're under camera observation, and we've shown this man's face to each road gate. No one has seen him before."

Vladislov Galenko stared into the muzzle of a .38 revolver. "Sir, I apologize. Raise your hands, please." Galenko took the whole thing as a huge joke, but one he both appreciated and, obviously, had gone through before on his own territory. Another guard frisked him.

"Okay, that's enough," Hudoff growled.

"Sir, raise your hands, please." The .38 was leveled at Hudoff. The guard reached into his jacket and removed the high-velocity .32 automatic that Hudoff always carried. He looked up at the camera and held up the gun. "Can you get the serial number off this, please?" he spoke into the camera. There was only a brief hesitation. "Okay, it checks out as the serial number for Bernard Hudoff. You can let him through."

"No way," the guard said. "Put the shift chief on the line. When *he* okays it, Mr. Hudoff, or whoever this man claims to be, can go through."

By the time they were finished Galenko was nearly in hysterics from laughter. They walked down a long hallway in the headquarters building, an almost surrealistic passageway darkened at one end and with the dazzling glare at the other of the midday sun. To each side were displayed pictures of past glories that began with the now-ancient Mercury program. Galenko stopped by a sweeping color photograph of five men floating in zero gravity, three Americans and two Russians. "Ah, your Apollo, our Soyuz," he remarked of the 1975 joint orbital mission. They continued on, their heels echoing hollowly on the hard polished floor.

"That guard," Galenko inquired. "What will you do to that man who was so quick with his weapon?"

"Promote him." He tapped the temporary badge on Galenko's jacket. "I'll have you a permanent security badge before the day is out."

Galenko smiled. "How quick you learn. Now, back to our discussion of before?" Hudoff nodded.

"As I said," Galenko spoke quietly, "they will not enter into negotiations. You have nothing to offer them."

"Nothing?"

"It is really simple. How many special guests will be here for the launch?"

"Government types and national figures, um, including the VIP bleachers and in launch control, say four thousand."

Galenko's smile was drawn, sad. "Four thousand of the world's leaders. Not only the politicians and the scientists, but the writers, the artists, the poets—"

"Yes, I know," Hudoff said impatiently.

Galenko would not be hurried. "All of them exposed to a nuclear explosion. You did not say the yield of those devices—"

"Four hundred kilotons."

"And six thousand from the world press?"

"Could be. Maybe more, not less."

"And with all the other guests and the visitors you will have a crowd of, let us say, five hundred thousand people within reach of the most dangerous elements of an explosion. That does not yet include the spaceship and its crew. It does not include the launch teams. Or the many astronauts who will be here to monitor the launch. Or . . ." His voice trailed away.

"I see what you mean," Hudoff said finally. "What could we possibly have to measure up to *that* kind of target?"

They stopped, alone and lonely in the corridor. Galenko turned to the American and placed a hand on his shoulder. It was many things in that gesture, a bond they were sharing.

"All these people, and you, and myself, my friend," Galenko said slowly, "we are all the hostages of this Zoboa. *We* also are to be counted among the victims."

Hudoff studied the man from the Soviet secret police, so different at this moment from that other world beyond the spaceport. "No," he said finally. "That's only a part of it. I understand now what you were getting at. They fire that bomb at launch nine days from now and this terrorist bunch turns the whole goddamned world upside down. The majority of the world's leaders will die or be so badly burned and injured they'd be better off dead. Another half-million people suffer the same fate. The whole space program is shot to hell. The VAB and our most critical installations here are flattened, gone." He took a deep, shuddering breath. "And for dessert we have world anarchy."

Galenko, listening carefully, finally nodded. "And overnight, Hudoff, the balance of world power shifts. What does the world see? That the United States cannot protect itself—*or anyone else*—against terrorists."

131

They walked slowly, almost to the elevators. "You mean," Hudoff replied, "that the balance of world power shifts clearly to Russia. You'll grab it and—"

A sharp laugh from Galenko caught Hudoff by surprise. The Russian gestured wildly in an emotional response.

"Grab it? Hudoff, you *fool!* You, all of you here, by your failure to stop that bomb, will hand over world leadership on, how do you say it? On a silver platter, *whether or not we even want it.*"

✠ 10 ✠

CONFRONTATION

Vladislov Galenko went through Hudoff's office like a teen-aged computer hacker through IBM headquarters: fascinated, impressed, hungry for more. They were surrounded in Hudoff's expansive, inner office with row upon row of electronic equipment and computers. Security here at the Kennedy Space Center had an awesome sense of the future. Galenko ran his fingers gently over radar console readouts, TV monitoring screens, computer panels, international clocks and direct comsat links, illuminated maps of the entire spaceport area and greater areas of Florida beyond the spaceport itself and the coastal beaches.

Galenko looked at his host. "One thing is for certain, Hudoff. *We* do not need equipment like *this* for our launch areas."

Hudoff laughed. "You sound like your tourist bureau. Of course you don't. You don't have bleachers or a press site or guests from around the world. You bring in a handful of people every now and then from the countries you control. If you find someone wandering around your countryside it means only one of two things. The poor bastard is lost or he's trying to run away. Either way you'd probably shoot him."

"You are wrong, Bernie Hudoff. It is not the policy any longer to shoot people for such things."

"Oh? Since when?"

"Since we bring efficiency experts into Russia. No more shooting. Everybody to Siberia." He winked at Hudoff. "But I must say your weather is much nicer here than Baikonur. That is pretty much what you call a shitty town, and it is a hundred miles to the launch center, and in between we have an enormous amount of nothing. But," he shrugged, "that is why it is there in the first place."

They stood together by the great picture window looking northward, toward the cubical monolith of the VAB and the two launch complexes beyond. The view was magnificent and—

Several warplanes exploded into being almost directly before their eyes, perilously close to the window as they howled past in tight formation. The engine thunder was devastating, rattling the window and shaking the walls. Galenko whirled around, beset with instant fury. Face contorted, he shouted at Hudoff:

"And that is another thing, my crazy American friend! You want security, yes? *Hah!* And *bah*, too!" He waved his arm wildly at the window. "Right across that river you have all those madmen, led by a crazy woman and her brother who also is mad, and a Nazi fighter pilot, and ... and ..." He was spluttering now, pent-up accusations pouring from him. "And drug fiends! Yes, *I know*, Hudoff! Drug fiends and drunks and they *all* have those machines of the wars, all the fighters and the bombers, and they fly anywhere they want, madmen, and you are mad, too, because you cannot tell me for certain they did not hijack those bombs today!"

Galenko's face was beet red, his anger ebbing from him now as, with eyes bulging, he threw himself into a chair and gasped for breath. He glared at Hudoff, who stared back, his face showing no emotion—and then Hudoff broke into laughter.

"The stolid, stoic, unemotional, cold, pragmatic Russian," he said finally. "What the hell just happened to you?"

"It is not so funny, you clumsy bastard!" Galenko shouted.

Hudoff returned to his desk, the laughter and his smile ebbing quickly. As he took his seat his demeanor changed. "Damn you, Vladislov, you're right. I *don't know* for certain." He stabbed a button on his desk. "Judy? Get me Elliott right away, and tell Jack to fire up that chopper and stand by. Oh, and pass the word, *officially*, that I will be having Vladislov Galenko with me, and his temporary security pass is good anywhere on this site." He hesitated. "As long as he is in my company, that is."

He looked across the room at Galenko. "*You're* a crazy bastard," he told his opposite number. "But God help me, you may be right."

"Hah!" Galenko shouted.

They spotted the car at the far end of the airport road, sparkling red and blue lights and even the headlights flashing on and off as if the deputies bringing Charley Morgan back to Shiloh felt the moment deserved its own celebration. "Hey! There she comes!" and "There's Charley!" rang out along the flight line to the office of Morgan Aviation, where more than a hundred friends and supporters spilled onto the ramp by the main hangar, whistling, cheering, and applauding. To the right of the sheriff's car thunder rose in waves to beat across the field and mix with the siren suddenly set wailing by the grinning deputies. The thunder of engines turning over, engines small and chattering to great monsters of many thousands of horsepower, grinding over propellers heavier and larger than many of the automobiles parked at the field.

The car came to a hard stop, tires squealing, in the midst of aircraft and crews. Charley's friends, laughing and shouting, crowded about her. She climbed from the car, turned slowly to offer a dazzling smile to *her* crowd, and cried, "Right on!" Fists went up all about her and the mob thundered the phrase in response. Charley kissed each deputy on the cheek, Bill Santiago came forward to close the driver's door and bade the deputy goodbye with a grin and an upraised middle finger. More applause and cheering as the car pulled away.

Her permanent cadre of pilots gathered about her. Karl von Strasser held out his beefy arms and she threw herself against him for a fierce hug. "See, little one?" he told her, the others hanging on every word. "You spend a little time for a drive in the country, you cast your spell over the big bad sheriff, and you are back here in time for the big party!"

A thick finger tapped von Strasser's shoulder. "Quit hogging the hugs, you Kraut bastard," he heard the voice of Lars Anderson. "I'm cutting in." Laughing, Charley let herself be wrapped in Anderson's grease-stained bear hug. She looked up at moistness along the corners of his eyes. "Lars," she said softly. "I didn't—"

"Hesh up before I say something stupid," he growled, pulling away and walking off toward the flight line. Charley couldn't believe the outpouring of relief and emotion for her. There was Bill Santiago and Tim Ryland, the tall figure of Jay Martin standing above the heads of the others, winking and throwing her a wave, and Ken Masters, and Sherri Taylor squeezed her way through the others and flung herself about Charley. She was laughing and crying at the same time. "I never thought I'd be so glad to see a woman who looks better than me, Charley!" she wailed, and broke into the laughter of relief.

Charley's feet nearly went out from under her as a furry mass, sensing the emotions of the moment, slammed against her. She grabbed at Magnum and threw her other arm out for support, and Abe Lansky was there, laughing with delight like the others, and her brother booted his dog in a familiar way and now Charley was crying as she hugged Marty, and she didn't know why. She held Marty at arm's length and kissed him, looking beyond Marty at the others, searching for a face in the crowd.

"Where *is* that son of a bitch!" No one needed to ask her who the son of a bitch was. Bannon had been gone most of the morning and questions were being asked about his flying in the show. Marty gripped her hand.

"Haven't seen him, Sis, but he left word he'd be flying with us."

Charley nodded. She glanced at her watch, nearly gasped at the time. "Everybody! I love you! Now get your tails back to your planes and get ready!"

They drifted away. Charley saw Abe Lansky again. "Abe!" she called and hurried after him. She touched his arm. "That was good of you," she said to him. "Thank you."

"The bail?" He smiled. "It was nothing, Charley, but you might have needed it."

"I didn't use it, Abe, but like I said, thanks for the thought."

He started to answer but she was already calling to the German pilot. Lansky's raised arm fell in mild frustration, and he motioned for Yusuf Hamza to go with him to their B-25 bomber. Most of the crews had gone to their planes for a final check before they would slide into their positions for the show.

Charley walked back to her office, arm around von Strasser's waist. He smiled to himself; the girl had a new spring in her step despite the scene with the arrest. "Karl," she started, hesitating, squeezing him tightly as they walked. "I'd like to ask you something."

"You ask anything."

"Bannon's never made any really close friends. You know what I mean? Except you," she added. "There's something special between you two."

"There is a wall he keeps about himself," von Strasser explained. "There is an element of caution in that one that is strange. It should not be there, but it is."

"Karl, what could possibly have made him turn *me* in to the sheriff?"

"That is a question everyone has been asking. Including me," von Strasser told her. "I do not know the answer, but there must be a reason we don't understand."

"I'm *trying* to understand!" she exclaimed. "But damnit, being dragged off to jail like that—"

"I thought, Charley," he told her quietly, "it was more like a parade. And a triumphant return, I should add."

She grinned up at him. "Well, it *did* turn out pretty great. . . ."

"Charley, do you believe Bannon would want to hurt you?"

She felt the question was unfair, but Karl never said anything without meaning. So she put aside indignation and answered him directly. "No. I don't believe that for a moment. But," she added hurriedly, "you said yourself he has a wall about himself we don't understand!"

"You are pushing, Charley, and there is no need. My little girl has her feathers ruffled—"

"Don't start the Dutch uncle routine with me, *Major*."

He laughed with her. "My only advice is not to make a final judgment until you know more. All right? You ask for my advice and I give it to you, Charley. Besides," he hugged her about her waist, "you knocked him kit from strudel with that punch."

"My hand still hurts," she giggled. "Next time I'll kick him in the gonads."

"How foolish. How can he then make love to you?"

"Karl!"

He laughed. "It is all right, Charley. I have known for a long time. It is no one's business." They were almost to her office when he stopped and faced her. "Charley, you know there are terrible stories about me that many people say."

She frowned and nodded. "I know."

"Do *you* believe those stories?"

She was aghast. "Never!"

"Other people believe such things. Why not you?"

"They don't *know* you!"

"Then there is a part of Bannon we also do not know. I suggest we *both* wait until we find out."

"All right, Karl, I—"

"*Charley! Look!*" She snapped her head around, saw her brother, pointing as he shouted to her. She turned with Karl to look across the field. "Good God—"

On the far side of Shiloh, holding perfect formation, red and blue lights flashing, sirens screaming, a row of helicopters rose like a tidal wave of lights and growing thunder above the distant tree line. They advanced across the field in the form of a breaking wave, air slamming down from the combined rotor wash, kicking up a pounding front of dust and grassy debris. Pilots in taxiing planes and along the flight line looked up in wonder and no small disbelief and then, acting on precision command, four of the helicopters lifted above the others and banked off to the sides of the airfield, maneuvering into a wide turn just beyond the perimeter of the field boundaries.

"What in the hell—" Charley started asking questions and realized there was no one yet on the ground to answer. She looked at Karl, who smiled and shrugged. "Military. They have a way about them. There," he pointed. "The machine with the police badge—"

"I know that ship!" Charley exclaimed. "I saw it early this morning." Von Strasser gave her a penetrating look. "It was at Bannon's hangar. He told me something about the NASA security chief visiting him, and—"

"Later." Von Strasser took her arm and started her on the way to the lead helicopter now on the ground by her office. They walked quickly through the blizzard of dust and blowing debris. Charley turned from the office and stood before the helicopter so the pilot could see her clearly. She held up her right arm with her middle finger out stiffly, and then moved her hand rapidly back and forth before her throat in the unmistakable signal to the pilot to kill power. He glanced at the men standing just outside the cabin and one man nodded. They heard the engine cut and the thunder began at once to recede. "Asshole!" Charley called out, and went with von Strasser into her office. A group from the flight line followed her.

Inside her office, the door closed behind them to hold down the wind from the slowing rotors, she looked at the four men. She recognized Bernie Hudoff, the same man she'd seen that morning. Another man wore the full security guard uniform of NASA. Two civilians, strangers, stood with stone faces just behind them.

The heavyset man had a strange look on his face. He was staring, obviously making a tremendous effort to keep his emotions checked. Startled, Charley turned to look at von Strasser. Karl and the stranger had an almost frightening eye contact. Karl's face was pure hate. He seemed caught off guard, thrust up against something hateful and dangerous. She spotted something else. By their eye contact alone, without a word spoken, Karl and the stranger had agreed to keep their silence. Charley looked beyond the group, out to the flight line, and her eyes widened. Armed troops had stepped down from the helicopters and were standing on the alert by their machines.

She turned back to the four men. "You're the security man for NASA?" she said to the one she'd recognized.

"Yes, ma'am. My name's Bernie Hudoff and I head all security for Kennedy and," he hesitated a moment, "for Canaveral. Are you Charlene Morgan?"

"Who the hell are *they?*" she pointed to the others.

"That's not important, Miss Morgan. I—"

"You're in my office. You're on *my* property. Tell me who they are or get them out of this office."

Hudoff hesitated. He saw the beefy man by her side, smiling. He knew instinctively this was the German he'd heard about, this von Strasser. And he had the *feeling* that the ice here was a bit thinner than he'd anticipated. He also knew better than to fire his big guns before they might be needed. So he nodded.

"Lou Elliott, NASA Security." He nodded toward the second man. "Joseph Horvath, United States Secret Service." He laid emphasis on the last four words for the effect he wanted. Then he went to the last. "This is Vladislov Galenko. He's the guest of the American government for the upcoming shuttle launch. Anything else?"

"That will do. Tell me what you want, Mr. Hudoff. You've already messed up my airfield."

"The tower cleared us, Miss Morgan." She showed surprise but said nothing. She'd wait him out.

"Miss Morgan, I—"

"Your identification, please," she broke in, changing her mind on the spot. It was time to do some of her own rattling of the cage.

He stiffened and a flush moved along his neck. He

wrestled with himself, then nodded and reached for his badge and ID wallet. "Of course," he said and held it out for her. She didn't give it a glance.

"Go ahead, Mr. Hudoff. *Now* tell me what you want here."

"What I want is ... Miss Morgan, I want all your pilots here, in this office, immediately."

"They won't fit. There are too many of them."

The first touch of exasperation showed. "Then in your hangar. That will do fine."

"My pilots are busy, sir. We have an airshow we are about to fly."

"I want them here *now*."

"You're *ordering* me? And them?"

"Damned right I am. I'm sorry to do it this way, but—"

"But, hell, mister. If you're ordering and not asking, let's see your warrant."

"My *what*?"

"Your warrant for our arrest."

Silence fell heavily between them. A cheek muscle twitched in Hudoff's face. "Miss Morgan, you don't seem to understand—"

"*Your warrant.*"

Something snapped. "I do not *need* a damned warrant. I—"

"Mister, I know who you are," Charley told him coldly. "You have full authority on that government installation over there," she gestured to the east, "but you are off the reservation *here*. You are on private property and—"

"Hey, mac! It's called trespassing!" a voice called out. They turned to see Mad Marty grinning from ear to ear. He was obviously enjoying himself. From the faces on the other pilots who'd drifted into the office, that same enjoyment was passing around quickly.

"*Mister* Hudoff, unless you have a warrant, or you're making a citizen's arrest through civil law enforcement, in which case you had better be damned sure of what you're doing or I have full legal action against you, you are way over your head. You are officious and you are

141

insulting, and I am rapidly coming to dislike you very much."

Charley turned to point at Horvath. "He said you're Secret Service. Are you?"

"Why, uh, yes, I am."

"Your identification, please?"

Horvath fumbled for his ID wallet as Hudoff fumed. Horvath held up his badge and ID card. "All right, whoever you are," Charley went on. "You're government. You're on private property, which is open to the public unless you're told otherwise. Are *you* arresting us? You have the right, but the same conditions apply to you as they do to Mister Hardnose, here."

"No. I am *not* making any arrest."

"Thank you." Charley stabbed Hudoff with a scathing look. "Since you won't explain, but prefer to demand, you really leave me no choice."

"Choice for what?" Hudoff asked. He looked bewildered. The one they called Galenko seemed to be having a fit. Charley didn't know if he was choking or . . . could it be he was *laughing?* It didn't matter.

"I am asking you to leave this airport immediately. You are on my private property. You are interfering with civil air commerce."

"You're asking me to leave? With all that—" He pointed outside to the helicopters and armed men.

"I am."

"The hell I will!"

"Then, sir, with these people as my witnesses, I notify you that you are trespassing after due notice, and I am *ordering* you the hell off my airfield."

Charley smiled expansively, totally out of character with the person rubbing Hudoff's nose into something he'd never expected. "And if you do not depart these premises, and that *is* the legal term, Mr. Hudoff, then according to the laws of the State of Florida you are guilty of trespass after warning, which in this state is a *felony*, and I have the right to arrest you and hold you for the proper authorities, *and I damned well will!*"

She was getting hot under the collar, not wanting to, but

obviously losing it with the heavy hand brought against her. Hudoff had gone beyond his own cool approach.

"Try it!" he shouted.

Charley turned to her desk, yanked open a drawer, and turned again with a .357 magnum in both hands, pointed unwaveringly at Hudoff. The hammer came back with a ratchety click that sounded almost as loud as a gunshot. The smile was gone and Hudoff faced a very grim woman.

"You, sir, are under arrest."

Silence. No one moved. Until a voice called out loudly, "Hotcha damn!" Heads turned to Bill Santiago, grinning like an imp, his accent heavy with his Cuban background. "I tell you, meester, that womans she mean whats she say. You wiggles your ass and she blow its away! I seen hers do this theeng before!"

Grins spread among the group, but they didn't belong. Quickly von Strasser and Anderson moved into the heated impasse that threatened sudden violence. Lars Anderson stepped between the gun and Hudoff. He didn't say a word, but wagged his finger back and forth as though he'd caught a little girl stealing cookies.

Von Strasser stood before Charley, his hand out. She looked up at him and he nodded, also silent. She handed him the revolver. He eased the hammer down and slipped the gun into his belt and turned to Hudoff.

"This is more than enough." There was steel in his body and his look and his voice. Party time was over and no one needed to voice that fact aloud. "Tell us what you want. But let us not hear *orders*."

Hudoff took the measure of the big man before him. Hudoff had met men like this one before. The last thing he needed now was bullshit, from himself, the one they called von Strasser, or anyone else. He nodded. "You're right. I thought you were informed we were coming here," he hesitated, "on official business."

"Hey, he can *think!*" Mad Marty called out from the group. "Ain't that wonderful?"

Hudoff whirled, stabbing a finger at Mad Marty. "I don't need any of your crap, sonny!"

A huge dog, snarling horribly, raced from the crowd

before Hudoff. He stared into a mouthful of enormous teeth.

"Don't bite him, you dumbass dog!" Mad Marty shouted. "You'll get food poisoning! Get your bushy ass back here—"

The dog backed up slowly, deep angry snarls coming from his throat.

Charley leaned against her desk, shaking her head. "This is absolutely crazy. Hudoff, please tell us what you came here for?"

He had control again. "I apologize," Hudoff told her. "When you understand what's involved, we'll both forget this. I promise you I'll get this over with at once. And I am asking for your cooperation." He glanced at his watch. "Can you spare a few minutes from your pilots?"

Charley looked at von Strasser, who nodded. She gestured to Wendy Green on the far side of the office. Not a word was exchanged between them. Wendy leaned to the public announcement microphone. "All pilots report to the hangar. Everybody to the hangar, please. Move it, boys and girls."

The pilots stood before the briefing platform in the hangar. Armed men guarded all the doors. Hudoff stood on the platform with the microphone in one hand. He looked at Charley, who nodded. Hudoff's voice echoed through the hangar.

"Some of you people already know me. For those of you who don't, my name is Bernie Hudoff and I'm the head of security for our spaceport complex. What I have to tell you is information that's shocking. It's also highly classified. The press has nothing on it. We're counting on you to keep it that way because we trust you."

A murmur went through the crowd as an almost visible ripple across a quiet pond. Hudoff wanted desperately to judge its intent and effect. He was dealing with an unknown factor here. Nothing in his background even remotely prepared him for negotiating with a band of men and women who were not only certifiable lunatics, but also people of tremendous technical skills *and* combat experience and an enormous potential for help or damage.

"Most of you at one time have served your country as military pilots. Or crewmen. I'm glad of that, because I'm asking you right now to think in terms of war. Not open combat, but something far more insidious. And more dangerous. To those of you who haven't served before, you're needed now. But I've got to ask *all* of you not to repeat outside this building what I have to say to you. Does anyone here object to that condition?"

"*Jesus Christ, get on with it, old woman! We've got a show to fly!*"

"*Yeah! Get to the point, willya!*"

Hudoff had a sinking feeling. He caught Horvath's eye and a barely perceptible shaking of the head. The message was clear. *As an inspirational source, Hudoff, you're a stinker*. Hudoff felt a flash of anger. Dumb bastard! He took a deep breath.

"Okay, you've got it straight," Hudoff continued. He was confused about whether to try the emotional or the flat-tone approach. Nothing seemed to be working. He could feel the hostility spreading swiftly through the group before him. What the hell had gone wrong with his patriotism approach? He ran all these things through his mind, discarded all options, and went for the facts. "Early this morning," he went on, "an unarmed Air Force transport was forced down near Lake Okeechobee. We don't know who attacked the military aircraft. We're still lacking details. But we do know that transport was carrying highly sensitive material and that its capture poses a tremendous threat to the security of our country."

He could feel his words lying sluggish and gravid among these people. Men and women were looking at one another, wondering what in the hell was going on. Murmuring rose and fell like gentle swells through the hangar and whispering became the signature of their discontent. They were not so much curious as wondering what they were even doing here when intense need waited right outside on the flight line. Hudoff thrust directly at his audience.

145

"Once they were on the ground," his voice rang out with more melodrama than he intended, "the crew was murdered in cold blood."

Again that stirring, the rising drone of voices climbing above whispering, and then the shouts. *"What is this? Meet the press?"*

"The son of a bitch can't get to the point. I'm going back to my airplane!"

"Screw this!"

"Damnit, listen to me!" Hudoff shouted into the microphone, a silly act that only came through the loudspeakers as scratchy noise.

"Who is this crazy bastard?"

"Hey, Charley, you talk to him! I'm flying!"

Near the platform, Mad Marty caught his sister's eye. Charley nodded, and Marty took the signal to climb up the stairs and stand alongside Hudoff. Mad Marty held up both his arms, waving them back and forth until the crowd quieted. He gestured to Wendy Green and she tossed him a second microphone. Then he turned to look at Hudoff, and everything he said went through the microphone so they could all hear.

"Mister, we really don't know what's going on here, and you're obviously from the government, and you're all upset, so why don't you get to the point. *What has this got to do with us?*"

Whistling, cheering, and applause rose quickly from the pilots and died away as Marty gestured for silence.

Hudoff looked from Mad Marty to the crowd, back to Marty and again to the crowd. "I *told* you . . . unknown aircraft forced down an Air Force plane and murdered its crew, and we have lost sensitive material that affects our national security."

"Jesus Christ but he's a long-winded bastard!"

"Hey, Marty, you talk with that asshole. We're going!"

Hudoff exploded. "Goddamnit, you people want it straight, okay, you got it!" he shouted. "This airfield is filled with fighter planes. Any one of you people flying these fighters could have forced down that military transport! Any one of *you* people!"

A woman pushed her way close to the platform. "My

name is Helen Fowler," she called into the silence that met her move. "You make it sound like we also killed that crew."

Hudoff looked down and blew it all away. "Madam, that is certainly possible."

No one spoke. The temperature in the hangar seemed to drop like a rock tossed down a well. "Your name is Hudoff, you said?" she asked.

"That's right."

"Well, Mr. Jerkoff, fuck you." She turned and walked straight for the nearest exit, many pilots following her.

Hudoff's voice followed them from all sides. "We're not accusing you! We need your help!" Most of the pilots stopped for a last look at the man they obviously judged to be a lunatic. "We've simply got to know where you were between five and seven o'clock this morning. Once you do that, you're clean. If you *can't* do that, you'll be detained for further investigation and—"

The last straw snapped. Jay Martin, standing a head taller than those around him, pointed his finger toward Hudoff. "I wouldn't tell that mother fucker where I've been for the last *year*," he announced in a loud voice. He turned for the exit to the pilot lounge, a stream of men and women following close behind. Derisive hoots and cries drifted across the hangar to the platform.

Hudoff turned to face an infuriated woman moving quickly to him on the platform. "I've *tried*," Charley snapped. "Goddamnit, but I have really given this everything I've got. Cooperation up the ying-yang. I've broken into our schedule, gotten my pilots pissed off at *me* because of *you*, you . . . you asshole. You just accused these people of harboring the men who killed an Air Force crew in cold blood!"

Her arm snapped out toward the exit. "Get the hell out of here! Get out and take these clowns with you! You come back on this field without a warrant, *any* one of you, and I swear to God in heaven I'll have your asses in jail so fast I . . . I . . ." She took a deep, shuddering breath. "You want to check out my people, Hudoff? All right, you son of a bitch. Start with me. And for openers I wouldn't tell you the time of day!"

The sounds of engines running up drifted into the hangar. No one spoke for several moments. Hudoff placed his microphone in a slow and exaggerated movement onto the platform table. When he turned back to Charley he was in full control of himself, a man who obviously recognized the futility of all that had just transpired. He spoke slowly and comfortably.

"Have it your way, Miss Morgan. *For now.* We'll do through channels what I couldn't accomplish just now on a direct basis. But as far as you're concerned, we're not interested in you."

Charley studied the man she felt had lost all his marbles. But he was too calm, too sure of himself. She glanced to her side at her brother and several pilots still with him.

"You're *not* interested in me?" she said finally. "I thought you wanted to know where all my pilots were this morning. Including me. After all, I could have shot up that Air Force plane and killed its crew."

Hudoff sighed. "We know where you were at six o'clock this morning when you blitzed that motel."

Charley's eyes widened in disbelief. She stared at her brother, whose expression was also one of total surprise. Not von Strasser and Lars Anderson, who were hanging on to one another and shaking with laughter.

Charley shook her head slowly. Comprehension swooped down on her. She looked in the distance, unseeing, totally preoccupied with her own thoughts. *So that's why . . . but how could he . . . my God; Bannon . . . that's why Bannon told the sheriff . . . that son of a bitch . . . he knew all this time!*

✦ 11 ✦

AIRSHOW!

There's only one thing better than eight good-looking busty broads in golden halters and golden hotpants and golden boots and all with golden hair, and that's eight *great*-looking chesty broads who have all these attributes plus dazzling smiles, who are hot-stepping it to *Flashdance* booming out from the loudspeakers along the crowd line. Fifty thousand people whooped and cheered and whistled and shouted their approval as Sherri Taylor led her seven Golden Girls along the taxiway before the crowd, dancing and high-stepping in a glittering golden display of beauty and precision as they neared their eight golden T-34s. Eight crew chiefs in golden flight suits waited for them to assist them into their planes and keep the performance moving for the crowd. The music stopped for the appropriate space of silence, the crowd hanging on the next move, and Kentucky Derby trumpets blared from the loudspeakers as the first crew chief held up his hand and brought it down smartly, and as his hand came down Sherri Taylor fired up her engine. One after the other, like drum majorettes on a football field, they started engines and the first booming roar washed over the crowd.

"And to your right!" the narrator called to the crowd. Slim Larson had been handling the pizzazz for this airshow for years. Face weathered by sun, hair bleached to a feathery white, his voice carried the inflections and tone of an old-time professional news announcer. Which he was, and making bundles of the long green up north when he decided snow higher than his ass and incipient frostbite was a ridiculous way to grow old, and he kicked it all and came to Florida and spoke to crowds about beautiful girls and magnificent airplanes.

"Watch that black high-tailed beauty, folks. Look for the flare, which tells us—" He paused as a bright red flare shot into the sky with appropriate *oohs* and *aahs* from the audience. They stood on tiptoe or chairs to see thirty young men and women in brightly colored jumpsuits double-timing into the black-and-gold Caribou jump transport, and the bugles had faded and a fast-tempo rock music pounded in time to the steady tramping run of the skydivers. Two more engines fired up with great blasts of smoke, and the Caribou wheeled smartly onto the taxi ramp, moving slowly before the crowd, thousands of people waving enthusiastically and the flight crews and jumpers waving back. Around back of the crowd, almost concealed by rows of campers and vans and motor homes, pilots and crews were manning their planes, getting ready to prime and start engines for their taxiing.

But all eyes were on the big black Caribou, and as it moved slowly between the crowd and the line of golden Mentors, it kept the attention of the audience. The music changed to a deep bass thunder, a heavy drum beat with brass overtones as the eight golden trainers turned smartly and taxied in tight formation behind the Caribou. The crowd continued to show its appreciation for the precision movement of the golden planes, and then the Caribou was lined up on the runway, the eight Mentors behind, and Larson held them hypnotized as thunder rose louder and louder and the black plane started rolling and lifted from the ground in only eight hundred feet. It pulled up sharply and seemed to poise in the air as behind and beneath the dark shape eight golden planes surged forward in two formations of four planes each, and as they neared takeoff speed all the

Mentors suddenly trailed long streamers of sparkling golden smoke and above them the black Caribou turned away sharply to the left and the golden Mentors banked to the right and flew around the edge of the crowd and it was a bangup way to get things going. In the distance, from another runway, mostly unseen by the crowd, warbirds took to the air in a steady stream, staying low and turning away from the audience.

Which was busy watching a wholly impossible sight. A young man in a heavy flying jacket and a seat-pack parachute banging against his legs, his face partially hidden beneath flying goggles and a leather helmet *and* a white scarf, tapped his way blindly along the taxiway, cane in one hand and the halter for the huge seeing-eye dog, also wearing dark glasses, leading him toward the blue-and-gold airplane standing alone on the line. Mad Marty stumbled and wove a precarious limping path to his T-28, berating the dog and the world in general. He pawed and fumbled his way up the side of the airplane and turned with unseeing eyes behind him. "Get up here!" he shouted. "You know I can't see and you got to fly this here thing!"

Larson kept the crowd broken up by describing what was going on and the people watched with awe as the huge dog leaped into the back seat of the airplane. The blind man leaned into the back cockpit, adjusting a harness by feel, removing the dog's sunglasses and replacing them with a leather helmet and goggles that fit the animal splendidly. Magnum turned to the crowd and lifted a paw and received a thunderous ovation. Moments later the pilot was in his seat and screaming signals to the flight line crew, and one man held aloft a flare gun and fired a long spume of confetti that drifted down over the airplane. The T-28 fired up, belching smoke, rocking back and forth on its nose gear, and a jeep with flashing lights and sirens screaming pulled up slowly before the airplane to lead it down the taxiway. Waves of laughter followed jeep and plane as they passed before the crowd which had the chance to read the big sign at the back of the jeep.

Slim Larson juggled the crowd's attention between the taxiing T-28—weaving and jerking suddenly as the blind man struggled to follow the jeep—and the Caribou climbing steadily overhead, its engine drone becoming thinner as it climbed for altitude. It moved with a glow of gold, the eight Mentors led by Sherri Taylor flying in wide formation around the Caribou. The T-28 spun about several times before the crowd, rocked dangerously from side to side, spat and belched smoke and then howled with power as Mad Marty firewalled the throttle. Wings wobbling sickly, it staggered into the air and seemed to fall behind trees on the far side of the airport. As it disappeared from sight a huge fireball rose into the sky, mushrooming upward from just beyond the trees, giving birth to thick oily smoke. Screams and cries swept the crowd, but Larson pointedly ignored the frightening sight and held up one hand to look into the sky. A dozen girls in cheerleader outfits joined him on the narrator's platform, chesty and long-legged, and began dancing to fast-paced booming music.

"Keep your eyes on the sky! Ladies and gentlemen, we're getting close to that moment when we open the Strasser Air Circus extravaganza with a fantastic leap from the heavens! Thirty young men and women will hurl themselves into the sky from ten thousand feet and they will not, I repeat to you, *will not* open their parachutes until they are seconds away from certain death! If you blink you may miss a sight you'll never forget. This is *your* moment, and now you can see the Caribou on its final jump run, I'm listening to the pilot and the jumpmaster planning the final critical seconds and we're waiting—*there they go!* Look at them falling—*here they come!*"

No one really heard him any more. Enough shrieks and yells and cries soared from the vast crowd to drown out any words as thirty bodies trailed thin plumes of multi-colored smoke, the skydivers holding perfect formation as they plunged with frightening speed at the earth. Fingers were being chewed, knuckles pressed against teeth, hearts pounding as they fell closer and closer and then, spurts of powder as the first chutes cracked open and thin popping sounds came down from the sky as all the chutes opened, and Larson counted aloud with the crowd until they had all thirty and then he shouted, "Look! Another one! He's falling!"

Falling he was, the flag jumper, who pulled his chute open at four thousand feet, a great square canopy with red, white and blue stars, and blue smoke from one boot and red from another as he released a huge American flag to hang beneath him. He cut spins and whirls and turns, going through chute acrobatics, and "There they come! Sherri Taylor and her Golden Girls!" And the eight gleaming golden Mentors raced down from the sky and set up a huge double circle about the flag jumper, engines snarling, smoke streaming in great circles as they kept formation with the flag jumper and as he neared the ground the Mentors peeled away to slide back into perfect formation. The jumper landed on his feet to roaring applause directly before the narrator's platform, waving at the crowd as he picked up his chute and several beautiful girls ran out to accompany him to the platform. Everyone's eyes turned to the sky, where dazzling lights appeared in the air as the Mentors turned in a tight formation from north of the field, all landing lights and strobes on, trailing their smoke, diving for a gut-squeezing pass down the runway, tucked in wing over wing, the lower planes' propellers barely inches above the runway. They climbed easily and broke out from their southward run to turn eastward, over the highway and toward the river, and Larson kept talking about them as the formation shifted before the crowd to hold their attention.

And hold it naturally, so they wouldn't see or hear all hell breaking loose from the north. Major Karl von Strasser and his gang of aerial thieves come to steal from the past and hurl it before the thunderstruck crowd.

The crowd was still watching the precision movements of the receding Golden Girls when a swelling roar pushed down against Shiloh Field, throaty and coughing, pouring out of the north, the first wave of an immense explosion tugging at clothes and pushing like a soft pillow against bodies everywhere. The thunder beat heavily as its source rushed closer. "My God! *Look!*" Larson cried over the loudspeakers and then went silent, for why compete with a thunderbolt from the heavens? All across Shiloh heads turned eagerly to the north, looking into the bright sun and thin blue sky, trying to distinguish form from the haze shimmering brightly over the trees. At first the onlookers' eyes watered; they blinked, saw spots, and felt that greater crash of inrushing sound. Then a thin heartbreaking wail, piercing all else, the frightened cry of the siren calling the air raid alert. Other sounds lifted above the thunder and the siren mewing thinly: men shouting to one another, feet nearby pounding on concrete, jeeps racing like square-boxed, noisy little muppets racing pilots to their planes for the emergency scramble. The loudspeakers crackled tinnily and a voice called hoarsely, frightened, imploring the fighter pilots to save the field and all these innocent souls who are about to die.

The thunder rolled downward in waves so heavy now they made normal conversation impossible. Children clung to parents, hands searched for other hands, and the fury of the sound weakened the knowledge that this was a *show*. Realism leaped the boundaries from make believe to *omiGod!* as three bombers crashed out of the haze, menacing in their shapes, their thunder now angry and body-punching as they went for the runway. Frightened voices cried out via the loudspeakers, tremulous with the moment, begging instant defense with the calls of "Quick! Turn those flak guns around! No! No! We're all gonna *die!*" Before the gaping, staring sea of fifty thousand people, men swung long-barreled anti-aircraft guns in the direction of the speeding bombers so close now that people made out the open bomb-bay doors, the machine guns jutting like porcupine quills from their bodies, sunlight glinting from curving plexiglas. The first guns opened fire, long tongues of flame leaping into sight from the barrels, and who for a moment would have thought *propane* rather than high explosive?

The speakers boomed. *"Ach! Verdamnt Amerikaner machines! Gunners fire! Schnell! You shtupid peoples, aim der guns!"* Again the anti-aircraft batteries and smaller banks of machine guns fired. *"All pilots! All der flieger. All der flugerhorns! Man your planes! Into der shky! Rauss! Rauss! Uppenzee undt fly!"*

The engines of two Messerschmitts turned over with shuddering coughs, smoke banging back from the engines. Two German pilots ran for their planes, mechanics waiting for them. No time for parachutes! Save the field! Guns boomed, engines roared, voices shouted, children screamed and shrieked and the fighters punched away, kicking back dust, rushing down the grass to get into the air while there was still time.

Time; ah, it was handled so neatly. The Messerschmitts banked steeply to get to the bombers because Bill Santiago sat on a high tower to the side of the crowd, headset-and-microphone comfortably on his head, watching everything with his practiced eye. "All right, the bombers come back up with the power, you got it, B-25s, let's cob it, you got the two Messerschmitts coming around from your right, very good, bomb bay doors are open, you two Messerschmitt pilots, get a little altitude there, you'll be right behind the wake of those bombers and we don't want you crimping metal, that's good, pyrotechnic people, on your toes, watch for the bombers to cross the red marker flag and then give it to 'em, B-25s get ready for the explosions, Messerschmitts, come on! Get in there to shoot them down, this ain't no picnic, you know, 25s be ready to break left at the south boundary and the ME's stay with them, all fighters in holding position in Square One, start coming around to begin your runs, dive bombers give me a call and your status . . ."

Towering fountains of flame ripped upward from the runway as the B-25 bombers struck. The explosive charges of black powder, balsa wood, gasoline, and assorted soft debris, shaped for maximum upward effect, went off with blasts so powerful that the concussion wave plucked at clothing, sent people reeling back, laughing and half-crying in sudden fear and immediate laughing release, and the B-25 closest to them caught their attention. No American star on the side of the fuselage but a shining crumpled beer can, just for that extra touch, and then all eyes were on the flames spurting from the bomber guns and from the attacking Messerschmitts. One fighter wheeled suddenly, wings vertical to the ground, and it fell crazily away from the runway, skidding and wobbling as it dropped behind the trees and an enormous explosion tore upward. As quickly as the blast raced over the crowd the loudspeakers "miraculously" carried the voices of the bomber gunner. *"I got him, Skipper! I got him! A flamer! That's one Nazi less who can hurt our women and kids— Look out! Here they come again!"* Children screamed and pointed. Voices rose from the crowd. "He's behind you!" "On your tail!" "Look out! Look out!"

More thunder, higher-pitched this time as airplanes started coming out of the sky in steep dives, other bombers racing in low in a concerted attack and an enormous sheet of flame erupted for a thousand feet, the sound of the blast again crunching into the crowd, and thick black smoke poured upward, drifting with the wind over the thousands of people who loved the feel and smell and taste and punch of such marvelous hysteria. More bombs, more smoke, more jeeps dashing back and forth, more guns firing, sirens wailing, men and women shouting, falling dead in marvelous histrionic departures from life, blood spurting from uniforms as they fell, kicking and writhing.

"All fighters! Return to the field! Schnell! Shtop der sightseeing! Schnell! Gettenzee back here! Der rotten Amerikaners dey are here again! Help us!"

A motley formation bunched loosely in the sky droned in from the north. Larson dropped the ersatz cries of the Germans and went to straight narrative to keep his on-their-toes audience fully informed as to what they were seeing. A huge Boeing B-17 Flying Fortress thundered along the left side of what gratuitously passed for a formation, the pilot—Tim Ryland— flying as if no one

156

else might be in the air. The other pilots kept a slight distance from the four-engined bomber so nothing would interfere with the crowd view of the historic machine. Again the uproaring flames and thick smoke, perfect settings for the bombers and fighters following to race through for a greater impression of speed and fury.

From high overhead two Avenger torpedo dive-bombers hurtled downward, air-driven sirens shrieking painfully as they plunged toward their targets. They pulled out to trail a series of more explosions, and then it was every man (and woman) for himself. Pale gray and shining-blue Skyraiders ripped "enemy targets." A B-23 Dragon released a stick of bombs, its bright red-and-white tail stripes an unexpected flash of color in the skies. The bombers raced in, turned over the river, and came back for more attack runs. The Flying Fortress, Mitchells, a Havoc, a Dragon, Avengers, Skyraiders, a single Marauder, a British Blenheim making the main attacks.

The fighters came in as lethal wasps and hornets, engines screaming and guns hammering. The number of fighters doubled and tripled. To the crowds who first saw the swarming Mustangs, Corsairs, the Hellcats and Wildcats and Warhawks, the gleaming lone P-38 Lightning, the Airacobra and Kingcobra, the lone Thunderbolt and the Tigercat and still other ships, the sudden appearance of a literal cloud of T-6 and SNJ trainers, along with a mixed bag of T-28s and T-34s, Japanese-made Fuji fighter-trainers and odd models, meant they were *all* fighter planes. The bombs exploded and the guns hammered, Larson at the microphone was near hysteria, ambulances dashed back and forth through the smoke, anti-aircraft batteries crackled and boomed, flames leaped upward, men screamed and died, bodies ripped into the air from nearby explosions, tumbling like the straw dummies they were sickly against the ground.

The Japanese had yet to make their appearance, and seven Zero fighters escorting Val dive bombers and Kate torpedo bombers raced in for a splendidly vicious strike. No matter that they were attacking a German airfield;

157

it was a *target* and that's all that mattered. Soon the air swirled with American, British, Japanese, German, and Italian fighter planes, as well as more than forty powerful trainers whose pilots had themselves the time of their lives shooting, bombing, and strafing, and performing ridiculous maneuvers.

The best was yet to come. Through the thick and thin of the maelstrom of furious combat, three old camouflaged C-47 transports hove into view in line-abreast formation, holding steady altitude fifteen hundred feet above the ground. Hands rose like quills above the human sea on the field, pointing to the doors yawning wide open in the sides of the transports. Above and behind and off to one side of the assault ships droned a protective escort of twenty more fighters and trainers. As the transports rumbled into final position, several escorts dove against the runway, strafing and bombing, their machine guns ripping up the earth in stuttering bursts of heavy fire.

Then the transports were in position and the aircraft beneath them, anywhere over the field, mysteriously skidded and slipped and turned out of the way as the C-47s each disgorged twenty paratroopers in perfect rhythm, multicolored skydiver canopies blossoming in the sky (so who cares about bright colors?), the troopers coming down with weapons at the ready. They landed just off the runway, gathering in perfect discipline, young men and women dashing about with great verve to concentrate their firepower. Immediately they were attacked with a formation of ground vehicles and German troops; the Nazi assault armor made up of one tank, three armored vehicles, two bread trucks and jeeps rushing about, and an old fire truck. Anything that could defend the German airfield against the *verdamnt Amerikaners*. Automatic weapons and rifles fired with great abandon, hand grenades flew through the air, and the staggering and flopping of the dying was a sight to behold.

From the north, brought in with perfect timing by Santiago, appeared a formation of German bombers and fighter escorts. They raced across the field, *their* machine guns blazing away; and as they passed by (with everyone's attention on the aircraft so that the dead and dying troopers had time to regain their feet and rush into position for further combat) deafening explosions rocked the field. More flame! More debris! More smoke! And the voice screeching through the loudspeakers, an anguished cry. *"Verdamnte schweinhunt! Dumbkopfs! Schmeggeggies! You haff bombed our own fuel tanks!"*

That wasn't quite all. Dead center in the field stood a small building, a perfect old wooden outhouse with a half-moon cut neatly in the door, and emblazoned at the top with a German eagle and swastika. There's a war going on but when nature calls, it sings an irresistible song. A German soldier in steel helmet and dragging his rifle ran through machine gun bullets kicking up dust about him, dodging hand-grenade explosions, leaping and twisting in his desperate need to reach the outhouse. The door slammed shut and the building rocked and teetered from side to side as the crowd roared. A bomber raced overhead and explosions bracketed the outhouse. The door flew off and the German soldier stood in the doorway in white longjohns, trousers about his ankles, shaking his fist. Another bomber came by and the "bombs" exploded with a gush of flame and smoke, hurling the soldier through the air as the outhouse blew up. He staggered to his feet and ran wildly off, holding up his pants, and smoke pouring in a stream behind him.

The crowd was convulsed . . .

Hudoff and Galenko stood in the midst of the crowd, jostled by cheering and whistling spectators, children scampering about their feet. Acrid smoke from the steady explosions drifted across the field, bringing Galenko to wrinkle his nose. "Stinks like burning cabbage," he grumbled.

"It hasn't hurt your appetite any," Hudoff observed. "That's the fifth hot dog you've had this afternoon."

Galenko stopped in mid-bite, raising his brows. "So?" he retorted with *smrfs* and chomping noises, his mouth full. "If I do not taste, how can I make report to Moscow on secret American recipe?"

"Sure. *And* a sixpack of Coors to go along with it." Hudoff grinned and gestured to take in the entertainment in the air as well as on the ground. "From the looks of things, your day hasn't been all that bad. I just about had to hold you back from those drum majorettes."

"You have dangerous imagination, my friend," Galenko replied, wiping mustard from his chin with his sleeve. "I am *observing*, you understand?"

"Sure I do." They walked from the food concessions to the flight line, where thousands of adults and children moved through the lineup of fighters and bombers that had landed from their parts in the show. Men and women wearing shoulder and breast patches reading Valiant Air Command, along with full back patches of the Strasser Air Circus, sat on the wings or before the planes, signing autographs and photos held up to them by their enthusiastic audience. In the air the Golden Girls were going through tight maneuvers directly over the runway, and as they broke in a tight formation, two fighter planes dove toward runway center from opposite sides of the field to begin a duo aerobatic performance. Galenko stopped beneath the wing of a torpedo bomber. His bemused expression was gone as he stood so close to the war machine.

"We talk serious for a moment, Hudoff?"

"Sure."

"These people are crazy, Hudoff."

The NASA security chief sighed. "Shit, I know *that*."

"You should never permit people to talk back to anyone from security," Galenko said critically. "That is unforgivable. I would have thrown the Morgan girl into jail *at once*."

"Sure, but there's a problem."

"What can be the problem!" Galenko said, exasperated.

"This isn't Moscow."

"So what is the difference?"

"Legally, she was right. Damnit, Vladislov, don't you understand? *I'm* the one who screwed up."

"You are *all* crazy!" Galenko shouted, his arms sweeping wide to take in the entire field. "You have emergency with—"

"*Stop.*" Hudoff snapped. "Watch what you say."

Galenko nodded. "I was going to say you have emergency with these people. You do not know guilty or innocence, so," he emphasized his words with a shrug, "you *must* presume guilt is *somewhere* in them. Until you find out which one you arrest them all!"

"Bullshit."

"Why bullsheet?"

"Because we work within the law. Because we're only *guessing*. Because there isn't a single specific charge I could bring against these people to hold them. Sure, sure, I could swear out a warrant and have them arrested, but—"

"Do it, Hudoff!"

"*But* they'd be out in an hour. They'd make bail and there isn't a judge around here who wouldn't give it to them."

Galenko blinked. "You mean even *judge* would not keep them in prison?"

"Not without good reason. Or to use more of the legal term, not without good or sufficient cause."

"What happened this morning is not good cause?" Galenko was honestly incredulous.

"The cause doesn't justify wholesale arrests, Vladislov. That's the way the law works."

Galenko's face worked as he struggled to reply. He gave it up as a bad job, grabbed Hudoff's arm, turned him around, pointing as he did so to take in the explosive, roaring mayhem across the airfield. "And what about all *this*, Hudoff? Look for yourselves! This is like war! Why do you even permit it? *It is stupid!*"

Hudoff jerked his arm free. He couldn't give up this moment to needle the KGB agent. "You, my fine feathered Russkie, are too goddamned serious. And these people are having a wonderful time, which I've come to understand *you* can't even do any more, your head is so far up your ass."

"Playing war is a wonderful time?"

"Look at those broads over there, Vladislov!" He half-

161

spun the KGB man around to direct his gaze to the drum majorettes filing by, a stream of young beauties returning to their bus. "Do *they* look like war to you?"

"Bah! You avoid what we are talking about, Hudoff!"

"No, I'm not," Hudoff snapped, struggling to keep his face straight. "Your problem is that when all this is over you're going back to Russia. There the women all look like Ernest Borgnine and *here* they look like these kids, and you can't—"

"Stay serious!" Galenko roared. "We are talking serious, my friend. All these planes, these bombs, *that Nazi*, all this is American way to glorify war!"

Hudoff sighed. Even a kick in the nuts couldn't get a message across to this Ivan. So he quit the routine with the young and beautiful women. "Glorify, hell. We're not glorifying anything. We're paying respect to our war history. What you're seeing is a living memorial to that history. What the hell's wrong with that?" He stared Galenko straight in the eye. "Shit, man, we *won* the goddamn war. So did *you*. That's worth celebrating."

"Is horsecock!" He waved an expansive arm to sweep the entire field. "You never see things like *this* in Russia!"

"You're as full of shit as a Christmas turkey, my friend," Hudoff threw back at him. "Are you telling me there are no military parades in Moscow? No May Day review with troops, planes, tanks, artillery, missiles, and—"

"That is different. That is national holiday."

"Well, I got news for you, buster. Any fucking time we want to have a party we have it. We don't need no goddamned annual communist bullshit parade. Furthermore, you don't have any war games, right? No maneuvers for your army or navy or air force. Sure! And I guess those war monuments I've seen in Kiev and Leningrad and Moscow and Odessa and Kursk and Kharkov are all for figure skating, right? You've just forgotten the whole war, right?"

Hudoff had worked himself into a near-frenzy. All his frustrations from the botched meeting in the hangar rose up in him like bile and collected in his mouth and he *had* to spit it out. And now he had this commie—

He grabbed the Russian by the shirt and they were nose to nose. Hudoff had to shout over the roar of Mustang fighters screaming low overhead. "Vladislov, you're one of the best intelligence agents I've ever worked with or against, but I'll tell you this . . . as sure as God made little red apples, *you* are a fucking asshole!"

He stomped away, feeling angry with himself for losing his temper and yet filled with a burgeoning ebullience that had him nearly skipping along like a kid. He felt wonderfully lighthearted. He heard Galenko cursing him and running behind him. Hudoff didn't turn around. He kept walking, right hand raised, middle finger extended rigidly.

The bubbles didn't last long. No longer than the end of the show. Hudoff and Galenko moved with the crowd toward the parking lot and then turned down the taxiway leading to the mosquito control hangar. He'd told Bannon to meet him there right after the show ended, and had his helicopter waiting out of sight behind the hangar. He still wasn't sure what they were going to do, but he knew he had to clamp down and hard on these crazy bastards and their flying hoopla. He went into Bannon's office and dragged out two deck chairs. He dropped heavily into one, lit a cigar, and motioned Galenko to the other. The Russian sat with him, then without a word held out his hand to Hudoff, who in turn reached within his jacket and withdrew the flask of Jack Daniels. Galenko took half the flask's contents in one long swallow.

They watched the big torpedo bomber rumbling toward them, the wings folding back and to the sides like a bird tucking in enormous wings. Bannon brought her around smartly and ran the engine to high power, the thunder from the huge radial engine so close to them almost shaking the fillings in their teeth. He shut down the Turkey and was climbing down and walking toward them while the prop was still grinding around.

Hudoff introduced them. Bannon didn't twitch when he caught the name. Before he could ask questions Hudoff took care of the preliminaries. "Vladislov is here as the officially invited guest of the White House. He judges all security for their cosmonaut. He's a good man to have around. And so you won't need to ask, we don't keep anything from him." Bannon nodded to Galenko; it was clear the Russian appreciated a man who didn't foam at the mouth with stupid questions.

"What went wrong in that hangar with the pilots?" Bannon prodded Hudoff. "Ain't like you to drop the ball like that, boss."

"Chalk it up to not understanding maniacs as well as I should," Hudoff told him. "I screwed up. You want it on parchment?"

Bannon waved away the subject. "Okay, boss. But what's next? You're not one to just drop the ball."

Hudoff showed a flash of touchiness. "I'm not dropping a damn thing, Ace. I screwed up. I didn't say I *lost*. There's more than one way to skin the ass from your flying buddies. Nothing has changed, Bannon. We are still in deep shit."

"How you going to do your skinning?" Bannon pressed.

"Well, you see this big, beautiful airfield, Bannon?" Hudoff said expansively. "Well, I can't just arrest everybody. Like your little lady said, no cause, no warrant, no nothing."

Hudoff smiled and Bannon waited. He'd seen this look before. The canary feathers were about to appear in the mouth of the big, bad cat. *"But I can close this field under the authority I have by declaring its traffic a hazard to operations of the federal space transportation system."* The smile broadened. "You might tell your asshole friends, Bannon, not to count me out too quickly."

"Can you really close Shiloh?"

"You can put that in the bank and draw immediate interest, Ace. The law is specific. There is contingency planning. Right now my people are waiting. They'll roll military vehicles onto those runways. A grasshopper won't be able to get off them. We'll impound any helicopters here. My men are ready to take over the control tower. I have the authority to request full cooperation from the FAA. In short, Bannon, I can lock this place up tighter than my Aunt Minnie's crotch, and she sewed her knees together thirty years ago."

Bannon nodded slowly. He reached for the flask still in Galenko's hand, unscrewed the cap, nodded a salute to Hudoff, and drained the flask. "Well, I got to hand it to you, boss. That's a pretty neat package you've got to close us up."

"Damn right it—"

"But it won't work."

Hudoff stared a moment, then shook his head. "You been flying too high, Bannon. You're low on oxygen to the brain." He paused to study his agent. "Why the hell won't it work?"

"You intend to check out all aircraft before they leave here?"

"Yes. I damned well do."

"And the crews?"

"What the hell's the matter with you? Of course that's what I'll do!"

"What about the fifty thousand people leaving here on the roads?"

Hudoff sat straight up. "Fifty—the roads?"

"Boss, look across this field. There are two main roads leaving Shiloh. One goes north and the other east to U.S. 1. At least ten or twenty thousand people have already left. Cars, trucks, campers, trailers, motor homes. How do you know that anybody you're looking for *hasn't already left?*"

Galenko stared at Hudoff. "Can this be? You did not seal off the *roads?*"

"I never thought, I mean, it's the planes we want to check out and—"

"Man, you just don't see it, do you?" Bannon asked, as gently as he could. "Bernie, *listen to me.*" He pointed to several runways where planes were lining up and waiting for the signal that the field was out from under the airshow restrictions. "See those planes? You're thinking about a hundred and fifty warbirds. Bernie, those are just the *show* planes. You know what you're looking at over there? There's more than a *thousand* private planes waiting to leave here *right now.* You got everything from Cherokees to King Airs, for God's sake. There are *several thousand people* lined up waiting for the runways to open. You going to shut down this field, order them all back to parking places, and keep them here while you question everybody and inspect the planes?"

Bannon turned away, spun about and held Hudoff's gaze. "For the record, you don't have both oars in the water right now, boss-man. No way. You'll be here for a *week*. In the meantime you got fifty thousand people waltzing out of here on the roads. And even if you *could* check out every car and van and plane, what in God's name do you expect to *find?* You think they brought the bombs *here?* You want to question *our* pilots, you can still do that, but all you'll get is the old Bronx cheer."

"What is Bronx cheer?" asked the puzzled Galenko.

"Can you read lips?" Bannon asked him.

"Why, I—"

"Try this for size." Bannon stuck out his tongue and blew a raucous raspberry to the Russian. He turned back to Hudoff, but before he could speak, Hudoff's pager sounded. He shut it off and removed a slim, powerful radio from his jacket. "This is Tophat. Go ahead."

"Sir, Green Six here. If you're going ahead with your plan to close this—"

Hudoff didn't let it go any further. "This is Tophat. *Cancel.* I repeat, cancel. Withdraw all security personnel and equipment immediately."

"Sir, I'd like to confirm that again, if you please."

"Oh, *shit*. Green Six from Tophat, cancel Trinity. I repeat, cancel Trinity. Over."

"Yes, sir. Confirm cancel Trinity. Over and out."

Bannon offered Hudoff a look of respect and appreciation. "That was a smart move, boss-man."

Galenko studied them both. "What is Trinity?"

Bannon took the query. "It's what you might call a nice touch, Mr. Galenko. Trinity was the code name for the first atomic bomb test in 1945."

"Wonderful. You people are so sentimental." Galenko leaned back in his chair, arms crossed, shaking his head. A sudden roar caught his attention. Engine thunder rose and swelled from across the field as the tower began to release the planes in flights of two for takeoff from two runways. Every few seconds four planes began racing down concrete to take to the air. It was like watching cattle with wings rushing through a chute and soaring into the afternoon sky.

"They'll be moving out of here like this for a couple of hours," Bannon commented.

"I haven't got a couple of hours," Hudoff said. "I need to get back to my office where I can throw up in peace."

Bannon nodded, smiling. "I've got a discreet line to the tower. They can get your chopper out of here to the southwest and keep you under the traffic."

"We'll take it. Call them," Hudoff said as he stood. "By the way, do those warbirds also leave here for the night?"

"Uh uh. That's what I've been trying to tell you. Almost all of them remain here for the whole weekend. Besides, we've got a gasser of a party tonight. These guys would rather drink than eat."

"You taking your lovelorn, Bannon?"

"Yeah. I'm taking Charley. What the hell is it to you?"

"You *were* taking Charley. Now you're going to be at a security meeting tonight. My office, ten o'clock sharp."

"Goddamnit, I—"

"Tough titty, Ace. Besides," Hudoff said, wrinkling his nose, "now you got time to take a shower. God knows you need one."

They walked off, leaving Bannon with a full head of steam and no way to vent his sudden anger. He turned and let loose a terrific kick at the nearest chair. It flew into the air and smashed a window to Bannon's office. He howled with pain, holding his foot and dancing on one leg like a crazy man.

SUNDOWN

"He looks just like a one-legged man in an ass-kicking contest." Lars Anderson stood by the flight line fronting the maintenance hangar of the Strasser Air Circus, holding his usual huge wrench in one hand, tapping it gently in the palm of his other great paw. He motioned with the wrench and the crowd of pilots broke into laughter at the sight of Mitch Bannon hopping wildly on one foot, gripping his other ankle with both hands, and cursing a blue streak.

"Never mind *him*," a pilot sang out from the group, elbowing his way forward. "Lars, baby, *I need you*. I need you right *now*. I'll walk your dog or kiss your ass or I'll even hump that ugly wife of yours—"

"I don't have a wife," Lars growled. "Would never let one of them critters get near to me."

"I know," John Busby said and flashed a grin. "But I really need you, man."

"What's your problem?"

Other pilots crowded closer behind Busby, obviously ticked off because they'd let him get first crack at Anderson. "I got a pretty bad mag drop on runup today. It was just enough to let me fly the show, but after, when I checked it, it like to shook my engine to pieces. I can't fly with it like that tomorrow," he added unnecessarily.

"You bring a spare?"

"Well, uh, I—"

"You asshole. How many times we got to tell you dummies to bring the spares of your most critical parts! You know how many goddamned different kinds of mags go into all these planes," he waved a grease-stained hand, "we got on this line? Go check the parts bin. If we got it, you're in luck. If we ain't got it, you forget the party tonight and get your ass to Melbourne or Orlando or wherever and *get* the part. Now, *git*."

Busby flashed him a grin and started off. "Hold on!" Anderson shouted. "You 'spect me to drag that piece of junk you fly here by myself? Taxi it up here and park next to the Tigercat."

Busby nodded as he took off at a trot for the parts shop. Immediately the other pilots shoved forward and a babble of voices rose from the crowd. "Lars, my right brake is locking!"

"Hey, you got some metalflax lines? My carb heat hose went to hell on me today . . ."

"Jesus, Lars, can we get a heliarc weld on a busted tailwheel? *Please?*"

Fading brakes, bad mags, shot plugs, EGT gauges, oil pressure lines, cracked cowls, nicked props, leaking fuel lines, stuck valves, broken cables, loose bolts, burned manifolds; they brought to Anderson a litany of diseases, ailments, and illnesses of their mechanical birds, beseeching and pleading for immediate mechanical ministration to bring their heavy iron or fabric creatures back to health for the airshow the next day. And they all closed their beggars' plaints with the same singsong cry of "Lars, baby, if I don't get it right Charley will ground my ass for the show . . ."

Anderson finally gestured to the motley group of young and old before him. He gave them a collective don't-shit-me look and moved a powerful arm to take in the warbirds assembled like hungry vultures about the hangar. "See those planes? Every one of them is sick. They're tired, they got cramps and measles and tummy aches

169

and crippled wings, they got bad mags, lousy plugs, burned valves, scorched exhausts, bum carbs, broken lines, prop governors going ape . . . they got rashes and fever and everything else you can think of and *you all* want them ready by the morning. That's *early* morning, right at sunup, y'hear me, worms? Sunup for your test flights, understand?"

He fixed a fierce glare to his face. "Remember the rules. No airplane flies in the show after it's been worked on without first doing a test flight. *No exceptions.* Anybody got anything stupid to say?"

No one spoke and no one expected anyone to walk into *that* trap. Anderson smiled. "Okay, now. You write down what's sick with your bird and—*holy shit!*" He dropped the wrench and before it struck the pavement he was dashing madly away from the group, yelling as he went. A Mustang rolled along the taxiway toward the maintenance hangar in the gloom, its pilot going through careful S-turns left and right to see where he was going. No one sees straight ahead over the long high nose of the P-51 fighter.

But as the Mustang moved from right to left, preparing to work back across the taxiway, a figure in dark clothing shot out from between the row of parked planes to the side. A figure that *glided* instead of running, a smooth movement on the concrete, but with body rocking from side to side and arms moving to some unheard musical beat. "Crazy son of a bitch!" Anderson yelled and dove headlong for Wilbur Moreland. He hit Moreland with a crash that knocked the breath from both men. Moreland's skateboard flew wildly out from beneath his feet as he went down with Anderson.

The Mustang propeller that would have sliced them into chopped meat in a split second passed sickeningly close overhead, and the landing gear rolled bare inches from Moreland's nose. He looked at Anderson, startled, still not hearing anything. A headset over his ear booming music from a tape recorder hanging from his shoulder had kept him in oblivion from the world. Moreland started up and a big hand slammed his head down. "The tail, you dumb bastard! Stay down!" The wide stabilizer of the fighter edged over their bodies.

Anderson climbed slowly to his feet, his face purple. The other pilots dashed up in time to see Anderson holding Wilbur Moreland by the throat with one hand and trying to stuff his headset with his other hand into Wilbur's mouth. "How many goddamn times I told you not to wear that fucking headset on this fucking flight line! You crazy bastard—"

They pulled Anderson away. Wilbur Moreland grinned at him. "Weren't *that* bad, Mr. Lars," he said, still grinning. He rubbed his chin and worked his jaw back and forth and then wiped saliva from the headset. "I saw that airplane—"

"You didn't see shit. You come whizzing out from them other planes and that pilot didn't see you and you didn't see him and—" He took a deep breath. "Wilbur, why must you use that damn foolish skateboard *and* shut out everything with that headset?"

Wilbur Moreland was tall, lanky, freckled, and blessed with a friendly grin that would have made a Doberman smile back. "It's the beat, Lars, *it's the beat*. You just *got* to go with the beat." His fingers snapped and his body squirmed as he listened to the beat.

"Dumb fucker ain't even got on his headset and he's hearing music," Lars said with disgust. "Wilbur, you dumb shit, if you weren't the best damn mechanic I ever seen in my whole life I'd throw your ass off this field so fast . . ."

A pilot handed Wilbur his skateboard. "Put a headlight or something on that damnfool contraption!" Anderson roared. He studied Wilbur's lanky form, finger-snapping and rocking. "Where the hell were you going anyway?"

"Miss Taylor wants the brake lines checked on her airplane. Said she was a'gettin soft brakes today," Wilbur explained. "So I guess the smart thing to do was go fix it where it is instead of towing it all the way up here and bothering you with it."

Anderson wanted to kill and hug Wilbur at the same

time, but he just kept his stern I'll-kill-you look. "You know you'll be working all night?" he told the boy.

"Sure do, Mr. Lars. Soon as I finish with Miss Taylor's airplane I got to check the throttle connection on young Morgan's bird, and then I'll be coming to the hangar."

"Move it, Wilbur. But for God's sake, *be careful.*"

Wilbur grinned and before Anderson could stop him he had the earphones back on his head and the skateboard under one foot and he went sailing down the taxiway, fingers snapping, body weaving to "the beat."

"If he don't get killed," Anderson said to his bemused audience, "it'll be a miracle. But what can I do? He *is* the best damn mechanic I ever saw!"

The sounds of the skateboard on pavement and snapping fingers drifted away in the twilight.

Anderson and the pilots started back to the hangar. Rick McSorley, who had a Mustang waiting for a new right tire, nudged Anderson. "You really going to work that kid all night?"

"Damn right. While *you're* partying, hotrocks, and then sleeping, he'll be working. Just so *you* can be a hero tomorrow."

The pilots smiled. They'd been through this routine before, but they knew it was true enough. "What time do you go to sleep tonight, Lars?" one man asked.

Anderson offered him a tired smile. "Jim, what's sleep?"

No one laughed.

Perfumed soap suds rose in fragrant billows from the marble tub. Charley Morgan slipped deeper within the water, luxuriating in the heat, the perfumed oil, the caress of the fan turning slowly above the tub. "I don't think I'm *ever* going to leave this thing," she murmured. She felt weary in every bone, and the big marble tub in her private apartment over the hangar office was a godsend.

"You'll be getting out soon enough," she heard the voice of Wendy Green as she placed a glass of cool white wine on the side of the tub. "Big time tonight, remember? The whole gang's looking for you at the party."

Charley lifted herself just enough to slip a hand from the billowing suds to reach the wine glass. She sipped slowly. "Which one?'" she asked.

"Well, I thought you'd make the rounds. You know, the hangar party first, and—"

"That's *not* a party. It is a foul-mouthed, nasty brawl where all the children vent their temper tantrums."

Wendy laughed and nodded. "True, true. They do get a bit rowdy there." She eased herself to a lounge chair and sipped from her glass. "It's the kind of party I like. I think I'll catch up with Bill there."

Charley's look was a clear reprimand as she took in the oil-stained flight suit. "Then what are you doing here and what are you doing still in those clothes? Santiago is crazy over you. He'll be biting his nails until you show up."

Wendy offered a lopsided grin. "Uh huh." She chuckled. "He'll be there. The waiting will do him good." She gestured with her glass. "Besides, you've had a rough day. Someone's got to look after you for a while."

"You've got a man out there who loves you and you're worried about *me?*"

"Look who's talking!" Wendy hooted. "What about you and Mitch?"

Charley thought about the words for a moment and then shook her head. "What about me and Mitch?"

Wendy didn't hide her exasperation. "Right now it's just you and me, Charley. No boss lady and number one girl, right?" She waited for Charley to nod before she went on. "Okay, then. Just between us girls, if you like. He loves you and you love him. What's so complicated about *that?*"

"We're a long way from that, kiddo."

"Bullshit. Go tell fairy tales to someone else. I know you since you were a kid. And I know *him.*"

"It's *not* that simple, Wendy."

"So what's there to be complicated? My mother always told me that where there's love it's always simple. You know, him-her and he-she, Tarzan and Jane and—"

"I have a date tonight, Wendy."

"I know, I *know*. Bannon's picking you up and—"

"It's with Abe Lansky. Not Bannon."

"When the hell did that happen?"

"When Mitch broke our date." Charley scowled. "Big evening. We were going to drop in at the parties, and then we were all set to go to the Hilton for dinner and dancing. I think Bannon was even going to wear a *tie*." Charley sighed. "I was looking forward to this so much . . ." Her voice trailed off.

"What happened?"

Charley shrugged. "Mr. Wonderful called me, said he was sorry but he had to work tonight, said he'd give me a raincheck and then," Charley gestured and soap suds flew, "he hung up." She looked up at Wendy. "Then Abe called. I'll be damned if I'd turn *that* invitation down."

Wendy nodded in agreement. "This thing tonight with Mr. Wonderful," she added to the sarcasm. "Charley, you thinking what I'm thinking?"

"I don't even want to *think* about it, Wendy."

Wendy went right on despite Charley's words. "You think he's making a run?"

Charley's face showed immediate anger. "How would I know?" Her mood changed and she pushed aside her desire to avoid the subject. "Oh, I don't know," she said with frustration. She looked up, her face pained. "Damnit, Wendy, why does he still run pot? He doesn't *need* to do it. I mean, he doesn't need the money or . . . I don't know." She shook her head. "Jesus, he drives me crazy."

Wendy didn't laugh. It wasn't a joke. "What drives you crazy is that he supplies your kid brother," she said slowly.

"How'd you feel if Marty was *your* brother?"

"He might just as well be," Wendy said, a note of reprimand in her voice. "I've helped raise him, remember?" She plunged on suddenly. "And what's so bad about Bannon bringing in the stuff for Marty? He *needs* it; he really does. I'd rather see him get it from Bannon than from some scumbag on the street. Besides, dealing with Bannon means he won't get busted."

"How do you mean that?" Charley's eyes narrowed.

174

"Oh, God, we're playing games again." Wendy drained her glass. They were obviously into an area touchy to Charley where other people didn't tread. "Charley, look, it's no secret that Bannon has some very strong contacts in the sheriff's department. And it's hardly a secret to anyone that your kid brother is whacked out of his mind half the day and all through the night. He's on a steady diet of grass, beer, wine, and God knows what else. *Everybody* knows it, lady!" She was reflective for a moment. "And yet," she went on, more calmly now, "he's never been busted. He goes his merry way as if he *knows* he'll never take a fall. There ain't no two ways about it. Bannon's got a very heavy blanket covering the kid."

Charley shifted in the tub, lit a cigarette, and dragged deeply. She took the moment to think over their conversation, then shifted suddenly. "Wendy, I—God, how could this have slipped my mind! Wendy, that big ape from NASA ... remember when he came busting in here today?"

Wendy laughed. "And went out on his ass; right. What about it?"

"But how did he know?"

Wendy's face showed her own confusion as she faced the question. "Why, he told us. I mean, he said Bannon told— No," she interrupted herself, "it was that deputy who said Bannon told the motel manager, right?" Charley nodded. "Then," Wendy continued, "you told me the sheriff confirmed Bannon spilling the beans. None of *that* makes the first bit of sense, but, well, you're right. How did Horrible Hudoff get into the act?"

"Obviously," Charley said slowly, "because they're on this hunt together. About the Air Force plane, I mean."

"That figures," Wendy agreed. "They're supposed to work together, anyway."

Charley was suddenly intense. "This was at the back of my mind the whole day, but we were so busy I—" She shook her head and sat upright, water splashing from her. "Wendy, Bannon told the sheriff *long before* the NASA man knew about it."

They stared at one another, their faces reflecting the search under way in their minds.

"It ain't kosher, that's for sure," Wendy said to break the silence.

"But how could Bannon have known!" Charley began to tick off the points on her fingers one by one. "One, we fly the B-25 and we do the number on the Paradise. Two, sometime while we're out flying, it seems this unknown group comes down on the Air Force. They force down the transport and, according to what Hudoff tells us, they kill the crew." Her face sobered. "It's a bad scene all the way around. But somehow, Bannon knows about that. And he knows, or he's figured, that the government is really going to drop the hammer on us until we can establish we weren't flying fighters and were in the air at the time the transport is forced down. Follow me so far?"

Wendy nodded. She had a strange smile on her face but didn't speak.

"Okay, next," Charley tapped another finger, "knowing what he does, no matter how he finds out, Bannon calls the Paradise and lays it on the manager that I'm the baddie who busted up his party. The manager in turn, somewhat hacked off at the world by now, calls the sheriff, they get a warrant, and bingo, I'm the star of the party."

"Right so far," Wendy agreed.

"And I want to kill Bannon because—"

"You nearly did. That was a hell of a shot, kid. You could have put away Marvelous Marvin with that roundhouse."

"I thought I'd broken a finger." Charley giggled suddenly, her hand over her mouth. "I wouldn't dare tell this to anyone else. I broke a nail." She paused a moment. "*And* my bra strap."

They smiled, then returned to the matter at hand. "Bannon set me up to be arrested," Charley said in fast review.

"But not to hurt you," Wendy appended.

"I know! Obviously it was to clear me with the feds.

And he did it. *But how did he know what was coming down before anyone else knew about it?"*

Wendy sighed. "Charley, you ain't figured it yet?"

"Yes and no. What I *do* figure is almost too bizarre to believe."

"Are you, ah, getting the idea that there's more here than meets the eye?"

"To put it mildly," Charley confirmed. Her face grew serious. "Wendy, could he have been pulling the wool over our eyes *all* these years?"

"You mean is the bastard really a knight in shining armor?" Wendy shrugged. "It's possible. But if Bannon ain't a bastard, he's one hell of a great actor. Tell you what. I got connections no one else knows about." She pointed a finger at Charley. "Including you, so don't ask. But I'll do some checking on my own."

Charley leaned back and began to gently wash her legs. "You do that, and I'll do a little nosing around myself."

"Oh? With who, maybe you'll tell me?"

"Lansky. My date tonight, remember?"

Wendy showed a sour face. "*That* putz again."

"I thought you'd be on *his* side. I don't understand you, Wendy. I mean, you of all people would be—"

Wendy stepped into the breach quickly. "Why, because he's *Jewish?*" She lifted both arms and beseeched heaven silently. "I'm supposed to adore him because he's a Hebe like me? Charley, you're church people. So was Adolf Hitler. *And* Mussolini and—"

"I get your point," Charley begged off.

Wendy grinned. "Come to think of it, as far as *I'm* concerned, he's about as Jewish as any raghead."

"Raghead?"

Wendy made exasperated sounds. "You *know* . . . a sand monkey, a wog, a . . . a dune ape." Charley just stared at her. "Oh, for Christ's sake, an *Arab*."

Charley gave her a disapproving look. "For a Jewish broad you're one of the most bigoted—"

Wendy laughed with delight. "Bigoted? *Me?* No such thing. I'm just anti-Semitic. I hate A-rabs."

"All right, I get your point. But," Charley came back,

177

studying her nails, "that doesn't change the fact that he's a perfect gentleman. He's charming, and a delightful dinner companion, a marvelous dancer—"

"I'm going to throw up."

"*And* from what I hear he's a bona-fide Israeli war hero."

Wendy's response was vehement. "He's a *schmuck*."

Mario del Passo stepped down from the cabin of the swift jet helicopter that had rushed him northward from Miami to a private heliport on an estate bordering the Banana River in Cocoa Beach. The dapper little man from Interpol wore a natty silk suit and a homburg and carried a rosewood attaché case. Hudoff met him with a warm handclasp. "Mario, I'm grateful for this. I know you're a busy man and—"

"Tut tut, Bernie. Think nothing of it," the Portuguese told him as they walked to a waiting sedan. "The atom makes bedfellows of us all, you might say. And who knows? I might need your help if this insane affair ever visits my country."

They settled in the rear seat of the car. The driver turned to them. "Mario, you know Joe Horvath?"

Mario smiled. "Secret Service. But he fits his cover well. Mr. Horvath, at your service. Do you really sell much life insurance?"

Horvath offered a half-smile. "I thought my cover was air-tight."

"It is, it is," del Passo said with a broad smile. "Outside of this car, Mr. Horvath—"

"Joe; please."

"Very well. Outside of this car I know nothing." He felt the necessary amenities were behind them and turned to Hudoff, who in turn motioned for Horvath to roll. "You indicated time was even more pressing than before."

Hudoff reviewed for him the events of the day, leaving out nothing, including his own fumbling performance with the pilots at Shiloh Field. "If we were right, then we were on their trail without losing a minute," Hudoff finished. "But I don't believe these people really

178

had a thing to do with it. They're crazy, and most of them have shit for brains, but they're absolutely loyal."

"And you have also concluded there may be one or more skunks in their woodpile?"

"Absolutely. But we have no idea who they may be. My, ah, plant has eliminated just about all the suspects I had considered as prime candidates." Hudoff held his words as Horvath drove from the service road onto A1A and turned northward. "There are still some unanswered questions about a few of these people. That's why I called you in for help, Mario. These people move across national borders the world over. Interpol could have many leads I never even thought of."

Del Passo removed a cigarette package from his jacket. "You don't see many of those," Hudoff commeted of the sleek black container with the name Fribourg & Treyer.

"No, but it fits my status as a successful British businessman," del Passo explained as he lit up. "I intend for people to see this package and other little hints. It will occupy them for a few moments, at least, and I learn much by watching other people reflect on past and foreign associations. Now, Bernie, why the rush *tonight*?"

"I'm meeting with several of the pilots. Not the regular run of the mill. Abe Lansky—"

"I know his name."

"I thought you would. And his sidekick, a tub of butter who goes by the name of Yusuf Hamza. I don't want you at that meeting, but we'll tape everything and I'd like you to listen to every word later on. It could prove interesting."

"We will get a good voiceprint that way," del Passo noted.

"Also, I can arrange a business meeting. He's an international dealer in—"

"Guns, bombs, explosives, all manner of weapons. He is a merchant of death." Del Passo sighed. "But highly respected. I know about him. I can have the meeting set up through an office in Brazil. Those are details. Go on."

"That's it. I've got a bad feeling about this cat. Nothing I can pin down. I'd like you to feel it out."

179

"Absolutely. Who goes with you?"

"Galenko."

Del Passo chuckled. "You are getting back to your old habits, Bernie. And I had thought you were settled down with a nice quiet job, your slippers, a pipe, and a dog."

Hudoff showed surprise. "Everything except a wife?"

"I don't talk about wives. I do not wish to irritate my friends." Del Passo leaned forward. "Joe, you and I are having dinner together while our portly friend plays spy."

"Anything you say, Mr.—"

"Mario."

"You got it, Mario. Where are we going?"

"I don't know. You will take us wherever it is." Del Passo removed a slim notebook from his jacket. "For years I have waited for the opportunity to sample what is known as good old Southern cooking." Mario del Passo had an impish air about him. "While we discuss matters of such grave international import, Joe, we shall dine on a Southern repast. I have with me this list of delights so highly recommended. I would like to go somewhere so we may try, if not all, at least a goodly portion."

"Yes, sir. Mind reading it to me?"

Del Passo glanced at Hudoff, leaned back, and read from his notebook. "Corn pone, hush puppies, butter beans, black-eyed peas, country fried steak, fried chicken, collard greens and turnip greens, fried okra, baked beans, turnips, pig's knuckles, pickled pig's feet, potato salad, cole slaw, lady peas, cheese grits, barbecued ribs, beer and lemonade—"

"Stop!" Hudoff cried. "Mario, do you have any idea in hell of what you're talking about?"

"Yes. I am an expert on international cuisine."

"This ain't international. It's American Southern."

"I got just the place, Mario," Horvath called back from the front. "Over in Cocoa. It's called Mama Lo's. It's a black joint, it don't look like much from the outside, but it's got the best damned food in the whole world."

"Mario, I should warn you. You're going into a rough black part of town," Hudoff said, frowning.

The dapper Portuguese laughed. "I have had lion steak in the Kenya bush, fried grasshoppers in Angola, buffalo stew in Zimbabwe, leech pie in Nigeria—never mind. And you feel I should worry about Florida?"

"Damn right. The blacks you ate with in Africa are natives. The blacks over here are civilized. *That* makes them dangerous."

Horvath eased from the highway in Cocoa Beach with a right turn. Hudoff looked up to see the Hilton Hotel before them. "I get off here," Hudoff told del Passo. "After you stuff yourself silly—and Joe's right, Mama Lo's is the best damn eatery in the world—I'll catch up with you back here. We have a private suite under the company name of Pentacostal Oil."

"You have a charming touch, Bernie. Goodbye, give my best to the darling of the Kremlin. I'm looking forward to seeing Vladislov again. He hates me."

"Why?"

"Because he has *never* beaten me in chess." Del Passo smiled. "And he never will."

Hudoff and Galenko stood several feet back from the golden sheen of the penthouse entryway. A television camera stared down at them and they both stared back. A disembodied voice spoke from a concealed speaker. "Ah! Gentlemen, you are right on time, I see. Please." They heard a dull metallic click. "Come in, come in." The door swung open. Hudoff and Galenko glanced at each other. They shared the same thoughts. *Nice touches. Good security if you're a simple burglar. The real defenses are inside.*

Abe Lansky stood just within the hallway. They saw a tall and well-proportioned man with curly hair, a slender moustache, and in an evening tuxedo that Hudoff judged on first glance to cost at least fifteen hundred dollars. A long, thin cigar. Just the right touches of gold, not obtrusive but properly evident. *Very upper crust, tremendously self-confident, reeks of money. A man accustomed to power and dealing in that power. Just the kind of opponent that tested them. Now why,* mused

Hudoff briefly, *did I categorize him as part of the opposition?* He put aside his negative thoughts to open his mind to the moment. This one was *not* going to be a pushover.

Beyond Lansky, waiting in an anteroom glowing in gold leaf and obviously expensive paintings, stood the fat one, Yusuf Hamza, also in a tuxedo, but rumpled and ill-fitting. The clothes did not like Hamza, and clearly he disliked the clothes. He was a man of the fields, not this ornate retreat at the top of the 2100 Tower on the sands of Cocoa Beach.

"You're Hudoff from NASA security," Lansky greeted Hudoff with extended hand. "I remember you from this morning at the airport. You were, ah, quite entertaining." He shifted smoothly to Galenko and shook hands with him. The door closed silently behind them. "And you are our guest from Moscow, no doubt. I did not get your name, sir."

"I am Vladislov Galenko, here with the official cosmonaut party for the cooperative shuttle flight between our countries."

"Yes. Of course," Lansky replied with a thin smile, making it clear within the restraints of propriety that he really didn't give a shit whatever Galenko had to say.

"You appear dressed for dinner," Hudoff noted aloud. "If we're interfering, I apologize. We can come back when it's more convenient."

"Not at all, not at all!" Lansky was expansive, suddenly even warmer and more inviting. "Come on in. I've been expecting you and you're most welcome. My time is at your disposal. Follow me, please. The terrace. It's delightful this time of night over the ocean."

They followed Lansky into an enormous living room with a heavy Mediterranean flavor to its decor. Lansky stopped by a wide table bedecked with flowers, silver trays, and gold furnishings. He extended a box of cigars. "The finest Jamaicans, gentlemen. Please, help yourselves."

"Thank you, Mr. Lansky," Hudoff told him, eyeing

the cigars but shaking his head. "This is a business visit. Some other time."

Galenko stepped forward, reached around Hudoff, and grasped a handful of cigars. He tucked them within his jacket as he smiled broadly at Lansky. "Ah, but *I* am *not* on duty like this one. Thank you, comrade! And I accept your hospitality. I will have scotch and soda. Chevas, perhaps?"

"What? No vodka?" Lansky asked with a laugh.

"Vodka, my dear friend, is for peasants. And for anti-freeze in terrible Russian cars in winter." He moved a cigar beneath his nose. "This is *good* tobacco. Like you say, the finest. Also not for peasants, hey?" He boomed with laughter. He was enjoying himself hugely.

Lansky nodded to Hamza. His portly sidekick waddled to a huge, ornate bar. Smoked glass with gold trimming. Gold statues. Gold mixers. It even had a bar rail, and Hudoff would have bet a buck to a nickel it was also gold-plated. Or solid gold, for all he could tell. What he did notice and tuck away in the back of his head was that there should have been a bartender. There should have been a serving girl. Lansky had a staff of six to run this penthouse, but the place was empty except for the four of them. And that did not fit. But that kind of speculation was also a dead-end.

"He'll bring the drinks to us," Lansky told his guests as he led them to the wide terraced balcony facing the ocean. A strong surf cast its soothing sounds up to them. Music from beach parties mixed with the sound of the waves. Lights from the shrimp fleet dotted the ocean, and to their left loomed the brilliant lights of Port Canaveral, and just beyond, the lighthouse and high towers of the Canaveral launch center. The Kennedy Space Center lay well beyond that. A lonely searchlight pierced the sky, and they heard a distant drone as a huge jet transport floated in from the dark Atlantic skies. They stood for several minutes, taking in the salty night air and the feel of the ocean. Hamza brought the drinks and stepped back to a respectful distance.

Hudoff took a long sip of his drink and gestured with the glass. "Mr. Lansky, we're very short on time, and I hope you won't mind my being as frank as possible and getting down to the reason for this visit."

Lansky surprised him. The effusiveness evaporated. He remained suave but cool, somehow different, as if he'd shifted mental gears.

"I know," he said.

"From the look on your face, you seem to know a hell of a lot," Hudoff said quickly.

"You certainly do not mince your words, Mr. Hudoff. You just told me you wish candor. I give it to you and you appear upset. So neither of us will play the cat and mice game, yes? Let us cut the mustard, Mr. Hudoff. Have at it, sir."

He continued his chameleon routine. Of a sudden, as if the switch were now fully thrown, he was sharp, hard, every inch the professional. He didn't give Hudoff a chance to respond to his statement, but added his own clincher. "You have already checked me out on your criminal computer system. The whole NCIC search. Then you went through CIA to the FBI, and you brought in the national security agency. *And* the Pentagon." Lansky smiled. "What a waste of time, money, and effort, Mr. Hudoff. What a petty charade. You had only to ask *anything* and you would have had your answer at once."

"What you say is true," Hudoff confirmed, and received an appreciative look for his honesty from Lansky. "That's my job. It doesn't matter what anyone *offers*."

"A child's game. Mr. Hudoff. Alphabet blocks and toy pianos. So let me save you some more of your most precious time. You are aware I own this entire building." He paused for effect, and it was working. Hudoff felt as if he'd been caught with his hand in the cookie jar. "You also know I own the Paddock, the Arabian breeding farm north of Ocala along Highway 441. I own three thousand head of cattle on the Bar Two spread east of Gainesville, and a piece of the Blacknail Ranch west of Fort Pierce." Lansky smiled, a cold expression without warmth or humor. "I imagine this matches what you have already learned. As well as my stock holdings in export-import firms, in air express delivery,

184

in a home electronics firm. You are also aware of my position with the Israeli government and its, well, let us call it their security office. You knew all this before you came here tonight, and yet—and I find this incredible—" he paused to set his glass on the terrace ledge before turning back to impale Hudoff with icy contempt—"you felt it necessary to play your little detective charade by coming here to, shall we say, check me out? You know I have top clearance in security matters with the government of the United States."

He paced slowly, playing every word for its maximum effect. "So why, Mr. Hudoff, do you waste all this valuable time, as the sands flow through the hourglass, when you *should* be somewhere out there," he gestured with a flourish, "looking for those bombs that were hijacked earlier today?"

Hudoff had come up short and frozen his body and his facial expression. Galenko didn't bother with the self-control routine. He snorted in a sound of surprise and acceptance that this man was far more than they had believed. Hudoff recovered quickly and followed his old maxim that, when in doubt, go for the throat.

"How the hell do you know about those bombs? There's no way Washington told you. We haven't even passed the word through the system yet."

Lansky smiled. "You are guarding so carefully what must be the worst-kept secret along this entire coastline!" Lansky eased into a chair, crossed his legs, and toyed with a cigar. "Mr. Hudoff, do you believe for one moment those pilots at Shiloh haven't already figured out what's happened? Do you, *can* you possibly believe they bought your childish story about sensitive electronic equipment being involved?"

This time the laugh was genuine, but compounded of contempt and disbelief. "At least half those people, before whom you made a complete fool of yourself today, flew military aircraft at one time that carried atomic weapons. They know the score! You told them a transport was flying from Guantanamo to New Mexico. Any fool could add that up. Your story to them is equally as thin as your excuse for coming here tonight with," he added with a neat twist, "your Slavic hound for company."

Galenko raised an eyebrow but ignored the bait. This was still Hudoff's party and, if nothing else, Galenko was a man who listened quietly and had great patience. He was pleased to see Hudoff still hammering home, still pushing and twisting to find something never intended by this Lansky person.

"Do you know *why* those bombs were hijacked?"

Lansky's hand stabbed to the northeast. "There's a *shuttle* out there! It's not a *pyramid*."

Galenko chuckled aloud. "Not bad, not bad."

"Who do you think is after the shuttle, Lansky?" Hudoff was staying tight with the questions.

"Ah, the *first* question that has meaning. I was beginning to wonder if you would ever ask me what is really important." Lansky gestured with diffidence, an acknowledgement that he was humoring Hudoff. "I'm certain," Lansky went on, "that you've already put the question to Israeli intelligence, and the name they gave you was Zoboa."

Hudoff nodded slowly, his expression one of confirmation. *But it wasn't. Hudoff had never contacted anyone from Israeli intelligence.* Were these details he himself considered so secret already common knowledge passed among the cooperative security agencies? My God!

"Is this Zoboa for real?"

"Most likely it is. I don't know for sure. And if the name Zoboa is not a red herring," he nodded to Galenko for the expression, "then it is a real organization. You, sir, are looking in the wrong places. Every organization needs a leader. Find *him* and you start to unravel your mystery."

Galenko stepped in with a heavy tread. "What is this name we want?"

Lansky appeared to be genuinely surprised. "You really don't know?"

"No, goddamnit," Hudoff snapped, "we don't."

Lansky leaned forward, fingers clasped tightly, rocking back and forth. "Jabal." He paused. "That is the man you must find. *Sadad Jabal.*"

He rose to his feet and stood with his back to the balcony to look down on Hudoff and Galenko. "So you will know what you seek, I will tell you certain things. This Jabal is a master of electronics, completely at home with computers and advanced systems. He is no technician, no matter how capable he may be. First and foremost, he is absolutely a fanatic. He's dedicated to freeing the Muslim world from the clutches of America *and* Russia. He'll do anything to set the Arab world free."

Hudoff looked at Galenko. "I've heard that before."

"Prophets with long beards. Set their people free from capitalism and communism so ayatollahs slaughter them at home. Is old bullshit, I think," Galenko said with disdain.

"The Arabs are hardly anyone's slaves," Hudoff added. "Except of their own leaders."

Lansky wet his lips. "Are you confusing what I tell you with what *I* might believe? This Jabal has his beliefs. They are fanatical. You are both devils. You are worse even than the Jews like myself. And the only way to get to the devil is to use a weapon that is so mighty that it *must* hurt." He became expansive, gesturing with every phrase. "And what better than to blow up a shuttle, with all the world watching, with an atomic bomb! You are still burdened with the legacy of *Challenger*, Mr. Hudoff. Everyone in the world who can watch a television set will be watching for *that* to happen again. And the Arab world, and much of the other third-world nations, cheer the death of *every* American."

Hudoff refused the bait. "Where's this Jabal now?"

Lansky laughed. "Ask of the wind, my friend, ask of the wind." His face sobered. "If I knew I would tell you instantly. But he is like a zoboa itself, I think. No one knows what he looks like. I have never seen a picture of him. He trusts no one. That means, of course, that he is *here*—"

"In *this* country?" Hudoff interrupted.

"Of course! *Here.* Right here in Florida, no doubt. And if I know how these people operate, *and I do, Mr. Hudoff, I most certainly do know*, then he considers this operation much too important to trust to underlings. So Sadad Jabal *must* be close by. And like the wind he is invisible, but with deadly effect."

"Bullsheet," Galenko growled. "Is impossible to be invisible. Hide like dog, yes. Invisible, no."

"Then you find him, Mr. KGB agent."

For the first time Yusuf Hamza moved closer. His contempt for Galenko came through unmistakably. "It could be, Russian, that *you* are Sadad Jabal."

"Do I look like Arab dog?"

"No. More like a pig. Jabal is a *name*. He could be anybody, including you."

"You are crazy. And stupid," Galenko said with growing heat. "We have cosmonaut aboard this shuttle! You think we would kill one of our own?"

Hamza sneered. "How humanitarian. It would not be the first time you Russian pigs have killed your own people to serve the Kremlin's orders."

Galenko snarled like a bear and his huge arm moved faster than their eyes could follow under his jacket. In the blink of an eye a 9-mm automatic locked solid on Hamza. Hudoff didn't move from his seat. "You're my guest in this country, Vladislov. Guests don't go around killing people because they piss them off."

"It would help clean the air," Galenko said quietly.

"Put away that fucking piece!" Hudoff shouted.

It went slowly back into its holster. "For now," Galenko said very softly. "I am *your* guest," he told Lansky. "To you I apologize for my behavior."

Lansky nodded.

"But keep his leash on tight, yes? If he gets loose—"

"Vladislov, just shut the hell up, will you?" Hudoff turned to Lansky. "He apologized. I sure as hell apologize to you. Please, may I ask some more questions?"

Lansky was obviously more amused than ever. "By all means, Mr. Hudoff." He gestured to Hamza to cooperate.

"You're Arab, Mr. Hamza?"

"Yes."

"What would you do if you were Sadad Jabal?"

Laughter bubbled wetly from the porcine Arab. "I

would never be caught. *Never!* Does that surprise you? You do not understand the intensity of such people as Jabal. You will find him invisible because he will make no demands of you. None. You are his prisoner in time. If I were Jabal I would not change a thing. Time is his weapon. Time presses heavily on you to act. All he needs is to wait, concealed, invisible. And your clock ticks and ticks and ticks. It is like radioactivity, remorseless, timeless. Ah," he laughed suddenly, "that is good, that analogy. Because with every passing minute, with every new tick, the bomb grows in your minds, in your presence. *It shortens your future.* It is the Arab way. To throttle a man, they do not need to choke him. They stake him out in the desert sun with wet leather thongs about his throat. Then they wait. Look at your faces! You believe this to be an Arab atrocity. Your own American Indians used this method. As the leather dries it tightens. Tick, tick, tick. The Chinese water torture. Tick, tick, tick."

Sweat beaded on Hamza's upper lip. His skin had a glossy sheen more pronounced with his growing intensity. He glanced at Lansky. Nothing there; Lansky had gone poker-faced. He was letting Hamza carry the ball, and Hamza was a pig rolling happily in the mud of incipient fear.

"What makes you so certain," Hudoff asked carefully, "that Jabal would act in such a manner? This using time, as you say."

"This is Christian country!" Hamza cried with sudden fervor. "You, who have had this bomb for so long, are protected by your own propaganda that you are the most beautiful, the strongest, the richest, the most *invulnerable* people on this planet. You *believe* this. It is in your culture, your religion; it is everywhere. So Jabal must find a common language, yes? Music is a common language. It needs no interpreters. But there is . . . there is," he frowned, searching for the right words, "yes! There is *terror*. It is more than fear. It twists the gut. Terror needs the ticking of time to be truly effective. *Terror is music. Everyone understand it.* A metronome. Tick, tick, tick. And why does it work so well here in

America? You can't even see it? *You have a schedule.* You plan every hour, minute, and second. Everything by checklist. Everything according to system and procedure. No margin for error. *Tick, tick!* The closer your countdown goes to zero, so does the countdown for the bomb!''

His eyes gleamed and he leaned back against the wall, perspiration darkening his shirt, making his skin glisten in the terrace lights. For several moments no one spoke. Hamza's intensity had reached them all. Hudoff had the urge to tell Galenko to go ahead and shoot the son of a bitch. But that would only have proved just what this man was saying. *And he wasn't the enemy. He was warning them in every way he knew how.*

''That,'' Hudoff said finally to Lansky, ''was a hell of a performance.''

''You heard him. I hope you *listened*,'' Lansky replied.

''I listened. I've never heard something like this before described as *music*.''

''Then try this on for size, Mr. Hudoff. We are both trying to *help*. American attitudes sometimes make such an effort extremely difficult. Yusuf is telling you not to wait up at night for the ransom note to be delivered. To him, Jadad Sabal is a musician, and when he plays, his victims move to his dance of terror.''

Lansky moved closer to Hudoff, stared at him directly. ''Money and lives are the drums and cymbals of Sadad Jabal. You, like all Americans, think in terms of money. He is out to reshape your thinking in terms of lives. *He must destroy the shuttle at liftoff because the world theater will be packed.* And when he sets off that bomb to destroy the shuttle, he will also destroy most of the world's leaders at the same time. It will be the greatest international symphony ever played.''

Hudoff took a deep breath. There was something missing here. All this bullshit about cymbals and drums and ticking sands was missing the boat. ''Let me get something straight. Or your opinion on this. Am I to accept that Jabal and his Zoboa crew don't care about the human lives involved? That tens of thousands of people will die?''

"Of course he cares!" Lansky retorted with unexpected intensity. "He cares as much as any Westerner. He cares as much as *we* cared for Dachau and for the Gulag, for Hiroshima and for Buchenwald. *He chooses to emulate us.* Would you condemn him for *that?*" Lansky laughed harshly. "Would you condemn him for obeying Mohammed? For his love for Allah? For ridding the world of so many infidels?" He stabbed a finger at Galenko. "I'm sure he has talked about the vacuum in world leadership that the Russians must fill when this bomb kills off this globe's leaders and proves America inept at protecting its own house."

"If we're such infidels," Hudoff said with a sideways glance at Galenko, "it wouldn't seem to make much difference between Americans and Russians."

"Oh, but it *does!* Ethnically the Russians are so much closer to the Muslim world. Millions of Russians are Asiatics. Millions of Russians *are Muslims.* Yes, there *is* a difference."

"What the hell's the difference!" Hudoff said, on the edge of shouting. "If we're all devils—"

"You see?" Lansky broke in, clearly convinced he was fully in control of the exchange. "You're angry with the reality of the situation. You're angry with *me* and you have received the information and help you came to ask me for. You rail at the sky for raining on your parade. *Mr.* Hudoff, Sadad Jabal knows how to use such anger. No; wait," he said to ward off the interruption he saw coming. "If you are not incompetent in this matter then there's nothing to worry about, am I right? But if there is some doubt and you are worried, and not even you would deny this, then this Jabal fellow has you very firmly by the balls."

Hudoff *was* angry. "He's not the first of his kind, Lansky. We'll get the son of a bitch and—"

Lansky almost pounced physically, so swift was his lashing out suddenly. "How? Where? And *when?*" He raised both arms to heaven and looked back at Hudoff. "You'll do all these things *after* the bomb goes off? What a marvelous American solution!"

"Where will you be when we launch *Antares?*"

As he intended, the question caught Lansky off stride. But the Israeli came back even faster.

"I wouldn't miss that show for anything on earth."

Galenko looked from one man to the other and back to Lansky. "And the bomb, Mr. Lansky. You do not worry about the bomb?"

Lansky's hand rested over his heart. "Me?" He looked wounded to the quick. "Of course not! My dear Galenko, why would *I* worry? I'll be watching, of course."

He smiled with great self-satisfaction. "On television, of course. From Orlando."

✠ 13 ✠

FIRST NIGHT

Mad Marty Morgan licked the salt from the edge of his margarita glass. He made smacking sounds with his lips and offered Sherri Taylor a grin of pleasure. A carefree, idiot grin. Sherri grinned back. Mad Marty was one of her favorite people. Anyone who took on the worst of adversity as this young man had done was at the top of the heap in her book. She'd been described many times as a daredevil. She loved the term and everything it meant, and when she tried to imagine how she would react to losing a leg—a whole fucking leg, for God's sake!—she was filled to bursting with pride for and admiration of Mad Marty. She was proud in yet another way. The inner circle of airshow pilots centered about the German major, and Mad Marty had never invited a woman to one of their evening soirees before the big weekend performances. They'd dragged her along to their favorite beachside haunt, the plush Grotto restaurant lounge on the water's edge of Port Canaveral. It was a marvelous setting with the lights of boats gliding past the picture windows, the sparkling lights of the huge tracking ships across the port inlet and the sky glow beyond of the space center.

Damned good club, Sherri thought with pleasure. A terrific broiled Maine lobster and dizzying drinks and wonderful music and these crazy people. *Her* kind. Major Karl von Strasser and Jay Martin in a deep and likely meaningless argument with gesturing hands and animated faces. Hoot Gibson, smashed out of his gourd, sprawled in his chair with pieces of lobster and glistening beads of spilled beer down his beard and flight suit. Bill Santiago had joined them "for wan leetle drinky poo" before he was to pick up Wendy Green for the hangar blast, but Sherri hoped Wendy didn't have her heart set on it. Bill had poured nearly an entire bottle of rum into his rib-gaunt frame and his eyes had been crossed for the last hour. Sherri wondered where Mitch Bannon might be, then remembered he had a date with Charley. The only bizarre element of their crowd was Tim Ryland, with his debonair, white-haired, impeccable manner. *He looks like Colonel Sanders,* Sherri thought with a renewed surge of giggling. *I wonder if the Chicken Colonel also wore pure white leather boots.* She heard someone talking about a dog, and Sherri tapped Mad Marty in the center of his forehead.

"I want to talk to you about your dog," she told Marty.

Mad Marty blinked. "Dogs don't *talk*, Sherri," he blurted.

"I want to know why you throw him out of airplanes."

"Sho he can be hero dog, thash why!"

"Maybe he doesn't like it, Marty."

"Loves it. *LOVES* it. Only chance damn dog got to be asshole hero."

"Your dog's an asshole hero?"

"Sure. God tol' me. Tol' damn dog, too."

"*God* told you?"

"Absorutely. God talks to us alla time when we jump. *Thash* how we know dog's an asshole."

Sherri Taylor took a deep breath. He was drunk, sure, but he'd never talked religion before. "What does God say to you?"

"*And* old Magnum. God talks to Magnum also. Thash how—"

"What does God shay—Jesus, I mean, *say* to you?"

"She say, lissen honky, the only thing that falls outta

194

sky is birdshit and assholes. Right? Me and Magnum, we ain't birdshit, so stands to reason damn dog is asshole hero. Course, damn dog is Swish, I mean, Swiss dog, maybe that's why he likes jumpin' outta airplanes.''

"Marty, did you ever ask your dog if he likes being thrown out of an airplane?"

Marty fixed her with a beady-eyed stare. "Ask him alla time. He loves it. LOVES it."

Sherri knew she'd hate herself in the morning. "What does Magnum say?"

"You really wanna know?"

The table was quiet, everyone listening as intently as their alcoholic haze permitted. Sherri glanced from one to the other and back to Mad Marty.

"Yes, I do."

"He says," Marty took a deep breath. "Bow wow." Marty's face dissolved into a lopsided grin. "Sometimes, nacherly, he says Bow fucking wow. Smart damn dog."

Laughter exploded. Hysteria had been on the thin edge for some time now and the *bow fucking wow* was all it needed to spill over. The pilots laughed and choked and howled. Cries of *"Bow fucking wow!"* mixed with giggles and roars. They turned red and tears ran down their cheeks.

"Damn dog talks better Bow fucking English wow than old Field Marshall Putzenheimer—"

"Who?" Jay Martin was emerging from a deep fog. "Who's that?"

Sherri gestured at von Strasser. "He must mean our resident kraut. Karl."

"Don't need no freakin' Nazi pilots," Marty said brightly. "I gotta great idea. We change Major Karl. Change 'em."

"Change him to what?" Ryland threw into the muddle.

"No more Cherman," Marty hiccuped. "Needs plastic surgery."

"You make him maybe Cubano?" Santiago asked.

"Nah," Marty said, waving his hands wildly. "Make his eyes srant."

They all said it at the same time. "Srant?"

"Slant. Slant eyes, right? We make him a gook. Japanesey pilot. Hey, suicide gook pilot!"

"He'll be our resident kamikaze!" Ryland cried.

Sherri pointed to the beefy German. "*Him?*"

"Uh-huh," Marty agreed. "Big goddamn Jap for shure."

Von Strasser rose ponderously to his feet, pushing out his beer-belly stomach. He raised his hand and brought it down with a tremendous crash against his stomach. People turned with the sharp report. "Sumo wrestler maybe I am," von Strasser announced. "Kamikaze, never!"

"Gotta be kamikaze, you dumbhead," Marty told him. "Sumo wrestlers spit. Don't fly."

"Karl, you'll make a beautiful kamikaze," Sherri told the German.

"He's too ugly," Jay Martin observed. "If my dog had a face like his I'd shave the dog's ass and walk him backwards."

"You don't have a dog," Ryland said.

"Well, *if* I had a dog—"

Sherri abandoned herself to the moment. "Karl Kamikaze! It's a wonderful name!"

"He don't *look* like a Jap," Martin said sourly.

"We'll *make* him into a Jap!" Sherri announced.

Ryland extended a butter knife. "You make the first incision," he said warily.

"I got the fork!" cried Gibson.

Santiago's hand flipped in a blur and a switchblade appeared in his hand. "Pointy ears. Gotta make his ears pointy!"

"Make room!" Sherri told them. Jay Martin swept her side of the table clear. Sherri dropped her purse on the table and began withdrawing her cosmetics. "I need a headband," she ordered.

"One headband!" Santiago called. Marty held up a linen napkin and Santiago sliced it with a blur. Sherri took half the napkin, rolled it into a flat headband, and painted a large red meatball with her lipstick on the center. "How do you spell kamikaze in Japanese?" she asked.

"Kamikaze," Ryland told her.

"Bow fucking wow?" Marty offered.

Sherri rolled her eyes and scrawled lipstick imitations of what Japanese lettering might look like. She moved behind von Strasser and tied the napkin about his head, centering the meatball, then tied the ends into a knot. She stood back to admire her work. Von Strasser squinted and grimaced in imitation of what a Japanese might appear to be.

"Tonight we drink!" Sherri cried. "Tomorrow he die!"

Chairs fell over as they stumbled to their feet, squinting and bowing to one another with terrible Japanese accents.

"Make suicide dive into Amelican freet!" Marty shouted.

"Kill tousands Mexicans!" called Jay Martin.

"Melicans, you asshole!" Santiago cried.

"Dive! Dive!" Ryland added.

"*Banzai!*" roared Karl Kamikaze.

"Flucking great soomerai!" Santiago called out.

"Banzai!" everybody shouted.

"The check! Who gets the check?" the waiter tried to shout over the uproar. The manager stood in a far corner, hands clasped together. He seemed to be praying.

The waiter extended the small tray with the check to the most sober-looking person in the group. Ryland stared at it stupidly.

"Sir, *please?*" the waiter pressed.

Ryland took the check, holding it at arm's length as if it might bite him, and passed it to Sherri Taylor. She smiled at the waiter and returned the check. "The fat Jap is paying," she explained.

The waiter took a deep breath and turned with the check to Karl Kamikaze. He broke into a huge smile and grabbed the tray. "Ah! Bavarian chocolate! Is good!"

He sank his teeth into the check and the plastic tray and bit off a large chunk. His eyes bulged as he bit down and then spat out plastic and paper. "Is Bavarian shit!" he bellowed.

"Banzai!" cried Santiago.

Mad Marty staggered around the table, leaned one hand on Sherri's shoulder and heaved himself onto a chair. He weaved from side to side and held out one hand. "*I'll* pay the goddamned check!"

Cries of "Banzai!" rang out again.

"Bow fucking wow!" cried Marty.

A scream from the front entrance followed his sudden outcry. A door crashed open, a woman screamed again, frightened shouts filled the air, and a huge dog scrambled through the flailing people at the entryway and dashed straight for the pilots' table.

"*Gottinhimmel!*" Karl Kamikaze von Strasser shouted.

"Good Lord!" Ryland yelled.

Teeth bared, foam speckling its mouth, snarling horribly, the big animal attacked with bone-chilling fury. The dog threw himself into the air and with a blood-curdling snarl sank his teeth into Marty's leg. Marty howled with pain as the dog's onslaught hurled him off the chair and dog and man crashed to the floor. Screams broke out from all sides as blood spurted from Marty's leg, spraying against terrified customers. Dishes and glasses scattered, chairs bounced in all directions, and people drew back as the great dog began dragging the screaming man across the floor. Jay Martin and Santiago grabbed at the dog which refused to break its grip, Ryland had Marty by one arm, Sherri Taylor was white with shock and fear and von Strasser in his kamikaze headband stood over the scene, cursing furiously and shaking his fist.

"*Verdamnte hundt! Schwein! Shtop! Shtop!*"

Martin and Santiago fell against the entrance door and as it burst open the dog dragged Mad Marty outside like a bloody sheep, pursued by the pilots and Sherri screaming, "Oh, my God! Kill the dog! *Kill the fucking dog!*"

"*Bow fucking wow!*" cried Marty.

A van screeched with locked tires to a halt by the entrance, the side door already open. In a mad scramble, everyone piled into the van. Except Sherri, staring open-mouthed at the insane uproar before her. Von Strasser leaned out, grasped her wrist, and hauled her into the van which was already burning rubber as Doug Callahan floored the gas pedal. They lay in a tumbled, laughing, hysterical jumble of bodies, Mad Marty patting the dog on his flanks.

He looked at the open-mouthed Sherri Taylor, drew a finger along the side of Magnum's head and held it up. "Whipped cream. Good. Want some?"

She couldn't talk. She tried to, swallowed, and finally found her voice. "But . . . your *leg* . . . I saw the blood where he attacked you and—"

Marty lifted up his trouser leg to reveal an aluminum limb with a plastic ketchup bottle taped to the leg. Everyone was grinning hugely.

Sherri saw the can of Rediwhip on the floor. She picked it up and sprayed the thick cream into her hand. She held it out and Magnum licked her hand eagerly. Sherri leaned back on the floor against the side of the van. She looked up at her drunken friends, then nodded at the dog.

"Bow fucking wow," she told them.

Karl von Strasser caught her eye. He was behind the others and he smiled. *He's not drunk*, Sherri realized suddenly. *He's not the least bit drunk. My God, he's been taking care of Marty all night long . . .*

"Where to?" Callahan sang out from the driver's seat.

"To the hangar!" Jay Martin answered.

"It's party time!" Santiago shouted.

"Oh, there are no fighter pilots down in hell," Mad Marty started their favorite song.

"There are no fighter pilots down in hell," Gibson echoed.

"The place is full of queers—"

"Navigators—"

"Bombardiers—"

And all together: "But there are no fighter pilots down in hell!"

"*Ja!*" von Strasser said, removing the headband. "Bow fucking wow."

Charley Morgan stood before the full-length mirror. She saw a stunning young woman, star reflections from jeweled earrings and her necklace. Bejeweled, in a body-hugging off-white gown, her golden hair upswept and a

199

slender tiara barely visible, she was a magical transformation from the girl in levi shorts, halter, and sneakers. She pirouetted before the mirror, smoothing the dress along her hips. She turned with a brilliant smile to Wendy Green.

"You like?"

Wendy stared and then shook her head in open admiration. "You look like a goddess. No wonder every hunk on the beach is crazy over you."

Charley turned to once again study her mirrored reflection. She nodded with satisfaction. "I don't think the word goddess is what I had in mind," she told Wendy.

"Hey, I call them the way I see them," Wendy countered.

"You have the name wrong. It's not Aphrodite. Diana will do. The goddess of the hunt."

Wendy's mouth opened to say "Oh?" but a sudden rush of sound covered her remark. She peered through the window drape. "Your knight in shining helicopter is here," she announced. "You're going in style, anyway," she offered in a grudging acknowledgement of Lansky's appearance.

"Abe's pulling out all the stops for the big romantic evening," Charley told her as she started for the door. She stopped and turned. "Don't wait up. Your man is waiting for you."

Wendy nodded. "I hope Bill doesn't see you first. I'd get kicked out of bed tonight. Take care."

She stayed by the window until the helicopter was out of sight. *Bannon*, she thought, *you're one dumb son of a bitch*.

Bannon came back on power at two thousand feet, letting the Turkey drop at a steep and steady descent toward the long skid strip on Cape Canaveral. He banked steeply, added a smidgin of power for the exact angle he wanted on a short final approach, and brought the heavy torpedo bomber down with a feathery touch. Red and blue lights appeared magically before him and he followed the ground control jeep into a large rounded hangar open front and back. Inside, he cut power, shut down the switches, and climbed from the airplane. A mixed group of Air Force and NASA people waited for him, and a sergeant pointed to a waiting car. "He'll take you to Mr. Hudoff's office, sir."

Bannon nodded, stopped suddenly. "You know how to work the bomb bays?"

"Yes, sir," the sergeant confirmed.

"Be sure to get that load of grass aboard."

"No sweat, sir. We'll take care of it."

Bannon nodded, went to the car, and settled in for the short ride. The car drove to a concrete wall that slid aside as the driver blinked his lights. Within the garage beyond the wall, guards checked out Bannon's ID and called in his presence. He'd never run into this kind of security shakedown before. It gave him a good feeling. Two guards accompanied him along a hallway and into the private elevator to Hudoff's office.

He recognized Horvath and Galenko. But he didn't know the husky black colonel in Air Force blue seated at the conference table. Hudoff went right to it. "Let's not waste time. Bannon, you know everybody here except Colonel Hank Rawls. He's my counterpart with the Air Force until this whole thing is resolved." Bannon nodded and looked at Rawls, sizing him up. *Very* professional. Pilot's wings and beneath them paratrooper wings. Tough, hard, smart, fast. Good; we can use all we can get like this one, Bannon thought.

The social amenities didn't hold with this group. Hank Rawls was all business as he studied Bannon and then turned back to Hudoff. "You meant what you said before? No holds barred? No social bullshit?"

"You heard right," Hudoff told him.

Rawls jerked a thumb at Bannon. "I know this one. What the hell did you bring this beach scum here for?"

Hudoff offered an enigmatic smile. "That's my business, Colonel. And you'll regard him as a full member of this security team."

"The hell it's *your* business," Rawls snapped. "We're dealing with *nukes*, goddamnit. This shit here is my business also. We've got him on the books as a drug runner."

Hudoff caught him off balance. "You're supposed to."

"You mean—"

"Do I have to spell it out A, B, and C?"

Rawls shook his head slowly. "No. I'll discuss it with you later."

"For the record, Colonel Rawls," Hudoff pushed, "*everything* you may say to me gets said to *him*. Screw your personal opinions. I'm asking you to accept my professional judgment here."

Rawls was fast. "All right. You mind a question?" He waited until Hudoff nodded. "What are we doing mixed up with pot?"

Hudoff shrugged. "I never touch the stuff myself. Any more social studies?"

Rawls showed a touch of irritation, stuffed it out of the way. "As long as we're on this subject," he paused to spread papers before him, then picked one up, "there is something I need to know." He gestured with the paper. "That airshow bunch at Shiloh? I have dossiers here. They're drunks, punks, old men, crazy women, a damned Nazi—"

"You mean Strasser?" Rawls turned to Galenko. The KGB man sat like a heavy statue in his chair.

"I do," Rawls said.

"Strasser is no Nazi."

Rawls held up the paper. "It says here—"

"I do not care what your paper says. The people who write such reports do not know," Galenko said. "*I* know."

Hudoff was studying Galenko. He remembered the look that had passed between Galenko and Strasser when they were at the airfield. A look that could have knocked down walls. Suddenly it began to fit. "You knew Strasser before?"

"Yes."

"For God's sake, *where?*"

Galenko sighed, his thoughts heavy with memories. "A prison camp. In Siberia. He was there for nine years when I arrived to take over as camp commander."

Rawls had a triumphant look on his face. "*See!* I told you—"

"You told only nonsense. You know nothing," Galenko said, a touch of contempt for hasty conclusions evident in his expression. "He was a prisoner because he was a fighter pilot. A very dangerous fighter pilot. The man shot down over a hundred planes. No one knows the exact number. He was even decorated by Hitler." Galenko's look was grave. "But none of this made him a criminal."

"Then what the hell was he doing as a prisoner?" Rawls demanded.

Galenko laughed without humor, a harsh chopping sound. "*You*, Colonel, were still a child in those days. Sometimes I fear you Americans are fools who live in a world of Ivory flakes. He was in prison *because we won the war!* Because Moscow ordered *all* German aces thrown into prison! And most of the bomber pilots as well. I personally interviewed Strasser. I checked all his records. His only crime is that he was a great flier."

Rawls and Galenko locked eyes until the American nodded finally. "This isn't getting us anywhere. I withdraw my comments." He turned stiffly to Hudoff. "I need to know what's happening *now*. You expressed a concern, Hudoff, that those pilots and their old military planes might be harboring the very people we're looking for."

"You're a charmer, Colonel," Bannon said.

"Can you tell me beyond any question of doubt that someone in that group might *not* be part of the hijacker's group?"

Bannon shook his head. "Nope. No more than you can tell me that *every* pilot at *your* field is above suspicion."

Rawls concentrated on Hudoff. "You said you'd run a check on those people. What about it?"

"We're doing that right now," Hudoff replied. He offered Bannon a brief sideways glance before continuing with Rawls. "I have our people at Shiloh, *now*, going over every plane on that field."

"Jesus Christ," Bannon said, disgusted, not hiding it.

Hudoff ignored him and kept his attention on Rawls. "Colonel, you told me you wanted to meet with us tonight based on orders from the Pentagon to coordinate all security search teams for this emergency. Is that correct?"

"Yes, sir."

"Colonel Virgil Padgett from Army . . . have you clued him in on this?"

"Yes, sir, I have. And Commander Arval Tilson of Navy. They've all been briefed and they have received orders to function under Air Force authority."

"Very good. Coast Guard?"

"That would be Bob Bergstresser. He's, uh—"

"His rank is commander," Hudoff said quickly. "But he's not military. In peacetime he comes under the jurisdiction of the Department of Transportation."

"They've yielded jurisdiction for the duration of this affair, Mr. Hudoff."

"And what about *you*, Colonel. Where do you stand in relation to *me*?"

Rawls offered a half-smile and shifted uneasily. "I'd hoped to work that out right now, sir. You know, establish lines of authority and—"

"Bullshit."

"What was that, sir?"

"Don't start filling my breakfast bowl with bullshit, Colonel Rawls. We are *not* going to have a sorority discussion as to who runs this show. *I do*. No arguments, no dialogue. *None*." He saw Rawls winding up inside for an angry counter of *Who's In Charge Here?*, and Hudoff was determined to kill that one before it ever got verbalized. "We work together, Rawls. Tighter than two snakes screwing in a tunnel. You and me. But I have the final say-so. I'm not interested in usurping your authority. I want and I need your cooperation. This is *my* responsibility. That's a NASA bird out there on the pad. This is a NASA facility. I know it far better than you ever will. That's enough reason for us to work together as a team. Do you read me, Colonel?"

"I do, sir."

"Do I have your full agreement?"

"Well, I—"

"Colonel, one more fucking hesitation out of you and I pick up this little old telephone, here," Hudoff tapped an orange phone on the side of his desk, "and I call a man by the name of Coke Stevens. Do you know that name?"

"I've met him, Mr. Hudoff."

"Do you know who he is?"

"No, sir. Only," Rawls added with obvious dislike for what Stevens represented, "that he's got some strong contacts in the Pentagon and—"

"Off the record, in this room only," Hudoff said with snap, "he has nothing to do with the Pentagon. His line goes straight to the Oval Office. Either you buy the package I just offered you or I have Stevens call the house on Pennsylvania Avenue and you are *off* this assignment. We are *never* going to repeat this conversation or have one remotely like it. What's your answer?"

"We're at your service, Mr. Hudoff."

Hudoff didn't ease off the tension flowing from his body. "Thank you, Colonel. Despite what you may think, you just went *up* a couple of notches in my book. What we're facing doesn't leave any room for pitter-patter." Hudoff shoved a cigar in his teeth and lit up. "Now, are we all through with your party invitation list?" He gestured to the thick file of personal dossiers Rawls had spread on the table. "You've been fussing with that college checklist so much you've fogged up the room. Are we through with that?"

Rawls caught him completely by surprise. "No, Mr. Hudoff, we are *not*. The military has certain advantages to it. We can trade fighter planes for information, as an example."

"You *can* be intriguing, Rawls," Hudoff said, but with no trace of antagonism.

"Yes, sir. You see, we've found a connection between a hijacking of nuclear materials in the past and those four bombs we're missing right now."

His words brought everyone upright. The room was almost electric with attention. Rawls couldn't help hanging on to the moment as long as he could. It would bring more parity into his relationship with Hudoff. "Sir, to be certain of the situation before I go any further, I can assume you've made no such connection?"

"What are you bucking for, Rawls? An extra stripe on your fucking sleeve? Get to it, man!"

Bannon gestured for Rawls' attention. "Colonel, any names? Anyone in particular?"

Rawls nodded and dropped his bombshell. "Wendy Green."

Hudoff turned to Bannon, ready for the fiery outburst he knew was coming. He didn't get it. Bannon stared for a long moment at the Air Force colonel and began to laugh. He motioned to Vladislov Galenko. "Sir, will you do me a favor?"

Galenko's lips were pressed together tightly. "Ask, Mr. Bannon."

Bannon pointed at Rawls. "Take him home with you. We got more than enough comics here."

"A nice offer, Mr. Bannon. But I will refuse it, if you do not mind. After all—"

"Shut up, the both of you," Hudoff snapped. "Rawls, even I have to admit that's one of the craziest things I've ever heard. Let's have the rest."

"Sir, do you remember how Israel got its first major supply of nuclear materials?" As he spoke, he watched Galenko from the corner of his eye. The Russian's face had lost any sign of levity from his exchange with Bannon. He was rigidly attentive now.

Hudoff bit down on his cigar. "I remember."

Horvath leaned forward. "Holy Jesus. That's right . . . *it was a hijacking.*"

"At sea," Galenko offered. "Yes, yes. I remember, too."

"An Israeli strike team, very efficient, very smart," Rawls continued, "hijacked a German freighter on the high seas. They didn't just take its cargo of high-grade uranium oxide. They commandeered the entire ship, held the crew prisoner, and moved that freighter under cover of torpedo boats, a submarine, and a cover of radar aircraft and fighter planes to a secret port in the Mediterranean. They kept the German crew under guard and offloaded the uranium and shipped it off to a secret

206

base. An Israeli crew took the ship back to sea, told the Germans to remain where they were for an hour, and took off in their torpedo boats." Rawls took a moment to light a cigarette and pour coffee into the cup before him.

"They assembled at least sixteen nuclear weapons from that hijacking," he added.

"They have more than sixteen," Galenko said quickly.

"Yes, sir, they do. At least forty or fifty. But they built their first bombs from that hijacking. And they have been able to exert a lot of pressure behind the lines, so to speak, because they have the bombs *and* the delivery systems."

Galenko smiled. "They are good at what they do. The Arab governments know that if ever they invade Israel now, every major Arab city and oil field will take an Israeli nuclear strike."

"Wait just a fucking moment," Bannon broke in, the temper he'd controlled through the exchange finally spilling over. "How in the hell does Wendy Green fit into all this? She's never even been to Israel!"

"That's true," Rawls replied, very cool and sure of himself. "But her older brother, Meier, was one of the Israeli commandos on that hijacking. Meier was one of the people charged with planning the mission. He was extremely thorough. He returned to the States to stay with his sister while researching a history of hijacking at sea. He was especially interested in rum-running during Prohibition days by some of our best-known gangsters, who used powerful speedboats to get through customs and the coast guard. There's no question he did his homework, and the Israelis adopted the tricks used during Prohibition. Whatever they added to the old days, it worked. They pulled off the uranium snatch without a single hitch."

"Where does Wendy Green fit in to all this?" Hudoff queried.

"Meier Green belongs to a secret sect within the Israeli military. They're fanatics just as much as many of the terrorist groups. Their sworn goal is to end all American aid to the Arab nations. Most people aren't aware that the United States has poured just as much money and military equipment into the Arab nations as it has to Israel."

"You know what this sounds like?" They turned to Horvath. "If what you say is true, then this Israeli group—"

"They go by the name of King David."

"Then this group seems to have the same objective in mind as this Zoboa bunch we're trying to track down."

"That's the dumbest—" Bannon began, and was interrupted by Hudoff.

"*Nothing* is too crazy to consider," Hudoff said harshly. "Nothing and no one can be ignored, and everything and everyone are under suspicion." Hudoff turned to Rawls. "But for the life of me I can't figure out why this King David group, or *anyone* from Israel, would do anything to hurt their strongest ally. *Us.*"

"They may be going for what you call an object lesson." Heads turned to Galenko, who returned their looks with impassivity.

"How would they do that?" Horvath led the questions.

"Let us say," Galenko explained, "and I say this only for example purposes, understand? Let us say the Israeli underground through this King David organization has the bombs. They continue as we face the danger now. We believe it is like Zoboa. They intend to explode one or more bombs at the time the shuttle launches.

"Only this is not what they intend, but what they want the Americans to *believe.* They permit events to roll right down to the final countdown and at the last moment they inform the Americans, secretly, of course, where the bomb or bombs may be found."

"But *why*?" Horvath persisted.

"It is an object lesson, a demonstration, if you please, of how effective they truly are. It is a powerful means of letting the American government decide that it is foolish to waste money and time and weapons on the Arab nations when the Israelis are so smart and capable as to having pulled off such a trick. It is—"

"*It is so much bullshit.*" Bannon had pushed back his chair until it enabled him to rest his back against the

208

wall. His boots were shoved against the table. Any other time Hudoff would have climbed his ass. Not now. He recognized the mood and setting that Bannon had created. "Galenko, that is the biggest pile of crap I've ever heard."

"You are quick to defend the Jews," Galenko said disarmingly.

"And you're a very smart sort of a prick who's trying to set up something here I don't understand, but you don't believe any more than I do. How's that for proper convoluted communist crap?" Bannon let the chair hit the floor with a bang as he came forward. "All this would be nifty," he said directly to Hudoff, "with one exception. It's great strategy on a chess board or on whatever passes for Friday-night television in bogeyman-land around Moscow. But, for Christ's sake, Bernie, you believe the Israelis would be showing us how smart they are and demonstrating to us why we should work with them, not the Arabs, as our best friends—*by killing the entire crew of that transport?* You know we'd never forgive murder in cold blood of Americans! In fact, it would be just about the *dumbest* thing the Israelis could ever come up with."

Bannon was on his feet in a sparks-flying staredown with Galenko. "Listen, you agitating commie bastard—"

"Bannon, enough of that!" Hudoff roared.

"Up yours," Bannon retorted. "Just remember what was said when this la-de-da started tonight. No holds barred and no social bullshit. Okay, *your* rules. Or you don't need me in this room one goddamned minute more."

Hudoff nodded. Bannon knew it was all his security chief could do to keep from cracking a smile. He turned back to Galenko. "Okay, let's have it *all* out on the table, Ivan."

"My name is—"

"Fuck *your* name. *Tell us Abe Lansky's real name.*"

Galenko's mouth clamped shut with an almost audible sound. Bannon stood straight. "So much for candor, frankness, and open communication between all the girls," he said acidly. He gestured to Hudoff. "Neat,

209

huh? Boris Karloff here knows so fucking much about the Israelis, but it just seems to have slipped his mind that Abe Lansky, the name, can't be real. The Israelis aren't crazy. *They never use their own names outside of their organization at home.* And we got somebody here who just came down with lockjaw."

Standoff. Silence. Bannon started for the door. "Where the hell are you going?" Hudoff asked quietly.

"I got to take a piss." Bannon glanced at the mute Galenko. "After what we just went through, it might not be worth coming back in here. Why don't you throw that asshole out?"

"Bannon, you ever think of taking a Dale Carnegie course?"

Their eye contact said it all. Bernie might just as well have said *Don't stop now . . . we got them on the run.*

Bannon didn't need to use the john. Inside the men's room, behind the locked door of a stall, he removed the microphone-and-antenna from his belt. He judged he had just enough range to make contact with Shiloh and talk to Lars.

210

✦ 14 ✦

DARK

They stood on the edge of the Twilight Zone, the
taxiway at its end wide and expansive, holding great
metal ghosts of warbirds on each side and then, like
railroad tracks joining in the far distance, the taxiway
seemed to narrow and the metal shapes diminish in
size. Lights flickered, glowed, shone, spun and danced
in an ever-changing coruscation. Blues, whites, reds,
greens, and ambers of all sizes and shapes, gaining
reflected life from the metal surfaces polished and waxed
with loving care so many dozens of times. Voices carried along the whispered breezes of the night, echoing
amidst the canyons of fuselages and wings aligned one
to the other in serrated rows. Here was the veldt of the
dark, the Shiloh of its own shadows. And the great
beasts in the distance would stir to life with rumbling
coughs, the almost-visible jaws of a huge cat yawning
and ending its stretch with a sudden roar. But no lions
or jaguars or pumas these; here the deep-throated cries
and chesty bellows were Cyclones and Merlins, Wasps
and Allisons, Lycomings and Kinners and Continentals
and their kin.

Beneath the wing of a great slab-bodied sky predator,
bunched shadows moved furtively. Eyes concealed by
the shadows peered just around the edge of metal. Lars

Anderson raised infrared binoculars to his eyes. The battery-powered system brought the darkest shadows into a green-glowing relief, and what had been invisible to his own night eyes leaped into startling clarity. "I got 'em," he whispered to the group huddled at his side. "They's wearing stocking masks, f'Christ's sake."

"What are they doing, Lars?" Wilbur Moreland asked, tugging at his sleeve.

Anderson slapped away the offending hand. "Just like Bannon said," he told his group. "Goddamn government spies. Ain't got the decency to come right out and ask us to show 'em these planes. Been glad to. But, no, they gotta sneak around like Ninja assholes. Guess it makes 'em feel like heroes." He turned to his group and a grin moved slowly across his face until he was beaming. "Everybody know what to do?" he queried them. They nodded and whispered assent. "Okay. Stu, you're first. Get set."

Stu Goodwin slipped out of his trousers. His friends stifled their giggles with a stern look from Anderson, who held out Stu's jet helmet and oxygen mask. Stu fastened the mask, checked his equipment. Anderson studied the government agents slipping from one plane to another. "Go!" he whispered to Goodwin.

The federal agents froze with the sound of the siren. They dropped deeper into shadows and scanned the taxiway. Jaws dropped and eyes stared in disbelief as a man naked except for a diaper and jet helmet pedaled furiously on a child's bicycle down the taxiway, siren howling and smoke trailing in a thick stream behind what was clearly an apparition of flailing legs and squeaking wheels. The agents looked blankly at one another.

"My God," an agent exclaimed. A Christ figure glided along the taxiway, arms outstretched in a perfect crucifixion, halo glowing above his head, robes glowing from within, his face beatific as the sound of angels' voices carried through the night air. "His feet aren't moving! How—"

Wilbur Moreland glided by, a ghostly apparition, his long robes concealing the motorized skateboard beneath his feet, batteries tied about his waist beneath the robes, small and powerful speakers and a cassette player strapped to his chest and back. Calyumite chemical light tubes had been taped together with a shoulder strap to create the halo. Without the merest sign of effort, the Christ figure flowed down the taxiway and, abruptly, vanished. Wilbur had shut off the batteries. Sight and sound were gone.

"What in the hell is going on here?" The question rattled among the agents huddled amidst the planes. "Did I really see what I think I saw?"

Anderson readied his next assault on their senses. "All set?" he asked the girls. Honey Fields and Marilyn Pappas nodded, two beauties who had for years made mockeries of the bras trying to hold them in. They weren't wearing their bras now. In fact, they wore only smiles and each a flower wreath about her head. Anderson looked through his group. "Jeff? Jeff, damnit, you ready?"

Jeff Clayborn pushed to the front of the group. He was a huge gorilla except for the neck and head, which were very much his own, protruding upward from the furry gorilla suit. "Get the girls on the platform. And remember, don't turn on them back lights until you pass that first taxi light."

"Got it, Lars." The gorilla head went on and the huge creature climbed behind the wheel of the jeep. The rear half of the jeep had a high platform, behind which was mounted the brightly lit FOLLOW ME sign for leading aircraft along the airfield. Lars signalled the jeep to start. Everybody got behind the vehicle and began pushing and running until it had enough speed to coast by itself. As it drifted away Lars studied the agents through his night-vision binoculars. "They're watching him. All they can see is a shadow and he should start up just about n—"

On the taxiway, Clayborn popped the clutch and hit the lights. Brilliant headlights stabbed down the taxiway; flashing red and white lights about the sides and rear of the jeep snapped into dazzling glares. Federal agents interspersed among the planes gaped as the jeep

213

rolled slowly down the taxiway, two stunning naked women seated on the back platform, both real and unreal, flashing into being in eye-twisting stroboscopic effect from the red and white beacons. The girls waved and flashed smiles, huge bosoms quivering with the rocking motion of the jeep. Baffled, intrigued, flabbergasted, the agents emerged from the shadows to stare after the apparition.

It held their attention to the north along the taxiway so that they neither heard nor saw the row of vehicles approaching from the south. Anderson stood at the big control handles of a foam fire-fighting truck leading a half-dozen jeeps, weapons carriers, and two more fire trucks. They rolled closer to the group of gaping agents. Anderson bellowed through loudspeakers.

"LIGHTS ON!"

Blinding floodlights speared the dark and exploded away the night. A dozen men in dark form-fitting slip-over jumpsuits and silken face hoods froze where they were or, startled by the savage light, stumbled out from beneath the aircraft. The trucks kept rolling forward.

Anderson raised a fist and his voice boomed out.

"FIRE!"

Powerful auxiliary engines and generators whined and screeched and howled into life, exhausts hammered the sundered night air, and the huge pumper trucks hurled forward enormous plumes and fountains of fire-fighting foam. A Niagara of the slippery, greasy white foam erupted along the taxiway, hurtled like a ground-hugging tidal wave beneath the planes and, like a living fog, raced after, attacked, and enveloped the stunned, cursing, sliding, slipping, falling, tumbling group of men caught so totally by surprise. The force of the foam from the heavy pumpers bowled them over, tossed them about like corks, bounced them off big tires and wheels.

"Hold your fire!"

The shrill whine and deep coughing roar of the pumps and exhausts fell away. Foaming spumes fell to the taxiway, shortened and died out with burbling gurgles.

The only sounds were those of idling engines and the moans and curses of the feds beneath the brilliant lights.

"Okay, move 'em up!" Anderson's voice crackled over the loudspeakers of the trucks. From behind the fire and crash vehicles the feds stared at a row of jeeps and weapons carriers moving slowly and inexorably closer. Every vehicle mounted a .50-caliber machine gun or a 20-mm cannon. The guns held belts of ammunition and were kept at the ready by individual gunners aiming them at the hapless agents.

"They look like Russian spies to me!" Anderson announced over the loudspeakers.

"No!" a voice called out from the sloppy mess of foam. "You don't understand—!"

"Show the sons of bitches we mean business! Give 'em a warning burst!"

Wicked blue and yellow flames erupted from the machine guns and cannon. A stentorian chatter of explosions ripped the night, hammered at the senses as the massive burst of firepower sent the foam-covered figures reeling back. Anderson held up his arm. The guns fell silent. A pathetic voice begging for mercy came from among the foam-trapped men. A man kicked wildly at the source and the whiner went down in a slippery flail of arms and legs.

"Everybody on your feet!" Anderson announced. "All you people are under arrest for trespassing. You're under arrest for attempted hijacking of these here planes! You're under arrest for disturbing the peace! When you take off them wet clothes you'll be under arrest for indecent exposure! Move over here by these lights and start stripping! Anybody tries to run we'll blow you into little pieces. Now, *git!*"

The federal men gathered before the headlights trapping them in a blinding semicircle. They stripped down to their underwear. "Ain't they purty?" a voice called from the darkness.

"All right, you commies start walking down this here taxiway to that hangar. Stay close together or you've had it!"

The trucks, jeeps, and weapons carriers rumbled and

coughed to form a guard escort of the men shambling along. Honey Fields, now wearing a jumpsuit, emerged from the shadows and climbed aboard the fire truck to stand by Anderson. She leaned closer to him.

"Lars, what if they find out all our guns are fakes? You know, that they're just propane gas and—"

"Shut up, Honey. I'm working real hard at looking mean, if you don't mind."

Honey giggled. "Can I have that one over there? By the right? He sure has a nice ass, Lars."

"Yeah. Well soaped, too." Lars patted her ample backside. "Anything you want."

Bernie Hudoff slammed a calloused palm against the table before him with the cracking sound of a rifle shot. He not only appeared to have lost patience with the indignities and accusations and petty nonsense of what had started out to be a gathering of forces to pursue the missing bombs, he was completely out of patience. He was dog-tired. He'd been on the go for sixteen straight hours. He'd been eating on the run. His flask of Jack Daniels was empty. He was distressed to see Vladislov Galenko lose his cool. Any other time that Bannon tweaked the people in the room would have brought pride to Hudoff, but all it did now was waste time.

And then there was the blue-suiter with the permanent dark tan. Colonel Hank Rawls, trouble-shooter and a prideful, almost arrogant son of a bitch. Beneath that blue suit and behind those dark eyes, Hudoff recognized fine qualities. But as long as Rawls was concerned about his human relationship with these people, he wouldn't be worth a rat's ass for getting the job done, and Hudoff would have to go over his head and bounce his ass out of this whole problem. But Hudoff *wanted* Rawls. Maybe the only way was for Rawls to see that he wasn't facing a closed coalition against him. It wasn't too often that an Air Force officer was closeted in a room with a top NASA official, a drug-running beach bum who was obviously a lot more than he seemed to be, one of the highest-level KGB agents of the Soviet Union, and a representative of the U.S. Secret Service.

"I've had enough bickering," Hudoff announced, making certain his gaze took in everyone at the conference table. "No more of this bullshit. No more digging at each other. I want specific inputs and results."

Now he leveled his eyes directly at Rawls. "Colonel, aside from all your questions about people, how do you plan to have the Air Force work with us, help us, or do whatever it is you're going to do, to find these four nukes?"

"You want me to drop my inquiry into individuals?" Rawls' expression was enigmatic.

"Yes. I damn well want you to do just that. You've got plenty of lieutenants and captains and majors who can handle all that, Colonel! We don't need to bury ourselves in chicken shit. Give me hard specifics I can put to use *now*."

"Well, Mr. Hudoff, I'm working on bringing in at least ten aircraft with long endurance times to help us detect the bombs."

"Detect?"

The interruption came from Bannon. He was sitting straight up and intensely watching Rawls. Hudoff gestured. "Shut up, Bannon. Let him finish." Bannon leaned forward, elbows on the table, his gaze locked on Rawls.

Hudoff didn't miss Bannon's sudden shift. He was poised like a cat with coiled muscles. *He's on to something*, Hudoff judged. *Thank Christ I had him here for this.*

"As I was saying," Rawls went on, showing his irritation with the drug-running beach bum who was polluting the meeting, "we're bringing in at least ten more aircraft with high loiter times. These are in addition to the aircraft we already have at Patrick Air Force Base. We have, uh, a small force of O-2 observation planes—"

"Numbers, Colonel, *numbers*," Hudoff said brusquely.

"Four, sir." Hudoff waved him on.

"And we have six OV-10 Broncos, as well as six Jolly Greens, but those are pretty well tied up on special assignment. The ten aircraft we are bringing in will be either O-2 or OV-10's so that we'll have twenty aircraft for the search-and-detect missions."

Bannon could barely contain himself. Hudoff watched as Bannon spoke with great restraint. "Colonel, uh, maybe I'm pretty dumb about such stuff, but how can you detect those missing bombs? The way those things are packaged, there's no radiation to pick up, so—"

"Why, that should be obvious to *anyone*. We never transport these weapons without first activating their signal transmitters—"

Bannon was moving slowly to his feet. "You mean trace signals?"

"Yes."

Bannon pushed back his chair and walked slowly about the far end of the conference table. Every eye in the room followed him. Hudoff started to tell him to get the hell back to his seat, but he stayed his own words. Whatever was going on between Bannon's ears showed in his face. A cheek muscle twitched and his jaw was set in concrete. He came around to Rawls, rested his hands on both arms of the colonel's chair, and leaned forward until their faces were barely inches apart. When Bannon spoke, his voice sounded like sandpaper.

"I want this absolutely straight. You've got radio transmitters in those bombs?"

"Yes. That's what I said."

"Those bombs have been missing since early this morning and they've been transmitting homing signals *the whole time?*"

"Y-yes." Rawls pushed his chair back and stood, his own anger coming out. "I don't answer your questions—"

"Yes, you do."

Rawls turned to Hudoff. "Who the hell is he?"

Hudoff had become a Cheshire cat. "For starters, try National Security Agency."

Rawls looked back at Bannon, disbelief stark on his face. Hudoff's voice carried to him.

"And Blue Light."

Rawls was staring now.

"And Delta Strike Team. *And* Counter Intelligence for—" Hudoff cleared his throat. "It's a long list, Colonel Rawls. Of course, you will forget everything you ever heard about Mitchell Bannon except that he is a drug-running miserable scumbag beach bum."

Rawls sat slowly. "Yes, sir. Bannon, I—"

Bannon was driving hard and not letting up. "You stupid bastard. *Why the hell didn't you tell us?*"

"I couldn't tell you! You weren't cleared for that kind of information and—"

Hudoff's voice skewered Rawls from the side. "Why didn't you tell *me?*"

Bannon turned to Hudoff, his thumb jerking in the direction of Rawls. "Does this asshole really work with us? Do you know what he's done? From the moment those terrorists got their hands on the bombs and for the next few hours, they're at their most vulnerable. They haven't had a chance yet to secure everything. They've got to move the bombs and store them, either together or, most likely, separating them. *That's been our best shot at finding them!*"

He spun back to Rawls. "Talk, damnit. We've lost enough time!"

Rawls had it back. He was stiff and more than a little nervous. He'd come to this meeting to tell these people how the Air Force would handle the search for the missing bombs and he'd walked into a den of wolverines. The only thing to do was to play it absolutely straight. He didn't know that much about Hudoff and he sure as hell didn't cotton to this beach b—to Bannon, but Rawls *did* know Horvath, and no one from U.S. Secret Service would have stood for a moment of this circus—*unless it were for real.* So Rawls didn't fight for position any longer.

"Each bomb carries a transmitter that operates on a discreet frequency for seven days, give or take one day. We activate them whenever we transfer the bombs."

"When do you start signal?"

"On the taxiway. We can get an accurate Doppler check and distance confirmation by testing with accurately known topography."

Horvath jumped into it. "Range?"

"Five miles."

"Is that direct or are you measuring by slant?"

They looked with surprise at Horvath. He'd been the silent man in the background. Abruptly he was in the center of the action. He knew from their faces what they were thinking. "I spent six years in anti-submarine electronic systems. *And* airborne ECM as well," he said to forestall questions. He went back to Rawls, waiting for an answer.

"Sir, that's slant direct. We're pretty low on the power."

Horvath nodded. "Separate antenna or contained?"

Rawls was visibly relieved to be off the personal hacking at one another. "Contained antenna, sir. We hook directly through the weapons casing to painted antenna."

"Can they detect the transmitters inside the bomb casings?"

"No sir," Rawls replied. "They're built right into a false hull, and they're not visible. They'd have to know about them before they got the bombs, and I don't believe that."

"That helps," Horvath told Hudoff and Bannon. "Even if they removed the devices from the packing cases, it means the transmitters will still be working." Back to Rawls. "I don't know if you said this before, but do you work those transmitters on locked discreet freq or do you have variances?"

"Locked discreet, sir."

"So you must use the Tattlers? Yes, that would be right. Model 7R2?"

"Yes, sir." Rawls' eyes were just a bit wider.

Horvath relaxed. "We've used those for years. Simple and reliable. The tracking or pickup system is just as simple and reliable."

"What do your pickup receivers weigh?" Bannon shot at Rawls.

"With self-enclosed antennas, six pounds."

Hudoff motioned for attention. "How many units do you have at Patrick, *right now?*"

"Four, sir. Those are permanent units we keep on hand for emergencies."

"This ain't no birthday party, Colonel," Hudoff snapped.

"No, sir."

"Rawls, how many units can you get?" Bannon asked.

"Why, whatever you need—"

"Two hundred. At least that many." Bannon did some

heavy figuring. "Can you get them here tomorrow morning?"

"I can find out—"

"Find out, hell!" Hudoff roared. "We don't have the time to *find out*. Where are they kept?"

"The closest shipping point is Langley. In Virginia—"

"I know where it is. Colonel Rawls, get them started here now."

"I'll have to—"

Horvath tapped the table. "Colonel Rawls, you're aware of my authority level?"

"Yes, sir."

"Pick up that telephone, Colonel. Order those units *now*. If you need to, pass on Code Victor Shangrila. Got it? Victor Shangrila. They can verify through DOD if necessary. *But do it now.*"

Rawls didn't flinch. He looked directly at Horvath. "I'll make the call, sir. But you're aware my ass could be in a hell of a sling for this. Going above my commanding general, I mean—"

"Colonel, which is more important? Your ass, *my* ass, all our asses—or those bombs?"

For the first time, Hank Rawls' face broke into a grin. He picked up the phone and punched in a series of numbers. The others sat quietly as Rawls went through an amazing transformation. He spoke as if he were a human computer, then stopped. He turned to Hudoff. "Where do you want delivery?"

Hudoff deferred to Bannon. "Straight to Shiloh Field. Morgan Aviation hangar. Let us know their ETA and we'll be waiting for them. One more thing, Colonel. Have them send at least four technicians who understand these things along with the units."

"Got it." Rawls turned back to the phone. When he hung up, he had a very satisfied look on his face. "Well, my ass is now hanging over the edge of the tree. They'll be on their way within the hour. A captain I know personally will handle the job."

"Thank you, Colonel," Hudoff told him. He turned to Bannon. "What's the plan?"

"We've got nearly two hundred warbirds at Shiloh.

Figure we'll be using a hundred and fifty of them for shows. The rest of the week they're available to go hunting. We can put these trackers on another fifty planes and helicopters. We can map-grid all of central Florida, which is the most likely place to look for the bombs. The military, through Colonel Rawls, can attend to south and north. We'll have a hornet's swarm of planes all over the middle of this state and from coast to coast. They're critical."

Bannon looked at Rawls. The colonel recognized that the earlier enmity was gone. Bannon was all business now. "Rawls, have you figured why you need our planes so badly instead of a mob of military jet fighters and similar equipment?"

Rawls smiled. "It took a while, but yes, I do. It's the range problem of five miles. With that short range, the *slant* range becomes everything. Anybody flying at fifteen or twenty thousand feet would virtually have to be directly over the bombs to detect the Tattler signal. But if you're low—"

Bannon nodded. "That's right. If our people fly at a thousand feet, let's say, that means they're covering a circle at least eight miles in diameter, because they'll pick up the signal from any direction. I didn't ask before, Colonel. What's the installation time in the planes for these?"

"You can carry them in your lap. We use Velcro to hold them in place."

"Colonel, will you do me a favor?"

"I surely will if I can, Mr. Bannon."

"I'd like you to be at Shiloh when these units come in. We may need some heavy authority on tap, and you're it."

"I'll be there."

"One more thing, Colonel." Bannon's face broke into a smile. "No uniform. You'd stand out like a sore thumb and—"

"Never mind, Mr. Bannon. If nothing else, I learn fast. I've got this hot beachcomber outfit from Jamaica, man, and I got this ghetto blaster, see, baby? And we are gonna get it *on!*"

They slapped palms, grinning at one another.

Von Strasser turned in from the beach road and parked in the carport. He shut down the van and sat quietly for several moments. The surf crashed only a hundred yards to his left. Music drifted from nearby homes. He was glad no one was about. He turned to look behind him. Marty Morgan was strapped in a captain's chair, asleep, but not well. Facial muscles twitched. *Even through sleep his body knows the pain.* The big dog lay at his feet, sensing that his master was less than well.

The German pilot went around to the side of the van and slid the door back. Marty looked at him through a haze of alcohol, drugs, and deep pain, diminished but not subdued by the agony that preceded his almost frantic intake of anything that would relieve him. "We go inside now," Karl told the groggy youngster. Magnum moved quickly aside, his eyes following every move as Karl released Marty's seat belt and supported him down the step to the ground. Marty leaned against the van, breathing deeply of the cool salty air.

"Whole world's at a thirty-degree bank," he murmured. "Either the world's crazy or my instruments' all fucked up."

Karl got a firm grip on the loose body. "We blame it on the instruments. Come." He saw Marty's face twist in pain as they climbed the concrete steps to the door. Inside, he leaned Marty against the wall until he found the light switches, then supported him through the tumbled debris about the floor until they reached the couch. Marty went down heavily and winced. He leaned back, eyes closed. Magnum sat by him, the dog's huge head resting on one knee. Without thinking, Marty's hand went to the animal and gripped his collar as if the handhold might stop the whirling in his head.

Karl glanced about him. There was something better about being here than anywhere else. The room bristled with models, pictures and paintings, parachutes and flying gear, aircraft instruments and radios, charts; all the signatures of men whose lives are in the sky. *And the other things, too,* Karl thought heavily. Not merely the beer cans crumpled in odd corners and beneath the tables, or the emptied whiskey bottles, but the marijuana pipes and the coffee cans in which Marty kept his supply. Marty stirred and opened his eyes.

"That was interesting," he said of the pain that had been whipsawing him through the evening hours. Karl nodded. What Marty called "interesting" would have brought many men to tears. Marty leaned forward, grunting with the effort, and opened a cigarette box. He kept his machine-rolled joints in these things. There were some in every room. Karl had learned his language. Jamaican Red and Colombian Green were his favorites. Marty lit a joint and sucked in fiercely, the marijuana cigarette glowing bright red at its tip. Again and again he took deep shuddering breaths. Karl said nothing because there was nothing to say until the drug reached the brain and relief began to flood Marty's system. He was almost desperate as he sucked in the smoke, swallowing it with deliberate effort. Karl watched until he saw the pink glaze in Marty's eyes begin to wane, until he knew Marty could again focus without seeing through a cloud of pain.

"Shit, man, I need a beer," Marty said finally.

Karl sat heavily on the other end of the couch. He disliked these moments, disliked talking about these things. "That will not help," he said after a long pause.

Marty drew another deep shuddering breath. "The hell it don't," he said, the smoke curling about his mouth.

Karl sighed, a heavy, almost despondent move as his shoulders slumped. "Only for the moment, my young friend." He turned to look directly at Marty. "I have been around pain all my life, and what cures only for the night makes it worse for the mornings that follow."

"This ain't for tomorrow morning, you fuckhead," Marty snapped. His irritability was almost palpable. "It's for *now*." He winced suddenly with pain and clutched at his leg stump. His teeth ground together with an audible sound. "Son of a bitch," he gasped.

Von Strasser didn't touch him. "It is that bad, Marty?"

Marty winced again and gasped for air. "Jesus, *yes*. Oh, my God, Karl, but this is a bad fucker right

224

now. . . ." He was rocking back and forth and not even realizing his motion.

"This stuff you smoke. The pot. Tell me truthfully, Marty. It helps?"

A hollow, mocking laugh came from the pain-wracked young man. "Does it help? Holy shit . . . grass, whiskey, beer, coke, *anything* helps . . . *nothing* helps. Find me something stronger, you Nazi son of a bitch!"

Von Strasser drove quietly and persistently toward what he needed to know. "Did you hurt yourself tonight?"

"You mean that shit with the dog in the Grotto?"

"Yes."

"Jesus Christ, Karl, that *always* hurts."

"It would be easier, you young fool, to pay the bill than play your stupid game."

Marty grinned. "Sure, but where's the fun in paying your bill when—" He stopped, gasping for air from a sudden intense blow of pain. He struggled to stand, but the pain wasted his sense of balance and he began to crumple. Von Strasser's powerful arms had him instantly. He lowered Marty to the couch with great gentleness and cradled him in his arms as he might soothe a hurt child. Marty's agony showed in his face. Blood trickled from his lower lip where his teeth had cut through skin. They held a deep, silent bond between them. Von Strasser did not talk. Holding was everything.

Marty moved finally, wiping the blood from his mouth. "That was a bad one, old man," he said through clenched teeth.

"I know. I understand pain. It is an old friend." He thought heavily, never taking his eyes from the hurt soul in his arms. "Marty, this is not good."

A small, agonized animal might have looked back at him, silent, unable to speak.

"We must do *something*," von Strasser said, more forcefully.

"They've already," Marty struggled for the words, "cut off the fucking leg."

"There are medicines, Marty. There are treatments that can help!"

Marty made it halfway up, sprawled at an angle on

225

the arm of the couch. "The only thing . . . to do . . . is for you to keep your . . . mouth shut." He clutched desperately at his closest friend. "Promise me that, Karl. Promise me, you son of a bitch! You know it would kill Charley if she knew . . . we can't tell her . . . can't . . ." Marty passed out.

Karl stroked his forehead gently. "All right, little one. We will not tell your sister." He knew Marty couldn't hear him. "If she knew you had cancer it would kill her, too."

✦ 15 ✦

SATURDAY

Lars Anderson stayed up all night. So did Wilbur Moreland and three other mechanics. They drank coffee until they were pissing every hour on the half-hour. It had been a hell of a night, getting ready for the Saturday early morning dawn patrol and the airshow scheduled for the afternoon. They'd held the federal agents shivering in their wet underwear until someone showed up from the local FBI office to take them away. Anderson and the FBI man, with whom he'd gone fishing many a time, grinned at one another and agreed to forget anything that happened during the night. Lars was glad for one small favor. He'd tried on Wilbur's headset and the wild rock music punched through his ears into his head and made his eyes roll. He ripped the headset from his ears and handed it back to Wilbur.

"How in God's name do you stand that there shit?" he demanded.

Wilbur gave him a cockeyed grin and snapped his fingers and rolled his butt from side to side. "You look like a goddamned snake," Anderson chided him.

"It's the beat, man, it's the beat," Wilbur sang out, feet tapping, gliding in circles, elbows flapping. "You gotta go with the beat."

"I'll beat your fucking brains in if you don't get to

work, Chikowsky or whatever his goddamn name is."
Wilbur grinned again and whirled around on his skateboard, balancing tools in each hand and whistling tune-
lessly to the uproar pounding through his headset. Lars
Anderson wouldn't have traded Wilbur for a dozen men.

Sometime during the night he saw Bannon's Turkey
gliding out of the darkness. He liked Bannon, but damnit,
he didn't cotton to this crazy stuff of busting the law
left and right on these dumb night runs of his. The
torpedo bomber came down like a feather and a tire
squealed like a whimpering puppy, and except for the
engine that was all the sound Bannon made as he taxied by to his own hangar, he rolled out of sight behind
the hangar and shut down. Anderson watched him go
into his office.

Planes came in during the night without too much
fuss. Just about two in the morning that big beautiful
helicopter that Lansky owned flew in from the east.
Lights blazed like a Christmas tree all about the chopper. The pilot set it down right on the flight line by the
office. Lars got a good look at Charley walking with
Lansky to the office door. They stood for a couple of
minutes like two kids coming home from a date to the
prom. Charley went inside and left Lansky standing by
the door. For some reason Anderson felt good about
that. Lansky had never fit into their group. Too big for
his britches. Hoity-toity or whatever the hell they called
it. It was a feeling.

At four o'clock in the morning Lars Anderson and the
other men skinning their knuckles the long night through
had the feeling they needn't have busted their chops
without any sleep. The first wave of mosquitos came in
on the sudden winds that began kicking up from out of
the direction of the swamps. "Oh, shit," Anderson said
as he got hit first-off. The skeeters that came in at night
like this were the biggest damned things Anderson had
ever known. They were worse than what he used to
fight off in Alaska during the summer months, and
them things was so bad they could fuck a turkey
flatfooted.

The rains began shortly after. First the winds and

then the mosquitos and the gusts got stronger, and they knew they were in for a hell of a squall line. Lightning chewed the night air and thunder boomed and rattled and banged against and through the cavernous hangar. Anderson went into his office and called the weather office at the Air Force base. "What you guys got coming in here?" he asked them.

"Hey, Lars, how you doing, man?" They went through the ritual social greeting and Sergeant Banks gave him the news. It was good or bad depending upon whether you'd slept a wink that night. "Don't expect your people to fly any dawn patrols this morning, Lars. We got a line of thunderbumpers from Daytona Beach all the way across the state into the Gulf. Moving about forty an hour. The whole mess. Gusts to sixty or seventy and we'll be putting the whole middle of Florida on tornado watch."

"How long will it be with us?"

"First line until about eleven and then there's a second pressure trough coming through about an hour behind that one. It's going to be a good day to log sack time, old buddy."

It got worse and then it went to hell in a handbasket. Wendy called from the office and told them there'd be no flying for the entire day. "Rest up, Lars. The weather people said we'd have severe clear late Saturday night and for the next couple of days behind when that high rolls in."

It could have been worse. The weather was too bad for test-flying the airplanes they'd worked on all night, but a lot of hangovers needed sleep to get rid of them. It looked to Lars that with all that weather they wouldn't see anything flying all day long.

So he was surprised as hell when the big Air Force Hercules turboprop came busting through the booming winds and the heavy rain like it was time for a Sunday picnic. His surprise got all the bigger when a couple of Air Force helicopters came bitty-bopping right over Highway I-95 to the west, flying barely over the tops of the bigger trucks, sort of slid east from the highway to the edge of Runway 9, and then marched right up to his hangar and set down.

What in the hell, Lars wondered, was Mitch Bannon doing in an Air Force helicopter?

He had the whole damn bunch in his conference room. Well, the weather didn't permit much else. It sure as hell didn't allow for much flying, and Bernie Hudoff was grateful for that. The maniacs from Shiloh cancelled their dawn patrol to wake up the county, and that didn't much matter because the thunder crashing about the sky and spearing into the ground had everybody awake anyway. They were on tornado alert and that also meant everybody had evacuated the launch pad where *Antares* stood bravely within its servicing structure as rain poured in small waterfalls down the walkways and beams and the rounded flanks of the shuttle and its enormous boosters. Whoever flew in this shit would come under instant and thorough surveillance. That meant, if anyone were trying to move those bombs by air, they wouldn't do too well.

You're lying to yourself, Bernie, baby, his inner voice ground at him in its maddening sing-song whine. Goddamnit, his inner truth was right, and logical thinking was as soggy as the world outside. What would keep someone from moving the bombs by car or station wagon or van or truck, for God's sake. *Nothing,* his inner self needled him. *Nothing at all. They could move the Taj Mahal in this weather and you wouldn't know a thing about it.*

He forced himself back to the moment. The rain might be a blessing in yet another way. It was tough to think in grim overtones when the Florida skies reached all the way to heaven with a rich blue tone and the clouds were right out of a commercial brochure and you saw all those great-looking broads on the beach and—well, there were psychological overtones to these moments. Thunder did more than rattle a man's cage. The kind of thunder they were having included a lot of cloud-to-cloud stuff. Lightning bolts ten miles long played in the skies beyond their vision and absolutely anviled the

230

world beneath. Windows shook and pictures vibrated on the walls and the deep rumbling got under your skin and made a man's balls tingle.

But not her balls, he thought with a sudden stupid chuckle. Maybe the damn weather was affecting him, too. Lightning flashed again and water ran in sheets down the picture window, and there was more lightning to highlight the silhouette of Irene Bellmaster, she of the NASA hierarchy in the vaulted halls of Sodom on the Potomac. Irene Bellmaster was the Associate Administrator for International Relations of NASA, responsible only to the Administrator himself and the Vice President, Keith Satterfield, who headed the National Space Council. The word had passed all through the system by now, and Hudoff was amazed he wasn't hearing it every twenty minutes on radio and television. Obviously the press had been either isolated from the story or they'd been told everything and were cooperating by clamping a lid on the whole affair. Hudoff had the idea it was the latter. Right in his own back yard he had a hellfire legion of newsmen who could sniff out a story faster than a dying camel could smell good whiskey. He knew they'd be storming *his* bastions soon enough.

But not yet. Right now there was Irene Bellmaster of the severely sharp chin and sharper nose and frosted hair and, for all he knew, frosted tits. It didn't matter. Irene Bellmaster was a tough cookie who knew her business, and her business right now was on the thin edge of blowing up in her face. *She* was the unfortunate responsible for the coordination, transportation, care, feeding, and coddling of the four thousand VIPs, their servants and retinues, who would descend onto the Atlantic coastline for the big fireworks show in only eight more days.

Irene was also an old friend, a fact they made certain never to reveal in public. They weren't bedmates. They were people who truly respected one another professionally. They trusted one another and in this business you just couldn't get belly-to-belly closer than that. She turned from gazing at the storm and fixed chrome-steel eyes on Hudoff.

"If we can, I'd like to get this sewing circle down to business," she said in a voice that was both level and laced with strychnine. Only Irene could choose a single phrase out of the entire language guaranteed both to piss off all the men in the room and give her the advantage of their sudden attention. "There is more to life than lunchtime in the space tropics," she added to her dig. She looked about the great circular table, her eyes flicking past Hudoff briefly but long enough for her to see she had his acquiescence. "When I leave here, gentlemen, which will be absolutely no more than one hour from now, I shall fly directly to Dayton, Ohio, where the Vice President waits to hear what emerged from this huddling but august body."

Fucking A! Hudoff said triumphantly to himself. He sat up straighter, gesturing with a pencil as if antagonizing a symphonic orchestra. "We've been over this now for two hours," he announced brusquely. "It all comes down to the fact that you're all free with advice, proposals, suggestions, maybes, perhapses, possiblies and could-bes, but *none* of you has ultimate *responsibility* for how this problem is to be solved. So I am going on the record as agreeing completely with Ms. Bellmaster. *And* we are going to put each and every one of you on the record as well. This is being recorded. The tapes go to both the President and the Vice President. When things start coming unglued, as no doubt they will, every one of you will be *on the record.*"

Hudoff shifted in his seat and flicked a cigar ash over his shoulder. "One person only in this room is exempt from what I've just said to you, and that is Mario del Passo, who is here at my invitation and who most generously has provided us assistance and invaluable information through his, ah, own contacts. I will ask him the same question as I ask you. He's agreed to respond as if he were a member of our own government, but do keep in mind that he brings to this meeting his special viewpoint."

Hudoff studied his audience. "One final word. What

232

you say now will live here, with your name attached to it, after you leave. You're going on the record. Unless extraordinary circumstances prevail, we're not interested in your coming through the back door after everyone else has left so you can second-guess whatever you say *now*. We don't have time for that. When I state your name, have at it, and please, don't stand on protocol or ceremony. For God's sake, put aside whatever political, security, diplomatic, or any other considerations that you'd normally use to temper your own feelings and conclusions. All right, lady and gentlemen, we'll begin with Joe Horvath of the United States Secret Service. Joe?"

Horvath had been on this emergency from the beginning, and that affected how he would answer. "No foreign government leaders," he said flatly. "Cancel the invitations. Don't expose them to the danger we know exists. There is absolutely *no* excuse for our bringing people here when we know we can lose them all. My summary is that until we have all four bombs back in our hands or know they've been destroyed, you keep the space center antiseptic. I will not comment on any decision to launch or not to launch." He fell silent as though a switch had been thrown.

"Louis Elliott is my chief security officer on this installation," Hudoff explained. "He's closer to the day-to-day security than anyone else, including myself. He's in the trenches, so to speak. Lou?"

Elliott wasn't accustomed to mixing with what he considered the stratospheric levels of government leadership, but he cut right to the quick of the matter *and* he held the attention of the room. "I've been here for a long time," he said slowly, and the simplicity of the man came through with telling effect. "I can't judge what you people judge. I'm against the launch. I say we shut down the whole complex, we close it off to everyone we can, and we go through this place like we're after termites. When we're able to confirm the bombs are *not* here, well, then you people know best what to do outside the gates of my space center."

He'd said "*my*" space center. He judged the matter

strictly from the immediate local level. Which might make the best sense of all. Hudoff didn't know. He might never know what was wisest. But this input might show him the way.

Coke Stevens cleared his throat when Hudoff nodded to him. "You people know my position," he said to open his remarks. "It's most unusual for me to participate in this sort of discussion. Usually I observe, I judge, and I pass on information. Sometimes, when I'm asked for them, I add my recommendations." He paused to look about the table. "I really don't know what the hell to say. I don't know what I'm *supposed* to say. This entire affair scares the bejesus out of me. I must restrict my expertise to what I know, and that is the executive office. My recommendations to the President will be," and he smiled as he realized he was contradicting his own words, "whether or not I'm asked for them, that no member of the executive branch of our government come within a hundred miles of this place until it is absolutely guaranteed safe."

He deferred to the next man in line. Arthur Low of the FBI was someone Hudoff wished wasn't even in the room. Mr. Paranoia could throw a monkey wrench into everything. He had a direct line to the director of the Bureau.

But now he surprised the hell out of Bernie Hudoff. "We can't knuckle under to terrorists," he said slowly. "That's a basic premise. We also can't be foolish enough to ignore what's real. They've got the bombs. What we've determined so far promises us a lot of trouble and perhaps even a horrifying catastrophe. I agree with much of what I've heard. My own position is not quite to shut down the space center, as Lieutenant Elliott feels, but to reduce operations to a volunteer-only skeleton crew. That goes for Kennedy, Canaveral, *and* the entire port area. Proceed from there on a step-by-step basis and make your decisions one day at a time. I'm aware that that seems to be, if not cautious, yielding to the threat. I can hardly imagine anything so devastating as four nuclear weapons out there ready to go off at any time. I look on these terrorists as mad dogs. That means anything can happen. We've dealt with mad dogs before, but they could never harm more than a very small number of people. I . . . I just don't know. I've recommended to the Director that we absolutely saturate the area involved with special agents and that we reduce to its minimum the danger to anyone not necessary to the search."

A heavy silence followed his words. Joe Horvath motioned for the floor and offered a general question. "Arthur, what about—"

Hudoff didn't let him complete the question. "I'm sorry. *No discussion at this time.* I made that clear. If anyone here can't accept that condition, step aside." He motioned to the next chair in line. "Roger Coats, CIA?"

Coats was a hell of a lot more confident than those people preceding him. "First of all," he said in a voice that boomed across the table, "we do *not* know who these terrorists are. We are working under a variety of suppositions. Not a single one can be counted on to be accurate. In our business we assume nothing. All we know is *what has happened.* Everything else is *might* or *could* happen. You've been told the terrorist group we're facing is called Zoboa. Maybe it is, maybe it isn't. *It could be anybody.* It's not our province to get into protocol or diplomatic areas. We may be dealing with a bunch of crazies who are using this whole threat against the Cape and the shuttle as a smokescreen *with a completely different target in mind.* It may not be political positioning they're after. It could be a straight money deal to sell those bombs. I have something less than kind words to say about the internal security system that let those bombs be snatched the way they were. In *our* world it was like grabbing candy from a child. All right, that's not the issue here. But our office is *not* going to be pushed or prodded into making any recommendations of the sort Mr. Hudoff is asking for until we have better information to go by. I abstain from an official proposal."

Bang; he was through. But his effect was disturbing and it went through the room like ripples from a rock dropped into a silent pond. Hudoff showed no emotion. Not the time or place. "Colonel Virgil Padgett, please?"

"I represent the United States Army," Padgett said. He sat stiffly in his seat, starched like a board of green lumber right out of the sawmill. "We're in a, well, a compromising position. We're minor tenants at the Cape with missile tests like the Pershing series. In essence, we must perform within many other requirements. I didn't mean a recital of our position, but it *does* color our attitude. I have been told, officially, to *stay out* of whatever operations are under way to regain the nuclear devices. Unless we're asked. No one has asked for our participation. I know little about what's happened. Under these circumstances, until and unless we're briefed fully as to all the ramifications involved, we cannot and we will not be badgered into making recommendations that—"

Hudoff almost lost his cool. "Colonel, I said to forego the political claptrap. Plain English, please. Are you going through that whole speech to say you have no comment?"

Padgett sat like a robot. "Yes, sir, I am."

"Okay, you've said it. You're out of this entire affair." With those few words Hudoff completely dismissed the prissy martinet and went on to his naval counterpart. "Commander Arvil Tilson: you represent Navy *and* Coast Guard, sir?"

Tilson was the first person at the table to rise to his feet before he spoke. He was a junior officer in terms of time in grade to the other military people in the room. That obviously didn't bother him personally, but he recognized that an inference might be drawn that could be detrimental to his Navy representation. "I'm not able to speak in terms of your measures to try to discover the missing weapons. Everyone I've heard speak here has validity to their remarks. The Navy doesn't launch from here like Army, Air Force, and NASA. We take our problems out to sea. The best I can tell you is *what we are doing* about all this. First, we're removing anyone and everyone from naval and coast guard installations not absolutely necessary to running our stations.

We will move all our nuclear subs from the Poseidon and Trident areas to sea station or reassignment to another base until this issue is clarified. We have asked for volunteers to join the ranks of Mr. Hudoff's security forces to provide all the help we can. We have weapons and electronics people at his service. Other than that, and speaking personally, I feel you are all making a terrible mistake in exposing civilians to a possible nuclear blast. Anyone not in military or government service should be removed at once from the installations involved here."

Colonel Padgett got in his question before Hudoff could stop him. "Commander, are *you* one of those people staying here?"

Tilson's smile was sad. "Yes, sir. I'm staying, although I admit I hate myself for it. For the record, however, I have already sent my wife and child from here back home to Montana."

Hudoff made a mental note to thank Tilson later for keeping his response brief and not allowing that prissy asshole from the Army a chance to turn the meeting into a sewing circle. He tapped the table for attention, and motioned toward Galenko. "I don't know how many of you people know this man. His name is Vladislov Galenko. He has been assigned by the Soviet government as the security coordinator for Cosmonaut Georgi Mikoyan, who is to fly aboard *Antares*. He has full clearance from the American government to participate in *all* security matters. For those of you who've heard rumors to the effect that Mr. Galenko is a member of the KGB, let me say that the rumors mean nothing. He *is* a member of the KGB, which means we are now represented in this room by the KGB, CIA, NSA, FBI, Secret Service, and quite likely other organizations of which even *I* am unawares. I value his opinions highly. I suggest you consider carefully what he has to say."

Galenko made a steeple of his thick fingers and peered over them slowly until he had made eye contact with everyone in the room. "So!" he said at last. "Certain things emerge. Your CIA spook is absolutely right. We have only theory to go by, rumors to guide us, as to *who* has bombs. Also, he is right when he says they may be far gone from here by now." Galenko smiled. "Even if he did not say that he was thinking, same thing. But you cannot accept what he says and be complacent. That is the word, I think. The danger is most real. I do not want to be preten—no, the word is presumptuous. My look at security is different from yours. My methods are different."

Again there was an interruption, but Hudoff wouldn't have stopped this one even if he knew it were coming. Irene Bellmaster signalled for attention to Galenko. "Mr. Galenko, my apologies for breaking in. I must ask this question."

He nodded, a bearish acceptance.

"If you were in the position of Mr. Hudoff, sir, what specifically would you do?"

Galenko smiled and then boomed with laughter. "You really want me to say this?"

She nodded. "Please."

"All rights, then. First, there would never be stupid meeting like this. Whole idea of democratic committee to meet terrible emergency is crazy! *It is insane!* The time to talk is later. Me? There would be nobody left in towns around here. *Nobody.* Why do you think Tyuratam and other places are so isolated? Why do you think Baikonur is a hundred miles from the launch pads? Ah, but I digress. *Everybody except the most trusted people out of all the launch installations.* I would have dogs everywhere. I would have strangers who do not know one another always watching one another. We are talking about killing tens of thousands of people and destroying whole space complex that costs billions and billions of rubles! Forget your guests. Forget the presidents and the poets and the popes and the princes and the philosophers. They can watch from hotel rooms on television! Why you people . . ." He wiped his brow. "I apologize, madam. I give you short answer. Clear everybody the hell out of space place *now*. Consider everybody a danger. Start clean and fresh, like Ivory flakes, like your television says." He had a gleam in his eye. "You have another saying. This will piss off the pope, maybe, but that morning when you wake up you will still have spaceport and not smoking hole in ground!"

Hudoff didn't give anyone a chance to comment. "I want you all to hear from Mario del Passo. I've explained his special relationship to us here. Consider his remarks as resulting from his position with Interpol, and *not* as a representative of the government of Portugal. Also, anything you hear from Mister del Passo is off the record. You will be called a liar if you even refer to his presence here. Mario, if you please."

"You have heard more than enough." Del Passo assumed the posture of a strict schoolmaster. "I will not explain what is unexplainable. First, this group called Zoboa is real. It is definitely an Arab-supported terrorist group, very well financed, very powerful. They *do* operate in this area. If they have the bombs, that is not yet confirmed. If they are the group that has the bombs and they intend to use them here, you will have no advance warning. No ransom, no blackmail. Only the bombs when they are ready."

He took time to light one of his special British cigarettes. "Since my last meeting here, I have followed through on several other matters. Mr. Coats, I believe, suggested that an Israeli group of intense fanatic might be behind the hijacking of the bombs and their use. I do not believe this to be so. But so you will understand, my contacts in Mossad are beyond any question. Mossad is in charge of all espionage and security outside the borders of Israel. Then, as Mr. Low will appreciate, there is Shin-Beth. It is the Jewish equivalent of the FBI and it deals with counterspy and security operations within Israel. It is completely divorced from anything to do with your situation here. We must also consider that Mossad has SOD, its Special Operations Division. This is the finest intelligence group in the world. It operates anywhere in the world. They are beyond suspicion. Mossad, in fact, will be sending three of their best men here to work with Mr. Hudoff. Finally, in respect to the Israelis, we considered that fanatic group known as King David. You may eliminate them from your thinking. They are ultraright, somewhere on the side of Genghis Khan, I should say." He smiled briefly. "But they are almost wholly supported by American funding. And, as you say with great wisdom in America, money talks."

He took a deep breath and sighed. "Even the most radical of the Arab governments will not work with this Zoboa group. Even the Arabs who are wholly dedicated to Jihad, their Holy War, would not participate against America as we believe Zoboa does. Not even Libya is that insane. I fear Zoboa is real, that it will attempt to strike as you have been led to believe, against a launch when *Antares* is released."

Coke Stevens glanced at Hudoff. "I apologize, sir, but this is critical." He turned back to del Passo. "If I could take a message from you to our President, Mister del Passo, what would it be?"

Mario del Passo shook his head slowly. "It is brief, Mr. Stevens. Change my name from Mario del Passo to Vladislov Galenko but change nothing he said. Are you prepared for wholesale arrests? Are your cherished civil rights, with which I agree and for which we recently fought in my country, above all considerations for the slaughter of hundreds of thousands of women and children? Is martial law beyond your consideration? Are you prepared when you find terrorists to hang them or shoot them on the spot, in public executions? *Because you must!* This is not a new age, Mr. Stevens. You are living on a new planet. Adapt, or what happens here will be just the beginning of a whole new wave of terror. America, my friend, is like the shark that terrorizes the sea but is prey itself to the remora. And the remora, like the terrorist, is a filthy leach and bloodsucker. I have had my say. Please, in deference to what Mr. Hudoff must do, ask me no more."

The wall about del Passo snapped into place with an almost audible bang. Hudoff let the murmurs about the table rise and fall like the tide and then he banged his knuckles on the table. "There are two more people I wish to have their say. We have two people with a much more personal, even intimate, concern with this issue. Sheriff Bob Hughes is the head of the sheriff's department in Brevard County, and by his side is Markham Powell, special assistant to Governor Kermit Bellamy of Florida."

Powell motioned to the man by his side. "Sheriff Hughes will speak for both of us, Mr. Hudoff. Before he does, I am going on record by noting that you have truly given us an agonizing situation with which to deal. Bob? Go ahead, please."

Hughes had had plenty of time to reach this moment. Hudoff knew the sheriff was way out in left field with this kind of power. He had given Hughes as much time as possible, and he knew the man by now was with it. "What I got to do is make a decision," Hughes said in a rasping voice and a southern drawl. "I got to decide whether or not to mess up the lives of a lot of people. I got civil defense plans in case of a hurricane to evacuate the whole coast of this county. We're ahead of the game there. But is this what we're going to do? How many more times do we hear about the bomb and then evacuate most of this county? Where do we put the people? After the second or the fifth time, most people won't go. Do we drive them out of their homes at the point of a gun? Of course not," he answered his own question. "So I got to gamble. With their lives and with mine. I been listening *so* careful to everything you say."

He looked around him at a group of people who were strangers and would always remain so. They didn't operate on his level. They never mentioned racial or ethnic groups, or babies, or criminals, or God knows *anything* to do with the real, everyday world. These people might as well be from Mars. "I'm not giving in," he said finally. "I just ain't going to do that to my people. Because there ain't no end to it. And there ain't no use in running like a whipped puppy with his tail up between his legs. We are not going to say one damn word about evacuation. Nobody here, which I've now found out, has the guts or the authority to order it. That's copping out. You're not going to do it to us. If that bomb goes off, I'll be here with my people, who elected me sheriff to protect them. They die, I die. But

241

I'll tell you this. If that happens, you're the people what killed them *because you couldn't do your jobs.*"

He rose to his feet and picked up his Stetson with the gold star on its front. "Let's go, man," he said to Powell, "there's nothing left for us here. I guess they can always send the governor a memorandum, for all the good that will do."

The two men walked about the side of the table and went to the door that would let them out into the main hall. Hughes grasped the handle and was hit with a blast of rock music that shook the conference room. Heads turned and stared at a tall black man with a red bandana knotted about his head, gold chains about his neck, a gleaming diamond hanging from one ear, a torn shirt, and, balanced on one shoulder, a pearl-covered radio. He did a double-take at sight of the sheriff's uniform, badge, and gun, snapped off the radio, slid sideways into the conference room, zig-zagging and rocking to the music still echoing about the walls. He slouched before the stunned Hudoff.

Colonel Hank Rawls, USAF, winked at the NASA security chief. "Hey, baby, wha's happenin', man? Huh, man? I jes' come from *the* party, baby. We done hooked up and we is in the *groove!*"

Hudoff stabbed a finger at Lou Elliott. "Get this crazy son of a bitch out of here!" he shouted, his face contorted with anger. Behind his scowl he was smiling. Rawls and Bannon had done it. They'd equipped every one of his old warbirds with the radio trackers to search for the missing atomic bombs.

Mitch Bannon didn't make the meeting in Hudoff's office. Nor did his name come up. He'd spent several hours with Lars Anderson and a few Air Force technicians going over the Tracker receivers preset to the beeper signals of the Tattlers aboard the missing nukes. Then they called Charley and she got her office group together, and they brought in von Strasser, and within two hours they had the pilots of every plane on the line at Shiloh for their briefings on what the Trackers were for and how they were to be used. That didn't take long.

When the briefings were over, the pilots looked at one another, agreed it would be a shame to waste the effort in getting to the field and, since the weather couldn't have been too much worse, they did what all sensible people do under those conditions.

Instant party.

Bannon left Rawls in the hangar with three dark-skinned beauties he'd gathered for his role as one more strung-out surfer bum joining the party for kicks. Bannon had his own jungle into which he would slip to do some tracking on his own. He went to a sealed-off room behind a false wall in his hangar and locked the door behind him. When he emerged ten minutes later, his best friend likely wouldn't have known him. His nostrils flared from small gold rings expertly placed well within his nose. A sloppy blond moustache and a wig of filthy blond hair adorned his head. He had two gold caps flaring from his mouth and he was smoking home-rolled cigarettes. Their tobacco was from Indian Lion packages which looked like, burned like, and smelled exactly like strong marijuana, but contained not the first trace of the THC hallucinogen. His clothes were suede and silk and gold chains and the accepted paraphernalia of the nether drug culture infesting the beach communities. Either walking or seated in the big Lincoln Continental reserved for such forays, no one could detect the flat .32 automatic with highvel cutting ammo in the holster taped under his arm, or the spring-loaded boot knife in his lizard-skin decorations. He had other goodies from his former trade. Piano wire strung in his belt. A buckle elaborately decorated to look like a derringer. It *was* a derringer—Magnum .22 with two rounds. He also had some special equipment loaded onto his body and his gear strapped tightly to his frame.

He took the back roads out of Shiloh and went south on I-95 to the 520 highway leading east into Cocoa. He drove through slowly. The blacks and Cubans knew his car. They knew every delivery vehicle in the business. They'd pass the word on down the line that Skyking was on the move. He took the high bridge east to Merritt Island and turned into a Fina gas station, slipped behind the garage, and went down a dirt path to pick up Tropical Trail where no one would see him come onto it. He studied his watch. He had exactly fifteen minutes for the special job, he'd cover his presence with a pot dropoff, and be on his way again.

It took exactly fifteen minutes, and soon he turned off 520 onto A1A amidst the high-rise condos, shopping centers, and cheaper old houses from the old days of missile glory. He cruised down A1A with the Lincoln's stereo shaking the big car.

He almost had Hank Rawls with him for company. The hidden background of the Air Force colonel had stunned Bannon. Rawls could be the stiff-upper-lip prick in uniform, or a hard-rocking, with-it knuckle-busting guide through whatever native quarter you hit. "My daddy was an undercover man," he explained to Bannon. "I grew up in two worlds. The old man would take me with him on his surveillance runs. He figured no one would pay much attention to a nigger wino and his snotty kid riding with him and he was right. You might say I learned the business right up front. It's what kept all us kids in our family off the shit. Pop made sure we saw the worst cases from the junkies. He'd drag us down to the street people and where they lived and then he'd take us to the lockups where they'd be screaming and puking and soiling themselves, screaming like all the devils of hell were stabbing them in the belly and their balls and in their eyes, which, of course, they were."

"The street's a long way from the blue suit," Bannon noted.

"Pop had connections. He was more than a hell of a cop. He kept a couple of kids from very influential families out of the slammer *and* the newspapers. He told their parents he wanted a payback. No money, no job influence. 'Get my kid into the Air Force Academy,' he told them. Then he told me I had to pass the entrance exams on my own or else."

"Or else what?"

"Or else I was going to be a crippled nigger kid with a busted head and he was going to attend to it personally." Rawls laughed. "I made it. I went through it real slick and majored in counter-intelligence and criminal investigation. I was a natural for that, of course. I never expected to be in Saigon doing that sort of shit, but I did. In a way that paid off. It took a month to scrub *that* stink off me, and when I got back I went into long training on the terrorist programs. The people in the Puzzle Palace figured rightly that with my super tan and my upbringing I'd be perfect for CID work. Here I am."

"You are making me feel much better," Bannon told him bluntly. "I couldn't figure that almost-smart college nigger routine you were waving around in Hudoff's office. It didn't fit. You walk too much like you've been down alleys and side streets."

Rawls laughed. "You hit the nail square, Bannon. You used the right words. The key in the white man's world, especially high government, is to be an *almost-*smart college nigger. You can be a genius and then they don't care if you got green skin and three nuts, or you can be *almost* as good as them. But never be equal to the top boys. Be almost as good or even better, but that equal shit really don't cut it." He studied Bannon in a new light. "Why all the sudden interest in me?"

Bannon sighed. "Because we've been missing a bet, Hank. Look, let's assume this Zoboa outfit is for real." Rawls nodded. "Now, except for a few Arab governments that really *are* freaked out, no one is going to back a group that will hurt the U.S. *so* badly that we'll get pissed off to the extreme and make mashed potatoes of wherever they call home. I learned something from an old-timer about what happened when the Japanese attacked Pearl Harbor back in 1941. He said that was about the dumbest damn thing the Japs could have done. They really didn't hurt us that badly, but they pissed off the whole country and made us look both stupid and helpless. He said that for the next four years the United States fought a war based solely on getting even. Territory didn't matter, money didn't mean a thing, but kicking the absolute shit out of the Japs was our real goal. And we did it. We beat them so badly we were almost apologetic for kicking them back into the last century. So what did we do? We dragged them back on their feet and—"

"And then *they* got even," Rawls laughed. "I got me a Toyota that's making my mechanic prematurely rich. Okay, I got your drift, beach bum. What follows?"

"If they have to squeeze support from the top paranoids of the Arab world, it means they've also got to produce a lot of their own money for operations. If Zoboa gets guns and stuff like that, it's not the same as having the bread to move around. What's the best way, the fastest way with the greatest return, for making a hell of a lot of money today?"

"Yeah, I get you," Rawls confirmed. "You run the happy stuff."

Bannon looked pained. "Please. *I* don't run that shit. I'm limited strictly to pot. Not much different from beer."

"Bannon, I *got* to ask. Where do you get the shit?"

"Would you believe DEA?"

"You really mean the *feds* are your supply?"

"Yep," Bannon said with a huge grin. "It even makes it legal that way. There's a government law that says the transportation of the stuff is legal so long as it's done by a city, county, state, or federal government agency. I never use the shit myself, so I'm not involved that way. Besides, the local law has been told just enough to keep hands off."

"Do you give it away?"

"Hell, no. Then I'd *really* be crazy. I sell cheaper than anyone else and I give credit everywhere. It's the same, I guess, as giving it away, but with one very important exception."

"I can figure that one," Rawls said. "They owe you."

"Yeah. And maybe tonight I can start collecting. I'm going downtown. The kids themselves don't know enough for me to lean on them, but the local dealers, they know who the big runners and the shippers are. I'm talking coke, horse; the heavy stuff where the big money lies. It's mostly in coke because it's the easiest to get for the high numbers."

246

"And you're going for the tie-in to what might just be a bunch from the world where there's a lot of sand and oil."

"You got it, brother. You're staying here?"

"Yeah. I'll mix with the turkeys out there, maybe do a tap-dance routine with that Wilbur kid, because he *is* way out, know what I mean, Sam? He hears the beat, it's in his blood, and that will make us bros."

Bannon laughed. "How late you want me to call?"

"If you live through the night, call me anytime. I'm the curious type."

He parked well in the back of The Pit, making sure the Lincoln had a straight shot for getting away. He set up his own Swiftlock. He locked the doors, but a single tap of a pressure point on the roof would unlocked both. No slowing down when he needed to make fast tracks. The same for the ignition. Pressure on an exact point of the steering column would start the car. Bannon never forgot those days of long ago when killing other people was the *only* way to keep from getting the deep six yourself.

The Pit was appropriately named. Clever bastards the way they designed it. You walked in, around a high bar, and then down into a huge pit with deep seats, cushions, low tables; the works. Around the outer rim of the pit the wood swirled away in deep recesses so that while you remained below ground level you had your privacy if you wanted to pay for it. *But you couldn't get out of the place in a hurry.* If you wanted out fast you had to run the gauntlet: fight *up* to the high ground and then get around that circular bar to make it to a doorway. So if you were inside and you got fingered for the wrong kind of people, they had you very tight . . . and you were at the bottom of the well with everyone else looking down.

Of course, there were ways to cut those odds. You could always kill whoever was in front of you and the rest would melt away fast. Bannon shrugged to himself. It had been a long time since he'd had to do that, but like riding a bicycle, you don't forget easily.

He wanted one person tonight. No big dealer, no special wheeler, no hot-rock coke jockey with a retinue of eager young snatches fighting for the right to blow him so they could get their expensive fixes for no more than an expert routine with lips and tongue. That was the trademark of Jackie Starr. Only Jackie Starr was a woman, and *her* retinue was of kids from ten to thirteen years old who were hooked beyond all redemption. They would do anything for Jackie because she kept them free of pain and agony and horror and nightmares. Jackie owned The Pit, and a whole line of pushers along the coast, from Sebastian Inlet on up to Port Canaveral. She was as twisted and sick as a gnarled hickory limb. Her mind had rotted years before from her own poisons, and yet she commanded a fortune in money and kept a small army to attend to her wants and be available to protect her. She was also, from her viewpoint, invincible. She had her little girls, and she got what she wanted from them. Naked little piglets or squirming pink puppies crowding about her crotch with wet lips and tongues flashing, fighting to get to the rot she accommodated between her legs. That's what she lived for. That's all she cared about. What Bannon knew that Jackie Starr didn't was that the first chance many of her protectors had to kill her, they would. What kept them from closing the books on Jackie Starr was that they didn't know where she kept her records, with their names, their deals, their crimes. Even if she were killed the records would surface. They'd buy it right in the neck.

Mitch Bannon knew where the books were. He'd known for a long time. He'd done a few favors himself. Where Starr dealt in mind and body rot with her drugs, Bannon had paved the way and smoothed some bumpy surfaces for the heavy gun runners: the Cubans he'd known in the past still living with their dreams of recapturing their homeland; even agents for the IRA, here to work with the Cubans for their own weapons. There were plenty of them. Bannon lacked the hard circle of drug runners and dealers, but he had a lesser number of people with firepower and he knew he could count on them.

He had planned on taking out Jackie Starr the right

way. Through the law. By the book. Clean and neat and no mistakes for lawyers to jump through later on technicalities. He knew when he left the airport tonight he couldn't do that.

Time had run out. Bannon never believed in the fine art of discussion, especially not when you faced four atomic bombs about to come down on a few hundred thousand people. That wasn't merely stupid; it was insane. Hudoff *had* to work through the system. He worked under a magnifying glass. And the rest of them: Coats, Low, Stevens, all of them, were so entrenched in the system they wouldn't step over the line even if they saw the bomb falling. So he detoured on the way from Shiloh into Cocoa Beach and The Pit. He drove onto Merritt Island and turned south along Tropical Trail to a big house on stilts at the end of a long dock. Jackie Starr owned it. She kept two men here at all times and a couple of dogs who'd grown fat chewing on people.

Bannon was going out on that dock right to those dogs and those two men, because somewhere in that big house were the books that Jackie Starr used to keep control over so many people. Bannon was going over the line. He was busting the rules. He couldn't take Hank Rawls because if he screwed up Hank would take the big fall with him. Besides—and he smiled with the thought—the *bad* man doesn't want anyone else along. He parked brazenly in front of the long dock, checked his equipment, took a long breath, and started down the dock. Right past the signs that read KEEP OUT! and BAD DOGS! and NO TRESPASSING! and the rest of that shit. He carried some very special equipment with him.

The dock wasn't just long; it was narrow. Two dobermans came at him like hounds out of hell, jaws wide, teeth white even in the night gloom. Bannon let them get about twenty feet away and he judged their speed carefully, and brought up the short-barreled shotgun he'd modified a long time ago for moments just like these. An intense flame burst forth with a loud *pop!* and the dobermans raced into a ball of fire that covered the entire dock. They were going too fast to stop and ran into the flaming sphere that was still spitting out big globs of blazing white phosphorus. Not even the most savage doberman can ignore flames in his eyes and nose and scorching down his throat, and then a thousand devils began tearing at the animals' skin and heads with fiery talons. The dogs screamed. They scream worse than a damned woman, and the dogs were burning alive and hurling themselves into the air, biting at their own flanks madly as the phosphorus stabbed deep into their blazing flesh. They whirled crazily off the dock into the water, *where they continued to burn*. Those parts of their bodies under water had relief. Their heads had sticky globs of white phosphorus and those continued to burn in the air. The animals, now insane with their pain, struggled to the shore and climbed onto land, where they burst into flames again as air reached the phosphorus. Howling madly, they raced away between houses. That would keep a lot of people busy, and the sheriff's deputies and fire departments would be answering hundreds of calls from people reporting the burning hounds of hell screaming through their neighborhoods.

Bannon dismissed all this from his thoughts; as the dogs spun away from him he was already crouched low and running toward the house. The two guards dashed out to the entrance steps, staring in disbelief at the flailing, burning dogs in the water. Bannon had already gone flat and he had a long-barreled .22 Magnum in his hands. No bullets. Hell, he wasn't going to kill them. He'd let them do that to themselves, but a bit later. He held the Magnum in both hands and squeezed off one round and knew he'd hit his man, and a split second later he'd fired again and the second guard took a slim frangible plastic needle into his body.

Bannon rose casually, brushed himself off, and walked up to the two men staring at him with the glassy eyes of absolute shock. Small wonder. A man takes even the tiniest dose of etorphin diluted down to the proper dosage, and that's all she wrote. Etorphin is an opiate known to few people and available to a tiny elite. It's the most potent mind-altering drug in the world, with literally ten thousand times the pain-killing properties of pure morphine. A tiny drop at the end of a dart fired into a rampaging elephant will knock the animal unconscious before it takes another step and likely will kill him. In tremendously diluted form, injected into a human being, it turns him instantly into a mindless robot who must, who absolutely *must*, obey whatever orders he hears.

Bannon stopped by the two zombies. "Throw your guns into the water," he told them. The guns splashed and disappeared. "Go inside. Disconnect all alarms and communications systems. Cut the phone lines. Disconnect all security and protective devices. Do it quickly and contact no one. Take no orders from anyone but me. Do it."

He went inside at a slow stroll, taking in everything with practiced eyes. Several minutes later the two men returned. "The ledger book Jackie Starr keeps. Where is it?"

"The fountain. It's hollow. The ledger is in there."

"Get it. Bring it to me."

He watched them work the handles of the ornate fountain in the huge living room. The water shut off, a door slid open, and moments later they handed him a thin leatherbound volume. He glanced at it a moment, nodded to himself, and slipped it inside the body armor vest he wore beneath his clothes.

"Do you have gasoline for the speedboats in the back?"

"Yes, sir."

"Bring up two cans. Quickly."

They came back with two five-gallon cans of gasoline. "Start along that wall," he ordered. "Spread the gasoline around the entire room. Get it on the drapes and the walls and then pour the rest of it on the floor."

That took just under three minutes. "Do you have a cigarette lighter?" he asked. Both men nodded. "When you see me walk out the front door, start counting aloud," he instructed. "When you reach one hundred, both of you take out your lighters, light them, and set the drapes on fire." He paused. "We're going to redecorate and this is how we clean up first. When the fire starts, sit down on the floor and watch it. Do not leave. You understand?"

"Yes, sir."

He turned around and left, walking steadily but without visible haste to the Lincoln, unlocked the car, got inside, started up, and drove away. He took a corner slowly four blocks distant and looked in his rearview mirror. The ball of flame climbed at least a hundred feet above the rooftops. *Two zombies cooked*, he smiled to himself.

The first half of his job for the night was finished. Now came the part he knew he would enjoy.

He moved slowly through the smoke and the noise and laughter, the shrillness underlying the musical gaiety of The Pit. His first move was to check out the muscle in the place. He recognized Bulldog and the Snake. He saw Hydra and Thor. They never used their own names. No one ever knew them by any other name. No one except Jackie Starr, that is. She owned them. A bunch of kids recognized Bannon and he received waves and hellos, half of them with their minds blasted into the middle of next month. The smoke and stink of the candles and incense, the stale beer, the pot and urine from kids who were too smashed even to remember to get up to relieve themselves in a bathroom. It was like moving in slow motion through an old Chinese opium den. He picked up on the undercurrent. There had been big business transacted with Jackie Starr recently. He knew it was coming through. A hell of a shipment of coke and heroin. She'd latch on to more than the coastline business. Now she could branch out into the Orlando area and even hit Daytona Beach farther north. Bannon didn't care about any of that.

He wanted to know who brought in the shipment. *Who was supplying Jackie Starr?* Because he'd had hints, subtle innuendos from a dozen sources. Some really big shit was coming through. They were all going to be in Nirvana. Valhalla beckoned; they'd soar through the halls of Asgard on steeds of the finest dust and powder man had ever produced. The supplier was new.

The very word *new* triggered Mitch Bannon's alarm bells from all sides. You didn't come into the delivery

252

business in one single whack without paying the tariff through your nose and up your ass. It was more than rolling in the stuff and in the payoff. It took time and patience and skills, it took extortion and blackmail and payoffs developed to a fine art to build the protective wall. Jackie Starr had all that. So if someone was being permitted to move in, they were paying a hell of a price.

Bannon wanted to know who they were. If all his past experience and his deep-rooted knowledge and his knowing this scene meant anything, then the payoff was the reverse of what you'd expect. To get heavy money, the new supplier would have to triple or even quadruple his quantity of goods without an increase in price over a regular shipment. If he brought in three or four million bucks' worth, he wouldn't find that in his paycheck. He'd get two bits on the buck: a mil for four times' worth that much. *You did that when you needed the money fast. You did that when you needed the money to fund operations that you didn't want anyone else to see.*

He stopped at the bar. This made the hovel legal. Jackie had a license and she served straight, good stuff that let her play her games. Bannon sat at the bar and sipped at tequila straight and took it all in, and he caught a glimpse of naked legs and buttocks through a curtain opened briefly and closed again. Muffled thumps and squeals and groans of pleasure from behind the curtain told him that Jackie Starr had made her hit and was now reaping her reward.

Bulldog slid up to the bar. They'd named him aptly. He had nothing between a massive bullet head and huge shoulders. Not even a trace of a neck. Four hundred pounds if he went an ounce. Used to be a pro wrestler. Bouncer. Muscle man. God knew what else. But that was all *used* to be. Bannon had run some very thorough checks on every animal in this sty. Bulldog didn't fit the mold. He had three kids and a wife and an ailing mother on a farm in Nebraska, and he sent them every dime he could and he wanted nothing more in this world than to get the hell out of here and work the farm. If he went one mile beyond the town limits, Jackie Starr would drop a package of information on Bulldog right in the lap of the drug enforcement crowd, and Bulldog would go up forever.

"You sightseeing, Bannon?" The huge human animal was pleasant enough. Why not? Bannon had never done him any wrong, and he was on the right side of the Dragon Lady.

Bannon shook his head. He half turned to make certain he had solid eye contact with Bulldog. "No. It's the millennium. The second coming. Time to get out from under before the world ends."

"You on the shit, Bannon?" Bulldog screwed up his pink features until he looked like a giant pink bowling ball as he studied Bannon.

"Nope. My head rings inside like Tinker Bell taking a leak on a chandelier. It's time, that's all, friend. Time."

"I think you're over the edge, Bannon."

"Think away." Bannon gestured. "The Dragon Lady has her retinue of nymphs down in the beaver pond, I see."

"We don't talk about that." An ominous tone rumbled upward from Bulldog's barrel chest.

"She closed her deal." Bulldog gaped at him. "I want to know who brought in the stuff."

"Man, you *are* crazy," Bulldog hissed. "I could kill you for—"

"Do you know who I am, Bulldog?"

"Course I know, you dumb shit!"

Bannon edged closer. "No, you don't know." He smiled and the air seemed to chill. "Bulldog, you ever play with silly putty?"

"*What?*"

"A lot of stuff looks like silly putty. You ever use plastique?"

Bulldog edged back a hair. "What the fuck are you trying to tell me, Bannon?"

"I'm wired, Bulldog."

"You're fucking strung up, you mean. You—"

"Shut up. Come closer. You open my jacket, very slowly, very carefully, *very gently*. Tell me what you see."

The big man leaned closer, eased open the jacket and his pink complexion paled. "God . . ."

"You'll meet him if you fuck with me," Bannon said quietly. "That's eight pounds of RDX Nine, Bulldog. If I squeeze what's in my other hand, mister, that eight pounds goes off. You can count on two blocks going. There won't be a toenail left to send home for memorial services to your kids on the farm."

"What the hell do you want?"

"Who delivered to the lady pig?"

"I can't—"

"Yes, you can. If you don't you're going to be very dead."

"So will you, you asshole."

"Yeah, but I already made out my will. I'm running out of time and I'm losing patience. Besides, I got something to bargain."

"Like fucking what, Bannon?" Bulldog was ugly and mean and wanting to hurt or kill Bannon, but he didn't dare move.

"I got your ticket out of here. That goes for Hydra and Snake and Thor. You deal with me and you all leave here in a few minutes and you never come back."

"Now I know you've lost your marbles. You know what she's got—"

"The dogs are dead."

"What?"

"So are Mike and Tony. *Very* dead." Bannon smiled. "They are fricasseed, roasted, basted, cooked to a fare-thee-well."

"Bannon, she'll—"

"I have the ledger, Bulldog. I'm wearing body armor. It's under the armor. Your ticket home to your family is under the armor. But there's eight pounds of RDX Nine between you and that ledger."

"What do you want?"

"I told you."

"A flight came in a couple nights ago."

"Where?"

"I don't know. It was long range. That's all I know,

255

man, and that's on the level. The word is out it's the biggest deal ever."

"Where did it come from?"

"Shit, I don't know that. I know they got past that fucking radar balloon somehow. You know, it was shut down for a while, and when the plane came through, it started working again."

That figures, Bannon told himself. "What about the other guys?"

"They know less than I do."

"You trust me, Bull?"

"Looks like I got to, with that silly putty you're wearing."

"If you ever trusted anyone in your whole life, trust me now. I want ten minutes in here without interruption. I want you and the rest of the circus people—Hydra, Thor, and Snake—outside. You don't let no one in. You close the goddamn doors. Ten minutes, that's all. Have your car ready. When I come out, I hand you the ledger. You're gone."

"That ain't good enough. She got a memory like a fucking computer."

"She won't for long. Yes or no. I'm out of time and I'm feeling suicidal."

"If you don't come out in ten?"

"Then I advise you to come back in and do everything you can to kill me."

"I will."

"No. You'll *try.* You'll never do it. Not you, not the four of you. I told you, Bull, tonight I am death. If you're going, *go.*"

Bannon didn't move. From the corner of his eye he saw the mountain of flesh slip through a beaded curtain. Thor left the bar and two girls took his place. Bannon turned. They were gone. He waited a minute. No one came through the doors. *Holy Jesus Christ, it's working . . .*

He checked his equipment, and he started walking. Around the curving end of the bar, down the six steps into the Pit. He felt the rage coming on him with the sight of the slack faces of the teen-aged wrecks on all sides. Faces slack, sallow, eyes glazed, dumb, and blank, and every minute they spent in this place they destroyed another week or a month or a year from their lives. Even worse, their brains were frying, steaming, overheating, and many of them would never come back. Tomorrow's street people, the sleepers beneath the bridges, the paper-and-rags legion of the future. Never fear, America; *these* kids are no problem except to themselves. He couldn't help the flashes of memory of his own equivalent years. Work, fight, hammer, *do* things; that credo worked. *This* would disgust a pervert.

He hadn't gone twenty feet across the center of the Pit without being offered a dozen pieces of ass, blowjobs, gang bangs; anything and everything he wanted or might want. He was a runner, he had access to the goods, he was the man they loved and loved to love. And this was where he'd earned that fearsome reputation as an inexhaustible cocksmith. These kids would brag to one another and anyone else who'd listen, and the stories spread like oil on water, of how *they* took care of *the* man. Bannon knew if he'd performed only a tenth of the sexual feats attributed to him on the beach he'd be in a specimen jar in some Ripley museum.

He put all this from his mind. He forced himself to recognize that if everything came down wrong, then these same kids, and all the decent ones who weren't strung out like limp catgut as were these horrors, could well burn, or be torn to pieces, slashed and maimed by flying glass and exploding buildings. He thought of that monstrous fireball and a hundred and eighty million degrees and the nuclear radiation, and with those thoughts storming his mind he yanked aside the heavy drape to the large alcove and stepped within the snakepit.

The word was right. Snakes of pink and sallow white skin. Gaunt eyes and skinny breasts and skinny legs and ribs showing, and scraggly pubic hair and bony knees and faces desperately lost in some limbo. Kids twelve and fourteen years old with the faces of women sixty or ninety years old. The faces he'd seen in the films out of the concentration camps of a war fought before he was born; horror and surrender and hopelessness, made all the worse by the stupid, simpering, grisly smiles they offered him. Three of the girls, naked buttocks showing scars and burn marks from cigarettes, squirmed between the legs of Jackie Starr, the one they called the Dragon Lady. She wore a huge loose chiffon gown, thrown up about and over her head so she was naked from the waist down, and the three piglets squirmed and sucked and slobbered at what might have been a single wrinkled teat instead of the revolting pubis which they labored so fiercely to please.

Bannon felt the bile storming up his throat and he fought desperately not to throw up right where he stood. He gritted his teeth and leaned down with a sudden frightening savagery. First a leg, his powerful hand about an ankle, hauling the child into the air and throwing her aside onto the cushions spread about the floor. Another one by the arm, another by her hair, every one he could reach, throwing them aside. Some looked at him with surprise, others with fear, still others with faces blank and showing eyes so hollow you could almost see the emptiness within.

"Out! Get the hell out of here!" he yelled, shoving with his hands and boots. The stench! Oh, my God, the stink ... ! Foul and putrid and acid-like against his skin, burning his nostrils. Jackie Starr pushed down her dress and looked up, angry with the interruption of her pleasure. She tried to focus, shaking her head to clear the fog. It didn't work too well. Bannon knew she looked up at him through a drugged haze mixed with pleasurable stupor, and now the jangled feelings of interruption that absolutely should not have existed. She glanced about her. Her eyes widened as she realized she was alone with Bannon, and with that additional level of shock she recognized him more clearly.

"My boys will kill you." She said it calmly, as certain of that statement as day follows night.

Bannon nodded. "Maybe. Only you're going first."

She came up snarling, pure vicious she-cat of poison, long nails curved to rake his face. Bannon's body didn't move; it didn't *seem* to move. He curled his fingers not into a fist, but extended before his hand, and he snapped his arm so that the knuckles acted as an iron bar, ramming into her upper lip just beneath her nose. Most of her teeth broke free from the blow and pain stabbed through the drug numbness, and she flew back onto the pillows, blood gurgling from her mouth, her face white, her hands moving to feel what in God's name had happened to her. Bannon dropped to one knee and moved forward. His thumb and two fingers of his left hand reached to grasp the thick muscle by the small hollow along the side of her neck and he squeezed. He had tremendous strength, he had muscle, nerve, and sinew in that grip; and Jackie Starr in that moment was pinned as helpless as a bug stabbed onto a board. The pain was so great that her eyes flooded with tears, and she could only gurgle instead of scream.

"This is just the beginning," Bannon said, his voice flat, calm and terribly deadly. "You closed a delivery a few days ago, bitch. Who'd you buy from? Where were they from? I want names."

He released the pressure so she could speak, and her foot snapped up into his groin. He didn't try to avoid the kick. He wore a kevlar cup with heavy padding and he knew she couldn't hurt him, and he also knew the shock of kicking him in the balls without effect would play its part in their little drama. He reached down again, this time in the soft flesh beneath her armpit just at the top of the ribcage, and his big hand closed on flesh and muscle and he lifted her into the air, dangling like a rag doll. The pain was terrible and this time she screamed, shrill and piercing.

Heads turned beyond the drapes, but no one paid attention. They'd heard a lot of screaming from behind those drapes. They'd been hearing it for years. The Dragon Lady was a screamer when she came. The young girls attending her screamed when the Dragon Lady pinched their nipples or labia as hard as she could. The pleasure from inflicting that kind of pain sent her into orgasmic frenzies. But Bannon didn't have time for the full theatrics. He dropped her and reached for her throat, applying just enough pressure to keep her from screaming or choking. But she could talk.

259

"Who delivered to you?"

"I . . . I can't . . ."

To be effective, keep the pain moving about the body. Thumb and middle finger into the inside of the thigh, squeezing with the force of pliers. She twitched and spasmed crazily as the long muscle mashed beneath his grip.

"Oh, God, don't . . . No, no . . . I'll tell you, I'll . . ." She went limp and her head fell to one side. Bannon sighed. Shit; the trick was hardly new. He reached out again and grasped her left hand and broke her pinky in a sudden twisting motion. Her eyes flew open.

"It gets much worse. Talk."

Her eyes were almost pink from the pain. Her mouth spewed blood and she felt stabbed with white-hot pokers from head to foot.

"Abdullah . . ." She gasped.

"The full name. Where'd they come from?"

She struggled to speak. "Abdullah . . . name is . . . Sulaiman . . . don't know . . . where . . . I'll . . . kill you . . ."

"Where?" he repeated.

She spit bloody drool in his face. He didn't flinch. "Kill me, you fucker!" She snarled as would an animal, her face contorted. He recognized madness when he saw it. He'd seen it before. Son of a bitch. He'd crapped out. And he couldn't leave her to talk. What the hell.

He reached into his inside pocket and withdrew a small metal atomizer. He slipped his hand beneath her dress and pressed down on the atomizer. A slight hissing sound. That was all. The combination of hydrochloric acid and fifty percent glucose solution sprayed her vaginal area. He might as well have sprayed burning gasoline on her. The acid turned her vagina into flaming agony, and the glucose at so high a solution swelled her labia and clitoris like a gas bomb going off beneath the skin. As he expected, her hands flew to her groin and her mouth gasped open. He sprayed a shot into her wide-open mouth. She twisted violently and tried to scream as agony seared her between her legs and in her mouth, but the glucose worked too quickly and her tongue was already several times its normal size. He replaced the atomizer, rose to his feet, and pushed the drapes aside to leave. As he was about to climb the steps, he turned. Every eye in the room was on him. He needed that. He *must* have these people see Jackie Starr *alive* after he was gone.

"She's OD'ing," he announced, gesturing to the concealed alcove. "Angel dust, I guess. Take care of her." He was just through the doorway when they reached her, her mouth foaming, her hands tearing the skin away from her vagina in bloody chunks. She'd be dead in a minute or two. No one in the place had enough sense to slice open her throat to get air past the passages swollen tight from her massive tongue.

Outside, he took one step forward and then ran sideways into the shadows of the building, the .32 automatic in his hand with the hammer back. No one moved in the parking lot, but he knew the bully boys hadn't left. Not yet. They had her record book, but they also knew that Mitch Bannon could be privy to the information that could put them away. They wanted Bannon disposed of. They'd had ten minutes. They knew his car: the big white Lincoln was a marvelous target in the night. If Bannon had figured these apes right, he'd be kissing his ass goodbye when he started the Lincoln. Assholes. He fingered the round studs on his belt. They activated a radio signal from the battery-powered transmitter strapped about his waist. The signal closed the ignition switch to start the Lincoln.

It also set off the four sticks of dynamite they'd wired under the car. It made a hell of an explosion as the gas tank blew and flaming chunks of Lincoln sprayed the parking lot. Bannon didn't watch the fireworks. His eyes scanned the parking lot and he saw them coming at him from left and right, two on foot and the other two in an old jeep. He went to one knee, steady, and drilled two rounds into the windshield of the jeep. And he knew he wasn't fast enough because he'd have to get out of the way of that damn thing, and the other two were already too close for him to get the both of them.

They didn't make it. Bannon was twisting out of the way and bringing the gun around when two dark figures emerged from the corner of the building and hit the two men running at him. Hit them with tremendous force. Billy clubs crashed into heads, ribs, and knees. Both men went down. Bannon stared. Who the hell—? Blacks. Big fucking blacks, behind the two apes, clubs tight against their throats, holding them helpless. The jeep had stalled, and Bannon saw a tall figure in the glare of the burning wreckage. A tall figure holding a .45 automatic against the head of the driver. The tall figure was talking and the driver was listening very carefully. The blacks holding the two men to the ground dragged them to the jeep and threw them in. The driver started the jeep and it burned rubber backing up and then shifted into first and tore out of the parking lot.

Hands grabbed Bannon's arm. He went with the pull rather than fighting or being dragged, and ended up in a heap in a darkened van already gunning it from the parking lot. Bannon heard the thin wail of sirens in the distance and knew they'd split with little time to spare. But who—"

"I figured you were still wet behind the ears and we'd have to take care of you." He barely made out the face and the broad smile.

"Rawls!" Bannon looked at the other men. Big bastards. "What the hell are you—I mean, how'd you know?"

"My boys followed you from Shiloh, old buddy," Rawls said, his grin even wider. "They're all official. I'm sure you're familiar with Blue Light?" Bannon nodded. "That's right," Rawls went on. "You were in that outfit once."

The elite killing teams. Special operations for Uncle Sam anywhere in the world. Every man a killing specialist.

"That's quite a performance you gave tonight. Did you get what you wanted?"

Bannon shook his head. "I got a name. Abdullah Sulaiman. That's all."

"Means nothing," Rawls agreed. "By the way, what the hell are you doing in that weird getup?"

Bannon removed the wig and the moustache and the

gold rings from his nose. "Didn't seem to fool you," he said.

"You can't hide your walk or your touch, my friend. Now listen to me. We never saw you tonight. You never saw us, right? But we got a car for you. And you're going to be drunk." Someone held a bottle of whiskey over Bannon and poured it onto his clothes. Rawls took the bottle and handed it to Bannon. "Chug-a-lug, baby. We want a good alcohol shot from you. You were picked up for drunken driving, oh, let's say, about two hours ago? Nine air police remember you giving them a hard time, so they threw you in the slammer at Patrick. Got it?"

"Got it," Bannon said as he took the bottle.

"Drink up."

"Sweet dreams," Bannon said. He finished the bottle. No use acting the drunk when you can be one.

God knew he didn't want to be sober anymore tonight.

✦ 16 ✦

TRANSITION

No one could ever tell that the pilots flew beneath a huge invisible anvil in the sky. With the Tattlers aboard all the warbirds and the pilots and crews understanding their purpose, there was the feeling that gloom *should* pervade their moods, certainly their flying. There's a world of difference between *should* and *did*. These were the same men and women, young and old, veterans and newcomers, who went out for every airshow and flew the razor's edge. At three or four hundred miles an hour, howling inches above a runway with heat waves rippling the air, with wind tumbling across trees, with vortexes and churning air from other propellers and wings, death is a constant companion. There wasn't anyone in the entire Strasser Air Circus or Morgan Aviation who hadn't lost at least one close friend when they slipped just beyond the edge. It doesn't take much.

Pilots died from carbon monoxide buildups in their cockpits. An entire crew of a B-26 went in when a propeller snapped and threw a blade into the cockpit that chewed the crew into dogmeat. Tom Garber took a Mustang with his fifteen-year-old daughter in the back seat down a runway, flying inverted, a perfect pass flown with the precision he'd exhibited for years. He hit a burble of air; something went wrong and instinctively he pulled back on the stick. Normally that shot the fighter into a steep climb. *But he was inverted* and everything was reversed, and when he pulled back on that stick it took only a split second for the fighter plane, pilot, and daughter to vanish in an incredible blast of flame that spewed burning debris for a thousand yards.

It happened in ways no one expected. Tod Wilkins was an old-timer who'd been flying more than fifty years, and he spent a day in high heat and humidity flying airshow maneuvers in several different planes. Then, because his face was florid and he was tired and burning energy like water through a hose, he went up in an old de Havilland biplane, graceful and gentle, a young pilot in the open back seat behind him. Wilkins was flying straight and level, as calm as seated in his easy chair at home, when heat prostration did *something* to him. His body pitched forward onto the stick and the de Havilland dove straight in from three hundred feet. It didn't burn, but it buried Wilkins and his friend eight feet deep.

Many times just getting to and from the airshows was the killer. The whole Strasser gang flew down to Texas for a great warbird reunion and flew madly for five days and no one even scratched the paint on any airplane. On the way home the gang separated in poor weather. Three Mustang fighters slipped into gentle rain that concealed completely the Texas Killer, a huge thunderstorm embedded in the rain. Four men died. The storm tore their Mustangs to shreds. The single biggest piece they found was an eighteen-inch solid-steel chunk of one fighter's engine. The one pilot who survived was helpless. He pulled back all power and lowered his landing gear and hung on for dear life and the storm spit him out at maybe a hundred feet, just enough room for him to zap the power and climb out with his wheels through treetops.

So it happened. Most of the time it happened so fast there wasn't much—really, anything—you could do about it. And so the pilots didn't talk about killing *themselves*. It's always the other guy who's going to buy the farm.

Always. Many of the pilots who flew from Shiloh were grizzled veterans who'd been through a whole damn bunch of wars. They had hundreds of missions. They'd been shot up and they'd shot down more than their share of enemy planes. None of them should have been alive. It took skill, it took guts, and above all it took luck in the right place at the right time. They'd imbued the younger fliers, male and female, with the same philosophy. Don't be stupid; that will kill you. But you've got to be crazy. Like the people who scale the vertical walls of mountains, or trek across killer glaciers, or go down into the sea and antagonize sharks. Or those raving idiots who jump out of perfectly good airplanes. The pilots took up the skydivers and watched the beautiful young people fling themselves out of their airplanes, plummeting earthward like stones trying to clutch at the earth, and they tumbled and swam through thin air and formed pinwheels and stars and they were wonderful, spirited, lovable lunatics.

You lived on the thin edge and it was worth it, because you breathed deeper and you honed life to a fine madness and it was all sweeter. Above all you never forgot that Fate had an enormous and barbed finger it could really stick into you. Every pilot who flew the airshows had at one time or another gone through formation flying drill with Will Player. He'd retired from the Air Force after a lifetime of combat in the second world war, in Korea, *and* in Vietnam, and he'd flown, literally, to every nation in the entire world and to both the north and south poles. He drank a minimum of a pint of whiskey and smoked four packs of cigarettes a day and had done so for forty years, and his eyesight was perfect and so were his hearing and depth perception and reflexes, and he passed every medical test known to man, and despite the whiskey and the cigarettes his lungs and kidneys were perfect. Will got hit with prostate cancer and died three months later.

All these were elements of the lives of these men and women, the young and the old, and it was their creed and their way of life. So when Sunday morning rolled around, with the sky a severe clear for a hundred miles in every direction and the wind blowing cool and steady and the sun outdoing itself, they taxied for their dawn patrol takeoffs in their iron beasts light and heavy and small and large and every one of them now had something in common they didn't have the day before. Within each plane was a small black box with a red bulb. The bulb would flash only when it picked up a broadcast signal on a discrete frequency: the signal being transmitted by the missing four bombs. When the light went on, a small computer within the black box gave out a reading of range and bearing.

"Everybody knows their position on the grid," Wendy Green radioed all the planes on the common frequency for the dawn patrol. "Stay with the grid, people. I know you'll all look like old fogeys to the people on the ground, but we need exact coverage. Fighters are cleared for takeoff. Roll at your discretion. One last check, good buddies. Everybody squawk zero four three nine for your transponders. Fighters, you have the runway."

They bored out with their waspish thunder, behind them the bombers rolled, and then the transports and finally the trainers took off, everybody swinging into the prearranged altitudes and headings they would fly for the dawn patrol. Bannon led a group in his Turkey, Strasser was already gone with several formations of fighters, Mad Marty and Magnum and two observers were in a Beaver mixing it up with a bunch of trainers and liaison ships. They scattered like huge metal geese.

They had a newcomer with them. Charley Morgan had her B-25 out for this mission, and in the right seat, new to it all, sat Bernie Hudoff. The medium bomber rocked and swayed and widened Hudoff's eyes. He'd gone along to find out just what kind of sky coverage his "lunatics" really could provide. Behind Charley and Hudoff sat Jay Martin, filling in as flight engineer, spare pilot, and observer, and they had three mechanics riding in the back, with a second Tracker device. The thunder of B-25 engines in the cockpit is an awesome experience, especially with the monster propellers thrashing around only a few feet from the pilots' seats. "My God," Hudoff finally commented on the intercom, "this is like going over Niagara Falls in a barrel. What's all the bouncing?"

Charley pointed to the other bombers ahead of them. "We're in their wake. It's the turbulent air coming back from the props and the planes. Once we hit the beach we'll spread out and it'll calm down."

They flew across the rivers toward the beaches, Charley talking with Patrick Radar to confirm permission to fly north through the restricted areas of the space centers. "Everybody heads up for the cable," she radioed on the air-to-air frequency. Hudoff felt his muscles tightening as he looked through the windshield at the great steel cable reaching upward to secure Fat Albert at the high end of its tether. "That's a hell of a sight," Hudoff said finally. "I'd hate to hit that thing."

"So would I," Charley said easily. "It could slice a wing off like a hot knife through butter."

They swung about the cable and Hudoff's nervous feeling grew swiftly. "Do you always fly so close to that goddamn thing?" he asked with irritation.

Jay Martin hit his intercom behind them, laughing. "Mr. Hudoff, we're not playing horseshoes. Near misses don't count up here."

That was all the excitement they got on the dawn patrol. Two hours of flying at two thousand feet, enough to clear all TV towers and stay safely above populated areas, but low enough to trigger any signal from a bomb that might be concealed beneath them. The formations began to drift back to Shiloh, still flying their grid patterns, Wendy Green bringing them in groups to the traffic pattern and using two runways to land them quickly. They came downstairs from the "patrol" in twos and threes and taxied to the flight line, wheeling smartly to their assigned parking positions so the paying crowd could walk among the aircraft and see and touch and feel before the airshow began and the flight line became dangerous with whirling propellers, barking exhausts, and rolling heavy iron.

Hudoff eased his way down from the B-25. He felt *different*, as if he'd entered a new world. And the word "lunatic" had taken on entirely new meaning. He wasn't yet aware of what had happened, but a couple of hours in the ceaseless thunder and demanding skill and performance of a North American B-25J Mitchell bomber had brought to Bernie Hudoff a respect for these people he'd never dreamed he would feel. Instinctively, because of this new experience, Bannon's role, and the enormous coverage they were giving him in gridding the sky to try to locate the nuclear weapons, he assumed a protective, almost possessive feeling toward the same people he'd always held at a distance and whom he'd never before understood.

He walked down the flight line to the Turkey with its huge wings lying almost flat against the fuselage after Bannon folded them during taxiback to the line. "Anything?" Hudoff asked, already knowing the answer.

"Wish there was," Bannon told him. There was little else to say. Hudoff knew the Trackers would remain in all aircraft from now on until the scheduled launch of *Antares*. Every time a plane flew it would try to work a new area of the invisible sky grid to increase the coverage. The two men walked together toward the Morgan flight office.

"By the way," Hudoff said easily, "you look like shit."

"I feel like shit," Bannon grumped. "Spending the night in an Air Force slammer ain't my idea of a positive social life."

"That's a pretty good lump on the left side of your chin."

Bannon fingered the tender, reddened swelling. "Son of a bitch got me from behind."

"He belted you in your face *from behind*?"

Bannon grinned. "He had a hell of a hook, I guess."

Hudoff fell silent for several moments as they walked through the rows of planes. "You heard about last night?"

"Heard what? Sirens? I heard them, all right. Lots of things. Get your hands up, honky mother fucker. You're under arrest, white shit. I heard a lot of *that*. Also a cell door. When they slam it hard the sound gets through to you."

"You familiar with the name Dragon Lady?"

"Sure. Terry and the Pirates, right?"

"Don't play games with me. Jackie Starr."

"*That* one." Bannon made a sour face. "Pukesville, boss. Strictly the lowest of the low. Big dealer on the beach. Real scummy. The law would like to bury her in a box and throw away the key."

"They don't need to bother anymore."

"Oh? Who got her?"

"Why'd you ask that?"

"She breaks deals with her runners. A hundred people I can think of without trying would like to do her in."

"Someone did. Or she did it to herself. They found her in her beach place, screaming and out of her mind, tearing up her body with her fingernails. Convulsions, the whole works. I talked to the medical examiner. He has her down as an OD."

Bannon shrugged. "Figures."

"Someone also wiped out her digs on Merritt Island." Bannon shrugged and didn't comment. "Two dead in the house. Burned to the ground. Or to the water, I should say. Her four bodyguards have split the scene."

"That figures also."

"Where's that big Lincoln of yours, Bannon?"

"Stolen. About three days ago. Turned it in to the sheriff and the insurance company. Why? You trying to sell me a car?"

Hudoff looked at Bannon, not speaking for a while. "It's amazing," he said finally. "Absolutely amazing. If you were at the crucifixion, Bannon, I'd bet everything I owned you'd have thirty witnesses you were in Rome throwing Christians to the lions."

"Nice try, boss. You got your history screwed up. Christ was a Jew, remember? They didn't have any Christians for fifty or a hundred years after the big parade on the Appian Way."

Hudoff didn't say anymore about the Dragon Lady or what had happened last night. He was certain he *didn't want* to know a thing.

The roar spilled down the taxiway like bubbling surf. Hudoff stopped, staring at the crowd pouring from the

270

big hangar at the end of the flight line. People yelled, whistled, and shouted, crowding about several people Hudoff and Bannon couldn't see from their position. The crowd opened a space and they heard a bullhorn crackling. "On your mark, get set, KILL 'EM! GO!"

Two figures shot out from the crowd. Hudoff stared at a muscular figure with huge arms propelling himself toward them in a blur of motion in a wheelchair. To his right a strange apparition gained on the wheelchair and began to edge ahead: a bigger hunk of muscle and two powerful arms holding ski poles, stabbing madly into the concrete, sparks flying when they dug in. Hudoff didn't believe it. *He was a paraplegic*, strapped to a mechanic's workstool mounted on wheels, and was beating his way, rowing or poling or whatever the hell it was, racing the legless man in the wheelchair. The shouts and yells and screams followed them down the taxiway to where several beauties in bikinis and hotpants held up a ribbon for the finish line. They went through with the paraplegic scant inches ahead of the man in the wheelchair and scraped to a stop. The bullhorn carried to them. "It's Rollins by a kneecap! Rollins wins again!"

Hudoff turned back. "You son of a bitch!" the legless man shouted. "You cheated! You stuck that goddamn pole into my spokes!"

"Fuck you, gimpy! You're just jealous because I'm always beating your ass!"

"What the hell you calling me a gimp for! I ain't got no fucking legs, you asshole!"

"Well, if you did you'd fall on your ass, you clumsy son of a bitch!"

The legless man reached out to grab Rollins by the hair and yanked him wildly to one side. The wheeled stool fell over and as he went Rollins hurled the wheelchair on its side. Both men tore into one another like pit bulls, fists flying, cursing, hammering clublike blows on each other.

"You know, the only thing they're not doing is kicking," Bannon observed.

"We've got to stop them!" Hudoff shouted, starting forward. Bannon grabbed his arm. "You want to get

271

yourself killed, you'll mix it up with them. They both got arms like gorillas. Might as well try to break up a couple of dogs. And they'll *bite*, too."

Hudoff turned to Bannon, his eyes showing disbelief. "This goes on, I mean, they do this—shit, I don't know what I mean."

"They've been having that race for three years, boss. Rollins always whips Carter. Carter keeps saying Rollins cheats and they end up beating the crap out of one another."

"What do they do here?"

"What else?" Bannon gave Hudoff a *you-are-stupid, man* look. "They fly the airshows with us."

"They don't have any legs!"

"*They* know that. Rollins flies left seat, Carter's in the right. Rollins works the throttle and the stick and Carter uses hand controls rigged to the rudders. They talk all their maneuvers through before and as they do them. They're terrific. They've even won a couple of aerobatic competitions."

Hudoff shook his head, muttering "crazy bastards" and other imprecations. They reached the last plane on the display line when the hangar loudspeakers boomed into life.

"Now hear this, boys and girls. Now hear this. The suds competition for passenger seats for the airshow begins in fifteen minutes. All sponsors must have their contestants in front of the hangar in ten minutes. I repeat, all contestants must be in front of the hangar in ten minutes. No exceptions, no exceptions. Get with it, people."

Hudoff had a look of resignation on his face. "What's that all about?"

"They're giving free rides," Bannon told him.

"During the airshow?"

"Uh-huh."

"You mean while you maniacs are trying to kill yourselves you take up *passengers?* People *want* to go?"

"They sure do. But they don't take just anybody. They have a contest first."

"What kind of contest?"

"Beer."

"They drink beer just before they go flying? Bannon, that's the dumbest—"

"They don't quite *drink* it. You've heard of a wet T-shirt contest?"

Hudoff's eyes narrowed. "Yes. What about it?" he snapped.

"This is a wet beer T-shirt contest. Obviously, it's for girls only. Nice girls. Preferably the bigger the tits the better."

"You're kidding."

"See for yourself." They walked to the platform set up before the hangar. A big transparent plexiglas tank had been set up on the platform, and a huge beer truck had just finished filling the tank with foaming suds. A rock band slammed away on one side, balloons drifted into the air, and the crowd grew to more than a thousand cheering, yelling enthusiasts. Wendy started off the contest by calling out rules no one listened to. All that mattered was the applause meter. Three girls would win rides during the airshow. According to von Strasser's rules, they must wear parachutes, even if no one else aboard the plane in which they were flying had similar equipment.

Twelve pilots led their amply proportioned contestants up the steps. They wore bikini bottoms or hot pants and flimsy, bursting-tight T-shirts straining from within. The rules called for each girl to leap into the tank and be dunked by two extremely enthusiastic helpers. Doused in beer, smacking lips, the girls then climbed up steps to the platform and walked before the audience to incite massive applause, shouting, foot-stomping, or any other noise they could register. A huge red dial on an instrument face read off the applause levels. The noise was deafening. Hudoff stared from the lovely scene before him to Bannon.

"Don't tell me they wear the wet shirts in the planes. Please don't tell me that, Bannon."

"Of course not. They take them off first."

"And?"

"And what?"

"What do they wear?"

"You heard Karl. They wear a parachute harness."

"That's *all?*"

"You ever see a pair of gorgeous boobs squeezed together in a parachute harness, boss?" Bannon rolled his eyes in mock ecstasy. "It pushes them out, makes the nipples hard, and—"

"Bannon, do these people realize what the hell is going on out there in the real world?" Hudoff was almost at the point of shouting. "Do they even comprehend what's hanging over their heads?"

Bannon looked at him without a trace of levity. "Yeah, Bernie, they realize, they *know.* But tell me something, man. Does walking around with a long face do any good?"

"Well, no, but they could be serious, for Christ's sake, and—"

"*Why?*"

"Why?" Hudoff echoed. "It's obvious! They could . . . well, I mean . . ." His voice trailed away.

"Any one of them could be killed today, Bernie. Or burned, or maimed. Whatever. They face that every time they fly. You want to tell them they should wear long faces because the world stinks? They're *alive,* Bernie, and until someone turns out their lights they intend to use every minute they got. You know what's wrong with you, boss?"

Hudoff studied Bannon. "Tell me."

"You need a good piece of ass, that's what's wrong with you. You need to walk around buck-ass naked for a while. Then you'll remember that it hurts to hang your shield on your dork, and it just ain't worth it."

"Let's go have lunch," Hudoff said. "You're buying. Then I got to get back to the mill. Call me about seven tonight."

"I still think you ought to get laid." Bannon waved an expansive hand at the girls screaming and giggling on the platform. "Take your pick."

"Fuck off," Hudoff growled.

"You got it all wrong, boss. That's how you settle a tie in a bathing beauty contest."

They started the Sunday show at two o'clock sharp. Lars Anderson was missing from the flight line. He had some last-minute adjustments to make on one aircraft. Wilbur waited for him in the jeep as engine thunder rolled over them. The Golden Girls rose in a burst of glittering glory, the flag jumper did his thing out of the first jump plane, music blared, kids screeched, and the big Merlins and Cyclones and Double Wasps took over the field. Anderson came out to the waiting jeep, sat on Wilbur's skateboard, and howled in fury, "Get me out to the line, you asshole!" Anderson shouted. "I don't want to miss that hero act!"

Wilbur shifted gears and turned sharply. "Ain't no need to get het up, Mr. Lars," he said, teeth jutting forward in his irrepressible smile. "They done shifted some acts around, so we's got time. They going to put out the divers first."

They rolled across the field. The smell of high octane mixed with buttered popcorn and smoke oil trailing the planes crashing their way into the sky. Music, flags flying, tens of thousands of people, a gorgeous sunny day. *Jesus, but it's good to be alive!*

Wilbur stopped the jeep and looked up, squinting in the brightness. "There they are, Mr. Lars." Anderson caught sight of the Caribou with trainers and fighters flying escort, the loose gaggle of Golden Girls reflecting sun like a brilliant searchlight off in the distance. Wilbur banged his hand on the steering wheel and stomped his feet on the metal floorboard. Anderson sighed. Wilbur was with the beat. He was no longer of this world. He looked up again. The big jump was just the prelude. He grinned to himself.

Inside the Caribou engine thunder battered the senses and almost drowned out conversation. The skydivers, mostly young men and women and a few old-timers who didn't have any sense, lined up before the door, anxious to make their final fast shuffle away from the plane. Through the open door and windows they saw the fighters and trainers holding formation. It was a hell of a feeling to know that all that horsepower was out there to boost your act.

A whistle blew and they looked toward the jumpmaster at the door. "We got a few moments," he announced through loudspeakers spaced along the overhead so they all could hear. "You assholes are heroes." Arms with clenched fists went up to the accompaniment of grins. "You can hear how the narrator's bullshitting the crowd—" He turned up the volume on the radios receiving the crowd narration.

"... up at the sky, and now, from your left, at twelve thousand feet, twenty of our finest young men and women will demonstrate a death-defying, heart-stopping free fall for more than two miles straight down! If they miss a heartbeat in their critical plunge through the air, we'll be watching a terrible sight—"

"Turn off that shit!" a girl called. The jumpmaster grinned, held up a middle finger, and killed the radio. The jumper behind the irritated girl pressed closer to her ear. Bob Witherspoon shouted to Becky Goldblum: "I hope we get out of here on time!"

"Why? You got a hot date down there?"

"Did you see that airline captain," Witherspoon asked, "who's got the hots for Charley Morgan?"

Becky nodded. "I saw him! Big hero. Carries a potato in his jockey shorts to impress everybody. What about him?"

"He talked Charley into giving him a spot in the show!"

"*What?* I don't believe—"

"She did it, all right!" Witherspoon laughed suddenly. "I don't want to miss his act!"

"What's so great about him?"

"He gave Lars Anderson a hard time!"

Becky began to smile and nodded, sharing his grin. "Was Lars pissed?"

"Enough to eat nails, and you know what *that* means!"

A bell clanged, lights flashed, the jumpmaster blew his whistle, and they all shouted, "GO! GO! GO!" shuffling forward and diving headfirst from the Caribou.

They fell for ten thousand feet, popped the chutes,

and went through their skillful grandstand act before the guests of honor in crowd center, front row. Becky picked up her chute and joined her jumper friend. "Bob, is that it over there?" she asked, pointing.

He followed her arm to see a brightly painted single-engine plane taxiing along the crowd line and about to move directly before the eager tens of thousands. "That's him. C'mon, there's Lars over there. Let's get by him."

Lars Anderson, Wilbur, and several other mechanics stood together in a group behind a fire truck, arms folded and relaxed, yet with a sense of furtive impatience about them. The brightly colored Cub aerobatic trainer taxied slowly by them. In the cockpit with the side panels open and locked beneath the wing sat a large man with golden wavy hair and moustache and a brilliant smile. He waved to the crowd and they waved back.

Witherspoon stood by Anderson. "That our hero, Lars?"

"Yep," Anderson said, powerful arms folded over his belly. "Old Smilin' Jack hisself, I reckon."

"Did you do what I think maybe you did?" Becky asked.

"What kind of dumb fool question is that?" Anderson growled. "I'm just standing here like any rubberneckin' tourist and enjoying the show."

Becky sidled up to Anderson. "Lars—?"

He smiled down at her. He was all innocence. "Now look here, Becky, girl, what was there to do? Miz Morgan, she tells me to make this here fella with all that hair and them rabbit teeth a big hit with the crowd." He shrugged his shoulders and brought forth a little-boy look. "Now, I admit that this here airliner fella *is* a real smartass. He thinks his poop don't stink like everybody else's."

A devilish smile replaced the saccharine smirk. "I always follow orders. Miz Morgan wants him to be a hit, then he'll be a hit, awright."

The Cub taxied beyond them and was almost before the VIP and guest bleachers. They all heard a sudden popping explosion as the prop spinner flew off and ahead of the Cub, clanging and bouncing along the concrete. Laughter broke out slowly and began to build. Lars and his group shared huge grins and chuckled with the surprised expression of the pilot. He turned to taxi around the propeller spinner and the airplane rocked as an aileron twisted slowly along its connections and fell in a whirling motion, bouncing and flopping behind the propeller airstream. Laughter swelled. A tire exploded in a cloud of white powder. The pilot's mouth hung open in shock. The wing closest to the crowd emitted an ear-stabbing screech and sagged slowly downward until the wingtip dragged along the taxiway. Oil sprayed out of the engine, blew back in the propeller blast and drenched the plane. An oil line mysteriously located beneath the instrument panel broke and dumped black gunk over the pilot. He waved his arms wildly as the propeller fell from its mounts and bounced crazily on the taxiway. The tailwheel broke off and expired in a loud whistle. Suddenly the rudder wobbled and then tumbled backwards. The plane continued to fall apart as a smoke bomb went off in the engine compartment and poured out thick orange smoke.

The crowd was hysterical. Guests and VIPs choked with laughter, beating their knees and each other on the back in roars and giggles. The pilot felt his engine choke and die, steam geysered upward, and the fuselage bent in the middle, sagging like an old rag.

Lars Anderson looked at his close audience. "Now, that there is what I call a *show*," he chortled.

Wilbur Moreland jabbed an elbow into Anderson's ribs. "That's what *I* call a show," he said, close to drooling.

Three T-34's taxied past, pilots in the front seats and a topless girl in the back, lovely boobs pushed up and out by their parachute straps.

✠ 17 ✠

MONDAY IS FOR DYING

"It's like another planet. I never really thought of an airfield this way before." Bernie Hudoff stood with Mitch Bannon on the end of the long concrete stretch that was the main runway of Shiloh Field. For two miles ahead of them concrete edged out to the horizon, narrowing almost to a point at its far end. To each side of the concrete span, grass spread outward. That was all. A concrete ribbon narrowing to nothing and an empty sea of grass.

"We call it the 'morning after,'" Bannon said. "It sort of gets you. Like the world's gone to sleep."

"Where the hell is everybody?" Hudoff asked.

"They're out searching." Bannon waved his arm to take in the barren wasteland where the warbirds normally parked. "Every ship we have that can fly is out there. One hundred and eighty-two of them. Everybody who can fly or act as observer is upstairs in the spamcans and the warbirds. They're all working new grids. They'll refuel at different fields and they'll fly until it's dark."

Hudoff nodded slowly. "Your people are crazy, Bannon, but I'm getting damned fond of them. They just might tip the odds in our favor. We've got forty military ships flying out there, but that doesn't hold a candle to your people." He sighed as reality crowded his thoughts.

279

"We're supposed to launch that damn shuttle six days from now."

"I know. I—"

A sharp beeping tone interrupted him. Hudoff switched off the tone and gestured to Bannon. "Your office, Ace. I need the security phone."

In Bannon's quarters he unlocked the concealed phone, worked the appropriate codes, and handed the instrument to Hudoff. The NASA security chief listened for several moments, said, "No. Let's have everything you've got right now." He listened for another several minutes. "Keep things on hold. I'll be there in less than thirty minutes." He handed the phone slowly to Bannon, who replaced the set within the file cabinet.

Bannon glanced up at Hudoff. "It doesn't sound good."

Hudoff didn't answer for the moment. He brought out his flask and took a long slug, capped it with a flourish, and finally spoke. "I just lost a good friend. Mario."

"What the hell happened?"

"He was murdered. They made it look like an accident, but it was murder. A truck hit him broadside when he was getting out of his car. Right in the parking lot of the Hilton. The man they found in the truck cab was a junkie, stoned out of his mind. No driver's license. No ID of any kind. He sure as hell couldn't drive, and whoever was driving slipped away." Hudoff sighed. "Shit. He was the best I ever knew."

"It looks like fun and games are over, boss-man."

"Yeah. We're getting down to the hard knocks now. Look, I got to—"

"Take off. I'll keep you on tap from here. Anything breaks, you'll know immediately."

"Take care, you dumb son of a bitch," Hudoff said in a strained tone. "I don't want to—" He broke off and hurried from the building to the helicopter waiting in the back.

Ken Lewis didn't mind looking for missing atomic bombs. He liked the program. He was well northwest of Shiloh at five hundred feet in his Stinson L-5, drifting low over the countryside, watchful for television and radio towers, but otherwise as carefree as a bird. At barely 110 miles an hour he clattered along over Highway 40, slicing through the gentle rolling hills of the Ocala Forest, keeping one eye on the world about him and always holding the black box with the dark red glass in view. He turned short of Ocala to miss the city, figuring he'd come back at fifteen hundred feet for a legal sweep along the grid lines marked on his chart. There was Highway 326, which cut north from 40 and then bent around to the west. Lewis kept a careful watch for military jet fighters that liked to chew up the Ocala Forest airspace on mock bombing runs, as well as for any heavy jet traffic at Jumbolair, the huge private strip of Nautilus Sports Medical Industries, where Arthur Jones kept a private 747 and other huge and smaller jets. He caught sight of the north-south strip and could just make out the private field of Jim Garemore when the red light flashed. He didn't hear the buzzer in the clattering racket of his cockpit, but there was no mistaking that light. It stabbed at him and made his heart beat faster—and the light winked out.

"Jesus Christ!" he yelled to himself, stomping rudder and shoving on full throttle and hauling the stick over hard to bring the L-5 around in a tight circle. Obviously he'd passed right through the extreme range of the transmitter in the bomb and he had to get back fast to pick it up again. He started to bring up his radio, then realized he was too low for anyone except a private receiver at Ocala Airport. Sure as hell he couldn't tell *them* he was hot on the tail of a missing atomic bomb. He concentrated on his flying, jotted down his position and time on his chart when the red light flashed. He continued in the turn for 140 degrees, snapped out level, holding his breath and *There! There's the son of a bitch again!* He kept turning, studying the ground, and then he picked up the similarity already nagging at the back of his mind. A big semi-trailer gravel truck on Highway 326. He raced low over the truck and then pulled up steeply and flew off in a straight line, judging time and distance. Sure enough, at five miles the light went out. He turned to come back from a different angle this time, keeping sight of the truck, and just at five miles the light flickered and then stayed on.

Lewis cursed. He couldn't reach anyone who mattered by radio, and he didn't want to lose that truck. He grabbed the 35-mm camera from the back seat, checked his film loading and exposure, and dove for the truck. He came in behind, cursed and remembered to set the camera on motor action, and took the L-5 down to treetop level. He held the camera aimed at the truck as he sped by, the motor clicking off half a roll of film. He saw the truck heading for a huge rock quarry. He passed well ahead of the truck and started his turn to come back from the other side to complete the film roll.

He banked into a tight turn and flashed across the road—and the first he knew that he'd flown into high-voltage power lines was an intense green flare and a billion knives of howling energy stabbing through his body and brain. The power lines tore away the left wing like confetti, and the L-5 tumbled end over end like a broken toy and smashed into the ground. Ken Lewis was dead well before that final act of destruction.

The German pilot's fist crashed down on Hudoff's desk. "It is past time to stop this polite nonsense!" von Strasser shouted. "You pussyfoot around and you wail like a child because a pilot is dead. All right, *he is dead*. But you are a fool to think Ken Lewis is not talking to us from the dead."

They looked at von Strasser as if he'd lost his marbles: Bannon, Charley Morgan and her brother Marty, and Joe Horvath from Secret Service. "They say dead men tell no tales," von Strasser went on with tremendous intensity. "The people who make such stupid remarks are not photo analysts. If they were, they would see what we can see here," his hand slapped against the photo blowups from the camera that survived the destruction of Lewis's L-5.

"A road and a truck," Hudoff said, far from buoyed up by the German's positive attitude. "Just a road and a truck—"

"No, it's more than that," Bannon broke in quickly.

"Karl's right. There's a whole story here right in front of us."

"Lewis was a student of mine," von Strasser broke in. "I not only taught him to fly, I knew his habits. Above all, he liked to fly low. *Very* low. These pictures confirm it."

Charley lowered a photo she was studying. "Mr. Hudoff, this is Highway 326. It starts off 40 that goes through the Ocala National Forest. It's a bypass to get around Ocala that takes you direct to 441 or to I-75."

They crowded around, and von Strasser tapped a pen against another picture. "See here? The Mastriana quarries on both sides of the 326 road. Ah, and in this picture," he shoved another photo before the group, "see this embankment? That is what you call a berm. It is a high embankment at the end of a runway to deflect a jet exhaust. It is at the south end of the Nautilus runway, here," he identified the semicircular formation on the picture, "and you can also see, to its left, part of the buildings of the old Vanderbilt estate."

"It's obvious what Ken did," Bannon picked up the photo interpretation. "He got a signal of the Tracker. And then he lost it. So he did the *only* thing to do. He cut a tight turn and came back, and then by cutting in and out of the edge of an imaginary circle line he could tell generally where the source was. *But it was moving.* Now he sees the same truck he's been seeing as he maneuvers around, and he puts two and two together and it adds up to gravel truck."

"Why didn't he call in by radio?" Hudoff asked.

"I've flown that L-5," Marty Morgan added. "It's got your basic one radio and that's all. The only radio contact he could have made from his position, even if he'd climbed, was on unicom, either one twenty-two eight or one twenty-three. And what would he tell them? Blab it over the radio that they had an atomic bomb in the neighborhood?"

"So," von Strasser said with unquestionable emphasis, "he does the smart thing. He takes pictures. He knows when he comes back maybe we blow up the pictures. Computer enhancement and such things, and

283

we can track down the truck. But," the German shrugged, "he is too excited. He is not, after all, a combat pilot, and even we made mistakes. He stays low for his pictures and he flies right into the power lines. He is dead, but the pictures talk to us."

"There are hundreds of gravel trucks like this one in this state," Hudoff said, a bit more harshly than he intended. "I haven't sat on my hands since we developed these pictures. I put a reconnaissance jet over that place at high altitude. Didn't want to make it obvious we were interested. The photos are, um, right here. See those trucks? Fifteen of them, and each one is exactly like the others."

"But I know that outfit," Charley spoke up. They looked at her and waited. "The Mastriani name is from the former holders. They haven't owned it for a year or more."

"Who owns it?" Hudoff asked, pen poised over a pad.

"I'm not sure of the name. It's no secret. I mean, Lansky knew all about it. He helped them close the deal. Part of Aramco, I think."

"That is Saudi Arabia," von Strasser said to Hudoff.

"You can find out for yourself later," Charley said impatiently. "It's an investment deal. You know, the owners don't even go near the place. All hired help. I don't know *who* works that quarry but I'll tell you this—they're crazy. I mean, *real* crazy. You can't get into that quarry. You push through the gate and they shoot at you."

"Wait a minute," Bannon said, snapping his fingers. "That Arab deal never went through. It's British, I think. Sutterby; yeah, that's it. They're into mining operations all over the world. They picked up the place."

"I don't care *who* owns the joint," Hudoff said brusquely. "To get in there and inspect those trucks I'll need a warrant. I'll have to—" He looked up as the door opened and Colonel Hank Rawls entered.

"Your secretary said to come right—"

Hudoff waved him in. "You know about these photos?"

Rawls glanced at the table. "Yes, sir. We have copies of them and I've had our intelligence team doing a study. That's one of the trucks from the Sutterby open mining operation. We got a blowup from the photo recce ship and ran the serial number on the vehicle through Florida motor bureau."

Hudoff blinked. "That's damn good, Rawls. Now we have another problem. Even with national priority I need a federal warrant to get into this place. Extraordinary or mitigating circumstances notwithstanding, that's the law and—"

"We are talking about the end of the world for this place!" von Strasser shouted. "And you waste time with legal pimples!"

"We've been through this before," Hudoff snapped, "and—"

"Dumbkopf! Will you tell all the thousands of people who die you are sorry because of your stupid law! The only law you must follow is *martial* law!"

Bannon edged closer to the table. "Bernie, he's right."

Hudoff glared at them. "You heard Miss Morgan. That crowd shoots at people. With a warrant I can go in there with force and—"

"And by then," von Strasser said, his words acid, "the bomb will be gone. *Vunderbar!* What a solution!"

"Bernie, listen to me," Bannon said, leaning on the table. "You and the colonel, here, never spoke to us. You keep your ass clean. *We* go in ourselves. Our warbird bunch."

Rawls almost sneered. It was the perfect moment to continue his public contempt of Bannon. "With *what,* beach boy? Popguns? You think that with a couple of deer rifles and shotguns you can—"

Bannon looked at von Strasser. "Ryland's ship has live guns, Karl. It's in the hangar right now."

"What kind of guns?" Rawls snapped.

"Fifty calibers. The whole plane is loaded with them. We can have the live ammo aboard in twenty minutes."

Hudoff stared. "You're serious?"

Marty Morgan smiled. "Mr. Hudoff, we got Molotov cocktails. We got napalm. We got oil sprayers we can ignite."

Strasser banged a fist into his hand. "*Ja!* Load with the napalm! It is best for this."

"What the hell are you people talking about?" Rawls said loudly. "A Latin American revolution?"

"Where'd you get that kind of stuff?" Hudoff asked.

"What's the difference?" Bannon shot back. "We made it. Paint stores, cleaning chemicals, gasoline; that sort of stuff."

"The whole idea's ridiculous," Rawls said with authority. "Besides, while you people have been *talking*, we've been doing just what our *Luftwaffe* friend here has been wanting to do. Hit them hard. There's a special law that enables us to move in wherever we suspect nuclear weapons are involved. We invoked that special law. We've moved in there with two combat choppers loaded for bear."

Strasser motioned for the others to remain quiet. "Two helicopters? An air strike if you need it?"

"Yes."

Von Strasser's eyes narrowed. "I suppose you sealed off all the escape routes, the exit roads, *first?*"

Rawls looked as if he'd been hit in the face with a fish. "Why, I didn't, I mean—"

"*Idiots!* They will be giving them an invitation to escape!" He half-spun about. "Bannon, stop *talking* with these children. If you want a chance to get that bomb, *do something now.*"

Bannon reached out to grab the telephone, punched in a number, drummed his fingers on the desk until he had an answer. "Jay? Bannon here. Don't argue, no questions, just do exactly as I say. Load up Ryland's B-25 with the napalm bombs. The *real* ones. Four of them in the bomb bay. Make sure the ship is fueled. Get it in front of the hangar and start the engines. I'm on the way in by chopper and I'll be going straight into that airplane to take off. No questions, damnit!" He slammed the phone down and looked at the others. "*Let's go!*"

They piled out of the office in a mad rush, leaving Hudoff and Rawls staring at one another. They didn't wait for the elevator but trampled their way down the stairs and rushed from the exit to the heliport on the expansive lawn. Bannon fired up as Charley, Marty, and von Strasser came in behind. They were startled to see Joe Horvath. "What the hell are you doing here?" Bannon shouted.

Horvath waved him on. "I wouldn't miss this for the world. Besides, if you get your asses in a sling I can lend official status to what you're doing!"

Marty clapped him on the shoulder and banged the door shut. Bannon slammed power to the chopper and left ground in a precarious swinging climbout. As they raced toward the river, Marty grabbed the radio to Morgan Aviation and made contact with the office. "Callahan, this is Marty. We've got an emergency, so just get cracking with what I have to say. Charley's with me and she'll confirm. I want the Beaver on the line and the engine warmed up. Stand by one." Marty looked at von Strasser.

"I go with you," the German said. "One to fly and one to throw things." He motioned for Marty to continue.

"Callahan, that red foot locker, the metal one we keep locked up in the electronics shop, bring it out to the Beaver. Just put it aboard. Got all that? Great; we're on the way in."

They pounded across the river and flashed over U.S. 1. "I can see our ships!" Charley called. "They've got them running!"

The B-25 sat on the line, both engines running. Callahan was taxiing the Beaver from its parking spot nearer the B-25. The big jet Sikorsky chopper Jay Martin owned was rolling slowly toward the other planes, and two L-5's were swinging around, pilots at the controls, back seats empty.

Bannon dropped the chopper in a hard landing, killed the switches, and everybody piled out and ran to their waiting aircraft. Charley and Bannon hit the ladder into the B-25 and started up into the cockpit. A startled mechanic scrambled from his seat. Charley took left seat and Bannon was in the right. He turned to the mechanic. "You just became a flight engineer! Close the hatches and button her up!" His brain seemed to shoot into overdrive. "Wait a second! Did Callahan load the bomb bays?"

"Yes, sir! Four—"

"Never mind anything else; button her up!" He signalled to Charley to roll out, then grabbed the radio. "Shiloh, you read the twenty-five?"

"Go, Shiloh." He recognized the voice of Max Youngstein.

"Whoever calls in, tell them to go to one two zero point one fiver for common frequency. I'll talk to you again when we're airborne. Clear us for takeoff. We're rolling."

Charley swung the bomber around, pouring full power to the engines as she turned onto the runway and they rushed down the concrete. Bannon looked down into the glass nose. The machine guns were empty. No ammunition belts. *Goddamnit!* He knew there hadn't been much time, but he'd still hoped. He tuned in to the common frequency on 120.15 megahertz and heard Marty telling the tower they were taking off from the taxiway. They didn't need much more room than a helicopter. Jay Martin's voice came in. "Hey, hey, two-five, this is Big Box and I'm airborne with four others aboard and we got Massapequa One Sixteens aboard and with you."

Charley glanced at Bannon, puzzled. He hit the intercom switch. "Jaybo's in the air. He's got four people with him and they're armed with M-16 autorifles." She nodded and Bannon went back to common frequency. "Okay, everybody balls to the wall for the Sutterby quarries. Ignore the restricted zones, I repeat, ignore the restricted zones. Straight through, you can follow us. We're looking for a gravel truck. Keep your Trackers alive and humming. You'll see the red light when you get within five miles of the right target."

They watched the huge Bithlo Towers, nearly two thousand feet tall, drift by them and Charley put the nose down for added speed, the big Cyclones hammering madly to each side of them. Bannon took the time to check the bomb-bay systems, the doors, and the releases. He called the mechanic up. "Rick, you stay the hell away from the bomb bays, got it? We'll probably be dropping in a while."

Rick's face was pasty white. "Mr. B-Bannon, what are we after?"

"A gravel truck, son. They ran out on the contract to do my driveway and I'm pissed off." He went back to common freq. "The two-five here. Can you see ahead of us, twelve o'clock our position?"

Beneath them were thick forest and a glimpse of the ribbon of Highway 40. Far ahead two plumes of black smoke drifted thinly on the horizon. Bannon tapped Charley on the shoulder. She nodded; she had the smoke in sight. Bannon felt sick. "Everybody stay alert," he called. "I think those two Air Force choppers that went to the quarries to investigate are down." It didn't take long to confirm the worst. He knew what had happened. The two heavily armed helicopters had gone in fast, then slowed, coming down in a hover. But no one shot at them, no one resisted, until they were maybe fifty feet up. Then gunners within the quarry, concealed and having perfect targets, opened up at point-blank range.

The results came into focus as they saw into the quarry: flames licking about crumpled wreckage and the smoke now heavy and shredded by the wind.

Charley came over the quarry tight and Bannon grabbed the controls, rolling swiftly in an opposite bank. "We're dead meat until the others get here!" he shouted over the engines. "Keep her wide until we have Jaybo here for cover!" She nodded, followed his instructions to fly in a fast circle, low and wide. Bannon looked down. Goddamnit, Karl had been right!

Bannon hit his transmit switch. "Two five to the circus, *every* damn truck down there is gone! Let's spread out over the roads. The twenty-five will take Four Forty One to the north, the lead L-5, you take Four Forty One south. Beaver, take the I Seventy Five highway north. Jaybo, you copy?"

"Big Box here. Go."

"I want you to hit Three Oh One for about thirty miles

289

and then come across to Four Forty One. Have you raised highway patrol yet?"

"Yeah, babe. They got the word. They said they'll stop every gravel truck in the whole damned state. I agree. Whoever's got that beauty could transfer from one truck to another at any time."

"Got it, Jaybo. Second L-5, stay on Three Twenty Six West, all the way to the coast."

He didn't even know the pilot's name in that ship. "Copy and wilco, Two Five," came the immediate answer.

"I got a truck! I got a truck! We're right on him!"

Bannon cursed to himself. "Who's calling in? Identify and give your location!"

"Uh, this is Marty and Karl in the Beaver. We're over Highway Forty and the truck is heading east, just coming out of Silver Springs. That mother is really hauling ass, too. We, uh, we confirm the semi, and, uh, we're chasing—"

"This is Highway Patrol. We copy your exchange and we will have vehicles blocking the highway on the east end of the bridge over the river. Once he hits that bridge he can't go anywhere."

"Holy shit! They're shooting at us! We got some bullet holes . . . goddamn, there goes the windshield!"

"Uh, circus leader," a call came on their frequency, obviously from someone who didn't know what call signs to use, "tell your, uh, man we have cars moving into position, and—"

"I heard you! But they didn't! The sons of bitches are still shooting at us!"

"Pull away from there!" Bannon called.

"No way! We're staying glued to that thing and—Jesus, we been hit again. We're okay, we're okay."

Bannon fumed. "Damnit, *shoot back!* You hear me, shoot back!"

"With what, you fool!" He recognized von Strasser's voice. *"I am in a toy airplane and I have a boy and a dog! That damn footlocker is locked! We can't—"*

There was a brief period of silence. "Hey, everybody, Jaybo here in Big Box. The Beaver's okay. Must have had their radios shot up or something, but I can see them both in the bird and they're fine. The highway troops down below got the truck. It tried to break through their roadblock and they clobbered him but good. The truck's down a ditch on its side and burning. They got the driver, repeat, they got the driver."

"Circus, this is Highway Patrol. We've got eight trucks so far, but no lights from the Trackers. I repeat, no lights from the Trackers. Over."

"We may as well go on home, Two Five. Jaybo here. We'll hang in with the Beaver in case they have any problems."

"Roger that, Jaybo," Bannon called. "Good—" His voice stopped in mid-sentence. Charley's hand gripped his forearm, nails digging deeply into his skin. He winced. What—

Charley thumbed her transmit switch. She spoke with amazing calm. "All aircraft from Two Five, all aircraft from Two Five. *We have a Tracker light. I repeat, we have a Tracker light.*"

Bannon looked at the ominous black box on their instrument panel. The red light flashed at him. He felt his blood run cold. The first truck must have been a decoy. They had almost lost the bomb they'd found. But the boys on the ground were good; they picked up immediately on the message.

"Circus, uh, the Two Five, please confirm you have a Tracker light. Over."

Bannon took the radio. "You got it, sweetheart. This is the B-25 bomber and we're over Highway I Seventy-Five and, uh, I estimate about ten miles south of Paynes Prairie."

"Big Box is coming as fast as we can. Stay with him, Charley!"

"Roger, Big Box." Charley called. "We're flying north, coming up on Micanopy. Oh . . ." A heart-gripping silence for a moment and then Charley's voice came on the air again. *"Dear God, the truck is heading straight for Gainesville."*

"Charley! Bannon!" They heard von Strasser's voice. "You know what that means! *Go after them! Do anything you must do to stop them!*"

Charley looked at Bannon, her face stricken. "Mitch, there's ... a hundred thousand people there. The university ... there's more than fifty thousand students ... and the bomb ..."

"Fly the airplane, goddamnit!" Bannon snapped at her. He peered ahead. "I see it, Charley. If that thing gets into the city we can't touch them. It's up to us, kid."

She bit her lip, white teeth cutting skin. "What do you want me to do?"

"Get ahead of them. Get over the prairie and then start your turn back. When you come around I want you at exactly two hundred feet on the altimeter. That's about seventy feet above the ground. *Stay directly over the highway heading south.* Got it?"

She nodded. Bannon shouted to the youngster riding with them. "Rick! I'm going to open the bomb bays when we come around the turn and I want you to confirm they're open all the way!"

"Yes, sir!"

Charley flew like an old veteran, everything smack on the money. She thumbed the intercom. Her face was a ghastly white. "Mitch, this could be ... this could be goodbye for us. If we hit that truck with the napalm it will ... it will set off the atomic bomb, and we'll ..."

He laughed harshly. "No way, lover! Those things have to be set off with an electronic trigger. They're made to blow apart if they're hit with any kind of real blast. The only explosion you'll get is the charge in the bomb that blows apart the mechanism. Now shut up and fly, damnit!"

She gripped the yoke with both hands, threw all her strength into the rudders, and brought the bomber around in a wicked, perfect turn. Charley snapped back to level flight seventy feet above the highway, holding two hundred and twenty miles an hour, dead level, dead straight down the long concrete span. Bannon hit the bomb bay door handle. The B-25 rocked and rumbled as the doors opened into the wind blast.

"They're open!" Rick screamed.

"Hold her straight, Charley. You've got to be dead

center. There's the truck, coming around that last bend . . . he's coming down that hill. Steady, steady, hold her steady . . ."

They were just short of proper range. He'd counted on that. He snapped the first release and the five-hundred-pound bomb fell away. Then the second, and the third. Before he released the fourth and last bomb a huge glare flashed off the highway and the hill ahead of them as the first napalm bomb exploded and sent a hundred yards of blazing hell down the road. Then the second bomb lit off in a huge rose blossom of sticky fire, covering the highway, sending panic-stricken drivers wildly into the marshy ground to the side of the highway. The third bomb went directly beneath the speeding truck and exploded.

"Pull up!" Bannon howled, and grabbed the copilot yoke and yanked back, stamping left rudder and throwing the yoke over to the left. Flames roared up from the ground and a shock wave hit the airplane like a giant fist. Heat mushroomed upward through the open bays. They saw the fourth great splash of napalm well beyond the truck, burning harmlessly along the side of the highway. They were in a steep bank, turning hard, watching the truck hurtling down the road, an enormous streaming fireball, and then the explosion ripped upward from the gas tank of the truck and buckled the connections between the cab and the trailer, and then another blast shattered the trailer and sent great chunks hurtling in all directions.

"T-take it," Charley stuttered, and as Bannon nodded to her, Charley put her face in her hands and sobbed uncontrollably.

✝ 18 ✝

T-MINUS 5 DAYS AND COUNTING

Amber suns hung in misty glowing space, diminishing in size and curving away into darkness until they were only a glow. Beneath each light walked a guard in Air Force uniform, armed with a submachine gun and accompanied by an attack dog. For the past several days Patrick Air Force Base, directly south of Cocoa Beach, had become an armed camp. Colonel Hank Rawls had brought down the hammer with telling effect. Any security infraction meant immediate arrest. Two airmen who failed to respond to passwords on the flight line had already been shot; one was dead. Three civilians also walked through the heavy fog, an armed airman and dog following behind.

Joe Horvath had never been so animated. Hudoff felt that he was seeing the man for the first time. "I still can't believe it. Damndest thing I ever saw. An ancient airplane, a girl and that crazy Bannon at the controls, a terrified kid working as flight engineer, *and they nailed that truck.* Just like they'd been doing it all their lives. Christ! Can you imagine what could have happened if that truck made it into Gainesville?"

Vladislov Galenko walked heavily, hands gripped behind his back, thinking hard. "That is a wonderful story, Mr. Horvath. One day maybe you will write a book. All

American heroes write books, I think. But in the meantime, if you please, Moscow is asking for confirmation. They have, shall we say, more than a slight interest?"

Horvath flushed; they didn't see it in the amber glow from the flight line. "Yes, sir, we have confirmation and Washington has asked that you personally make the call to Moscow. There's no question. We picked up traces of plutonium all over that highway."

"What did you announce to the public?" Hudoff asked.

"We told them the truck was carrying chemicals that converted to phosgene gas when it burned," Horvath answered. "No one argues with that kind of problem any more. We shut down the highway through the prairie. The only way to pick up all the plutonium that was scattered around is to dig down at least two feet and remove all the soil. We're doing that now."

Galenko stopped, studying the two Americans with him. "You are aware that as of tomorrow, you have only six days left?"

"You think we're forgetting that?" Hudoff shot back.

"No, no; of course not. Forgive me." Galenko seemed to make a sudden decision. "Hudoff, a question just between the two of us, please." He glanced at Horvath. "Your ears will stop working, I hope? Thank you. Now, Hudoff, when you talk with your Bannon you ask him about many people. But you never mention the name Sadad Jabal. Tell me why."

Hudoff admitted to himself the question had merit. "Because I want to see what he comes up with from his own sources. That's important. I've heard the name Sadad Jabal. I got that even from Mario before he was killed. Then we got the name of Abdullah Sulaiman. We don't know how real either name is. *Then* we got the word that some Saudi Arabians connected with Aramco were behind the buyout of the quarries. *That* turns out to have been a British outfit called Sutterby, and *then* we discover we're dealing with an absentee ownership deal. Sutterby bought it, but it was a paper transaction only, and there are at least four more buyers and sellers between Sutterby and the people who are running it now. We've dead-ended. We'll crack the nut, but for the time being, we wait. I know; this was a long answer to a simple question, Vladislov, but I'm trying to let you see *why* we're doing things the way we are."

They resumed walking. "You make good sense, Bernie." He chuckled. "I enjoy that. It does not happen very often, my friend."

"Vladislov, do you know what you get when you cross an ape with a KGB agent?"

"When you do what with which?"

"If you mate a gorilla with a KGB agent, do you know what the result is?" Hudoff persisted.

Galenko frowned. "I never hear of such thing. No. What do you get?"

"A retarded ape, you asshole." Hudoff slapped the Russian on his shoulder. "C'mon, let's have a drink. I'm buying."

"Why would KGB agent do such a thing?" Galenko asked.

Hudoff threw up his hands and walked off down the line.

Fog turned ordinary lights into glowing wonders. Along the Patrick flight line minor suns burned into the darkness. At Shiloh Field the beacon flashes swept the night with alternating beams of green and white, and scattered throughout the field pools of light glowed and flashed from rotating beacons and strobes where mechanics and owners serviced their planes. Ghosts glided slowly in the distance: the lights of jeeps and trucks moving with exquisite care in the misty shrouds.

Lars Anderson stood in the shadows of his hangar, the diffused lights reflecting from his glasses. He peered through the gloom at the Morgan Aviation hangar, his face screwed up as he squinted to see through the mists. Something was wrong over there. In the shadows, wrapped in the shrouds of gloom, a van moved slowly. *Their lights are out. That's bullshit.* He made out dark figures revealed suddenly by the van dome lights as the doors opened. They went directly to a side door. The light went out. Anderson listened intently as metallic sounds came to him, then a wrenching of metal and a door creaking open. He knew that sound. The entrance to the hangar and the museum. The son of a bitch always squeaked like that. He heard men grunting as they moved something heavy. It banged gently against the metal door jamb. The door closed.

Anderson gripped a huge wrench in his right hand. He'd used Old Faithful more than once to scatter assholes who poked around where they had no business to be. He moved past the empty van and stopped by the hangar door, feeling the bent metal where they'd forced it open. He slipped inside, pressed against the door to keep it quiet. Something else these people, whoever they were, didn't know about.

Inside, he flattened his body against the hangar door. In the reddish gloom of the emergency EXIT lights he saw only the great predatory shapes of fighter planes. By now he was seeing quite well in the dark. There; across the hangar display floor. The door to the museum. *It's open. It shouldn't be. The bastards are in there. It don't make no sense.* He crossed the hangar, brought the huge wrench up to strike, took a deep breath, and stepped through the doorway.

A flashlight snapped on, nearly blinding him. He stared at a figure wrapped in black from head to foot, some crazy Arabic writing on the forehead. Anderson didn't think. Not in a moment like this. The wrench came down with the speed of a striking snake. He felt hard metal crunch into soft flesh and then heard the thin cracking of bone. The flashlight clanged against the concrete floor and went out. Anderson sidestepped instantly to keep from being a target. He heard the man he'd hit, moaning on the floor. He wasn't interested in him. There were others here. He hefted the wrench and began stalking the sounds that were coming to him from several feet away. A light snapped on from the side. Instinctively he turned into the light and just as quickly he realized his mistake and thought *You dumb shit . . .* and he heard the whirring sound for an instant before a steel beam tore into his head.

It wasn't a beam but it had all the horrifying impact of one. Anderson realized the wet smacking sound he'd heard was *something* that crashed into his forehead and sent blood bursting outward and he felt as if his eyes and skull were on fire, and somehow he knew that sharp metal was imbedded deeply into his forehead and by some crazy reasoning he knew it had penetrated his sinuses and through the incredible pain he heard his wrench clanging to the concrete floor and bouncing a few times and he knew he must move, he must absolutely move to where he could get help or he'd be a dead man. He turned and stumbled against the doorway and he heard the van starting up and rubber screeching on the ground outside but he didn't care, he needed help, *I must get help or I'll die.*

Through the door. Keep going. Keep going. Lift the foot. Put it down. Lift the other foot and move it forward and down. That's it. There's the hangar door. Where's the fire alarm? I can get help if I set off the fire alarm. Can't see too good. Blood in my eyes. Pain blinding me. Keep going. Keep going. Through the door. That's it. I'm outside. Turn right. Walk to the office. He stumbled against the side of the building, fought for balance, and struggled onward. *Keep going. Almost there. Office. Gotta get to the office. Phone. Help there. Almost there* . . .

"Jesus Christ, woman, this is *wonderful.* I don' believe it am going to happen, this take so long." Bill Santiago's belly was on fire and he was as rigid as a steel rod and his heart was pounding as he fought madly to get that goddamned fucking too-tight stupid flight suit off his woman. He'd held her breasts and kissed her madly and got the zipper open partway and tore her blouse with his hands going inside and he was mad, *mad* to bring his lips and mouth up against those beautiful breasts and chew on her nipples, and Wendy had maneuvered herself on the couch so she could open his belt and his trousers and she had his pants down about his ankles and his shorts shoved down with them and he was going crazy, fighting that goddamned suit and he cried out, "*Help me, woman,* in name of love for Jesus and Mary I'm going to explode, help me get that goddamn suit off you and—"

"Easy," she panted, wildly lubricated to make love to her man. She sat up straight on the couch in the pilot's office lounge, twisting and squirming to get her arms free of the restricting suit.

"I cut the fucking thing off, Wendy! Give me my pants, I use knife. Fuck the suit! I buy you a hundred of them and—"

He stared at her. Wendy had gone rigid, every muscle frozen, her eyes bulging wide, and her mouth opened and he knew from the strangling sound she was going to scream, but he couldn't turn from the way he was pinned down on the couch. "Let me the fuck up!" he yelled but she didn't move and then she *did* scream, loud enough to break the fucking windows, he thought, and she screamed again and again and he fought his way up, pushing her back, twisting around to see what in the fuck she was screaming about and he almost screamed with her—

A monster loomed just outside the glass door to the office. "Holy fucking Jesus shit!" Santiago yelled, shoving Wendy from the couch and grabbing for the switchblade in his boot, but it was too late, the monster moved, the green light from the airport beacon reflecting off his shape and flashing from his metal helmet or skull or whatever the fuck it was and then it came crashing through the glass. A violent crackling, smashing, breaking sound and glass flying everywhere, Santiago throwing his body clumsily over Wendy Green and shouting. "Stay down! I kill that son of a beetch!" He had the knife out and the blade snapped open, and he lunged forward ready to strike but his feet couldn't move, tangled as they were in his trousers and his jockey shorts and he threw away the knife as he fell, and he saw the monster falling toward him and they both hit the floor with a tremendous crash. Wendy was still screaming but she'd scrambled from the couch to the counter, and if nothing else, Wendy Green could scream and do the right things at the same time. She hit the lights and dashed around the counter to Santiago, a .38 revolver clutched in both hands to blow away that alien son of a bitch lying face down, flat on the floor. Santiago pushed the gun away, got to his knees and heaved the monster over, and stared down at Lars Anderson splashed everywhere with blood, a Ninja throwing star imbedded deeply into one eye and his skull. His teeth clattered together like a skeleton as his muscles convulsed, his other eye opened and stared at them, his body arched in a final terrible convulsion, and his life fled.

Mitch Bannon and Karl von Strasser walked slowly from the lifeless cold of the county morgue in Titusville. "I hated coming up here," Bannon said after a long silence. "But I *had* to know for sure. Thanks for coming with me."

Von Strasser glanced at his watch. "We have time to get to the airport for the services. It is all right. Everything is arranged?"

Bannon sighed. "Yeah, it's all set. We'll do it just the way Lars wanted. No minister or any of that crap. We'll fly the missing man formation and scatter his ashes just the way he wanted."

"You have the ashes?"

Bannon hefted the leather bag with the sealed blue vase within. "Not much left of a big man."

"Bigness is not in the size, Bannon. He was big, he *is* big, he will always remain so to us. You know that."

"I guess you're right, Karl."

"Why did you need to talk with the coroner?"

"Well, it's obvious Lars died from that thing in his skull. But obvious isn't always the way it looks. He could have been shot or drugged or anything and *then* they drove that thing into him. But it turns out its just the way it looked. It was the throwing star that killed him." They got into Bannon's car and drove from the parking lot onto U.S. I heading south.

"Whoever they were," Bannon said, breaking the silence they'd held for a while, "they were insiders."

Von Strasser showed his surprise. "I thought the door was forced?"

"It was. But it was also a fake. They bent it just enough to be visible, but they didn't break the lock."

Bannon looked straight ahead. "That was supposed to lead us into thinking it was a ripoff of some kind. It wasn't. Nothing was missing. And whoever got in had a key."

Von Strasser didn't seem surprised. "So." The one word was a statement all by itself. "We have traitors among us."

Bannon nodded. "They're more than that. I know the mark of the pro in this business, Karl, and these people were real businessmen."

"Careful, Bannon, you are giving yourself away."

Bannon chuckled, but there was no humor to the sound. "Karl, I haven't fooled you from day one."

Von Strasser smiled, again a sharing. "No, Bannon. I also know the mark of the professional. But this time I am talking about you." He glanced at Bannon. "No one else knows."

"Well, thanks for that. These people who nailed Lars . . . I don't believe they were after him."

"No. Lars was a wonderful man and a very brave man, but you need more than bravery. He was not very smart when he went into that hangar."

"He did that, all right. No use in carrying a twelve-pound wrench into a museum at night. He saw something, he went in to check it out. I didn't tell you this, but he also did a number on one of those people."

"How?"

"We found plenty of blood on the floor. There were some drops away from where Lars got hit and then worked his way to the office. The blood type doesn't match that of Lars. So he got in a lick before they killed him."

"Any other leads?"

Bannon shook his head. "I wish there were. It's dead-end time."

"Anything missing? From the museum?" Von Strasser shook his head to answer his own question. "No, that would be stupid. There's nothing worth breaking into that building to steal. Not with several people, not to kill a man. So there's more to it than we know."

"We don't know shit," Bannon said with some heat. "Just that a very good man is dead."

"Where is the weapon that killed Lars?"

Bannon reached into his jacket, withdrew a leather wrapping and handed it to the German. He unfolded the leather, and held the throwing star. "It is the Ninja star. But," he said after a moment's hesitation, "it is also one of the favorite weapons used by the Islamic assassins."

"Which could have meaning to it," Bannon remarked, "or is supposed to lead us down a blind alley." Bannon pounded the steering wheel in frustration. "Christ, I'd like to pull in one of these shadows around us . . ."

Von Strasser carefully refolded the leather. "Bannon, do you know the name of Jadad Sabal?"

"Nope. Should I?"

"Yes. Remember it. And look for him or any sign of him."

"Don't be so goddamned mysterious, Karl. Who is he? Or she, for that matter?"

"It is a man. An Arab. A total fanatic. He might be Libyan or Egyptian or Algerian or Lebanese; no one knows. But his name is like a holy flame in the Middle East. All the words for him. Terrorist, murderer, fanatic, torturer, revolutionary; they are all part of Jadad Sabal. The word, Bannon, is that he is operating here in the States. Perhaps right here in Florida."

"How come you know so much about a camel driver?"

"Bannon, there are many German engineers in the desert. Some of us work the oil fields, or computers, or we teach mechanical and hydraulic engineering. There are other Germans who build missiles and weapons. Those Germans can never return to Germany. But they all keep in touch. The contacts remain open anywhere in the world. We learn things. We get names. Jadad Sabal is a name I hear again and again from these Germans, along with grave warnings."

"Anyone know what he looks like?"

"No. He is a shadow; a ghost."

"Yeah," Bannon said acidly. "A ghost with three atomic bombs under his robes."

302

He fell silent as he turned into the road to Shiloh Field. As they drove closer to the warbird operations area they saw the crowd. More than a thousand people had come for the final services for Lars Anderson. As Bannon and von Strasser drove up, they watched four Mustang fighters pounding down the runway, the Merlins roaring their cry of the lost soul. They would come back when called by radio to fly the missing man formation.

Bannon and von Strasser climbed from the car. "Well, everything is going to happen exactly as Lars asked."

"What can I do, Bannon?"

Bannon pointed. "Join that group over there. The pilots and the crews. Lars asked that the people he worked with and flew with get together in their best clothes for the ceremony, and then hoped they'd all have a cold beer on him." Bannon gestured to the big Sikorsky helicopter. "I'll be going up in the chopper with Jay Martin."

"Very good, Bannon. You will feel my hand on that vase when you release his ashes," von Strasser said, very somber.

Bannon climbed into the big Sikorsky helicopter. "Wind her up, buddy." Jay Martin was dressed in a tuxedo, dress shirt, and silk black bowtie. He looked uncomfortable. "This is what Lars asked for," he said by way of explanation to Bannon.

"I know. Okay, we'll leave the door open. I'll hook up a harness by the door to scatter his ashes."

"We going over the ocean?"

"Nope. I'll tell you later. Just take her up to a hundred feet, around the field perimeter once and then come upwind of those people down there. When I ask you to, hold her in a hover a hundred feet up."

"Got it."

Jay Martin flew the big helicopter with great care, a personal touch added to his usual skill. The helicopter thundered around the field. Bannon called on open frequency. "Mustangs, start back now for the missing man formation. You'll see the chopper hovering near the guests and friends."

"Uh, roger that, fella. We're on the way in. Two minutes."

"Jay, watch for the fighters. They'll come in from the south. When you see them, make for the crowd and give me the hover right at the edge of them. Not over. Just at the edge."

"You got it, babe."

Jay Martin flew the Sikorsky to the exact position requested. The Mustang fighters howled over in tight formation and, as one Mustang pulled up and away to represent the man missing forever from their ranks, Mitch Bannon leaned out from the open door of the helicopter and, exactly as Lars had asked in his will, sprayed his ashes into the tremendous downwash of the helicopter blades into the upturned faces of all his friends.

Bannon carried the big basket of food, wine, and beer from the station wagon to the big airboat tied to the dock at Kars Park on Merritt Island. To their south stretched the raised concrete ribbon of the Bennett Causeway, waters of the tidal basin reaching eastward to the spaceport spread before them. In the early evening the lowering sun cast its long shadows. It was a feeling they both needed. Charley stopped in midstride as she carried gigging spears to the airboat.

"You know, Bannon, I can't believe he's *dead*."

Bannon closed the loading door to the wagon and came to her side. "Lars is dead. Put a big period to that, love. And if you're concerned about our taking a break so soon after he's buried—"

"*Buried?* You mean that last laugh act of his is what you call *buried?* The last thing Lars ever did was to make the dry cleaners of this town richer."

Bannon grinned. The hysteria and laughing after the ashes sprayed forth from the helicopter had taken a lot of sting from Anderson's sudden death. "The man had his own way, that's for sure," he said agreeably. "Short of an Irish wake, that's one of the better ways to go. Most people talk about you but they're either laughing or cursing, and Lars had it both ways." Bannon finished loading the airboat. "Now, this was *his* favorite way to let it all hang out. Get into one of these things and push off into swamp country and the tidal flats and get back on an eyeball basis with old Ma Nature. He said he preferred gators to most of the humans he knew, and that a trip out into the swamplands for a night was worth a month in the mountains."

"All right," Charley told him with a mock pout, "I won't let this be a funeral dirge. I'll enjoy myself. I *promise*."

"That makes two of us." Bannon looked about him and checked their gear. "Looks like we got it all. All aboard, sailor."

Charley settled herself comfortably against heavy blankets and cushions. She reached for the ice chest and brought out two beers, snapped them open, and handed one to Bannon. "Where to, Ace?" she asked, settling back in.

He took the padded bucket seat, checked the controls, remembered he was still tied up, went back and released the lines and returned to the seat. He didn't climb up. On impulse he went back, held Charley by her hair and kissed her deeply. No grabbing, no wild passion. A deep, longing kiss. Charley held him for a long moment afterward, squeezing her body tightly against his. Then she leaned back, shuddering with a long sigh.

"Sometimes, Bannon, you are Mr. Right."

"I needed just *that*," he said.

"So did I." She sat up straighter. "Hey, this is supposed to be a dear-departed celebration and a break for us, remember?" She shook off the somber mood and asked brightly, "Where to, admiral?"

He settled back in the seat as they drifted slowly from the dock and fired up the big aircraft engine. The smell of gasoline and oil wafted across them like perfume. He throttled back to dead idle and still they shouted to be heard. "We're going where the tourists don't roam," he told her. He was genuinely happy. "The frogs are zippadee-do-daaing in the Kennedy channels. That spells dinnertime for us."

He brought in gentle power with a throaty hum and

they seemed to levitate slowly across the water. "Isn't that a restricted area?" Charley called out.

"You got it, love. And that's why the tourists don't roam there. Got special clearance from NASA's chief spy. This way the guards won't be taking pot shots at us."

"God, that's a gorgeous sunset. You arrange that, too, Bannon?"

"Sometimes it pays to have connections, babe. Hang in there." He went to higher power, and the airboat roared and blasted and boomed across the river. They reached the shallows of the canals and driftways and Bannon eased off the power. They slipped beneath thick overhanging growth and Spanish moss. Life abounded everywhere, all manner of birds, fish jumping from the water, and along the near banks they saw raccoons peering at them from behind their masks.

For the moment all was at peace with the world.

Night fell with a gentling hush along the rivers of the coastline. The sunset seemed to have spread a velvety glow that remained in feeling well after the sky darkened and the new sounds of the night made their entrance. Well to the south of where Bannon and Charley Morgan drifted through thick growth, the prow of a powerful cabin cruiser sliced with foaming spray through the river, then eased forward as the engines throttled back. Within the cabin two men stood easily before a control panel, studying glowing lights and slowly changing digital readouts. One man pointed to an amber light as it glowed to prominence and began to blink steadily.

"Looks like it."

"Hang in there. Let's see the numbers."

Red lights flickered, glowed, brightened and changed rapidly. The man at the cruiser controls reversed power and backed slowly, then went again to idle. "Good. There it is," his companion said. "Depth finder also checks. Anyone around us?"

The man studying the panel display scanned the waters about them with binoculars. "Nobody around."

"Okay. It's below us and ten feet to port. Let's bring that mother up."

His companion worked switches on the control panel. A clear *Ping!* sounded and the men grinned at one another. They turned on a powerful searchlight pointing straight down beneath the cruiser at the river bottom and looked through a glass panel. Through the brilliant light they saw the water stir. The *Pings!* continued behind them. Large gasbags along the bottom inflated steadily and rose upward, pulling a net behind them. Details emerged from the murkiness and reflected light. The gasbags broke the surface with a sloshing sound. Suspended in their midst was a Mark 62 atomic bomb.

The two men swung a metal arm over the side of the cruiser and winched down a cable with a grappling hook. They reeled up the bomb, swung it inboard. "That's it . . . that's it . . . come to Papa. *Easy.*" They lowered the bomb to the deck, secured it with bungee cords. One man leaned over the side with a long pole and sharp blade at its end. He jabbed at the gasbags, air hissed steadily, and with a trail of bubbles the bags and net sank to the bottom. He turned to his companion.

"Let's go. Take it due north past that Air Force base."

"Emergency! Emergency!"

The computer-generated voice screamed its shrill warning. Alarm bells clanged and intense red light flashed swiftly on and off, a surrealistic bloodletting.

"Red Alert! Red Alert!"

Sirens wailed, shaking walls, echoing down corridors with physical punching force. Bernie Hudoff sat bolt upright in his desk chair, every muscle rigid, his mind refusing to accept what tore at his senses in searing light and battering sounds.He heard and tried to separate in his brain the alarm bells, the computer voices shrieking of imminent danger, the pounding of feet along the corridors, frightened voices calling thinly, doors slamming. Hudoff rushed to the large plate glass window of his office in NASA headquarters, staring into the night, trying to see *anything* that was different, that would confirm the awesome reality chewing and overwhelming him. His arms spread out to each side, palms flat against the window; his face pressed against the glass to get closer, to see better. He knew his eyes were bulging, his features distorted with fear he couldn't control. He shook, wildly angry with himself for his shaking limbs, his treacherous nerves that palsied so badly, and he felt his bowels watery and all the world and everything beyond and behind and everywhere vanished in a light beyond all light and savage knives hurtled into his eyes and Hudoff screamed and screamed.

The light *whoosh*ed upward, racing away from within his office, streaking with clawed touch from his skin and his eyes and his knees began to give and he felt his bowels give way and he was soiling himself, crying out in fear and rage and he wanted to stop the screaming, but now he saw the fireball, the monster, the ultimate mushrooming rose of death, angry and violent and churning within itself with a billion hateful, killing devils, the fireball consuming everything it touched, boiling and twisting upward, shooting into the night sky on a glowing purplish stalk, hideous and malevolent, and in front of the stalk and the upward crashing base surge of dust and smoke he saw the livid white scar of the shock wave tearing toward him, snapping trees and picking up the locomotives and the freight cars and hurling them into the air like plastic toys. Thunder was everywhere, in the air and the structure of the building and in his head and his stomach and running foully down his legs and he saw the big service hangars exploding like balsa wood and tinfoil, ripping outward. There went the television tower, twisted like a paper straw and battered aside and the thunder grew louder and *there!* the shock wave, it's here and it smashed into the glass and he was being sliced, cut, slashed, skewered, and he felt each individual piece of his body, still stabbing into his brain with agony, as the bloody chunks and pieces of himself whirled and splashed through his office and he saw himself at the window, what was left of him, crimson spray and pink shreds and—

"*Mr. Hudoff!*"

What?

"*Mr. Hudoff, please! Mr. Hudoff, wake up. WAKE UP!*"

He stared at his secretary. Her hand shook him violently. The motion stopped as his eyes came open. "Sir, you've been having a terrible nightmare. You ... you frightened me." She was shaking. "I mean, you screamed and—"

He gestured to signify enough. "Thank you," he said simply. "You're right. It was a bad dream." He felt the perspiration soaking his clothes. "It was a *very* bad dream. You're very kind. You can, uh, go back to your office now."

She looked at him with a mixture of sympathy and pity. "Yes, sir," she said quietly.

He didn't move until the door closed behind her. He squeezed the flesh on his left hand to make certain he was awake. He stared at the plate glass window. Everything was normal. No cuts, no bleeding, no disaster. But he shook. His stomach felt twisted and his brain seared. He rose slowly to his feet on shaky legs, braced himself against his desk for a moment and crossed the room to the window to stand before it.

His body shook uncontrollably and he burst into sweat again. *My God, I can't do it ...*

He walked backwards slowly, feeling behind him for his desk, then sat heavily in his chair. He brought out his flask, opened it, and held it to his lips. He couldn't drink. He just could not take a drop. It wouldn't do any good now.

His subconscious had told him what the danger they faced was *really* like.

He buried his face in his hands, shaking.

"You're not gigging for frogs." Charley Morgan snuggled against Bannon's broad chest, relaxing her body against his powerful frame.

"Frogs? At a moment like this?" He held her tighter, her body soft and warm against his. He kissed the back of her neck.

"You have a point there, Bannon," she said, smiling. "I—"

Lights stabbed through the darkness in the distance: great searchlight beams crisscrossing the launch pad where *Antares* stood within its huge service tower. In the salty mists of the beach the lights showed an eery glow as if spearing through light fog. Charley sat up suddenly. The lights seemed to have cut through the moment of calm. She moved away from Bannon and turned to face him, her knees drawn up and her arms tight about them. He recognized the signs of something that had to come out of her thoughts.

"You mind some questions, Bannon?"

He sighed and opened a beer. He offered her one; Charley shook her head. "I really need to talk with you." She looked about her. "This seems like the perfect time and place. No phones to ring, no one to bother us. Don't know when we'll have this chance again."

"You look very determined, Miss Morgan," he said, hoping his mock severity would ease the serious mood that had come on her so suddenly.

"How did you know I needed that alibi?"

He blinked. "Oh. The motel blitz."

"Yes. You knew I'd need a cover story. You knew it before anybody else even knew about that Air Force plane being forced down. I thought you were a real son of a bitch." She thought for a moment. "Not that you aren't," she added quickly, "but not in this case."

"What's there to say? You needed a cover and you had it when you needed it. What's wrong with that?"

"Bannon," she said, a weary tone to her voice, "please stop the baby-faced horseshit?"

"Okay." He kept his expression blank.

"There's only one way you could have known. I should have figured it. I mean, all the times Hudoff kept showing up at the airport. How you always manage to stay out of jail when they should toss you in solitary and throw away the key." She took a deep breath.

"Bannon, you're a cop, aren't you." No question; Charley was making it a statement.

"Well, sort of," he allowed.

"*Sort of!* What kind of pussyfoot answer is that?"

"Charley, I don't go around arresting people. I never *arrested* anyone in my life," he protested.

"Oh, you're a clever bastard with the words, Mitch

Bannon. You know damned well that the word cop covers a lot of territory."

"Goddamnit, Charley." He fidgeted with the beer can. "You're not *supposed* to know. I mean—"

"All this time you've let me hate you for the miserable, rotten, son of a bitch that's your reputation!" She stared at him. "I'll bet all those stupid stories about you on the beach, you know, with all those beach blanket bimbos, are also just a lot of hooey and you—"

"Now just a damn minute. It isn't all fairy tales, Charley!" He grinned. "I was only doing my job, you know?"

"I'll bet." She glared at him. "Give me that beer," she told him, and took a long swallow from the can he extended to her. "You're not local," she said, thinking aloud. "That wouldn't make any sense. Hudoff wouldn't bother even talking to you then. So that means you're government, doesn't it." Again a statement instead of the query.

"You're doing the talking, Charley."

"Oh, screw off, Bannon. It's past time for silly games. You *are* government, aren't you!"

"Yeah."

"How long?"

"Long time, honey."

"Since you've been down here? I mean, at Shiloh?"

"I haven't *been* down here, as you put it. I was brought here on assignment. No need to tell you my cover. Crop duster, mosquito control, the warbirds. It's all made to order."

"But . . . but *why?* I mean, all these years—"

She was recognizing this man as a different person, someone she had never known, who had lived his life with her, in all his association with her, behind a façade. Now he became the serious, hard professional, as if he'd tossed aside a camouflage net so she could see the real Bannon. He took a long breath and even a hint of mockery was gone from him.

"I've been here because of the one thing we've always been afraid of," he said slowly. "Bernie Hudoff is one of the best security men in the world. We've been dealing with terrorism long before most Americans even learned how to spell the word. We knew that one day our most important, our most valuable, our most *vulnerable* assets, people and places, would become targets. The atomic bomb has always been in the forefront of our thinking. One day someone was going to try just what's happening now. This Zoboa outfit, or whoever they are, getting their hands on nukes and hitting us right in the underbelly. Here at the Cape. So I've been here for all these years, living the life you and everybody else sees, but always watching. Watching, and waiting." He lifted the beer can in mock salute. "Well, babe, now the waiting is over. It's here, as big as life, and that's what it's all about. Life or death. That's the name of *this* game."

"Wait. Wait a moment." She shook her head and gestured with both hands to stop his words. "You've been here all this time, and what people know about you—no, that's wrong, what people *think* they know about you, I mean, you run drugs . . ." Her voice faded away. "My God, Bannon, *you're a drug runner!*" Her voice became shrill. "Why in God's name do you do *that!*"

"Like everything else, hon. It's a cover. It works. It opens contacts."

"It's filth!" she shouted.

"So's a nuke going off in your face," he said quietly.

"I don't mean that! *You,* of all people . . . you son of a bitch, *you even supply my kid brother.* Marty . . . he's just a, a baby, for God's sake!"

"He's no baby."

"He's *my* kid brother, *and you hooked him!*"

The anger she expected from Bannon didn't show. If anything, he retreated within a shell. "There's more to it than that." His voice was so low she could hardly hear him.

"Mitch, what can there possibly be to *know?*" she asked in a voice of anguish. "Drug runners killed our father . . . and the man I've been in love with is the same man I've hated because he keeps my brother supplied with the same stuff . . . the same stuff they killed my father for!"

Tears ran down Charley's face. Bannon took both her hands in his. "Look at me, girl." She blinked rapidly. "No, I mean *look* at me." He waited; she held his gaze. "You said you wanted the truth tonight."

"Y-yes."

"No holding back?"

"Damnit, *no!*"

Bannon's face was like stone. "All right, Charley. I'm not keeping Marty hooked. I wish it were that simple."

Her eyes widened.

"Charley, he doesn't take the stuff just because he likes it. He needs it."

"Needs? You said he wasn't hooked—"

"He's not. He has codeine if he wants it. He has morphine if that's what he wants. I'll get the kid anything he wants to fight the pain. But he has to do it his own way. Take something to dull the pain but keep his head clear enough to fly, to, well, to do what he wants to do."

"*The pain?*"

"Yes."

"For . . . for what?" Her lower lip trembled. Bannon held the hands of a frightened little girl.

"Marty has bone cancer."

She made the sound of a hurt small animal. He held her hands tighter.

"He's dying, Charley. He's dying, and he doesn't have more than a year or two, and he intends to stay a man until his time runs out." She stared at him, not seeing. "Damnit, Charley, *listen* to me! You can't let him know that *you* know. That would kill him all the sooner. Do you understand that? *Don't feel pity for yourself.* And sure as anything can be he doesn't want pity from you or me or *anyone*. Do you understand?"

She nodded, mute. She struggled for her voice. "Who . . . who else knows?"

"Karl and me. That's it. And now you." He shook her hands gently. "Charley, you with me?"

"Yes." Strength flowed back into her face. "Bannon, why did you let me hate you for so long?"

*   *   *

"There are times," said Corporal Aaron Maynard of the Cocoa Beach Police Marine Patrol, "when I wish people whose bedrooms overlook the canals would have the sense to draw the drapes." He smirked at Lieutenant Cliff Autry, whose look made it clear Autry figured his partner for a shameless liar. "Of course," Maynard continued hastily, "there are times, like this one, when I, ah, when I ..." he held back his thoughts as he adjusted his binoculars to study the couple twisted strangely in sexual embrace, "when I am intrigued by the muscular contractions of the bipedal creature we call woman."

"You mean fucking," Autry said with casual disinterest.

Maynard looked up from his position at the wheel of the police cruiser. Autry sat outside, smoking a long thin cigar, his practiced eyes taking in everything in all directions from the boat moving with the gentleness of great power cut back to purring idle. "Hey, Cliff," Maynard called, and the slight change in his partner's voice brought heightened attention to Autry.

"Yo. What's up?"

"Cliff, what's the range of this gimmick they put in here?"

For a big man with huge arms and a barrel chest, Autry could swing with acrobatic speed off the foredeck into the cabin. He did just that, hitting the cabin deck with a heavy thump. "It's five miles," Autry said, looking over Maynard's shoulder. "You got something?"

Maynard turned, a shade paler. "I sure as shit do."

They both stared at the Tracker light flashing red. "*Goddamn!*" Autry hissed. "Stay with that thing." He grabbed binoculars and scanned to each side of the cruiser. He expected nothing from the east, where the canals stabbed between endless rows of private homes. But to the west ... "I got a light to the west," he told Maynard. "Stay with it while I use the radio."

He snatched up the microphone. "All marine units from Amberjack, I have a Code One. Repeat, Amberjack has a Code One." He reached up and slapped a switch to ON; a thin whine could be heard above the engine rumble. "Autofinder is on," Autry continued. "All units work off our signal. We have a suspect in the water, white cruiser, three miles two niner zero degrees our position, moving north." As he talked, he signalled Maynard to go to full power. The engines ran up to a powerful roar to bolt the cruiser forward and throw back a huge bow wave and a wake behind them. Autry brought up the binoculars again.

"All units from Amberjack! They've spotted us and they're cutting around into Thousand Islands. We're going full chase. All ground and air units get with it. Request helicopter chase. Ground units cover the bridges. It looks like they're going to try a run through the city. We'll try to get to them first, but they've got a good start on us. Amberjack out, but we'll stay alive on this frequency."

Maynard was trying to slice across the path of the cruiser racing away from them. "Cliff! You better get the heavy stuff out!" he shouted.

"I'm ahead of you," he heard. Autry placed a high-power scope rifle in a rest alongside Maynard and loaded another for himself. He checked his service .357, brought out a wicked riot gun, and hit the searchlight on the foredeck and the red-and-blue flashing lights. "Give 'em the siren," he ordered Maynard. "It won't make them stop, but it'll get innocent boats out of the way."

"They're heading for Snake Creek, damnit!" Maynard said.

Autry looked calmly ahead of them, judging speed and distance and closure angle. "Try to cut them off," he said simply.

"Jesus, Cliff, I don't know—"

"Give it your best shot, buddy. This is the big one."

Throughout the long coastal area of the spaceports, supporting military airfields, and civilian security and law agencies, red lights flashed in offices, cars, boats, and airplanes. Buzzers and beepers sounded. Computers signalled the word. *"We have a target. We have a target. All units move out as planned. All units move out as planned. Use Field Control Delta for command. GO! GO! GO!"*

From Patrick Air Force Base, two combat helicopters on standby alert wound up to full power and boomed into the air in curving takeoffs. Behind them a Jolly Green Giant of the Marines started to come to life, combat troopers with autorifles running from the alert barracks to the huge machine.

A jet chopper with NASA SECURITY on each side lifted from the headquarters heliport. The doors were off. Men on each side were strapped to cabin hooks. They held submachine guns at the ready.

Shiloh Field burst into sudden activity. Jay Martin was napping in the cabin of his big Sikorsky helicopter, but the alarm signal brought him awake and moving with catlike agility to the pilot seat. Across the tarmac he saw armed men running to the helicopter. He recognized von Strasser and Santiago. Two other men moved with them. Their weapons were at the ready in the Sikorsky cabin. Jaybo wondered where the hell Bannon was.

Throughout the city of Cocoa Beach, police cruisers and unmarked cars rushed to the dozens of small bridges and canal choke points. If necessary they could pour withering firepower into any boat that raced through the city. SWAT teams brought searchlights and riot weapons into position. NASA notified the Coast Guard to close off the locks leading from the tidal basins direct to the Port Canaveral and Kennedy Space Center ports and loading basins.

Two NASA cruiser patrols, powerful coastal boats used formerly by drug enforcement teams, moved out from their docks onto the canal waterways that led from the tidal basins west of Merritt Island to the launch center.

Aaron Maynard was giving it his "best shot." Their quarry was fast, but the police cruiser had tremendous power for just this sort of work, and Maynard knew where and when to cut inside the turns of their target. They closed the distance rapidly, lights flashing and sirens screaming. Hundreds of people poured out of their homes onto back yards and docks as the thunder

316

of engines and wailing sirens reached them. Boats any-where near the two speeding cruisers were tossed about like corks from the unexpected wake.

"Don't let up!" Autry roared from the forward deck. He had dropped to one knee, bracing himself against the cabin, the powerful rifle at the ready. He aimed for the fuel tank and got off two quick shots, knowing that the hammering, shaking jolts of his own boat made a hit unlikely, but just might cause their quarry to make a sudden turn that would bring Maynard even closer.

The aft deck of the fleeing boat sparkled with orange and yellow flame. Autry looked for the blossom of fire to follow and then threw himself flat on the foredeck as machine gun fire smashed into the police cruiser. Above and about him the slugs tore up planking. He heard the windshield shatter. The police cruiser lurched and be-gan to veer off from its target. Autry turned to look into the cabin through the smashed remains of the windshield.

Maynard stared at him, eyes unblinking. Autry saw his partner in deep shock, blood pouring from his shat-tered arm. White bone jutted through the spurting blood. "Damn!" Autry spat, fighting the now-rocking boat to get into the cabin. He threw himself past Maynard and yanked back on the throttles.

"Damnit, I'm okay!" Maynard gasped. "Warn the others!"

"Squeeze that arm above the break," Autry snapped. "I'll be right with you." Maynard was right. A few moments more wouldn't kill him, but it sure as hell could kill others. He grabbed the microphone.

"Amberjack to all units! We are taking automatic weapons fire from fleeing suspect. Exercise maximum caution. Repeat, we're taking automatic weapons fire from fleeing suspect. Amberjack has wounded aboard and we are breaking off pursuit." He glanced at his partner. Maynard was white, leaning against the side of the cabin, ready to fall. Beyond Maynard, through the side glass, he had a final glimpse of the fleeing cabin cruiser hurling back a great plume of spray as it raced down a canal lying between two rows of brightly lit homes and gaping people on their docks and back yards.

Autry grabbed a bungee cord from an equipment rack and bound Maynard's arm, twisting it tightly with the barrel of his revolver to form a tourniquet.

"Damn you, Cliff, *go after them*," said Maynard through a haze of pain and teeth tightly gritted together. "Look, they've got to come out on Eleventh. That's the only way out of that canal. Either they double back or they've got to hit the end and break to the west. We can be—uh—" he gasped with pain, "waiting for them."

Autry nodded, slammed the power to the boat, cut sharply to his left, and started for a canal exit. Maynard was right. They'd have to come out through there. "Amberjack to all units, suspect is north into Eleventh Street Canal. We expect them to break to the west and will try to hit them there. All units north of Eleventh be alert for the suspect to go through several bridges on the Madison Canal."

They raced in a wide curving turn. Maynard was in deep pain, but he'd picked up one of the rifles and was resting it in a crook of broken glass in the windshield, ready to fire. He offered Autry a sickly smile and nodded that he was okay. "You're a goddamn liar," Autry said aloud, then concentrated on his booming run into a narrowing waterway. There! Ahead of them ... Maynard was right, they were coming out of the Eleventh Street Canal like the hounds of hell were after them. Autry hammered the throttles and ran dead-on for his quarry. By his side Maynard pumped out round after round. The other boat turned sharply, threw up a great curving spume of white water, and Autry saw the telltale splash of fire. He ducked. Bullets whined and spanged over his head. Maynard couldn't get out of the way fast enough and Autry heard an animal cry of pain as another bullet found Maynard. That was it. Autry cut power, turned hard left, watching the other boat break out to the northwest.

"Amberjack has broken off pursuit. I have an officer badly wounded and I'm going direct for Cape Canaveral Hospital. Notify them I'm coming right up their back door and I want medics waiting for me."

He concentrated on his full-power run. Maynard was

slumped unconscious on the deck alongside him. Autry kept all his lights on and siren howling, cut around embankments west of the hospital, and drove the cruiser directly up the ramp onto the grassy surface beyond and killed the engines. The cruiser rocked violently and came to a sudden stop, heeled over sharply. Paramedics were already coming over the side to Maynard. "We got him," one said to Autry. "Please, give us room. We'll take care of him."

Autry climbed out to the top of the cruiser with his binoculars. In the distance he made out the white splash of wake against the dark water. An avalanche of sound poured over him as the military helicopters roared northward in hot pursuit. They looked like alien spacecraft with flashing lights and hammering blades. Autry climbed down and followed the medics into the hospital. To hell with the boat. His partner might need help, a transfusion, a hand held tightly. Anything. That came first.

The two men in the cabin cruiser, despite their enormous experience, outstanding skills, and heavy machine gun armament, knew precisely what they faced in the forces gathering against them. They had listened to every police conversation, monitored the NASA security channels, and overheard the messages between NASA and the military. They had eliminated their first opposition even though the pursuing police boat had survived the encounter. But from now on an avalanche of firepower would descend upon them, and they knew that everyone on shore, aboard boats, and in the air would be searching for the telltale wake of a speeding boat.

They cruised at almost dead idle through a weed-choked canal buried beneath thick overhanging foliage. A hundred yards down the canal, invisible in the night gloom, waited an oversized airboat. The driver sat well back in this craft, his high seat positioned just before the cage with the powerful engine and propeller, leaving the front and sides of the airboat free for full firing coverage. One man in the bow of the airboat flashed a light with alternating amber and green colors. The men in the cabin cruiser nudged one another with pleasure. They answered with the same light signal, then increased their speed slightly until both boats were alongside. They swung the bomb outboard of the cruiser onto the airboat, and both men followed. As they rushed away, one of the men from the cruiser pulled the pin on an incendiary grenade and tossed it into the cabin. "Go!" he called to the airboat operator, who nudged the throttle and swung sharply across heavy growth in the water to a cross canal. They were several hundred yards away when a fiery explosion tore across the tidal waters and a fireball lifted into the sky.

"Ah, very good," one man spoke for them all. "A beacon for them to follow."

Another laughed. "Moths into the candle flame."

"All units, this is Bearcat One." The Air Force captain peered through the forward sight of his heavily armed helicopter. A blast of flame tore along the swampy surface beneath trees well ahead and to his right. "Someone's nailed the target. We have a large fireball on the water and there appears to be a boat on fire. We're going in for a closer look. Bearcat One out."

In his big, clumsy but powerful Sikorsky, Jay Martin fumed and cursed. "Get off the air, you son of a bitch!" he shouted to the voice coming over his headset. As long as Bearcat One keyed his transmitter to call out, Jay Martin couldn't break in. The instant he heard the Air Force pilot close the call Jay shouted into his microphone.

"All units, all units, that burning boat is a fake! It's a fake, damnit! This is Tinkerbell, this is Tinkerbell out of Shiloh. I can see the burning boat, but there's an airboat beneath me that came out from under the trees, right where that boat started burning. It's heading due west to open water and—uh, goddamnit, uh, uh, *shit!*" The sound of tearing metal and loud banging noises came across into every headset and speaker of every radio tuned to the common chase frequency. Jay Martin's voice came back, strained. "We've been hit! Tinkerbell calling, we're taking fire from that goddamn airboat!

They're shooting at us with automatic weapons!" For a moment there were only more loud crashing sounds and they heard Jay shouting to his own men; he'd forgotten he was still keying his mike and blocking the frequency. "Open fire, you bastards! Get them! We're going down after them! Shoot, goddamn you!"

He released his transmit switch. Another voice came in. "NASA Two here. We have Tinkerbell in sight. He's going down to the deck and he's under heavy fire. Everybody get in there as fast as you can."

A deep coughing roar punched through the tall grass to the right of their airboat. Charley came bolt upright, eyes wide, looking about her. Bannon fell sideways in the airboat, struggling for balance. "Mitch, that is a *big* damn gator and he's hungry and he is *very* close to us and—"

Bannon made it to her side. "Damnit, Charley, it's just a gator, for Christ's sake! Haven't you ever seen one of those things before?"

He grabbed up a powerful flashlight to sweep the nearby water. Two glaring circles of red flashed in the beam and Bannon brought it back quickly, holding it this time on the garishly reflecting eyes. "Jesus, he *is* big," Bannon murmured. The gator opened his jaws wide and bellowed at them as it swam with frightening speed at the airboat. Bannon grabbed an oar on the deck and swung it in a single up-and-down motion to wallop the huge reptile squarely between his eyes. The oar broke in half and the gator stared for a moment, jaws closing, and slipped beneath the surface.

Charley grabbed Bannon's arm. "Mitch, this is crazy . . . I still *hear* it."

They listened to coughing, snarling sounds coming from a distant source. "What the hell is going on?" Bannon wondered aloud. He had a strange feeling, a flood of old memories of other sounds similar to these. But it couldn't be . . . automatic weapons stuttering thinly in the long dark and the persistent beeping sound coming from—

Beeping sound? "Damn . . ." He dove at their sup-

321

plies, shoving them aside, grabbing the emergency caller. By its side was a powerful battery-powered VHF radio. He switched it on to full volume and immediately they heard Jay Martin's voice.

"... got a signal! All units, this is Tinkerbell in pursuit of the airboat. We've got a Tracker signal! *That damn airboat's got a bomb on it!*"

Bannon snapped down the transmit switch. "Jaybo, Bannon here. Go to circus frequency. Out." He switched to their airshow radio frequency to leave the main chase channel open. "Jaybo, this is Bannon. You read me?"

"Gotcha. Where the hell are you?"

"We're in an airboat due west of the VAB in Gator Cove. Did I hear you right? You're after an airboat with one of the bombs? Over."

Harsh laughter from the radio. Charley stared at Bannon as he listened. "Buddy, you heard right. They're trying to shoot off my feathers. Hey, I sure hope you got some of that fancy hardware with you. Our target is coming north out of Snake Creek and that puts you right in his way."

"Roger that, Jaybo." He nodded to Charley. "You vector us if you can. I'll turn on the white strobe." Charley moved behind Bannon and hit the switch. An intense flashing white strobe speared the darkness about them.

"I've got you, babe," Jay Martin called. "Okay, they're about a mile or so from you straight-line but I think they got to do some turns to get where you are. Who's with you, Mitch?"

"I got Charley here."

"*Get her the hell out of there, Bannon!* Those people are loaded for bear and they're killers!"

Charley leaned forward to the radio. "Jaybo, cut the crap and keep us on top of things. Don't waste any more time or words."

"Jaybo," Bannon said immediately afterward, "she's right. What's our best move look like to you from up there?"

"We've eased back a bit. They beat the hell out of us. I got a couple of men wounded. Like I said, they're

322

mean dudes. Okay, it's best if you turn off your light. I think we can set you up to bushwhack them. If you get in first crack, maybe you can stop them long enough for the heavy artillery to get there."

Charley killed the strobe light the moment she heard Jaybo's recommendation. "Glad you got that light out. They'll pass east of you to stay north on Snake Creek. Move east about three hundred yards and lay low and—" A crackling sound and spitting static from the radio drowned out his words.

"Jaybo! Come in!" Bannon yelled into his radio.

". . . all in . . . hands. Hit . . . going down. Can't keep up . . . speed . . . guys have all . . . luck . . . look out for . . ."

The frequency went dead. "Damnit," Bannon snarled. He switched back to chase frequency, decided to hell with it. "There's no time to talk," he said quickly to Charley. "You heard it all. We'll get into position and try to hit them with everything we've got."

Charley had her wits about her by now. "That's terrific," she told Bannon. "And what the hell *do* we have?"

He pulled open a velcro tab to a long equipment bag and handed her a .357 magnum. He turned to get to the controls. "Bannon! What the hell am I supposed to do with *this*?"

"Use it!"

"It's a popgun, for God's sake. They've got an *atom bomb* out there!"

He was in the seat and advancing the throttle, the engine roar growing. "Get the hell down!" he shouted, then gestured at the revolver in her hand. "You shoot people with that, not the damn bomb!"

"What if it goes off?" she shrieked at him.

"You won't even have time to remember you love me. Big light and you're vaporized. Just like an instant haircut."

"Damn you, you idiot, I love you!"

"I love you, too. Hand me that riot gun, there, to your left." He braced it by his hip. "Now that flare gun, Charley." He stuck it in his belt. "Now get down low by the right side and brace yourself. Keep that gun ready."

Through their preparations and moving out they'd ignored the babble of voices from the radio. But the voice of Abe Lansky cut through all the shouting and chatter. "Bannon, if you read me, this is Lansky. Martin put down safely. I just passed him. I'm in the Boeing jet chopper right behind that target airboat. I'm coming over the Bennett Causeway now . . . I hope you're reading this."

"We got you, Abe. They still coming north along Snake Creek?"

"Affirmative. I'm switching back to chase freq. Stay low, you two."

Again Bannon switched channels, his hands flying between the controls and the radio. They were moving faster through heavier growth. Charley stared at Bannon. "I never expected Abe to be out tonight . . ."

"Get your head down!" he shouted at her. "And keep that gun ready to fire!"

She turned; almost at once she pointed and cried out. "I see them! Over there . . . in the shallows. Mitch, they're going *through* the shallows . . . heading for the shuttle strip!"

"Charley! The radio! Call it in!"

He saw her grab the radio and talk close to the mike. He went to full power, the wind and engine roar exploding to a furious crescendo. They smashed their way ahead, bouncing hard, slamming along the water. Bannon turned on a powerful searchlight mounted to a pole above his seat. Far ahead he saw the other airboat, its huge propeller sending back a glistening cloud of foaming spray and fog.

"Tell 'em, Charley!" he shouted as loudly as he could.

She leaned down low. "Morgan here with Bannon in the airboat! We've got them dead ahead of us . . . they're going for the landing strip!"

Directly above them several helicopters added to their thunder, lights stabbing ahead of them, racing with wicked speed over the water and the weeds and trees rising from the surface. Two military choppers, men barely visible as they leaned from open doors with weapons in their hands, flashed ahead of them. Conversation

324

was now impossible. The world boiled with energy, thunder smashed down like a billion kettledrums, and it all mixed with the wind, the boat smashing down and bouncing hard, helicopter blades and exhausts and the radio blatting out words they could no longer hear well enough to understand.

They tore ahead with surrealistic speed as high growth ripped past them, weaving about dark shadows Bannon knew were trees, hoping he wouldn't smash into a log or a gator. Then for a long moment they forgot any of their own vulnerability. Glowing coals arced into the sky from the airboat they were chasing. They barely heard shouted exclamations from their radio, but Bannon didn't need anyone to tell him he was seeing tracers from a heavy-caliber machine gun. His muscles tensed. Those damn fools in the security helicopters didn't know the ins and outs of a combat chase situation and they'd bore straight in, all full of piss and guts and vinegar. Their courage *without experience* would—

"Oh, shit!" he exclaimed aloud, his words torn away by howling wind and engine thunder. A rose blossomed in the sky out of a flash of yellow light deepening to orange, and finally the rose itself appeared, boiling red, twisting within itself and spilling out debris like a genie coughing blazing petals. Charley had grabbed the radio and turned it up to full volume and Bannon could barely make out the words. "This is Lansky. That airboat got one of the Air Force jobs. Direct hit. No survivors. Out."

Well, he knows how to handle his communications in a tight situation, Bannon observed to himself, and then forgot everything else. He gave the tumbling, spinning flames only a second glance. Looking up into the sky is a guaranteed way to run into what can kill you on the surface. He had an idea and shouted to Charley. "The radio! Give me the radio!"

She struggled to reach him in the jostling, smashing lunge of the airboat and got him the radio. He waited a moment for another transmission to end and snapped down the transmit button. "Lansky, this is Bannon. We've been gaining a little on them. Can you force them to the left? Over."

He heard a short, harsh laugh. "It's no fun down there, Bannon, but I'll pay them a visit. If you have any firepower, try to get their attention."

He cut off. Again, no wasted words. He saw the helicopter dip suddenly, swerving from left to right and back again, a swooping sort of falling-leaf maneuver. *He's a pro.* The thought rushed through his mind again and was gone as he threw his full attention before them. The world was a tremendous madhouse of noise, jolting blows to the body, a wild explosion of searchlights, strobes, glowing tracers arcing through the sky, and the flames of guns firing madly. Far in the distance a giant square moon hulked on the horizon: the huge VAB structure illuminated by floodlights. It was a hellish bedlam of sight and sound.

Charley's voice came to him in a half shout/half scream. "He's turning them! He's got them!"

The wildly maneuvering helicopter spat yellow flame from automatic weapons as Lansky took his ship down to the deck, reducing to a minimum his risk of being a target. Bannon saw the fleeing airboat racing from the shallows in a desperate new run for speed. It was working! Now he could cut across the line of their curve. He banged in full rudder, the airboat bouncing and skidding madly as he began his change in direction.

But it wasn't all that easy. Now they were in range and Charley had a rifle braced against her body, pumping out shot after shot. She couldn't tell if she'd hit anything, but she got their attention. Red coals flashed at them from the night, cutting magically through the tall grass. Bannon yelled at Charley. "Get down! Down!"

She lifted her right arm and held up her hand with the middle finger extended, dropped the arm and fired off another three rounds. Bullets tore up metal by her side. She hurled herself to her right, her expression one of complete astonishment, rolled again to the edge of the airboat, grabbed for the .357 magnum Bannon had given her before. Enraged, she sat straight up, the heavy revolver in both hands, blazing away.

"Hang on!" Bannon yelled. Charley looked up, saw a road above the water rushing at them, and with a muf-

fled scream dropped to the bottom of the airboat. They hurtled toward the road stretching through the shallows. Bannon hit the slope at an angle of seventy or eighty degrees. They struck with brutal impact that jarred every bone, shaking their eyeballs as the airboat struck hard land and flew up and wildly to one side. Bannon had already come forward and down from his chair, grabbing Charley's arm and throwing her in a great wheeling motion over the side of the airboat. He dove out after her and the world became a tumbling blur as they hit water several feet apart, barely able to see their airboat twisting through the air, engine screaming. Its shadowy shape seemed to expand magically until they saw that the shadow *was the other airboat* that had raced along Snake Creek on the other side of the road. The two airboats came together with locomotive force, engines howling, propellers tearing loose and flaying metal to shrapnel, hulls ripping with womanlike screams. A banshee cry tore through the swampy water as ruptured fuel tanks exploded. Two fireballs boomed across the swamp and huge blazing chunks splashed and bounced all about the surface.

"The road!" Bannon shouted to Charley. "Get to the road *now!*" She stared at him blankly until an enraged roar shook her body, a roar much closer than the hissing flames and helicopter engines and booming rotor blades: the bellow of an enraged gator splashed with burning gasoline. Several more reptiles thrashed madly in the water about them. Charley and Bannon swam for their lives, scrambling wildly up the bank onto the roadway. A huge gator came after them, eyes blazing in the reflected firelight. Bannon drew a revolver from an armpit holster and fired. A wet clicking sound came from the weapon. He hurled the useless metal at the gator and ran with Charley. A burst of machine-gun fire ripped the air over them as a chopper swung low, searchlight on the gator as the gunner ripped it into bloody chunks. It flipped wildly back into the water.

Bannon and Charley waved their thanks, turned to the airboat wreckage that had spumed along the shallows and the road. Incredibly, several men had lived through the crash and the fiery explosion. In the glow of flames and intense lights from the helicopters they saw men staggering onto a grassy bank. Just beyond them a helicopter came down hard onto a flat area. One of the men staggering onto the bank fired into the cockpit of the helicopter.

"My God, it's Lansky ..." Charley said hoarsely as the pilot dove from his cockpit door, a submachine gun in one hand. He hit the ground, rolling over and to the side, and came up with the machine gun blazing.

"Don't shoot! DON'T SHOOT! GODDAMNIT!" Bannon was shouting and yelling as he ran forward. He was much too late. Lansky was enraged and he was very good with his weapon. The man who fired at him stood stock still as the top of his head disappeared in a spray of lead and blood. Before he hit the ground Lansky had dropped to the ground, rolling, coming up with the gun again firing, and two more figures jerked and twitched wildly. They spun about and tumbled to the ground.

Bannon ran up to Lansky and grabbed his arm. "God-damnit, why'd you kill them?"

Lansky studied Bannon. "Are you crazy? They were shooting at me."

"You son of a bitch," Bannon railed, "they could have told us where the other bombs were!"

Lansky smiled thinly. "Of course, Bannon. Some day perhaps you will tell me how *you* will hold a conversation with someone while he's shooting at you from point-blank range. In the meantime—" He stopped short as he caught sight of Charley, splattered with oil and mud. "Are you hurt?" he asked.

She shook her head. "No ... I'm okay ..." She gestured at the bodies. "Do you know ... who they are?"

Lansky's face was satanic. He motioned with the machine gun, then rolled over the nearest body with his foot. The bloodied corpse with sightless eyes stared back at them.

"Jesus ... it's Hamza!" Bannon said hoarsely.

Lansky looked at them, his face mirroring anger, pain, hatred; God knew what. "You see this piece of shit!" he shouted suddenly, his rage exploding. "This man was my *brother!* This was the man who fought wars with me!" He emptied the machine gun into the corpse. "Bastard! Traitor!" he screamed.

Charley turned from the sight of the bullets blowing away chunks and sprays of blood. Bannon stared at Lansky and then at Hamza and back at Lansky, who trembled with outpouring emotion. "Now I know who this dung is! Do you know, Bannon? Of course not! *How would you know Sadad Jabal!*" He kicked violently at the shattered head of the dead man. Bannon grabbed Lansky. "Easy, easy," he said. "Let me have the gun, Abe." Lansky handed him the emptied machine gun. He stood with shoulders bowed, staring at the gory mess before them.

Wind howled with increasing force about them. An Air Force helicopter hovered to the side, its searchlights turning night into blue-white day. "This is Bearcat One," came the voice of a loudspeaker. "Is Mitch Bannon with you people?"

Bannon waved his arm in response.

"Please stand by, sir. NASA Security One is coming in to pick you up. By the way, Bannon, you were right. They had the nuke with them. Our people picked it up and it's safe. Thanks." The helicopter swayed as its pilot drifted off to the side, keeping the lights trained on them.

They watched another chopper coming in, settling gently, cutting power to idle. Bannon went forward. As he reached the helicopter, Hudoff climbed down from the cabin. "I just got the ID on one of those people who was in that airboat. That fat Arab bastard, Hamza! *Abe Lansky's partner!* Goddamnit, I'll bet Lansky's a thousand miles away from here by now!" He stabbed a finger at Bannon. "I want you to move heaven and earth to find that Jew son of a bitch! I want him alive! I want . . ."

His voice fell away as Lansky walked up with Charley, standing by Bannon. He looked like hell with blood and stains over his face and body. He moved unflinchingly to Hudoff until they were face to face like two

329

snarling animals. Lansky didn't snarl. He spoke clearly and with contained anger.

"Tell me, my friend. Tell me what you want from that Jew son of a bitch."

✛ 19 ✛

HANDCUFFS AND FRISBEES

Bernie Hudoff watched the flashing red and blue lights on the road shoulder behind him. One police officer stood behind and to the side of Hudoff's car; the other approached his open window. Hudoff had no idea what the hell was going on. He had been driving south in A1A through Cocoa Beach to reach the Air Force base when the police car came up behind him with lights flashing.

"What's the beef?" Hudoff asked the officer.

"Your driver's license, sir? May I see it?"

"Sure." Hudoff extracted the license from his wallet. "But you didn't answer me. What's going—"

"You're Mr. Bernard Hudoff, sir?"

"That's my picture on that piece of paper, officer." Hudoff was getting ticked with the courteous indifference. The officer ignored his questions and stepped back. "Sir, please step out of your car and come with us. Your car will be taken care of, sir."

"What the hell's the charge!" Hudoff yelled.

He didn't faze the young cop. "Sir, we haven't time to argue. You are not under arrest and you have not committed a crime, but we are under orders. If you don't come with us willingly—"

Hudoff pushed open his door. "Okay, okay, I got your message, bonzo. Gimme my damn license." He snatched it from the officer's hand and stalked to the police car. The second officer smiled at him, made sure Hudoff saw the handcuffs he'd been holding at the ready, and with great courtesy opened the door for Hudoff. "Sir?"

They parked outside the station, as silent as Easter Island statues, went through the back entrance, and walked on either side of Hudoff through an operations and communications room. Curious stares followed them, but no one said a word. Then it was up a flight of stairs, turning right into a narrow corridor with barred cells along each side. Policemen hustled scummy prisoners away from the cells. "God, they stink," Hudoff said aloud. A scabby prisoner grinned at him with broken teeth.

Hudoff realized suddenly that the entire corridor was empty except for himself and the two cops. They turned at the end of the corridor. Two rows of cells stretched before them. Another police officer stood by an open door. He nodded to Hudoff. "Sir, in here, please."

Hudoff stood like a rock. "You're putting *me* into a *cell*?" This whole thing was ridiculous.

"No, sir." The cop showed no resentment. "Mr. Hudoff, *please?*"

Cursing under his breath Hudoff walked into the cell and came to a dead stop before the beautiful woman standing by the far wall waiting for him. He knew she was something special by her demeanor, total self-confidence, business suit. This woman was accustomed to giving orders. By her side stood a police lieutenant. Hudoff saw the name Cliff Autry on the silver bar beneath his shield.

The woman extended her hand. Hudoff took it awkwardly. "Mr. Hudoff, I apologize for bringing you here this way. I am Jane Willoughby and I'm the mayor of Cocoa Beach. This is Officer Cliff Autry of our marine patrol."

My God, how can she be so gracious in a place like this? Hudoff wondered. Aloud, he was all business. "Autry. I know your name. Last night. You were the first to pick up on that boat."

"Yes, sir." Hudoff groaned inwardly. Another statue.

He turned to the woman. "I'm getting the picture fast," Hudoff told her. "You've heard things." He glanced at Autry; the one glance saved many words. "But why the secret hustle bit?"

Jane Willoughby seated herself carefully and invited Hudoff to take the opposite bunk. "Your time is valuable, Mr. Hudoff. So is mine." She paused and a smile crossed her face. "Obviously, we may have very little of it left."

He raised a heavy eyebrow and she smiled again. No humor went with her expression. "I shall be blunt, Mr. Hudoff."

"Do it, Mayor." He reached for a cigar, held it up, watched her nod, and lit up.

"A terrorist group has threatened to explode an atomic bomb in this area," she said with quiet, convincing strength.

Hudoff waited. Smoke drifted from his nostrils.

"Am I correct, Mr. Hudoff?"

"If you are then you know more than I do, Mayor." This time her facial expression was genuine. It was also one of surprise. "I don't know what you've heard," Hudoff continued. "You know about the four bombs that were hijacked. We *believe* that whoever has the bombs—the two remaining bombs, that is—will go after the shuttle launch area. But we don't *know*. There has been no contact, no word, no demand of any kind from whoever snatched those nukes."

"But *we*, here, *could* be a target."

"So could San Francisco." Hudoff leaned forward. "Look, Miss Willoughby, I'm not being difficult. But maybes and could-bes and perhapses don't mean much to me. The most likely target in this area *is* the shuttle and the launch area at liftoff. Period. More than that I can't tell you a thing. I just do not know."

"Why didn't you tell us? By us I mean the officials who are responsible for the people of this—"

He broke in with a gesture. "Please, Mayor. No Chamber of Commerce speeches. We didn't tell you anything because it wouldn't have accomplished anything."

"But . . . we have this entire community to protect!"

"Okay. Have it your way, Mayor. So let's say I told you. Right from the beginning. How would you protect your community with a little concrete information and a hell of a lot of speculation?"

"Why, we could prepare for . . . I mean, we could—"

Hudoff didn't want to do it, but he lashed out like a python. *"Go on, Mayor. Tell me what you would do!"*

He leaned back against the metal wall, sucking deep on the cigar, letting the smoke wreathe his face and lift slowly. She groped for an answer, and he slipped into the silence. "Mayor, you won't do a thing because there's nothing you *can* do." He shrugged. "Except, of course, hope that we find those two bombs in time. And if we continue to get help from your people like we did from this officer last night, we may do it." He glanced at Autry. "How's Maynard?"

Autry's reaction told him he was surprised to see that Hudoff knew his partner by name. "He's making it, sir. Thank you."

Jane Willoughby gestured suddenly, trying to emerge from the sudden confusion dropped on her by Hudoff. "We . . . we could *evacuate!*"

Hudoff didn't tell her what Sheriff Bob Hughes had to say on that matter. This woman was talking only to him and she deserved straight answers. "Ma'am, you'd evacuate? *To where?* How? And *when* would you do this? *You* tell *me* how much time you have to do all this. *You* tell *me* where that bomb might go off. You *could* be moving your people right *under* that fireball. If you do, you'll kill everybody who follows your advice."

She stared at Hudoff, devastated.

Hudoff eased off. "Mayor, I'm not being unkind, and I *do* appreciate your position. But please understand that we've been living with this thing for a while. You want to *guarantee* panic? You want riots? You want to kill people by stampeding them? Then tell them what you know, which is damned little, and that we're facing cold-blooded killers."

He dropped an ash carefully on the floor beneath his shoes. "You really want to help your community?"

"For God's sake, *of course!*"

"Then shut up. I'm not trying to insult you. *Don't say anything.*"

She glanced at Autry and then back to Hudoff. "You want me, all of my officials, *to lie?*"

"You bet. You learn fast, Mayor. *You lie.* You smile at them and you lie through your teeth because that's the *only* way you can help." He stood up. "Now, Mayor, will you please have your gorillas, as polite as they are, take me back to my car?"

"It's waiting for you downstairs, sir," Autry said.

"I should have known," Hudoff told him. He turned back to Jane Willoughby. "If this man ever gives you any trouble, Mayor, call me right away. I'll hire him on the spot."

Charley Morgan stood back from the monster. The creature was dormant, stripped of its flaming breath and the lash of thunder that had electrified an entire planet and carried men to and from another world a quarter million miles across the Sea of Vacuum. There, on a cratered and dusty surface that had never known the stirrings of life, men planted the flag, set down their scientific instruments, explored another frontier, and cavorted in the heady lightness of one-sixth gravity.

"I still can't believe it," she said finally as she shook her head at the five enormous engines that had lifted the gigantic Saturn V rockets from the same pads where the shuttles now poised. The monster lay on its side near the hulking VAB where the great rockets once were assembled and rolled out to their pads to fulfill dreams that went back to the time when men were first drawn by that cold, enigmatic orb in the night skies.

Bernie Hudoff was far from the moon. He was right here in the shadow of the giant now on display as a memorial to a dream grown nearly as cold as the lunar shadows. "Damndest thing I ever saw," he was telling Bannon as Charley joined them. "They just hauled my ass into jail past some of the scummiest gumbos you ever saw, they waltz me into this cell, and there's this stunning woman waiting for me. The mayor. I could hardly believe it."

"You must be talking about Jane Willoughby," Charley offered.

"You know her, Miss Morgan?"

"The name is Charley. Especially since we're no longer throwing daggers at each other. Yes. She was a friend of my father's. Did you know she was a state senator?"

"First, no, I didn't even know she existed. Second, I heard about a Jane Willoughby out of Tallahassee, but I didn't connect the two. And third, thank you, Charley."

"Think she'll go along with you?" Bannon asked.

Hudoff nodded. "That is a very smart, very sharp lady. Going along with me hasn't a thing to do with it. She'll do whatever is best for her town." Hudoff looked with genuine admiration at Charley. "Speaking of ladies, I'm talking to a very special one right now. I haven't had the chance to say thank you for a great many things. I get carried away sometimes with this job, and I don't candy to admit being wrong about people, but by God I was a hundred and eighty degrees out of line where you're concerned."

"You'll make me blush," she hesitated, "Bernie." She smiled and took his arm. "Underneath all that grizzly fur there beats the heart of a true gentleman. I'd almost forgotten what it was like to be around one."

"You keep bad company, Charley." They both looked at Bannon. Hudoff nodded in his direction. "You won't climb any social ladders with this lunatic around you."

Bannon sighed. "You're always a great help, boss."

"And he was so good at being rotten!" Charley exclaimed.

"I hate giving compliments," Hudoff replied, "but he's sure good at his job. He's rotten through and through." Charley squeezed his arm.

"Okay, back to work," Hudoff said gruffly. They started walking to the VAB. Hudoff gestured. "Look around you, Bannon. I can't think of anything we've missed." His gesture was meant to take in the entire operational area. "The whole launch complex, the astronaut quarters, museums, the press and VIP areas, fuel farms, the generating plants. Even the sewage pipes. Man, we have been through *everything* above *and* below ground. We even crawled through the transporters, the air conditioning systems and— A mouse couldn't get through the screen we have up."

"It won't be anywhere you've looked," Bannon told him. "It's all too obvious."

"Mind explaining that, Einstein?" Hudoff asked.

"Those bombs are four hundred kilotons, boss. That's four hundred thousand tons of TNT punch. *Each*. I'll bet you even tore the whole headquarters apart."

"Damned right we did."

"You wasted your time. They'd never be *there*."

"Bannon, what the hell are you talking about?"

"Yes, Bannon," Charley added. "You've lost me, too."

"Headquarters is about five miles from here," Bannon said. "It's too far away."

Charley looked at him with disbelief. "Five miles . . . only *five* miles, is too far away for an *atomic bomb?* Thats hard to believe. I mean—"

"Charley, they're not going after a city," Bannon said patiently. He held his words until they passed through the double-gated security barriers recently set up. They went into the huge vaulted structure of the VAB and again Bannon held his conversation. *Space cathedral* flashed through his mind, and then he resumed his explanation to Hudoff and Charley.

"Look, if they're after the shuttle then they've got to have a really powerful overpressure," he went on. "We lost *Challenger* early in '86 because it was *attached* to its own bomb. That was the external fuel tank. A man puts a gun to his head and shoots a bullet through his brain, things explode. That's what happened to *Challenger*. A shuttle like *Antares*, or any of the others, is designed to punch through thick atmosphere at better than eight thousand miles an hour. Even the external tank, especially since NASA beefed up all those systems, can take terrific wind loads. So if they want to knock out *Antares* with overpressure, they've got to get in close."

He stopped to let a huge loading crane rumble by before them. Several great shuttle external tanks were in vertical bays. Stacks of massive solid-propellant boosters and assorted nose cone and engine nozzles crowded the enormous building. Bannon felt let down, a sudden negative rush that caught him unawares.

"Hell, that damn bomb could be stuck in a tin can underwater, right off the beach to the launch pad," he said gloomily.

"Ain't no way, José," Hudoff snapped. He saw they were attracting attention. "Hold it for now. We're going upstairs."

They kept their conversation to idle chatter as they rode the great elevators to a height of five hundred and fifty feet above the ground level. Charley leaned over the rail, her helmet pressed against the safety screen that kept objects from accelerating with lethal speed if ever they fell from the top levels inside the building. People moved like tiny ants below, and even the biggest trucks were toy models. *My God*, she thought, *I'm at pattern altitude on my base leg for landing. . . .* They followed Hudoff through another security gate and climbed the final stairway to the roof of the VAB. The world spread before them as though they *were* in flight. Hudoff led them to the east edge of the roof. They looked down on the great crawlerway that led to the launch pads. To their right and the south loomed the structures of the Titan complex, and beyond that the slim needle shapes of the rockets at the museum on the Cape. Several orange launch towers stood like plastic toothpicks along the Canaveral beach line.

"You see that beach area beyond that launch pad?" Hudoff picked up their conversation, sweeping his arm to take in the beaches directly to their east. "I'll tell you for sure, Ace: there's no bomb on that beach and there isn't anything in the water. When I first took this job, I laid down metal detectors all along this beach for five miles north and five miles south. I've got anti-submarine detectors in the water for more than a mile straight out to the east. And to be extra sure, I've used new magnetometers. Everything there is. I brought in Navy demolition teams. I'll tell you right now there isn't a scrap of metal for two miles out we don't know about."

Bannon nodded slowly, looking about him. "So either

the bomb is already planted where this Zoboa outfit wants it—"

"Bullshit," Hudoff said immediately.

"—or they'll try to deliver it by plane at liftoff," Bannon finished.

Hudoff tapped a heavy finger against Bannon's chest. "Listen, Hoss, I know you people think you're all hot shit, and I even admit *that you are*." He glanced at Charley. "I've flown with the little lady here and she impressed the hell out of me, and I can't remember the last time that happened. But no one's going to get through the wall of jets and combat choppers we're going to raise on launch day. *No one*," he repeated.

"Well, you described it properly before," Bannon admitted.

"How do you mean that?" Hudoff demanded.

"The word was bullshit. Everything you just said is bullshit. Someone *always* gets through, especially if they're willing to dive right into their target." Bannon's look was almost pitying. "You better remember the Kamikazes, Bernie. Scared kids and old men up against the hottest defenses in the world and *they* got through. The divine wind, remember? Well, Zoboa's another divine wind, at least as far as those loonies are concerned. Boss, you could have your private Star Wars defenses all set up and someone *always* gets through. What are you going to do if they show up in a couple of jet fighters coming in at better than six hundred miles an hour? They've still got two bombs. You'll never know which plane's got the nuke and you sure can't get them *all* before—" He made a contemptuous gesture of the whole idea of stopping a concerted attack. "I'll tell you your best defense, boss-man. Find those damn bombs *now*."

Charley moved forward at the sight of Hudoff's troubled face. She rested her hand gently on his arm. "Bernie, I have to say something—"

"Please, go ahead."

"Bernie, I'm just a girl and I don't have any jet fighters of my own. My planes are from a war that ended more than forty years ago. But I can use the same stuff,

339

like aluminum chaff, that they were using way back then and I can knock out all your radar—you know, the stuff to track planes and fire on incoming attackers. And, Bernie, like I said, I'm a girl and I've never flown combat and I hate to tell you this, *but I can get through.*"

Hudoff studied them carefully. "You two make quite a pair. Real entertaining," he said sourly.

"Jesus Christ, Bernie, you want us to *lie* to you?" Bannon said with a touch of heat.

Hudoff smiled without humor. "There are times, Ace, when that would be better than the truth." He rested a hand on Bannon's shoulder. "No, of course not." He turned to Charley. "All your planes out again today?"

She nodded. "One hundred and seventy-one of them. We have a bunch of ships in maintenance. Ever since Lars was murd— since he was killed," she finished with a catch in her throat, "our maintenance operation has fallen back somewhat." She brightened. "But any time we get more than a hundred and fifty planes out on search we're doing okay."

She turned and pointed to the northwest. "See that high haze? Well, we won't be flying tomorrow. There'll be an inversion layer tonight that will give us a level of cold air over hot, and with the temperature and the humidity," she shrugged, "tomorrow morning you won't be able to see your hand in front of your face."

Hudoff wanted to be certain. "Fog early in the morning?"

She nodded. "Pea soup. Real thick. When the sun hits you'll see it condensing into clouds right on the deck. But as far as flying is concerned, it will be zero-zero."

Hudoff fell into sudden deep thought. "How long will the fog last?"

"I'm a pilot, Bernie, not a magician." Charley said, smiling. "But on the basis of what we've experienced here before, it should be breaking up about ten-thirty or eleven."

"Thank you," he said warmly, but with a touch of distance. What Charley had told him still had Hudoff deep in thought.

*   *   *

"Hey! Get another pony of beer, willya!" Mad Marty leaned over the edge of his chaise lounge and yelled to Wilbur Moreland as he zoomed into sight on his skateboard. Wilbur paid him no attention as he rolled to the beat, always the beat, his headphones clamped tight about his ears, fingers snapping, eyes rolling and one foot pushing. He barely avoided a wing tip, wobbled his way around a rudder, and clattered on down the taxiway. "Goddamn Wilbur, he don't hear for shit." Marty muttered. He whistled for Magnum. The big dog came to his side and sat, alert for further orders. "You go over there to the big German bastard, dog, y'hear?" Magnum looked at von Strasser and barked. "Okay, then, he gives you a can of beer, and you bring it back to me, and if you drink any, I'll kick your furry ass into the middle of next week. Go, dawg. Do it."

Magnum trotted across the bright green of articial turf, maneuvering adroitly amidst the lounge chairs, beach towels, folding tables with large pitchers of cold drinks, chips and pretzels, and drums filled with ice and beer. Sherri Taylor lay on a beach towel in a wickedly brief bikini beneath the afternoon sun. Two blonde teen-agers, lithe and beautiful, lay near Mad Marty. His head still covered with a turban-like bandage, Jay Martin sat beneath a beach umbrella, pensive and buried in thought, completely ignoring the beautiful young bodies nearby.

Von Strasser, Bannon, and Santiago sprawled about a table, smoking cigars. They were half-plowed, pleasantly drunk with hard whiskey and a hot sun. Von Strasser wore horrid Hawaiian shorts and a gambler's green visor. On either side of the group, large speakers boomed forth the body-pulsing tempo of *Flashdance*, each number interspersed with selections from Wagner's Ring of the *Nibelung*. The mixing of the dance tunes of the modern powerful beat with the massive rising crescendo of the *Ride of the Valkyries* made for an interesting, albeit senses-jarring, performance.

The big dog ambled back from von Strasser with a can of cold beer clenched firmly in powerful jaws. He stood obediently as Mad Marty took the can and then tossed an empty into the air near the dog. "Crush it,"

Marty commanded. Magnum snapped his teeth onto the can and closed his teeth until he had only crumpled metal in his mouth. "Well, don't just stand there," Marty told the animal. "Drop it over the side, you asshole."

Magnum walked gingerly to the leading edge of the broad wing of the huge transport plane, leaned over, and released the can. It fell fourteen feet to the concrete taxiway, clattering tinnily amidst other crumpled cans. The big dog lay down, satisfied with his performance. He looked up suddenly as a Hawker Sea Fury fighter came over low, the pilot pitching out for landing, the big engine and huge propeller sending a deep-throated, low moan of power across the field.

Jay Martin looked up and pointed. "First son of a bitch today who looks like he knows how to fly. All we've seen are assholes."

Marty slugged beer and belched. He liked the view from fourteen feet up, where they'd transformed the C-54 wing into their private lawn party. "Not assholes," he corrected beerily. "They're dumbshits. You gotta understan' the difference."

They sat up with mild interest as a pilot struggled down in a high-winged taildragger, fighting a crosswind, the airplane bouncing and rocking wildly from side to side before its pilot regained control. Bill Santiago hooted at the display. "I give you five to one that asshole he is wearing these Bermuda shorts. All pilots fly like that they's got to wear Bermuda shorts."

Sherri Taylor raised up on one elbow. "Why in God's name would they do that?" she asked.

Santiago smiled at her. He reminded Sherri of a large rat preparing to feast on a baby rabbit. "It easier," he said with mock severity, "when you wear thees Bermudas to scratch your balls."

"Sure," Bannon chipped in, "especially when you got three of them. Unlike Santiago, here, who, according to the legendary poems on the pisshouse wall, only has one."

"How the hell you know this?" Santiago demanded, his hours-long consumption of beer providing sudden indignation. "There ain't no signs on pisshouse wall. I look and I know."

"He cleans the walls every night," von Strasser observed.

"Besides, no one needs to read the crapper bulletin board," Jay Martin added. "Everybody knows he's got only one nut."

"How the hell *you* know anything, man?" Santiago growled.

"Wendy's selling pictures, man," Marty threw in. "Not only that, you spic bastard, if somebody buys a dozen copies she throws in a blowjob for free."

"Only blowjob you ever get is from you dumb dog!" Santiago shouted.

"Hey, spic!" Jay Martin called. "You know why a dog licks his balls?"

In perfect unison their voices rang out in a bellowing chorus: *"Because he can, that's why!"*

Sherri watched as the dog began vigorously to wash himself. "Well, he must have heard you loonies," she told the others. They turned to watch the dog, who ignored them all as his tongue worked furiously.

Sherri wasn't going to be put off by this bunch. "Marty, you think you could do that?"

He blinked. "Do what?"

"What your dog is doing," she said sweetly.

"I tried it once."

Sherri raised an eyebrow. The other girls looked up with sudden interest. "What happened?" Sherri asked.

"Damn dog bit me," Marty said with a straight face, until all the heavy looks evaporated into laughter and gasps as they choked on their beer.

Jay Martin sat straight up. "Jesus Christ," he said, and his voice was deadly serious, enough for his sudden change in tone and demeanor to command their attention. They turned to follow his gaze. A silver-and-blue T-34 taxied by the big transport, front and back cockpit canopies open, the pilots waving to them. They stared at the bearded man in the front seat.

"Son of a bitch," Martin said slowly, visibly shaken. "For a moment I thought I was going crazy." He looked up at the others, "He looked just like Lars!"

Sherri shook her head and blinked. "God, he really did."

They fell silent for several moments, feeling awkward at the sudden mention of their murdered friend. Karl von Strasser broke the emotional chokehold. "I miss him," he said with a voice of gravel. "Lars, he was a good man."

"Best damned mechanic ever born," Jay Martin added.

"It just don't seem the same," came the disconsolate addition of Marty Morgan.

Sherri sat up and lit a cigarette, her motions slow and deliberate as she studied the other pilots. Finally she gestured for attention. "I don't get you guys," she said, shaking her head. "He-men. Heroes. Sky kings with steel bars up your asses."

"What the hell gives with you?" Marty said angrily.

"With *me*? I wish it were only with *me*. Have you big boys heard yourselves? Have you listened?" She dragged deeply and blew out smoke. "Stop wallowing in your self-pity over missing Lars Anderson! The big bastard was my friend as much as he was yours. So instead of moaning like an old ladies' Geritol society, why don't you find out who killed him?"

"Yeah!" That from one of the teenaged bodies nearby. Bonnie Richardson sat up and glared at the group. "She's right. Why don't you find out who murdered Lars and kill *him*."

"Bloodthirsty little bitch," Jay Martin said, but not without agreement.

"And do it *slowly*," said the remaining girl. "Lars and my father were good friends. I can't believe you people just sit around and talk about Lars. Talk, talk, *talk*. Lars used to say to my dad that the worst thing anybody could do was to hurt one of the inner circle, because then he'd have to face everybody else. But all *I* hear is a lot of blubbering."

Bonnie had piqued Jay Martin's interest. "If we catch him, how would you kill him?"

"Cheez, mister. Just like I said. *Slowly*."

Jay Martin was amused and didn't hide it. "If I twist a rope around his neck, would *you* tighten it?"

"You bet your sweet ass I would," Bonnie said heatedly. "When you know somebody since you're a little kid, yes, you get even."

Marty Morgan looked from the young girl to Jay Martin and back to Sherri Taylor. "Well, it was Hamza who killed him. Hamza, or Jabal, or whatever his name was. That's why—"

Von Strasser was also sitting up now. A beer can disappeared into crumpled metal in his powerful hands. "No, I do not believe that, Marty."

"You don't think Hamza did it?" Mad Marty shook his head. "I don't get it. From everything I heard, Lansky was getting his tail shot off, I mean, the way Bannon asked him for help and he went right in there, balls to the wall, and he finds Hamza and naturally he blows him away. Pissed off the way he was, hell, I can understand *that*." Marty dismissed von Strasser's remarks with a deprecating wave of his hand. "You're all wet, Karl. Who else could it be?"

The German shrugged. "If I knew, you would know. But what I do not *believe* is that Hamza killed our friend Lars. It is too pat, too convenient. I simply do not believe it."

"I don't believe it either." They all turned to Bannon. He hadn't said a word through their exchange, but kept his attention glued to several young pilots playing frisbee behind a line of parked aircraft. They directed their attention to the group. Bannon kept studying a fat man of great girth but sure-footed athletic agility. He moved with surprising speed for his bulk and weight.

Jay Martin came up to Bannon. "That's Jack Acridge. Fat as a pig but don't let that mislead you. He was a collegiate wrestling champ and he's a damned good pilot. I think you know his old man; Gene Acridge?"

Bannon nodded. "I know him. I don't care how good he flies." Bannon pointed. "It's what he's doing *right now*." They watched Jack Acridge, the fat man throwing the frisbee with a powerful arm and astonishing accuracy. The frisbee sailed through the air to be snatched by another young but slender pilot, who whipped it back to Acridge.

"Goddamnit, *look*," Bannon said, impatient and exasperated that no one saw what was right before them. "Look at Acridge when he throws. He throws it sideways. He has to throw it sideways because *he's too damned fat to throw it overhand*."

They watched with Bannon. The slender pilot, Jim Lucas, snatched the frisbee in midair, drew back his arm behind his head, and hurled the frisbee so that it was perpendicular to the ground. Its lift was reduced over its motion when the flat surface was level with the ground, but in the vertical throw it had greater speed and a trajectory like that of a bolt hurled from a crossbow.

"Holy Jesus," Bannon said quietly. He glanced at Santiago. "Bill, you were with Lars when he died, right?"

"Yes, I am, and I never got it, I wants to tell you that—"

"That throwing star," Bannon broke in. "How did it hit him?"

Santiago had a look of amazement on his face. "You crazy, Bannon? It don' hit him, man, it *kill* him!"

Bannon talked to Santiago, but his eyes were on Acridge and Lucas. "Damnit, Bill, was it vertical or horizontal?"

"I don' know what the hell you talkin' about, Bannon."

Bannon turned and demonstrated with his hands. "Did it go into his skull this way, at a right angle to his eyes, you know, along the vertical line of his nose? Or did it go in level with his eyes, like this?"

Santiago's mouth made a quiet O. "Hokay, Bannon, now I knows what you mean. No, man, not that way. It was straight up and down, you know? Like this, man." He demonstrated with his own hands. "It go into his head over his eye and it push deep into his eye over here, like, man, part of it is in his brain and the other part is down through the eye and into his cheekbone, man."

Sherri and the two girls turned away, close to being ill.

Bannon ignored them. He turned to the other pilots. "Don't you get it? Hamza was a fat son of a bitch. He could never have thrown that star *overhand* with any accuracy! He'd have to throw it *sideways*, a horizontal throw, like the Acridge kid, there."

Marty stared back at Bannon. "Then ... it *couldn't* have been Hamza ..."

"You got it, kid," Bannon said with emphasis.

"So Lansky is lying?" Jay Martin queried.

"Goddamn, I can't figure it—" Bannon started, but stopped as von Strasser gestured.

"Lansky lies about many things," the German pilot said. "He is a businessman. All businessmen lie. He is a dealer in guns around the world. So he is a liar by profession. He is a lady's man and he must tell many lies with the women. But," von Strasser paused for added emphasis. "that is no proof that he lies about Yusuf Hamza, *or,*" he added quickly, "that he had anything to do with killing Lars."

"Karl, then why," Bannon asked, dead serious, "was he so damned quick to claim that Hamza was really Sadad Jabal?"

Karl von Strasser lost even a hint of the sarcasm that almost always accompanied his answers to serious questions. "Because perhaps Hamza's real name *is* Jabal. I do not know, you do not know, none of us here *know* anything! We don't even know if Sadad Jabal is a real person, or a figurehead, or the name of some organization. There is the John Birch Society. Its relation to John Birch at its greatest is specious, a ghost and no more. This could be the same. Everything, my friends, has a bottom line and the bottom line here is that Yusuf Hamza is dead. If he could still talk to us then he could answer the questions we are all asking like old women."

"Hear, hear," Sherri added from the side. She was ignored completely.

Marty turned to von Strasser. "Karl, who do you think killed Lars?"

The German cracked open another can of beer and took a long slug before answering. He wiped his mouth with the back of his hand, and he seemed to drift into time until they heard the hard, cracking voice of a no-nonsense Luftwaffe officer. "You tell me who was in that hangar that night," he said heavily, "and what they were doing when Lars found them, and I will answer *all* your questions." He belched, more with disdain than need. "But I also tell you this, and you listen to me carefully. We—all of us, Lansky also—we are all little bugs under glass. Everything we do is being watched. We eat, we drink, we piss, and they watch us and take pictures of us. So they know everything there is about any one of us and about all of us, and since they are so efficient, what is there to worry about?"

Sherri Taylor had moved closer. "I'll tell you, then, Karl, that *I'm* worried. You know, that nasty little thing we're not supposed to talk about that we're all looking for?" She looked about her and then moved closer to von Strasser so she was talking in a sharp whisper to him. "Aren't *you* worried about that damn bomb?"

Von Strasser smiled, and a powerful hand touched her arm with velvet gentleness. He smiled, and in that smile there lay great calm and strength. "Lovely lady, after Siberia . . . *nothing* worries me. I died more than thirty years ago. You cannot hurt a dead man, so I enjoy life and I do not worry. You, however, being of much beauty and able to choose your risks, you *do* worry, and—"

He never completed his sentence. A B-25 thundered directly over them, coming around in a wicked turning pitch-out, gear dropping and flaps sliding back, the big Cyclones popping and snorting like angry hogs as the power came off, and it swung around the far end of the field and greased in to a feathery landing.

"You see?" Santiago told them, pointing. "You talk about the devils, and he show up his ass every time. That is Lansky, no?"

Bannon nodded. "That's him."

"He lands that thing just like the person he is," Sherri mused aloud. Heads turned to her. "Like grease," she added, and rang up a chorus of smiles and chuckles.

They watched the B-25 roll to its parking spot before Lansky's maintenance hangar. It came to a stop with drill-sergeant precision, rocking gently on its nose wheel as Lansky stopped exactly on the marker line. As the propellers ground to a stop a van with CHARTER ELECTRONICS drove up to the bomber.

Mixed thoughts rose in Bannon's mind. He kept staring at the van as if trying to place a piece in some enormous jigsaw puzzle of time, events, names, and memory. He motioned for Jay Martin to join him.

"You recognize that van?" Bannon asked.

The question surprised Jay. "Who doesn't? They do all my radio work. They work on a lot of the heavy iron around here."

There was a lot more, Bannon knew. But he asked Jay Martin anyway. "What other, ah, work are they into?"

"C'mon, Mitch, what the hell are you after? Charter does the exec jets around here, they handle the more expensive avionics for most outfits in this area. Oh, yes, they also handle the best-of-the-line in home electronics. You know, super stereo and television, home security systems. They sell satellite dishes and they handle radar gear as well."

There was always the chance, Bannon told himself, that he had missed something in the past. So he played dumb and asked another innocent question.

"What kind of radar gear?"

"Bannon, nine out of every ten boats sitting up at Port Canaveral right now have a Charter radar system of some kind in them. They handle microwave for communications systems, they've got the contracts with the military for air traffic control radar, they work with the drug enforcement people where they use radar to catch the runners, you know, right across the spectrum."

Bannon couldn't hold back all of the smile that came to him.

Bingo!

✝ 20 ✝

MISTS OF MANY KINDS

Bernie Hudoff hated to do it. Not the grandstand lies to the press and to the nation and the whole goddamned world; shit, that was just part of the security business of hurling a blanket of near-truth over what you wanted to keep concealed. Keeping it hidden from the press was the same as keeping it concealed from the public, because John and Jane Doe out there in the everyday world were puppets controlled by invisible video strings of the network broadcasters, narrators, experts, announcers, and anchor men. Damned few members of the media were worth their salt, and those who really *knew* the ropes were terribly dangerous, because they could sniff out the kernel of truth in a whole grain silo of lies, and once they got their instincts going at ninety miles an hour they could tell you the color of Napoleon's underwear. If anybody cared. No one really did, any more, but just about *everybody* cared about the shuttle *Antares*. Some of the similarities to the ill-fated *Challenger* launch back in January of 1986 were terrifyingly close. That mission, too, had all the circus hype of someone very special aboard the flight who wasn't an astronaut. When they killed that teacher seventy-three seconds after launch, they killed the age of innocence that was part of the still-squalling newborn era of manned space flight.

Ever since then, when NASA departed the norm for a mission, everyone got a real tight grip on himself and prepared for the worst.

Hudoff couldn't shut out all the newsmen. In the appalling aftermath of *Challenger*, when NASA spokesmen fumbled the ball in trying to find *something* of worth to tell the public, they resorted to silence and all sorts of misinformation ploys *to the people who knew better*. Jay Barbree of NBC radio, whose voice was heard throughout the world, had been present at Cape Canaveral and the Kennedy complex for *every* manned launching outside the borders of Russia. Barbree knew a cockamamie spiel when he heard it, and while NASA was still reeling in shock and mumbling about not knowing why the multibillion-dollar *Challenger* shattered blue skies and seven lives, Barbree went to work, uncovered the failure of the solid rocket booster, and unleashed a Pandora's box of mismanagement and broken responsibility that was still echoing down the halls of space agency command. Barbree didn't just cover the story; *he was part of the story*. He could sniff out a coverup in the manned space business faster than the NASA field troops themselves could find out what the hell was going on.

We learn from history, Hudoff told himself. *And when we ignore the lessons of history, we're condemned to repeat our mistakes*. Way back in June of 1944, when vast Allied armies were poised to strike into the gut of Nazi-occupied France for the long-awaited invasion of Europe from England, Dwight Eisenhower, who commanded all the Allied forces, had wrestled with the problem of what to do with press people who were smart enough to understand the phases of the moon, the rising and falling of tides, and the time it took an armada of vessels small and large to travel from English ports to French invasion sites. If they figured it out on their own they were free to say what they wanted, and Eisenhower figured that was the most dangerous of all press events, because so many of them would be *right*, about the day and even the moment of invasion.

So Ike got real smart. He called in the best of the press people, swore them to full secrecy, and *told them everything they wanted to know about the oncoming invasion.* The reporters even went along with false stories to help mislead the Germans waiting behind a wall of fire and steel.

Bernie Hudoff mulled it over, got on the phone, and called Jay Barbree of NBC, Howard Benedict of AP, and a couple more of the really sharp cats in the press corps. Then he asked a favor. "*You* tell *me* the best people in this business who are down here. Then get them on the phone and I want everybody in my office at NASA headquarters at midnight. I'll lay it all out for you then." He had their names, passes, and escorts waiting at triple security gates, and when he had them all together he laid it on the line.

"I tell you just what the hell is going on," he said. "Then I tell you the lies I've *got* to tell the public. After that I ask you to lie for me. When this is all over all of you in this very select group have exclusive stories. You get *everything* first. Before I say anything else I'm going to warn you that you're all sitting on a volcano, and that a hell of a lot of people's lives may hang on what you say and do."

"One question." Bill Larson from the Seattle *Post*, who'd cut his teeth back on the old Vanguard rockets, raised his hand.

"Let's have it," Hudoff told him.

"You're going to have the rest of the national and world press come down on you like an avalanche when this is all over, whatever *this* may be, and you give us the exclusive."

"Could be," he said.

"What will you tell them?" she asked.

"To go fuck themselves," Hudoff said bluntly. "Compared to what we got here, their squalling isn't a pimple on a mouse's ass." He looked around. "We got a deal? If we do, all restrictions on you people and you people only are lifted."

"Let's have it, man," someone called out.

Hudoff gave it to them. When he finished, one newsman, who'd been in six wars around the planet, threw up. Hudoff didn't blame him.

One hour later his plan was working like a charm.

The real beauty of the Big Lie is that it permits you to cover your ass while you carry out other lesser, but equally vital, Big Lies.

Or they could be called diversions. Bernie Hudoff began to play his cards like the true poker player he was.

"Thirty seconds! Everybody knock off the shit! We're rolling video and audio. Goddamnit, watch those lights!" Bill Shell of World Television News was a man possessed as the final seconds counted down to the exclusive broadcast right from the edge of the launch complex of Pad 39A on the Kennedy Space Center. G. G. Helen Borchin stood exactly over the masking tape X on the ground, the dazzling floodlights of the launch pad creating a fairyland of swirling mist behind her.

The kid was right, Bernie Hudoff told himself, recalling Charley Morgan's forecast of dense fog during the night. He reminded himself to ignore his weather teams and call Charley when he really wanted to know what was going on. Tonight was his big bid, and the fog was heaven-sent. *Or courtesy of one beautiful young woman,* he appended with another warm thought of Charley. He forced his attention back to the moment. This G. G. was no slouch in the looks department either. Trim *and* busty, she'd added the perfect touch of a silk scarf tucked into a safari jacket for her live special report from the space center. The shuttle looming above and behind her resembled an incredible technological King Kong in the enormous cage of a servicing gantry.

"Ten seconds!" called out Bill Shell, and the startling confusion of the moment evaporated swiftly. A hidden voice counted down the seconds to four and then fingers replaced any sound. The lights came on and the video went out live across the entire country, and Hudoff knew it would be relayed by live satellite feed throughout the world and replayed again and again tomorrow.

"... and this reporter has uncovered the incredible danger posed to the astronauts of the shuttle *Antares,* as well as the launch teams and perhaps even the thou-

353

sands of invited guests who will be here in a few more days when *Antares* breaks free of earth's gravity bonds and soars into orbit. For days, the space coast has heard disturbing rumors of nuclear materials to be placed aboard the space shuttle. The space agency, and the Air Force is involved as well, has kept secret from the nation the existence of a thermofusion generator that was loaded into the cargo bay of *Antares* for tests considered so dangerous that NASA planned its experiments far beyond our planet.

"World Television News learned only a few hours ago, and we've taken this time to verify our facts, that the secret thermofusion generator is a critical part of a fusion energy experiment to produce enormous levels of controlled energy. The stated purpose of the generator was to accelerate its development as a power source for future space stations, perhaps even for the great *Pleides* now in orbit, certainly for future generation bases on the moon and manned flights to Mars. NASA's plan was to carry the generator into orbit aboard *Antares*, lift it from the cargo bay and attach it to a space tug, and then lift it to an altitude of three thousand miles for what we could call full-throttle tests."

The TV monitors showed expert editing by the producers and directors of the live news special. They were intercutting between G. G. Borchin and closeups of the *Antares*, zooming in to the VAB and other targets of opportunity, keeping a fast-paced delivery by G. G. and her team.

"But what NASA did *not* tell the public, or the astronauts, *or* the launch teams here at the Kennedy Space Center, is that the reason for sending the thermofusion generator to three thousand miles high for its tests is that the system uses highly refined plutonium, the same materials that go into the atomic bomb. And they needed this altitude in case the reactor within the generator ran out of control into what scientists call an uncontrolled chain reaction. In other words, there's the danger of the generator exploding like a small atomic bomb."

G. G. Borchin took a deep, shuddering breath, calculated perfectly to show her own fear and anger at what had been going on behind the scenes at the space center. "The words 'small atomic bomb' cannot possibly convey the magnitude of the disaster with which NASA has been flirting. At a conservative estimate, the generator could explode with the force of sixty to seventy thousand tons of TNT. That's four times greater than the atomic bombs that pulverized Hiroshima and Nagasaki back in 1945. The danger of the generator running away and exploding three thousand miles up isn't one we need to worry about here on the earth."

G. G. took an over-the-shoulder naked-fear look at the shuttle and the camera zoomed in to a tight shot of her face. "What this reporter learned a few hours ago, and that has everybody here on edge, is that the thermofusion generator developed a dangerous leak in the cargo bay of the shuttle. For the past several days this whole area has been in grave danger. According to highly placed official sources whom we cannot identify, there is and has been a real danger that the generator could have exploded at any time.

"That would have meant the explosion of a giant atomic bomb right here at the Kennedy Space Center. With us at the space center tonight, covering that side of the story, is Gene Maxwell. Gene?"

They switched to a remote camera where only the powerful lights brought clarity to the rugged features of Gene Maxwell, one of the grizzled old news veterans of the Cape days. "Thank you, G. G. I can't tell you how shook up everybody is here at the space center tonight. I'm standing on a service road leading to the long shuttle runway to the west of the giant VAB building. The fog is so bad tonight that this same building, which we can see from thirty or forty miles away on a clear night, is invisible right now, and it's only two miles from us. You can't see much of the special bomb disposal team in this fog, but behind me, right now, is the convoy of volunteer technicians and engineers who earlier tonight removed the thermofusion generator from the space shuttle, loaded it as quickly as they could into a giant sealed container, and then drove it through this thick pea-soup fog to the Kennedy runway. We'll be able to bring you exclusive shots of the generator being removed from the shuttle in just a few minutes—"

Hudoff smiled. *Damned right it will take a few minutes. We haven't even started the unloading of that biological container yet* ... He studied the screen again. This was the bitchy part, and he hoped they'd pull it off clean.

"... right now you can hear the roar of the engines of the huge Air Force cargo jet that's been at this field since earlier today. By the grace of God, or whatever good fortune we're enjoying at this moment, the huge C-5 Galaxy transport made a delivery during the day when the weather was clear, and was then grounded by this fog. However, NASA considers the dangers of an explosion from the leaking thermofusion generator so great that the volunteer crew of the Galaxy will be taking off at any moment with that dangerous generator aboard. It seems impossible that anyone would even try to fly in zero-zero conditions, but I spoke with the crew of that huge airplane, and they explained that the Galaxy can be flown completely by computer. The plan is to fly that generator out of here out over the ocean to a remote and isolated base where it can be made safe again. When that airplane takes off we should see an end to the wild rumors circulating through the space coast about danger from an atomic bomb, danger to *Antares* and the upcoming launch in just a few days. I want to remind—"

Maxwell looked properly startled as a monstrous roar overwhelmed him. He waited a moment, peering into the opaque fog. "We can't see the Galaxy," he shouted into his microphone, "but I'm sure you can hear it roaring down the runway, flown by its superbrain computer, and removing from all of us the horrifying danger of a nuclear explosion here at the space center. I can't emphasize strongly enough that ..."

Hudoff didn't need to hear any more of the television razzle-dazzle. He walked to his car, climbed inside and made sure the windows were shut. He activated his radio and scrambler. "Number One here. How did it go?"

"Like a piece of cake, sir," Joe Horvath reported.

"They took off like it was broad daylight. They're well above the fog layer and in the clear."

"The tankers set to rendezvous?"

"Yes, sir. Confirmation right on down the line. A KC-10 will rendezvous with the 747 at the scheduled vector, and air traffic control will make sure all other aircraft are kept at least a hundred miles from them."

"Great, Joe. Keep me on tap with everything as she goes."

"Yes, sir. By the way, Bernie. Congratulations."

"Thanks. One out."

Hudoff switched off and sat back in his car. In the dark he took a long swallow from his flask and enjoyed the quiet moment of lighting a cigar. My God, he'd done it. They had three shuttles at one time at Kennedy and they were more naked to losing almost their entire space program than anyone had realized. Well, *Columbia* at this moment was atop that 747 carrier ship on its way to safety at Edwards Air Force Base. They'd refuel in the air and fly nonstop to the California research center. The lie would come out soon enough, but for now, the lie was insurance. There was still that second shuttle in the VAB but—and Hudoff smiled with the thought—the wheels were already turning to solve that problem.

Wendy Green took a long slug of beer, shifted her body on the couch in the pilot's lounge of Morgan Aviation, and sat up slowly, swinging her feet to the floor. Alone in the lounge, she took a long drag of the Macanudo cigar and stared at the television set across the lounge. Some local news jock with pimples on his ass and a wart on the side of his nose was making noises about the *Antares* countdown continuing on schedule. Wendy started to get up to turn off the set when the scene shifted from a background stock shot of the launch pad to a swarm of warplanes racing across a field packed with people.

Wendy grunted with mild satisfaction. She didn't mind seeing her own boys and girls, and she paid attention to the newsman. "On the local scene, the famous Strasser

357

Air Circus will be putting on its usual weekend razzle-dazzle airshow, with the greatest planes of history performing for thrilled crowds at Shiloh Field . . ."

Wendy could look at the planes all night, but not the closeups of snotty kids and fat mothers milling about the hot dog stands. "Crock of shit," she said aloud to herself, crossed the room, and hit the OFF button. The room went comfortably quiet. She finished her beer, dropped the can in a wastebasket, belched quietly, and walked from the lounge to the main hangar. By her side was a large sign reading NO SMOKING! THIS MEANS YOU! Wendy offered the sign her extended middle finger and a plume of cigar smoke. She threaded her way through the warbirds to the opposite side of the hangar, still recalling the words of the newscast. "Razzle-dazzle, my ass," she muttered to herself. She stopped by the door marked MUSEUM ENTRANCE, opened it with her key, and stepped inside. She liked being in here alone, especially at night. With that fog settling down all across the countryside, there'd be little or no flying. She had hardly believed her ears when she'd heard that huge jet climbing overhead. The fog had picked up the sound and slammed it into every corner of the hangar, rattling walls and the roof and glass cases. Now the only sounds came from the distance, muffled, gentler as the maintenance crews performed last-minute checks on planes that had been ailing.

Sounds like that fit here, in their private museum of air war history. The place was filled with memories. Old flying clothes, pieces and parts of airplanes, all kinds of weapons with which men fought one another, instruments and souvenirs and parachutes; the paraphernalia of decades of jousting for keeps in the skies. She walked slowly through the aisles of history, nodding to familiar photographs and friendly faces looking down at her. She knew every picture, every painting, every airplane and exhibit and—

She stopped, her muscles rigid. She was unaware that her mouth was open and the cigar had fallen to her feet. Her eyes went wide and she stared straight ahead of her at the World War Two exhibit and the bridge they'd built to cross into the postwar era exhibits and she saw, but she couldn't believe it, and her feet began to move backwards and she heard her own breath coming hoarsely. She backed to the doorway and spun about to run frantically through the hangar, bouncing off wings and hard metal to the office door. She threw herself into the chair behind her desk, forced herself to breathe steadily, and lifted her telephone.

She tapped in the number and sat stiffly, again holding her breath. "Please ... please answer ... oh God, make it answer ... please ..."

They took crazy chances in the fog, but the message was imperative. Two sheriff's cars and a state trooper made it first to the office of Morgan Aviation, their flashing red-and-blue lights sparkling wildly in the blowing mists. They tried to calm Wendy, to make sense of her trembling fear. She refused to answer any of their questions. "W-wait for the o-others," she stuttered, clenching and unclenching her hands. Charley and Bannon showed up in another sheriff's car that had picked them up at a restaurant in Titusville. And an Air Force helicopter made it in, groping downward, guided by a circle of headlights to a near-blind landing. Bernie Hudoff and Vladislov Galenko followed Colonel Hank Rawls from the helicopter into the office. They arrived in time to see Charley holding Wendy by the shoulders, trying to calm her. "Wendy ... get a grip on it, girl. What *is* it?"

"I'll—I'll s-show you." She was shaking worse than before. "C-come with m-me ..."

She led them through the hangar and stopped by the museum door and turned to them. "It's—it's in t-there ... *be quiet.* Don't make any n-noise and f-for God's sake, *w-walk gently.*"

Bannon and Charley exchanged a quick glance. Both knew they were thinking the same thoughts. *She's gone out of her mind ...*

Bannon motioned to the others to humor her and to follow her without making a fuss. The deputies drew their weapons. They didn't know what the hell to expect. They crowded quietly into the museum. Wendy stopped halfway across the museum display area and turned to Bannon. "T-turn on the l-lights, please."

Bannon hit the switches and bright lights filled the room. He turned to see Wendy pointing with a trembling hand to the row of old bombs on display. "Th ... there," she forced out.

They looked at one another. Everything was calm, nothing out of order. Finally Charley nudged her. "Wendy ... *what is it?*"

Wendy stared straight ahead. "H-how many ... atom bomb replicas ... d-do we have here?"

"Why, two, of course," Charley said. "The models of the Hiroshima and Nagasaki bombs."

"N-now we g-got ... *three*."

The air seemed to freeze about them. Three nuclear weapons stood in a row before them. The third bomb hadn't been there earlier that evening.

Hudoff and Galenko stared, like the others, in disbelief. For the moment no one knew what to do. Hank Rawls went forward to the third bomb, a sleek shape with arrowlike fins. He knelt by it, not touching anything. He withdrew a small radio from his belt and spoke calmly into the slim mike. "Send in Mathers and Blum. Tell them to bring their equipment with them. Have them come around by the front of the hangar. I'll meet them there."

He stood up and spoke to Hudoff. "That team goes with me day and night."

"Nuke techs?" Hudoff asked. Rawls nodded, then spoke to the group. "Any of you with radios. Of any kind. Turn them off *immediately*." He did the same to his own unit. "Bannon, would you bring them in?" he asked.

Bannon went to the hangar door, returned with two Air Force technicians loaded down with equipment. They went to the bomb, checking it carefully, examining it from all sides. They ran special instruments about the casing, checked numbers. The lead man knelt by the bomb. It was Mathers. "Colonel, this baby is for real."

He rapped the side of the bomb with his knuckles.

Wendy gasped and bit her knuckles to keep from scream-ing. A dull metallic sound came to them.

Mathers smiled. He'd been with these things a long time. He stood up slowly. "Sir, there's four hundred thousand tons of big bang in here. It's alive and ticking."

Wendy collapsed to the floor without a sound. No one moved.

Hudoff motioned to Mathers. "Can you disarm it? Here? *Now*?"

"Sure thing." He looked at Rawls. "Okay to start, sir?"

Hank Rawls was Mister Cool himself. "How much time will it take, and do you need anybody else to help you?"

"About ten minutes, sir. We don't need any help. That ticking, colonel? It's a fake. This thing is on full safe right now. Somebody just put a clock inside it for fun and games."

Bannon left Charley with Wendy, still on the edge of hysteria, waiting for the sedatives to take hold of her shaken mind. He had things to talk over with Rawls. They'd waited until Mathers and Blum safetied the nu-clear weapon and then rolled the bomb onto a dolly to take it to the waiting air force helicopter. The chopper was gone and the bomb with it.

The two men walked together down the long taxiway with the ghosts of yesteryear parked on either side. The fog was breaking about them, and the world was a mixture of swirling mists with sudden openings to re-veal gleaming shapes that had managed to endure the decades.

"Well, now we know why your friend was killed," Rawls said to break the quiet of the walk. "They must have caught him in the museum. He heard or saw some-thing and went in to check it out and—" Rawls shrugged. No need to finish his sentence.

"Yeah," Bannon said with a tired sigh. "They killed Lars because there was every chance he could have identified them."

"Maybe he recognized someone," Rawls offered.

"Maybe, maybe, and more maybes," Bannon said unhappily. "You know what galls my ass, man? All the crap we've been through and we didn't even *find* the third bomb. They gave it to us on a silver platter! Not only that, the bastards knew about the radio trackers all the time. They've been leading us on a wild goose chase from day one."

"Bannon, they've got to be *very* sure of themselves to give up that bomb."

"Sure of themselves? Shit, the needle's so far up our asses we all got bumps on our noses. This whole scene is just to show us how helpless we are."

"Are they *that* smart, Bannon?"

"If they're not, you tell me who they are. I sure as hell don't know. A hundred times I was sure I had a lead that was perfect and every time it blew up in my face." Bannon stopped. "Hank, I haven't talked with Hudoff. Not since we found this little present tonight. Did Bernie say anything about going ahead with the launch?"

Rawls shook his head. "Not a word. They're convening a board tomorrow for a final decision. I'm on it, and I am recommending as strongly as I can that we do *not* launch."

"I can't believe that."

"What? Not launching?"

"No. That you'd recommend giving in."

"*Giving in?* Is that what you call not launching when you may have an atomic bomb exploded right in the middle of the party? For Christ's sake, man, we are talking about hundreds of thousands of people who—"

"Shit, don't start in again on *that*," Bannon said acidly. He stopped walking to look at the man who was his new friend. "Damnit, Hank, if we scrub this launch then they—*anybody*—can threaten us any fucking time they feel like it, and we'll knuckle under every time. Where the hell do we go from *there?* When do people like you say, well, this threat sounds real, but this one doesn't, or what? You going to throw dice to make up your minds every time you get a phone call that says we're going to blow up your neat little spaceport?"

"So easy," Rawls said smoothly, "so easy for you to

say. Keep the numbers low, Bannon. Let's say, oh, only a hundred thousand people. But don't use the word people. Don't use numbers. Start describing the human beings. The fathers, the mothers, and tell me the names of the children. Every little girl, one by one. Every little boy, one by one. Do it a hundred thousand times. Invoke the images, you son of a bitch. Invoke them with the flesh melting from their faces and the glass slicing into—ah, shit."

"Not worth going on?" Bannon said, testing Rawls.

"I could go on forever. You know what you're willing to do, Bannon? You're offering up martyrs on the altar of your fucking space schedules. What the hell do *you* care if they die, right?"

"They're going to die, anyway. Sooner or later everybody and everything dies."

"Oho! The dainty-skinned philosopher, right? What's the use in worrying because sooner or later we all crumble into dust, right? Man, but you are fucking quick and easy. Not so much with the *lives* of other people, but with *how* they are to spend their lives."

"If we give in, you're guaranteeing they'll spend the rest of their fucking lives in fear! They're scared already, aren't they, *Colonel*? Scared of *us* and our fucking bombs and scared of *them* and their fucking bombs, right? They've been getting the shit scared out of them since the big mushrooms climbed up way back in '45. So when do we say it's enough? When do we say fuck them and their threats? We recognize the reality of it, and we do everything we can to beat in their fucking heads, *but in the meantime we go on living.*"

Bannon took an angry step away, whirled back. "If they've got this bomb now, and they do, then they'll always be going for more bombs. One way or the other, Hank, if they're determined enough, *they can get the shuttle.* We're not a closed society. It's just not our way. And until we strip everyone out of this area and seal it off and make it an isolated camp, we are fucking vulnerable!"

"Jesus, Bannon—"

"No; hold it. What you said before makes a hell of a lot of sense."

"I did?"

"You said count and name off every one of those hundred thousand parents and kids, right? No one would ever do that; we both know it. But you *can* count off the names and the positions and the politics and the nationality of every one of the four thousand top world leaders, right? *They're the real target, aren't they!*"

"Of course. The target isn't people. It's the chaos that results from their being *here* when they're guests of our government. We end up looking stupid, no one trusts us any more, and there's a power shift around the whole world."

"Anybody *forcing* those fuckers to come here, Colonel?"

"What?"

"Why don't you *tell* all those special guests what's happened? Tell them we're under threat of a nuke? Give them the *choice* of coming here or staying home?"

"Who wants to go to a roast when you're the pig, Bannon? Of course they won't come."

"Would you recommend a launch if they *didn't* come?"

"No." Rawls was openly angry and defiant. "No fucking way, man. You better start naming off those kids, buddy."

"You know, neither one of us has the answer, do we?"

Rawls' laugh was harsh. "Shit, no. There's always the proposal that we *could* evacuate all the people from this area. Leave only volunteers absolutely essential to the flight and—"

"Bullshit," Bannon said, scornful of the idea. "It won't work. They'd still have us right by the balls. You can't keep these people out of their homes forever, and you sure can't evacuate them for every shot. All they'd need to do is make a phone call telling us they're bad people and they're going to blow up the joint, and we cave in."

"I still say caving in, as you call it, at least *this* time, is better than risking all those lives."

"Hank, do you know the single most essential item that's required for slavery?"

"*What?*"

364

"Damnit, it was a plain question."

"It's obvious. Power. Guns, money, position for power—"

"Bullshit. The one ingredient that makes slavery work is the slave. And you know why? Because he's afraid to die. Because he hopes. Because he'll do *anything* to stay alive, and so long as that word *anything* is in his vocabulary, you'll have slave masters."

"You talk big for a paleface."

"Fuck you, friend. That tan doesn't give you a lock on ancestral shit-kicking."

Rawls broke out in honest laughter. "Okay, okay, maybe you're right, maybe I'm right. Whatever. *My* hope, Bannon, is to fake out these mothers. Trick them into making their play. We're convinced the attempt will come by air, and we've got enough stuff to stop anybody who tries and—"

"Sure, sure. I've heard that song before. Do a little soft-shoe and you'll be even more convincing." Bannon took Rawls by the arm and started back to the Morgan office. "Let's get some coffee. I want you to do something for me."

"They say us darkies can be smelled in the dark, you know that?"

"What the hell has that got to do with anything?"

"I can smell trouble *from you* in the dark. So spill it quick before I remember that the only smart thing for me to remember is that I should have let those rednecks stomp in your head in that parking lot."

"So I owe you. Damnit, listen to me. I need access to your top-level radar."

Rawls studied Bannon. "Okay, all the funny stuff aside. Without one hell of a reason you really need top-level security clearance from Pentagon for—"

"I don't have the time. *You* don't have the time. I need access *now*." He looked straight at Rawls. "Even before we have that coffee."

"You're serious, right?"

"You asshole, I want you to help me find that bomb."

"I could get twenty years."

"Sure. And you'll hate yourself in the morning."

"Bannon, I rue the day I met you." He slapped Bannon on the shoulder. "Let's go do it. Maybe we'll have adjoining cells."

Magnum lifted his leonine head, looked across the debris of the living room at his masters, and slowly felt his eyes roll to the back of his head. Magnum groaned, a sound of canine misery that properly expressed the feelings of a huge dog suffering an equally huge hangover. His tongue lolled from sharp white teeth, and his entire frame shook from an unexpected beery belch. His nose wrinkled and his face took on an expression of surprise and distaste as the aroma of his own beery farts collected in a cloud about his body. He climbed shakily to his feet and turned to leave behind him the source of such nose-wrinkling fragrance. The swinging door flapped idly behind him.

Mad Marty stood precariously in the room center, wobbling dangerously, clutching a half-empty bottle of tequila in one hand, a joint dangling from his lips. He sneered at his German roommate, and when he spoke his words came out shouted-mumbling and slurred. "So what th' fuck, hey, Karl? You gonna keep me from flyin'?"

Try as he might, von Strasser knew his anguish showed on his face. He shook his head with sadness at what he saw in the younger man, and then he answered. "No. Of course not. I would *never* try to force you to do anything. Or not to do it," he added hastily.

Marty stumbled through the debris of the hours-long hard drinking session. He'd buried himself in an endless row of joints and an equally endless flow from various bottles. But the pain still penetrated the mists he'd forced into his mind, and he moved awkwardly, at times grotesquely, the spinning head and double vision aggravating walking in a confined space with only one leg. It was equally apparent he no longer cared what he looked like or what he might be doing to his body.

"Well, if you ain't gonna come down on me like a ton of bricks, ol' buddy, ol' pal, then *how*, I ask you, *how*," Marty ground out, weaving dangerously as he talked, "you gonna keep me down on the farm?" He broke into drunken hilarity, waving the bottle, splashing tequila on furniture and himself, sucking deeply on the joint, unaware of the burning marijuana scorching his fingers. "Thash hyshterical! Down on th' fuckin' farm! Oh, Jeshus, thas good!" He stared with mock, drunken severity at von Strasser. "You a fuggin' farmer or sumpin'?"

"No. No farmer," von Strasser said, sticking grimly to straight conversation, cautious not to offer advice or warnings. If he did that, he knew, he'd be talking to a bottle rimmed with pain rather than to what had been a bright, intelligent, skilled young man. "But there is a point, young Marty. If you are going to fly, as you say you will—"

"Fuggin' A, ol' buddy."

"—even *you* must walk to the airplane before you can fly the machine. Right now you cannot walk so well. In the morning you will be no better."

Marty gestured gaily with the bottle. "There'sh always the wheelchair, ol' buddy, ol' pal. Neat and nifty wheelchair. Got a horn and air brakes and, uh, a urinal, and—"

"Wheelchairs are for cripples."

The words fell upon Marty like clawing, hated mice. His face twitched and he forced himself to straighten his body. Drunkenly angry, he struggled for self-clarity.

"Karl, you calling *me* . . . a *cripple?*"

Von Strasser was again the former Luftwaffe officer, hard on the men he loved as brothers and led into combat. He brought steel to his voice. "You are a cripple only if you do not walk! If you continue to consume that garbage tonight," he gestured with contempt at the drugs, *"then* you will not walk in the morning, you will not be able to walk in the morning, and yes, then you *will* be a cripple!"

Marty hurled the bottle from him in a sudden motion of rage. It smashed against the far wall, sending a large framed picture sliding with a crash of breaking glass to the floor. Marty stood where he was, weaving. His face was flushed with his anger.

"Is that better, you Nazi sumbitch!"

Von Strasser kept himself cool and a little less stern. "Do not work so hard at dying, Marty." The pain began to show through on the face of the old German pilot. He knew what the youngster was enduring. "Dying is not difficult. It comes soon enough."

They stood almost as if embattled, staring at one another, all their words expended. Marty closed his eyes tight, wincing. Karl again felt the wave of empathy toward the young man, tried to feel the pain that had forced him to squeeze his eyes closed so tightly.

He could not know, of course, that Marty's sudden appearance of pain had nothing to do with the aches assailing his body. He had fought a battle, and he had won. His decision had been to offer his closest friend, the grizzled old German pilot, silence instead of the news Marty had received by telephone only yesterday.

"I'm sorry, Marty. I don't know of any way to tell you this. Your tests came back today." The doctor had hesitated, and it was at that moment Marty Morgan felt the coldness that would never again leave him.

"The most I can promise you is a year, but I wouldn't bet on more than six months."

Bernie Hudoff and Vladislov Galenko stood on a long plain of smooth rocks that moved beneath their feet. They shifted their weight to keep their balance. All their world came to the rocks beneath them, strange noises and the thick swirling mists of heavy fog rolling in from the cool Atlantic Ocean only a few hundred yards away. Hudoff took a quick slug of Jack Daniels and handed the flask to the KBG agent. He upended the flask and drained half its contents in a long, smooth pull, capped the flask, and returned it to the American. Hudoff wordlessly returned it to his jacket pocket, removed two cigars from another pocket, handed one to the Russian, then bit the end from his own cigar and lit up. He held the lighter flame for Galenko. They stood quietly for several moments, listening. The world trembled gently beneath their feet, a continuing vibration they heard and felt at the same time.

Soon the sounds began to mix: a deep thumping boom repeated endlessly, a coughing bass that laced easily through their bodies. Whirring sounds, huge chunks of machinery rising and falling, spinning, coughing, and barking. A terrible underfoot grinding as if some impossible Godzilla were rolling across the earth on monster treads, unstoppable, thousands of tons made of steel and iron, pulsing rivers of energy and howling diesels and blatting exhausts, all coming inexorably toward them.

Which was exactly what was happening. Another element in the plans of Bernie Hudoff was under way. *And it was working.* The 747 with *Columbia* on its back was twenty thousand feet in the air and on its way to safety. *Antares* was on its launching block at Pad 39A. But there remained the unnerving fact that *Discovery* was still in the VAB, and that a single bomb could take out the VAB and *Discovery* and so many booster elements. It drove Hudoff crazy. The fog and the help of his selected members of the news media was swiftly changing all that. To the world, the thundering jet departure in the fog was a C-5 Galaxy making the Cape safe from a runaway thermofusion generator—whatever the hell *that* was supposed to be. Now Hudoff was completing his burning goal to complete the separation of the three shuttles. *Discovery* at this moment was grinding its way toward them on the back of the enormous transporter, the huge carrying vehicle the size of a baseball diamond, with treads so monstrous that each single tread of the hundreds rumbling on this vehicle weighed more than a Volkswagen. With a speed of only one mile an hour, not even the fog was going to stop the juggernaut of several thousand tons from moving out of the VAB and along the transport "highway" of Alabama riverbed rock. Advance men walked along the roadway with radar dishes on their backs, and the driver-operators of the transporter, in conjunction with lights, computers, and men talking every foot of the way, were shifting *Discovery* from the VAB to the relative isolation of Pad 39B, well to the north of 39A where *Antares* stood within its service structure. There had been time, and the work would continue, to mount blast-deflection plates and thermal shields on the side of Pad 39B that would face southward, where any nuclear weapon might be expected to explode. The way to protect *Discovery* was not to count upon the blast and thermal shields deflecting any heat pulse or shock wave from an exploding bomb, but to absorb the blows in successive defensive layers. The first would stop the heat and would then collapse before the shock wave. By the time it collapsed, the heat pulse would be gone. The shock wave and blast would crunch the shielding panels. They would snap away as so much junk. The lessened blast would then howl through spaces left open just for that purpose, the relief of overpressure; and additional blast shields would absorb more of the blow. Hudoff had studied the pictures of concrete buildings in Hiroshima that withstood the atomic bomb that ground up that city. Then he went over the films of buildings subjected to nuclear blasts in later tests. He called the experts, he studied the patterns, and he ordered decisions turned into actions. The shields went up in around-the-clock shifts, and the moment the fog promised to come off the ocean, Hudoff spun more wheels. In a few hours the sun would be burning through the fog and they would move the transporter faster, around the curve to take it alongside and then well beyond 39A, where *Antares* would bear mute testimony to the dispersal plan's success.

Hudoff and Galenko had chosen to walk the roadway of river rock that could support ten thousand tons of moving mountain. They would be there when the sun brought an increasing glow to the fog, and they would watch *Discovery* ascend the slope to the pad where it would be bolted down, and three additional layers of blast shields folded into place from the servicing gantry arms.

Galenko drew deeply on his cigar. He had achieved an easy, deep relationship with this gruff American who drank whiskey so easily and profaned his subordinates, and had a mind of cutting steel. They spoke as confidants with enormous mutual respect of intelligence and ability.

"Moscow is not happy," Galenko said finally.

"Big fucking deal," he got for an answer. "So Moscow

370

isn't happy. Ring the church bells, kill the dogs; whatever. Send them a telegram, Vladislov. Tell Moscow there are two of us who aren't happy. Them and me."

Galenko ignored the sarcasm. He tipped his head to hear better as a foghorn blasted through the dark mists, then answered Hudoff's retort. "They are talking about withdrawing Georgi Mikoyan from the mission."

Hudoff stopped to look directly at Galenko. A surrealistic glow of red came and went from their faces as a nearby security car crawled as an advance scout of the monster grinding toward them. "Vladislov," Hudoff said patiently, "that sounds like coercion. You're pushing me. You, and Moscow, and whoever. Don't tell me they might yank your boy from the bird. I don't give a shit whether Georgi Porgi is aboard that shuttle or not. What I *don't* like is this messenger-boy act. What the hell do you want for an answer? A guarantee in writing we won't mess up his hair?"

"You are upset," Galenko said quietly.

"How the fuck did you guess?"

"What is your saying, Bernie? Up yours? With the finger like this?" He held up a rigid middle finger. "You would make a good Russian the way you jump from the handle."

"Fly off the handle, you mean."

"I mean any focking thing I say. What you did *not* give me time to finish saying, you hassholer, is that I have recommended *against* doing such a thing."

Hudoff started to reply, bit his tongue to prevent a precipitous response. This could turn into a touchy exchange, or they could continue to cement the bond growing between them.

"Why the hell didn't you say so right away?" he asked finally.

"What, and give up chance to chew up your ass?"

Hudoff chuckled and they started walking again as the rumbling, grinding thunder came closer. "You know what that machine sounds like?" Galenko asked. "Don't answer. *I* know. It is like standing at bottom of enormous glacier that is breaking apart at edge of the sea. It is a very impressive sound." He shifted abruptly in his remarks. "Bernie, when will your people make the final decision about launch?"

"Sunday morning."

Galenko was surprised and didn't try to hide it. "You will wait until only a few hours before launch?"

"I'll wait until the guests are to be brought here." He pointed in the direction of the viewing bleachers immersed in the fog, invisible to them. "If we go, those seats will be filled. If we scrub, they'll be empty."

"You are playing it—how do you Americans say it—very tight to the vest?"

Hudoff smiled. "That'll do."

Galenko smiled in return. "You feel so strong that you can stop an attack from the air?"

Hudoff nodded. "Look, my people have been beating me about the head and shoulders that you can't stop a determined air strike."

"They are right, Hudoff."

"But we're not talking about an attack by a large military force, goddamnit! We're dealing with one or two planes, one with a bomb and the other a decoy, *if* they even try it that way. They try to bring that thing in by air and we bring the whole damn hammer down on them. If they so much as show over the horizon we've got them cold. We've sealed off everything, the whole ocean area, to the east. The warnings are posted. We'll fire at *anything* that comes in from the ocean. I've got Navy radar planes with look-down coverage and vectoring. We've got thirty choppers working up to fifty miles offshore. Sixty fast boats. We'll orbit ten fighters in the air with missiles." He turned to Galenko. "*Now* what do you have to say?"

"They can get through. You are playing war with all these toys."

"*Toys!* Goddamnit, Vladislov, I've got enough firepower here to fight a full-sized war!"

"You are yourself saying, Bernie, this is *not* war. They need to get through but only *once*. They do not need to be accurate." He held up a hand to forestall another outburst from the American. "Unhappy fact is clear,

Bernie Hudoff. None of what you have done is worth anything if you do not know *where* they have the bomb."

"I wish you hadn't said that."

"Why?"

"Sometimes I hate the truth."

"Like you say about Moscow, that is making two of us." Galenko dragged deeply on his cigar. "Bernie, you tell me something."

"Let's have it."

"I suppose you will stay here for launch, no matter what?"

Hudoff shrugged. "Sure. What else?"

"What else is that if you stay, you may die."

Hudoff laughed. "Listen to you! My cognac-swigging asshole buddy from Siberia!" He turned and poked a thick finger against Galenko's chest. "If Mikoyan is aboard that shuttle when we launch, aren't *you* staying here?"

"How do you say it? Yeah, sure. What else?"

✛ 21 ✛

THE DAY BEFORE

One hundred and fifteen warbirds rolled down the two active runways early Saturday morning for the dawn patrol that would entice the crowds to the big airshow early that afternoon. Everything *seemed* right. Propellers turned and engines roared, but there was a sense of diffidence among the pilots and the crews. They spread out on their assigned runs through the county, but their feelings were hardly assuaged when Wendy Green sounded her cautionary note on the common frequency. "Baker Two Five formation on the active, be aware that Fat Albert's in the air and that all restricted areas are hot. No overflights or penetration of restricted areas, I repeat, no overflights or penetrations of restricted areas. Any questions? Over."

The reply came back in a flat monotone completely uncharacteristic of the "wild men and women" who flew the warbirds with usual verve and excitement. "Ah, Shiloh, this is Baker Two Five Lead, ah, we read you loud and clear. All areas are hot and eyeballs out for Fat Al. Sounds real thrilling. We're ready to go, Shiloh."

Somehow, Wendy Green couldn't bring up the wisecracks she used to send her pilots off on their roust-'em-out dawn patrol. "Baker Two Five formation cleared for takeoff. Roll at your discretion." She knew she sounded like lumpy cold oatmeal. The spirit was damp, the enthusiasm as lively as an obit column.

Everything was so damned normal, they were all on edge. They steered clear of the restricted areas. They didn't need Wendy to tell them the military was out in force, with hot guns, and as nervous as a bride about to be gang-banged by her new husband's seven brothers. They didn't *want* to fly off the Cape, not with Fat Albert hanging in the sky at the upper end of the tethering cable that could tear the plane of an unwary pilot to shreds. They all carried the tracking radios with the dull glass that would come alive when and if they ever sailed into range of the missing atomic bomb, but not that many pilots watched for the telltale blinking. They no longer believed in their importance to discovering the bomb and averting a mass slaughter. Too much had happened. Good people were dead, including the man who'd serviced these same machines and kept them humming for all of them. They returned from the dawn patrol subdued, defeatist, and off their feed. The warbirds came down hard and they bounced and swerved, and the extent of the piloting misery left its mark in the rubber scorching on the runway from tires swerving or being braked clumsily.

At two o'clock that afternoon they flew their show to a packed airfield. More than thirty thousand people crowded onto Shiloh and the weather was perfect, the wind a perfect ten knots out of the west. The bands played and the kids shrieked and men and women fell from the sky, the bombers struck with ear-hammering explosions and the fighters fought their mock battles, the Golden Girls put on their usual act to thundering applause. The crowd, as usual, loved it.

The pilots knew they were, in the words of Santiago, "for shit." Charley Morgan flew the airshow as air controller from the rear compartment of Bannon's big torpedo bomber, and from the gunner's seat she had a perfect view of the clumsy melee beneath her. Her long silences said more to Bannon than any words could have conveyed. The jitters were getting to the pilots.

375

They flew, at best, a lousy show.

Bannon couldn't blame them. Every one of them felt crippled and helpless. And they all sensed that the world they knew might well be rushing to its end.

The big television screen in the hangar told the constant change in time. A local station locked its video cameras onto the huge digital countdown display at the press site of the Kennedy Space Center, and gave local residents a constant update on the launch countdown for *Antares*, as well as any late-breaking news in the form of an information strip that rolled steadily across the bottom of the screen.

Few of the pilots and crews dragging themselves wearily into the Morgan hangar bothered to do more than glance idly at the screen in the corner of the hangar. As the last pilot returned from the flight line following the Saturday afternoon show, the clock read T MINUS 15 HOURS 48 MINUTES 37 SECONDS. The numbers changed steadily, rapidly for the seconds, slower for the minutes, and hourly for the left-sided readout.

The pilots and their crews sat dully on chairs or on the hangar floor, drinking coffee or beer as they waited for the debriefing that followed every show. The usual wise-cracking was absent. What was intended to be a debriefing started out more in the manner of a funeral dirge. Charley Morgan climbed the platform steps to the podium and microphone, and that in itself was a sharp departure from the norm. She wasted no time.

"I'll keep this short," she said without any preliminary remarks. "Today was the *worst* airshow I've ever seen. If you feel you're under too much pressure, damnit, then stay on the ground. *Do not fly.* Every one of you knows I'm not telling you anything you don't know. You were a bunch of schoolgirls up there today."

She shuffled papers before her, more for the deliberate pause than a need to consult notes. "The bombers flew sloppy formation. You were all over the place. And you fighter pilots ... you're supposed to coordinate among yourselves *and with the other aircraft flying with you.* Your air work discipline, or lack of it, was the

376

worst I've ever seen. You jocks were hotdogging it without regard for other pilots. You came close to collision several times. Now, you people flying the trainers. You looked like you were all first-time cadets at the controls. Just slop, and—never mind. The long and the short of it is that the feds were all over me and they've threatened to ground the lot of us until we prove we can do better. I've talked them out of cancelling our airshow waiver, but I'll tell you right now it wasn't by much."

She spoke to a hangar filled with men and women who showed the emotion of wooden Indians. Charley fretted over that; she'd rather have them angry with and shouting at her. This withdrawal was the worst kind of reaction to the danger hanging over them all. She knew that brow-beating these people wouldn't do any good. They *knew* what was wrong. But if she could get them to recognize themselves as slopping it out upstairs it might do some good. She honestly didn't know, and the fear of disaster right in her front yard gnawed deeply at her thoughts.

"Okay, enough of that," she said to change the mood. "Let's go on from here. As of right now we've got a dawn patrol set for tomorrow morning—"

"Time?" a voice called out. The interruption thrilled her. Just that one word, but it meant at least *one* pilot in the crowd was *thinking first of flying* ahead of all other issues.

"We'll shoot for the regular slot," she told them, feeling her own mood going into an upswing, her voice a touch brighter and clearer than it had been. "That's oh seven hundred on the nose. Now let me say this right away. We could have a change in that. It won't be from me, but I've got to keep the oh seven hundred hack as a maybe until we hear from NASA. I've no way of knowing if they'll make any changes in the shuttle launch time. Right now the countdown timer," she gestured to the TV screen behind and to her left, "is the update. Any questions?"

Mort Hackenberry stood up. "Charley, are those crazy bastards *really* going to launch?"

A murmur of agreement stirred through the assembled pilots. Charley held up a hand to quiet them down, and she shrugged. "Mort, I really do not know. As of right now, NASA says they're go. But for all *I* know they may have secretly flown the astronauts out of here. I have no way of telling if they're giving me the straight skinny or not."

More sounds of discontent from her flying troops. Inwardly she thanked whatever deities came to mind for the stirring even of anger from these people. Another pilot rose to his feet: Stan Baker. "Hey, Charley, you know what NASA stands for, don't you? *Never A Straight Answer!*" Hoots and hollers rose from the ranks along with chuckles and even a few touches of open laughter. *Keep it up, guys*, she told herself.

"Hey, we're getting away from the main issue, you people, and the issue is *us*. The official word is that NASA *does* want us to fly the dawn patrol in the morning."

Again the silence like a falling blanket, and again she waited for a single voice to pierce the shroud. "Hot damn! That's just great, Charley. NASA wants *us* to fly right over the area where an atomic bomb might go off at any time!"

The voices rose to spear the shroud. "He's right, Charley!"

"We don't owe NASA shit!"

"Why do they want us to fly dawn patrol, Charley?"

Charley wanted to kiss the man who'd asked that question. "Hey, I don't care what NASA wants. *I* want us to fly dawn patrol because it makes *us* money!"

Applause scattered through the group. "Right on!" was a sentiment echoed among the pilots.

Matt Stengel rose to his feet. Matt was a bear of a man with huge shoulders and a bushy moustache. He flew a Skyraider; he just about *needed* all that power to carry his hulk into the air. He stood until the comments around him died down. "Charley, I got to ask you this." She nodded to Matt. "Are *you* flying dawn patrol?"

Charley looked out at the sea of faces glued to hers. "My daddy," she said with a softer tone than she'd been using, "always told me nobody lives forever. You're damned right I'm flying. And I intend to stay in a pattern that keeps me as close to that launch pad as they'll let me fly." She held up her hand and paused another heartbeat. "But I don't want any pilot in that sky who feels they don't *want* to go."

Matt Stengel offered her a smile of booming radiance. "Hell, little lady, if you're flying, then I'll be right behind you!"

"That goes for me, too!" another man shouted.

"You can count on the Golden Girls," Sherri Taylor shouted.

"You're all crazy! Count me in!" boomed out another voice. More laughter greeted the remarks. *They've done it*, Charley told herself with near-disbelief. *They've broken the ice. They're okay* . . .

She laughed and motioned for quiet with both arms in the air. "My God, you're *all* crazy!" she told them. "Okay, let's get on with it. When we get through with this meeting, take a break and be back here at nine for a final briefing. I'll keep it short. I hate to bust up your evening this way, but NASA promised me a final update at that time."

Ken Masters was on his feet. "What happens after that?"

Charley frowned. "I wish I could tell you. Look, let's level with each other. Shiloh is at least twelve miles from the launch pad. Some of you may feel that's not far enough away from the pad if, well, you know, if that's far enough away to be safe. I don't believe we're in the slightest danger *here* if there is an explosion, of, well—"

Bannon went quickly to her side. He saw Charley faltering, and they couldn't let that happen. Charley looked at him as he picked up the microphone. "Hey, let's cut the mustard," he told them. "Anybody here who feels like leaving, you get the hell out of here. I mean that. Nobody can blame you. You've got to do whatever you think is right, what's best for you and your family. Christ, there's nothing wrong in being scared about an atomic bomb. It's a personal choice. I'm staying. So is Charley, and our crews. I sort of hang to the line

379

that there's a time for staying and a time for running. I don't like being *run out* of my own digs. I stay. So do Charley and Marty and Karl and all those people who sang out. But if you *do* decide to go for the safety you feel you've got to have, when you depart Shiloh make sure you make all your turns to the *west*. Anybody who crosses the river to the east and cuts the line to the launch area is going to have his ass shot off. So other than what Charley's told you guys, its a matter of taking one step after the other. Remember, those of you who plan to fly dawn patrol *must* be here for the final briefing at nine tonight." He cut it off abruptly, handed the microphone back to Charley, and stepped back.

The pilots began to assemble in small groups as an end to the meeting, talking furiously or concealing their doubts and fears in silence. A shrill whistle brought them all to look at Jay Martin standing on the wing of a P-38. "Hey! Enough of this happy horseshit, you people!" Bannon and Charley exchanged a quick glance. Jay might just put the right capper to this session.

"We're flying dawn patrol tomorrow and then NASA is going to launch their big bird, and then we're going to fly *our* show tomorrow afternoon, right? Because if those assholes in NASA *really* thought a bomb was going off they'd have cleared out their precious hides by now, *right?*" He raised a clenched fist and pumped it up and down. "Screw NASA! Let's take care of *right now, right!*" Both arms shot up in a grand Last Hurrah gesture. *"It's time to have a party!"* he roared.

The hangar shook from the spontaneous shouting response to Jay's verbal whips into the mood with which they were far more familiar. Whistles, cheers, applause, and shouts answered his call to arms.

"Wait a moment!" he yelled, gesturing wildly for them to hold it down. "We got a band!" he cried out. "We're gonna have a race. Wilbur on the skateboard against Nancy on her tricycle! We got a whole damn truck full of beer! It's all down by the terminal building! And it's on the house tonight! *Its free! Charley's paying! Let's go and get down to IT!"*

They poured from the hangar shouting and laughing

and back-slapping, unaware of how their mood had been so neatly maneuvered into their now openly expressed desire to share some hard drinking and partying. Charley held Bannon's arm. She shook her head in wonder. "I can hardly believe it. A few minutes ago these people were scared to death. I really expected most of them to clear out tonight." She gestured at the milling throng. "*Now* they're having the time of their lives."

"They might as well," Bannon told her. "You're paying for it." The crash of a rock band from huge amplifiers down by the terminal thundered across the flight line and bounced about the hangar walls. They winced and grinned at the same time. "It's an old story with this crowd, I guess," Bannon observed. "You can either be scared out of your skull and quit, or you get bombed and tell yourself you're having a great time. This bunch'll take the whiskey every time."

They saw Nancy Drake and Bonnie Richardson, two young lovelies who flew for Sherri Taylor in the Golden Girls act. Charley and Bannon went up to them. "Nancy, what's this about you racing a tricycle against Wilbur's skateboard?"

"The first *I* heard about that," Nancy retorted, "was a few moments ago."

"Don't worry about it," Bannon told her. "You're a setup to win."

"How come?"

"Its one of those three-wheelers for cross-country racing. It's got twenty horsepower," Bannon explained. "Besides, they're going to get Wilbur smashed out of his mind."

Nancy nodded, not answering as the four of them watched Jay Martin walking off with Sherri Taylor, Jay's hand flush against her curving buttocks. Bonnie Richardson sighed with the sight. "I don't mind saying I wish I was having some of that tonight," she said wistfully.

Nancy turned to her. "Honey, let me ask you something that Sherri's going to find out tonight."

"What's that?"

"Do you know what's white," she demonstrated with her hands as she spoke, "about this big and round, and, oh, about fourteen inches long?"

Bonnie shook her head. "No. What?"

"*Nothing!*"

The four of them broke up.

When the sun hangs *just* above the western horizon in the midst of an atmospheric sea of haze and mist, and you wait for *just* the right instant before the upper rim drops off the far end of the world, the final gasp of orange flame flashes a dazzling green in a display of solar colorama intended to impress the most distant of minds. On this last Saturday evening before the launch of *Antares*, Bernie Hudoff looked through the broad picture window of his condominium overlooking the Banana and Indian Rivers from Cocoa Beach. He saw the orange gasp and green flare, and it impressed him not a whit. It's difficult to feel an affinity with a star when the shrill and humorless verbal whip behind you, driving home with all the impact of a jackhammer, is wielded by Miriam.

Miriam, all one hundred and ninety well-turned and perfectly groomed pounds of her, was *Mrs*. Hudoff. And Mrs. Hudoff was laughing. Not with humor but with hysterical outrage, her face florid, her painted lips distorted in rubbery and quivering accusation.

"You son of a bitch!" Her arrows struck with deadly accuracy at both his ears. "Your own children! Your own flesh and blood, you bastard! You'd let them be torn to pieces and you would never even tell us a word!"

He'd been hanging on very well to his patience. Being shredded and having been dragged through many a wringer during the past week, that patience was evaporating swiftly as Miriam gained the acoustic pressure of an air raid siren. "There was nothing to tell—" He started his explanation for the umpteenth time, and as before she sliced it away like an unexpected circumcision.

"Liar! You lie! I heard it from Betty, and *she* knows. She *always* knows!" Miriam took in a huge breath, expanding her already swollen chest, and plunged on.

"She knows from her brother, down at the air force. My God, Bernie, an atom bomb right here in our own middle! How could you do this to your own children? Even if they lived, God willing, they would be monsters!"

"There isn't any atom bomb, Miriam. You've read the papers. Its an experimental thermofusion—"

"Thermo, shmermo! You bastard! I'm leaving, you understand? I'm leaving for the sake of our kids! And if you had an ounce of decency left you'd come with us." Miriam threw up her hands in a very visible, very histrionic cry to heaven. "God, where will we go?"

"Try the Himalayas."

Her hands came down slowly and her mouth drooped in concert. *"What?"*

"You heard me. The Himalayas. It's a nice time of the year in Tibet. I hear the monastery has a terrific view of Mount Everest. You'll be safe there, Miriam. The monks are sworn to celibacy and it's against their religion to eat meat. No cannibals."

"Have you gone crazy?"

"Not yet, but you're obviously doing your best to help me along. Are you really going?"

"I'm *going!*"

"Go *now.*" He smiled sweetly, bit off the end of a cigar, and stuck it in his teeth. Not a word was spoken as he struck a match and lit up and tossed the still-burning match casually onto the fluffy white carpet. "And go far, Miriam. *Very* far."

"I swear if you don't come with us I'll never come back!"

"You swear?"

"On my mother's grave!"

"She lives in St. Louis. How the hell can you swear on her grave?"

"You know what I mean!" Miriam screamed.

"I thought you were going?" He blew out a cloud of smoke. "Damnit, Miriam, you *promised.*"

"You *want* me to go!"

"That's good. Very good. You win a cigar. You're still here, Miriam."

"I hate you!"

"I should be so lucky. What the hell are you still doing here?" He crossed the room, pulled open the door to the hallway, pointed his finger at her. "Remember, you *promised*."

He whistled as he walked bouncily down the hall. That fucking atomic bomb had its good points, after all.

Colonel Hank Rawls, followed by two burly Air Policemen carrying MAC-10 9-mm submachine guns, stopped at the entrance to Fat Albert's control booth. He stood patiently while on-duty guards checked the identification of all three men, then waved them inside. Rawls studied the electronic control readouts for the giant blimp swaying in the dark high above them, suspending beneath its swollen shape the high-altitude surveillance radar for the central Florida coast. Rawls motioned to the duty officer. "Lieutenant, what's blimp height right now?"

"Twelve thousand feet, sir. We've got fifteen thousand feet of cable played out."

"Bring it down to four thousand feet. Keep it there until you receive orders from my office to change that altitude."

"Yes, sir." A clipboard appeared as if by magic. "Sign the authorization here, sir. Name, rank, serial number, and authorization code, please."

"You don't need this, Lieutenant. Just do it."

"No way in hell, sir. Meaning no disrespect, Colonel—"

Rawls took the clipboard. His smile barely showed as he signed as required. "Good job, Lieutenant."

"Thank you, sir."

"Get with it. Bring it down immediately."

Rawls and his two guards left the control room, the cable motors speeding up to engage the cable and begin dragging Fat Albert down to four thousand feet from its height of two and a half miles. As the motor whine grew in intensity, Rawls looked up at the bright strobe lights flashing far above him. He turned and walked to the parking area. Guards saluted him; he returned their salutes without missing a step. He saw the NASA security vehicle in the lot overlooking the beach and walked

384

briskly to it. He stopped twenty feet off, watching Bernie Hudoff standing alone, arms stiff, fists clenched, looking at *Antares* under its dazzling floodlights.

"Hello, Bernie."

Hudoff turned slowly. "Oh; Rawls. Evening, Colonel. Come join me."

They stood together several moments, both men studying the shuttle, knowing the danger that infused every molecule of their being, knowing how many lives depended on how well they did their jobs.

"Anything new break?"

"I think this Zoboa bunch is dicking us, Colonel."

"That's a new twist."

"I don't believe they ever intended to use a bomb against us."

"That's a powerful belief."

"Yeah. I wish it was true."

"The decision to launch or not come down?"

Hudoff shook his head. "Not yet."

"Got any ideas when?"

Hudoff sighed. "Yes. When I give *my* final evaluation."

"It's go or no-go on what *you* say?"

"Yeah. I'll trade jobs with you, Colonel."

Rawls shook his head. "No way. Man, I do *not* envy you."

Hudoff smiled in the half-light. "It's a funny world, Colonel." He turned to look directly at Rawls. "You ever have problems growing up because you were a nigger?"

Rawls hesitated only an instant. "Sure. Why?"

"Like I said, it's a funny world. Right now I envy *you*."

"Bannon, this is supposed to be a *briefing?*" Charley sat next to Bannon on the hangar platform, looking with amazement at the pilots milling about before her. "How can so many people get so drunk in so short a time!" she exclaimed.

"You buy good beer and whiskey, I guess," he told her. "And if I were you, I wouldn't waste any time getting with it. They're getting drunker by the minute."

Charley nodded to Wendy Green, who brought a police whistle to her lips and sent a shrill blast through the hangar. Eyes rattled in sockets and grown men and women shuddered as they turned to look up at the platform. The hangar became reasonably quiet. Before she spoke, Charley glanced at the countdown timer. Everything was right on the money and local time was 9:02 P.M.

"We have a go for the dawn patrol," she began. She hadn't counted on the response that bellowed and echoed about the hangar.

"Hot damn!"

"Whoo-hah!"

"Killer!"

"Atta girl!"

"You tell them momma humpers, Charley!"

She glanced at Bannon. "*These* are the same pilots who were ready to lay down and die a few hours ago?"

"That's them," Bannon grinned. "Girl, I'm telling you, while you got their attention, stay with it."

She turned quickly to the assembled pilots. "I want the first bird to have wheels up at six-thirty. Everybody flies for a maximum period of two hours. You *must* be back here no later than eight-thirty."

"What happens if we're late, Charley?"

"Fly north, west, or south, but *do not*, and I repeat, *do not* enter this restricted area, which includes Shiloh after that time and until the shuttle launches, or you will be fired upon. I really mean that, people. Security is tighter than a frog's rear end in a deep swamp. There'll be hot guns up there. If you're low on fuel or you have other problems, *put down at the nearest field* and just wait it out."

The questions came one after the other. "What's the scheduled launch time?"

"Just like it says on the boob tube, NASA's calling for liftoff at exactly ten o'clock."

"They say anything about a bomb?"

Charley shook her head. "No."

"Maybe it's a thermofusion generator, Charley!" a pilot called out.

"Yeah! Or the Batmobile!" another added.

"You believe them, Charley?"

"About what?"

"About it being safe to fly!"

"We all know flying's dangerous," Charley said, and she couldn't hold back her smile.

"The bastards'll have us flying right over the bomb, for Christ's sake!" a pilot shouted. There was no mistaking the tone of fear in his voice.

"Hey! You don't want to get lost, do you?" They turned to look at Marty Morgan standing by the platform. "That thing goes off, just follow the light!"

"Sure!" called another pilot. "To the end of the world!"

"Shit! That's gotta be better than Miami!" came another shout.

Bill Santiago came up to Charley's side and took her microphone. "Hokay! I don' wanna hear no more shits talk about Miami!"

"What do you want to talk about?"

Santiago held up his middle finger. "Hokay, hokay! This is for real now, you gots it?" The murmuring died down. "Is very simple," Santiago told them. "When you takes off in the morning you makes all your turns to the west. You gots it? To the west which is the opposite of the easts, hokay? You don' do that they gonna shoot your ass off and we got white people's chopped liver everywhere. And you flies your regular dawn patrol just like you always screws up when you hung up all—no, when you hungs over, hokay?" He blew a kiss to the pilots. "This the end of big briefing! Everybody back to the party!"

Bannon moved forward quickly and took the microphone from Santiago. He whistled shrilly for attention. "One more thing, people." He waited a few moments, searching the crowd for a particular face. "There's always the chance there'll be a screwup in the morning. We've been trying to get NASA to give us a safety corridor we can take to head out to sea if we have to, but you've got to stay above Fat Albert because of that cable. So even if you get permission to go through the restricted area, make sure you stay above—" He faltered, making sure the microphone was still close to his lips as he turned to Santiago. "Bill, you know what altitude they're holding for the blimp?"

Santiago shrugged. "I don' knows." He leaned into the mike. "Anybody here knows how high they flies the fat balloon?"

"Four thousand feet!" a voice sang out from the crowd.

Bannon smiled to himself. *Bingo!*

Bannon and Charley rode the airport jeep along the flight line, driving north to the old terminal building. Rock music pounded through the night air, vibrating the jeep, drumming at their ears. They watched the live band in a frenzy. "Who in the name of God are they?" Charley asked.

"Local group from the beach. They used to call themselves the Primitives—"

"I can believe that."

"—but they changed their name to Crescendo."

"I can believe *that*." Charley pointed to the tumultuous scene of pilots dancing, Wilbur going in crazy circles on his skateboard, and both men and women wandering about half-dazed.

"Bannon, that's been going on like that since nine o'clock," Charley groaned. "Those people are *smashed*, and they're supposed to fly in the morning, and—"

"Not to worry. It's almost Cinderella time."

"What?"

"Wendy cuts the power off at midnight. No power for the amps or the guitars or anything else. The band goes home."

"But—"

"The bar not only closes, Wendy has a crew to drive away with all the goodies. Also at the stroke of midnight, which is just about—"

Before he could say the word "now" the crash of noise loosely called music stopped in midnote. The silence was almost a physical presence. The lights went out and they heard the crash of a bottle and curses in the dark. Voices bellowed in protest. Charley and Bannon grinned at one another.

An engine started with a coughing roar. Headlights

snapped on and twin beams of light stabbed across the ramp. "What the hell—?" Bannon said for himself and Charley. The lights moved slowly but in their direction. Marching music boomed suddenly from speakers atop a truck. Floodlights sprang into dazzling light to each side and behind the truck. Coming across the field, weaving and lurching behind Karl von Strasser in a German helmet and banging on a great drum before him, came a line of drunken pilots, tooting on horns and kazoos. Von Strasser's voice thundered.

"Ve sing!" He waved an arm and pumped it up and down. "Ve sing *now!*"

The ragged chorus stumbled through the night air. *"Links! Links! Der obermeishter shtinks!"* von Strasser smashed madly at his drum and they picked up the words again.

"First der shtick undt den der rudder, but neffer vun mittoudt der udder!"

Charley tugged at Bannon's sleeve. "That's what you call sobering up?"

"For Christ's sake, Charley, they're singing, not drinking!"

Charley shrugged in defeat. "Get me out of here, Bannon. I give up. I simply *must* get some sleep."

"Your place or mine?"

"Bannon, for God's sake, *not now.*" She kissed him on the cheek. "Lover, I am really dead. Your place and a bed. And *sleep.*"

They drove to his hangar apartment. Charley moved like a zombie. Bannon settled down on the long couch with Charley wrapped in his arms. In the dark room he saw her face in the alternating green and white glows of the airport beacon. He snuggled her closer to him and moved carefully to kiss his woman. Charley snored gently. Bannon rolled his eyes and sat back. Charley was already in a deep sleep. Bannon leaned his head back on the couch and gave in to the inevitable.

He heard the drop falling from some great but unknown height, falling down and down to the pool of dark water. The drop splashed into the pool, and the tiny wave from the splash moved outward in all directions with a sound remarkably like an electronic *ping!* Another drop, and another, faster and faster, the pinging sounds becoming ever louder. Bannon's eyes flickered open. No water. No droplets falling. The pinging sounds coming from the concealed telephone in his locked desk drawer. Cursing beneath his breath, he disengaged from Charley, placed a pillow beneath her head and his jacket on her body.

He struggled to the desk, brought out the phone, and cupped his hand over the mouthpiece to keep down the sound of his voice. "Yeah, yeah, talk to me," he grunted.

"Security Three here. You got Security One on the way by eggbeater. Meet him. Confirm."

"I got it. Screw you, Mister Happy or whoever you are."

He disconnected, went to the bathroom, and tossed cold water on his face. He had just enough time to gulp down cold coffee when he heard the helicopter blades coming closer. He went outside. Salty mist hung in the air, the field was quiet, the long lines of warbirds loomed against the field perimeter lights like—

Bannon stared, blinked his eyes. For a moment there it—no, it couldn't be. He felt as if he'd swooped backwards through time. He stood at the end of the parking taxiway with rows of warbirds on each side of the concrete ribbon. At the far end they'd parked a bunch of Corsair fighters, their great wings folded upward until the wingtips nearly met over the cockpit. In the backlighting the row of wings were silhouetted. Bannon blinked. He could have sworn the wings had become a teepee. Far down the row of conical shapes a small fire blazed. Night crews taking a break in the cold air, seated about the fire. He saw their faces with amazing clarity. Four men, faces lined and old and weathered, staring into the fire. The scene could have been a thousand years ago. Ten thousand years ago. He saw a hand move to toss a stick into the fire, stirring the hot coals and sending embers soaring upward.

The climbing embers appeared to swell and mushroom in size and suddenly roar with power. Startled, he doubted his own senses until the approaching helicopter came into clearer view over the fire, its flashing red light along its gleaming belly mixing with the soaring embers and sparks.

Bannon jabbed the side of his head with his hand to knock sense back into himself. He knew he might never again experience so extraordinary a moment, as if he'd looked down through a crack in the walls of Time. But that was then and this was now, and as he walked toward the helicopter he saw Hudoff and Galenko and he knew before they said a word that they were going to risk *everything* in the next few hours.

✦ 22 ✦

FINAL NIGHT

Hudoff leaned from the cabin, holding open the door to the helicopter. "We don't have much time. Get in. We'll talk in here."

Bannon climbed inside and closed the door behind him. The cabin lights showed Vladislov Galenko seated on the other side of Hudoff. Inside the heavily sound-proofed cabin the idling rotors sounded no louder than a strong wind outside.

"We're go for the launch," Hudoff said.

"I figured you would," Bannon told him.

"But there's a change in the game plan, Bannon. Washington is still convinced this Zoboa outfit has the last bomb in their hands and they *will* try to set it off at launch."

"Then why the hell *would* you launch!" Bannon exclaimed, nearly shouting.

"Because we believe we can fake them out."

"How?"

"We've decided to use your crazy mob for cover."

"The warbirds? I don't understand—"

"The warbirds," Hudoff confirmed. "We want them right over the space center. We want every damn machine you can get in the air to swarm around Kennedy.

392

Bannon, no one will ever expect a launch with all you lunatics right overhead."

"You mean—"

"Christ, shut up and let me finish. You send up your dawn patrol. Just like you crazies do before your airshow schedules. But just before your people get in the air, we'll jam every radio frequency there is. No one will be able to use a radio signal of *any* kind to set off a bomb." Hudoff took a deep breath, glanced at Galenko, and looked back to Bannon. "Can your people fly the whole patrol without radio between them?"

"Sure. We can work it out ahead of time, but—"

"Screw the buts, Bannon. You've been telling me for years how great these people are and now you're going to have to prove it. Got me? I want them flying over everything *except the launch pad itself*. Jesus, make sure everybody understands that. They get within five hundred feet of *Antares* our gunships will be all over them like flies on shit."

Bannon nodded slowly. "Boss, let me tell you flat out the whole idea sounds absolutely crazy to me."

Hudoff grinned. *"That's* the whole idea! *It's so crazy that we're going to launch right through your planes."*

"That's not crazy. Its *insane.*"

"Okay, so it's insane. But if they're about a thousand feet away from the bird when she fires, they'll be able to handle the shock waves. Shit, Bannon, work it out among yourselves. Put your heavy iron closest to the shock wave of launch. Those things were made to take anti-aircraft *and* the kitchen sink. With that mob milling around, whoever's got the bomb will be laid back, waiting for everyone to clear out. They won't be *expecting* a launch—and that's when we'll hit the button. Damnit, you got problems about this *let me hear it right now.*"

Bannon was thinking as hard and fast as he could. "You said you'll black out all radio."

"Damn right."

"How will you communicate with the astronauts in the shuttle?"

"Cable and code scramblers. We'll plug into the shuttle and we stay plugged in—"

"It's too easy for someone to tap into the lines. Especially if they're the people who have the bomb. They'll *know*—"

"We've anticipated that. Hank Rawls came to see me after your little meeting with him. Damn good thing, too." He slammed a fist against Galenko's knee. The Russian winced; Hudoff paid him no attention.

"And that's why," Hudoff went on, "Vladislov Galenko, here, will be communicator for launch control. Blacky Moran will take the right seat of the bird for launch and Georgi Mikoyan, the cosmonaut, will get into the left seat as shuttle commander. *They'll be talking in Russian.* No one will expect that."

"Not exactly in Russian," Galenko added. "In original Ukrainian language. Not even many Russians understand that. Mikoyan is from Poltava. All Ukrainian. Me, also. It will work, Bannon."

"Wait . . . hold it," Bannon said quickly. "If you've got everything under control like this, why do you even need us in the air?"

Hudoff came back with an immediate answer. "Decoy, distraction, fakeout; call it whatever you want. Whoever this Jabal is, he'll never *anticipate* a launch, like I said, with everybody running around the sky right over the launch area. We're still going with the public announcement of launch at ten o'clock, but we're going to light the fire at eight sharp. No warning of any kind."

"There will be, as you say it," Galenko added, "fire in the tail and the space machine will be out of the danger area before anyone can make a move."

"Sure; it's all very neat. But what happens," Bannon asked, "if the bomb goes off *after* the shuttle flies? You've still got all those VIP's and the other people—"

"You let us worry about the people, mister. You just handle the flying part of this. I told you before, Ace, I don't think this Zoboa outfit even has the bomb anywhere near here. The way I see it, all this is a maneuver to hold our attention while they get ready to strike somewhere else. Besides, I've told you they could never get through what we'll have waiting for them."

"The way *you* see it?" Bannon shook his head. "Christ, Bernie—"

"Goddamnit, Bannon, do your people fly or not!"

Bannon leaned back and glared at Hudoff. "Okay. They'll fly. I just hope you're not wrong, man."

"Up yours, kid. I ain't wrong."

"You're going to be sunburned all over if that bomb goes off, Bernie."

Galenko chuckled and Hudoff slapped Bannon on the shoulder. "What the hell, you're the lover boy who tells me no one lives forever, right? Just remember this." He showed a macabre smile. "If I'm wrong, Bannon, I'll be wrong right at ground zero."

He shoved his hand forward. "We got to make tracks." Bannon shook hands with Hudoff, an extra squeeze added by both men. Galenko offered his hand, Bannon shook it firmly, and climbed from the cabin. He stood for a moment on the ground with the door open. Hudoff waved to him. "Happy landings, Ace!"

Bannon felt his eyes misting. "You too, asshole."

They were gone.

He brought Charley out of her deep sleep with a mug of steaming coffee close to her nose. Her eyes opened and closed until she realized it *was* hot coffee. She sat up, groggy, clasping the mug in both hands, sipping slowly. "What time is it?" she managed finally.

"Five. Go on; sip the coffee. I need you to be awake to talk to you."

"Bannon, you shithead, I could have slept another hour—"

"Not today, babe. We got to talk before you fly."

Charley's eyes were in focus. "You sound serious."

"I am. You awake enough for some heavy stuff?"

She drank more coffee, went to the bathroom, and returned with her face scrubbed from cold water. "I'm awake. Let's have whatever it is that's so important."

"While you were asleep I had some visitors." He paused a moment as an engine coughed and snarled and finally burst into life. Bannon related to Charley the full conversation he'd had with Hudoff and Galenko. To his surprise she caught even the subtleties.

"From what you said, then you think this whole thing, I mean, with the bomb, *is an inside job?*"

"Yes."

"From people who are already on the Cape?"

"And have been for a while. I can't prove anything but we're— Never mind, hon. This isn't the time for a round-table caucus."

"No; it isn't. All right, Bannon. What's next?"

"Where's your brother?"

"He said he'd be up earlier than the rest this morning. He had some work to do on his ship. He's flying the T-28 today. It's, ah, yes; behind the second row of T hangars."

"I need to talk with him. You know what to do?"

Charley finished her coffee and nodded. "Yep. I'll get Wendy and Callahan and a couple more. We'll brief the pilots as fast as they come in, and then I'll put both Wendy and Callahan in the tower. When the radios go out, if we're still working the tower, we'll do it with light gun signals."

"Great, doll. Let's go."

He dropped Charley off by her hangar and drove the jeep around the row of T hangars to find Marty. The big T-28 stood by a workstand, under bright floodlights. The big dog sat atop the engine nacelle. Marty was leaning over and into the rear cockpit as Bannon climbed onto the wing from the opposite side.

Marty looked up. "Hey, Mitch. Take a look at this."

Bannon leaned over to the rear cockpit, where Marty showed him a strange harness and parachute rig with unusual metal clips and lines. He glanced back at Marty.

"This looks like a rig for the dog," Bannon said.

"You bet. Lemme show you how it works." He whistled to Magnum. "C'mere, you dumb Nazi son of a bitch." Magnum scrambled down to the workstand, moved back to the ladder leading to the rear cockpit, and climbed into the back seat.

"See?" Marty said, demonstrating the system. "The harness fits right around him. This clip, here, acts like a

396

safety belt. But if this crazy dog jumps or falls out of the airplane then the clips break free, um, like this, and away his dumb ass goes."

Bannon tapped a black box secured to the parachute rig. "Automatic opener?"

"Yep. Set to pull at a thousand feet barometric." Marty smiled with satisfaction; underneath there lay a great deal more concern for his canine friend than his cavalier attitude indicated. "The little black box is the answer, Mitch. Dumb dog jumps he gets a good free fall and then the chute opens. Piece of cake."

"Magnum's jumped before, hasn't he?"

"Sure has. I'd grab his harness and throw his ass out of the plane, hanging on, so we'd go down together. He loves it." He pushed his fist against the animal's great head and rubbed hard. "Crazy Nazi dog."

"Okay, okay," Bannon said to end the social bullshit. He didn't have time for this, but to hit Marty cold at this moment would have been a mistake. "Come on down, Marty. You look like shit."

Marty worked his way down the mechanic's stand. "I *feel* like shit, man. What the hell did you expect? I been drunk the whole damn night."

They stood together on the concrete. "You do *not* look fit to fly. You don't even look as if you understand me, and I got some hard things to go over with you. Big changes."

Marty made a rude gesture. "Jesus, you sound just like Karl. You two make a great team. You know what? All you need are aprons to make first-grade mothers."

Bannon ignored the dig. "Let's get some oxygen into what's left of your brain. It'll help."

Marty hiccuped and added a foolish grin. "Got no oxygen in my bird. Ran out *last* time I got all scrungged out."

"Damn, I need your brains clear." Bannon looked around and pointed. "There's Lansky's B-25." He grabbed Marty by the arm to steer him along to the bomber. "I know he's got a full oxygen supply. At least, he did yesterday. Whole new system, in fact."

Marty frowned. "Abe might not like us using his stuff."

397

They stood before the airplane restored to better-than-new condition with all modern systems aboard. "I don't know, Mitch—"

"Jesus, where'd you get your sudden religion." Bannon opened the crew access hatch in the belly and pulled down the ladder. "Get the hell in there. Lansky won't mind. He's got the hots for your sister, remember?"

They climbed up the ladder and worked their way into the cockpit area. "This thing *smells* new," Marty said. He was in awe of the closest he'd ever seen to mechanical and electronic perfection and didn't mind showing it.

"Get in the right seat," Bannon said, pointing to the copilot seat on the right side of the cockpit. Bannon squeezed into the left seat, snapped on a pocket flashlight until he found the battery switch he wanted. He snapped it on and turned on low lights. The glass nose ahead of and beneath them gleamed from interior lights and the reflections of the floods by the T-28. "Open the windows," Bannon instructed. They slid open the cockpit side windows and a fresh breeze stirred.

Headlights moved on different roads like a string of broken, glowing pearls as the pilots and crews began to assemble at Morgan Aviation for the Sunday morning dawn patrol. They parked along the boundary fence and gathered in the lounge for last-minute coffee, doughnuts, and sandwiches. *And* any last-moment updates on the launch. By now a quiet resignation had settled within those pilots and crews who had decided to stick it out. Out of more than three hundred men and women who flew and crewed the planes, less than a dozen had left. No one harbored them any ill feelings. Besides, the ten adults who departed took more than forty youngsters from other families with them.

Wendy Green and Doug Callahan maneuvered the incoming crews beneath a hand-lettered sign that read ALL PILOTS AND CREWS IN HERE FOR LATEST BRIEFING. Everyone received a xeroxed copy of a map plot and the latest information on altitudes and grids to fly.

"We've changed the routine," they were told as Wendy

placed another paper in their hands. "Read this *and sign it.*"

"What the hell is it?" was the question most asked.

"It's a release," Wendy told them, leaning on the counter and smiling, her bust straining against the ever-present too-tight flight suit. "If you kill yourself, this turns over all your credit cards to us. Just sign it, will you?"

Charley emerged from her office and crossed the room, greeting her crews as she went to the front desk. She stopped by the counter. "Wendy, I'll be with Marty and Bannon out by the T-28. Keep everything going just the way you are. You're doing great. As soon as they can, have the pilots start engines and taxi into takeoff position. The moment we have daylight, get them into the air. We don't have time to wait for large formations."

Wendy stared at Charley, a pencil in her teeth, papers in both hands, besieged from all sides. She nodded, waved the papers in acknowledgement, and spoke through the pencil clamped between her teeth. "Mmmmrffkay."

"Terrific," Charley said with a laugh, and went through the door to the flight line.

Abe Lansky held a comfortable pace on the long curve of the airport perimeter road south of the taxiway and main runway, holding position within the long line of cars heading for the crew parking lots. Behind him, through his rearview mirror, he saw the first streaks spearing horizontally through the eastern sky, the first lance of the dawn rushing swiftly upward from the ocean horizon. Lansky would fly his B-25 today, a J model magnificently restored to the eye seeking World War II features. But inside, the most modern electronics and power systems available. His airplane was old heavy iron on the outside and the most modern of flight worlds on the inside. He glanced through the rows of T hangars as he drove and felt himself tightening his muscles, a rigid sensation of caution even as he continued to drive. He'd had only a glimpse of his bomber at the far end of two rows of hangars. *He'd seen lights on inside the windows of the B-25 cockpit. And he was flying with no other crew members for the dawn patrol.* It was the kind of solo performance he enjoyed; one man fighting the demands for skill and muscle of the bomber. No one should be aboard his airplane; *no one.* And he could think of no reason other than a fire or dire emergency for anyone even to touch that heavy iron.

Lansky eased from the service road onto a gravel path and killed his lights. He eased slowly in the near-dark to the hangars where he had his airplane fully in view. He sat immobile, not a twitch or motion giving any indication of the suspicion and questions running through his mind. This simply did not fit within any pattern he could judge. His hand tightened involuntarily on the steering wheel. Charley! He watched her appear from around the side of the hangar, look around the T-28. She shook her head, turned to look at the B-25, and headed for the airplane. Lansky watched, puzzled and quietly angry, as she climbed up the ladder. He didn't mind Charley going into his airplane, *but there was someone else already in the machine.*

Lansky climbed from his car, closed the door quietly, and began walking toward his ship. He stopped for a moment and removed a dull black featherweight .38 revolver from a shoulder holster. He brought the hammer back and resumed his stealthy approach.

Marty Morgan hefted the oxygen mask, checked the flow control, and held it poised before his face. "Okay. Got it set for a hundred percent. Let's have it, Mitch." He pressed the mask against his face.

Bannon looked at him with a headshake. "It don't work unless I plug in the other end, kid." He pointed to the hose coupling dangling beneath the mask.

"Yeah, I guess so." Marty offered a shitfaced grin, handed the opposite end of the coupling to Bannon. "C'mon, man, I'm dying over here."

Bannon checked the flow source first. He turned the system on, dialed in a flow rate of one hundred percent oxygen, and brought the hose coupling up to the source outlet. He pressed it in several times and tried to twistlock it in place. It didn't fit. He shoved harder but couldn't make the connection.

"Damn thing won't fit." Bannon said, grunting with his effort to connect the hose and not bend metal by forcing it into place. He turned to Charley, who knelt in the space immediately behind the pilot seats. "Turn your flashlight over here," he said

Charley held the light steady on the oxygen controls and outlets. Bannon inspected them closely and turned to the others with a puzzled expression on his face. He studied the hose coupling again, holding it up to the light. "You know what? This is crazy ... this stuff is brand new, just like the oxy system ..." His voice took on a more serious tone. "But this coupling, and this mask, it won't work in *this* airplane, because," he pointed, "see here? This damn thing is for a jet fighter." He lowered the coupling slowly. "I don't mean for *any* jet. This is *military hardware*."

Marty reached out and studied the coupling with bleary eyes. "You're sure of all that?"

"Kid, I'm *sure*."

Charley edged up closer, their mutual looks saying more than they had yet verbalized. "I know every plane our pilots own," she said slowly. "Every one. The type, the registration numbers, the serial numbers, the—never mind, *I know*." She reached out to touch Bannon's arm. "Mitch, *Abe Lansky doesn't have any jet fighters*."

"None that we *know* about, you mean," Bannon corrected. "We still *don't* know. All we know is that this oxygen gear," he gestured with the mask and hose, "is new and it's for a jet fighter type aircraft."

Marty leaned closer. "What kind of bird would it fit?"

"Air Force stuff," Bannon said.

"Like, a, uh, T-33?"

"It fits a T-33," Bannon said, his expression blank and his voice tone flat.

Charley wasn't accustomed to this game. Her eyes went wide and she gasped as she glanced back and forth from Bannon to the oxygen equipment. "That transport!" she cried. "Didn't Hudoff say those were T-33's that forced it down?"

"Yes."

"Then, oh, my God . . ." Charley went speechless.

"Son of a bitch," Bannon said softly, repeating himself again and again, slowly ramming his fist into his other hand. "*Now* it fits. Jesus, it's all coming together . . ."

Charley and Marty studied him, wanting desperately to hear what he hadn't yet voiced. Bannon looked up at them. "It was all bits and pieces for so long and none of it really mattered at the time, at *any* time," he added to his own words. "But it sure as hell does *now*. Marty, do you remember that party last week, two Fridays ago, when you people had the big blowout at the Paradise Motel?"

Marty nodded. "Yes, but—"

"Okay, Charley and I busted it up with our pass. That's not the issue," Bannon pressed. "I remember who was supposed to go to that party. Weren't Lansky and Hamza with you that night?"

"They sure were," Marty said. "Abe was right in the middle of that donneybrook when we went through the window and—"

"Never mind *that*," Bannon broke in. "You all came back in a bus?"

"Two or three," Marty corrected.

"We saw everybody come off those buses," Bannon said carefully. "*Neither Lansky nor Hamza was on a bus.*"

"That's right!" Charley exclaimed. "We did a head count. We were worried about those people, I mean, maybe they wouldn't be able to fly. Lansky wasn't with them. And *now* I remember!" she said with self-surprise. "Later that same morning, he landed at Shiloh . . ." She looked about her. "*He landed in this airplane.*"

Bannon nodded, his face grim. "But he didn't *take off* from Shiloh, did he?"

"Why, no . . . no, he didn't," she recalled.

"Which means," Bannon rolled on, "that he was *gone* for a couple of hours between the last time Marty saw him at the motel party . . . and when he landed at Shiloh."

"Enough time," Marty said slowly, "to get to another field and to get a couple of T-33's . . ."

"Marty, remember that van we've seen here at the field a couple of times? The one from Charter Electronics?"

"Sure do. In fact, it was here when that crew was installing new avionics in *this* airplane."

"Right," Bannon confirmed. "Charter Electronics also has the contract for servicing Air Force radar facilities at Patrick."

Marty stared. "Are you making a connection—"

"And they have the NASA contract to maintain the radar facilities on the space center." Bannon took a deep breath. "I've had Hank Rawls digging up everything he could on Charter. He found something and we all missed it."

"What?" Charley pushed him on.

"Charley, you've used Charter Electronics, right?"

She nodded. "For years. Why?"

"Who owns Charter?"

"Why, the Norden Company. *You* knew that! Jack Norden from Melbourne and—"

"Jack Norden sold out three years ago." Bannon's smile was grim and unfriendly. "And I knew who bought them out, and I couldn't make the connection until just now."

"*What* connection?" Marty shouted.

"Sutterby bought them out."

"So?"

"Sutterby also bought out that mining quarry north of Ocala, where we found that gravel truck. Sutterby," Bannon said slowly and carefully, "isn't a person. It's a holding company. A front, a blind. But Sutterby is the name behind the gravel truck operation that had one of the nukes. Sutterby owns Charter, which services radar facilities up and down the coast. With the Air Force and the NASA contracts under their belt, they have full access to all radar facilities, which *also means* they have full access to the security areas on the spaceport!"

"Bannon, I'm not sure I—" Charley wasn't given time to voice her question.

"Hank Rawls found out something else," Bannon said. "Abe Lansky is on that security list. He's cleared right to the radar installations on any government facility along the coast."

"But—" Marty began, and also was cut off as Bannon ran on.

"Lansky isn't on any of the employee or management personnel lists."

"Bannon, you're losing me," Charley said with exasperation. "What has all this to do with—"

"Damnit, can't you see? Lansky is the power behind Sutterby. He's *got* to be, in order to get onto the security list, because even though he doesn't work *for* Charter he can get that outfit to clear him or anyone else he wants into the most sensitive areas of Kennedy."

"Then where," Charley asked carefully, "does this other person fit in? This Sadad Jabal, or whatever his name is."

Bannon laughed harshly. "I can't prove it, but I'll bet my bottom dollar there isn't any Sadad Jabal. Not the way we think about it. *Abe Lansky is Sadad Jabal*. That's why he killed Hamza when he was hurt, so he wouldn't talk when they gave him drugs for pain if they hauled him to a hospital!" He gestured with the oxygen gear. "And *this* stuff for *his* jet fighter, here in his own plane, sort of wraps it up. What a perfect way to move stuff around! Just put aircraft gear into your aircraft. Who would ever suspect anything? He'd never fly high enough with other people aboard to *need* oxygen, so they'd never use it anyway. Besides, I'm sure he's got masks and couplings that fit this airplane. He just got sloppy and left *this* mask around because he figured no one would ever touch it except himself or one of his men."

"Then he knows where the bomb's hidden!" Charley exclaimed, her face white.

"Where it's hidden?" Her brother snorted with disdain. "Damnit, Sis, he owns Charter! He's planted the bomb. He's got it wherever he wants it!"

Charley grasped Bannon's arm. "You've got to tell Hudoff! Now! *Right now!*"

Bannon tapped his watch crystal. "We're too late. It's just after seven."

"Too late for what!" Marty shouted.

"My God, I forgot," Charley told him. "They've started jamming all the radio frequencies by now! *But we've got to tell Hudoff!*" she repeated.

"Tell him *what?*" Bannon said bitterly. "That he's the real owner of Charter Electronics? That he controls the Sutterby outfit? I'd have to explain all this. You know how long *that* would take? And even if I could do all that, it still doesn't tell us where the bomb is!"

His neck muscles stood out in his maddening frustration. We'll have to make a run in a plane or a chopper straight into Kennedy and hope to hell they don't shoot us down first. A hell of a lot of good we'll do *that* way." He looked with anguish at Charley and her brother. "What I need now is Lansky so I can *drag* it out of him! I need to—"

A dazzling light stabbed into his eyes. He spun about to stare into a powerful flashlight. He couldn't see but there was no mistaking the voice. Smooth and controlled and confident. "You need Lansky, Bannon? You got Lansky."

Marty started from his seat. The flashlight moved to show the .38 pressed against the side of Charley's head. "Go ahead, you crippled fool," Lansky told him, his voice a hissing challenge. "You'll be wearing her brains."

Marty eased back carefully into the seat. "Okay, okay," he said quietly, showing both his hands.

Lansky's smile was barely visible behind the light. "Go ahead, Bannon. You need me. You *have* me. What were you going to drag out of me, Bannon?"

Bannon sat casually in the pilot seat, half-turned to face Lansky. He held up his hands, moved one hand slowly, in full view of Lansky, to his shirt pocket to withdraw a slim cigar. He clenched it between his teeth, making every move in full view so as not to precipitate an involuntary trigger squeeze. He held a Bic lighter in one hand, but hesitated in lighting the cigar. Lansky's eyes narrowed and there came that smile again.

"A nice touch, Bannon. The rules say a man's entitled to a last cigarette. But your cigar will do just as well."

"I'm glad to hear that," Bannon said, again with that casual air that so puzzled Lansky. "You see, it's not the way you think, Abe."

"What might that be?"

"Well, to tell you the truth, Abe, you pull that trigger and *you're dead*."

Lansky laughed. "Brave man, brave talk. You're soft, Bannon. You won't let her die like this." He gestured, a small but vital movement with the gun. "But it makes no difference. Her, you, this stupid cripple here and a hundred thousand more. None of it truly matters." The revolver moved back and forth with his growing animation. "Everything is set in motion. You can't stop it, even *I* can't stop it now."

"Bullshit, Abe. You can't do a thing from here." Bannon motioned to the oxygen outlets and then pointed, moving his hand slowly toward them. "Listen to it, Abe. You can hear the oxygen coming out of that port. It's at a hundred percent. It's been dumping into this cockpit for quite a while now. We're all *soaked* in oxygen. You know what oxygen soak does, Abe. You pull that trigger, asshole, and it's goodbye for *all* of us, including *you*."

Lansky smiled again, but this time Bannon saw the hesitation, the touch of concern. "You're a poor liar, Bannon."

Bannon held the lighter directly beneath the oxygen outlet, the hiss sounding like a small tornado in the tense cockpit. Bannon's thumb poised rock-steady on the flint. It was his turn to smile, cold and confident.

"Then you won't mind if I light up, right? This ship explodes if I flick my Bic."

He chuckled at Lansky. "You dumb son of a bitch, if you pull that trigger the same thing happens, so—what the hell, man."

His thumb snapped down, flame appeared, Lansky's eyes locked onto the horrifying spurt of fire and the next instant a lance of flame shot outward from the oxygen port. Bannon's left hand had already shot forward to Charley's hair and he jerked her down and toward him in a violent movement, in the same abrupt move throwing himself atop her. Lansky fired instinctively as fire tore over his hand. Within the cockpit the explosion was deafening. Oxygen washed about the muzzle of the gun, answering the call of sudden new flame. The slug Lansky fired tore along the side of Bannon's face, tearing skin and burning him but not breaking bone. He felt flames above them.

Lansky fired again as his hair flared with the spreading flame. The shot went wild and shattered glass but it gave Marty time to kick out with all the strength of his metal leg. The leg cracked hard against the side of Lansky's head, hurling him against a metal bulkhead and splitting open his skin. He screamed from the flames in his hair. The gun flew from his hand and in that all-critical instant Bannon whirled from atop Charley and with all his strength drove his fist into Lansky's face. He felt bones break under his knuckles. Lansky tumbled backwards and his feet sought footing but he was over the open hatch and he fell clumsily, scraping skin against the sides of the hatch as he fell to the concrete below. Marty was after him in a flash, dropping through the hatch with feet first to crash against Lansky's chest and stomach, pounding air from his lungs.

Bannon came behind him, beating out the flames with his hands, one knee against Lansky's throat. He yelled up to Charley. "Use the fire extinguisher! Turn off that damned oxygen!" He looked at her brother. "Marty, get the hell back up there and help her!"

He turned back to Lansky, gasping for air, struggling from the great pressure of Bannon's knee against his throat. Bannon lifted his knee. Lansky stirred, moaning with pain and shock. His hair and scalp were charred, his face bloody from Bannon's fist and Marty's steel-booted kick. "Don't die on me, you son of a bitch," Bannon growled. He rolled Lansky over onto his stomach and brought his wrists together behind the small of his back, squeezing hard to keep them pinned.

Charley and Marty came down the ladder, staring. "Fire's out," Charley gasped. "It's okay up there now, and I turned off the—" She stopped with the sight of the long angry streak across Bannon's face, blood seeping down his cheek. Her hand reached out, shaking. "Mitch, I didn't know. I—"

He shoved her hand aside. "Marty. Your work bench. Bring me a roll of tape, *quick!*" Marty ran to the workstand, snatched up the tape, and was back within seconds. Bannon twisted the tape around Lansky's wrists, locking them tightly in a grip impossible to break. He rose to a stoop and rolled Lansky over again, then glanced at Charley and Marty. "The gun. Find the gun and give it to me."

Charley saw it near a tire, snatched it up, and brought it to Bannon. He jammed the barrel violently into the soft flesh beneath Lansky's chin.

"The bomb, you bastard . . . *the bomb; where is it?*"

Lansky tried to laugh and produced only a bloody rattle. Red foam bubbled at the side of his mouth. "P-pull the trigger, you fool." He coughed violently, spattering bloody foam before him. Hurt, burned, in severe pain, he was still defiant, his eyes almost glowing coals of hatred. "Kill me! It doesn't matter . . . nothing matters, Bannon! The bomb is set . . ." He laughed with a skeletal rattle. "We will watch the sun explode . . . together . . . for the last time."

Bannon shoved the gun harder against Lansky's throat. Marty pulled at his arm, wild to stop him. "For Christ's sake, Mitch, he can't tell us anything if you kill him!"

Howling thunder drowned his next words. They looked up to see a loose swarm of fighter planes roaring overhead. Bannon nodded. His anger waned before his thinking. Once again he had become the well-oiled machine, the professional in the jungle who needed information, fast, to save many lives. He turned and handed the gun to Charley. She took it with a hand she struggled to keep from shaking.

"If he moves, shoot him in the balls."

Charley looked at him as if he were mad. "Damnit, woman, whatever you do, *don't kill him*. Do as I say— you shoot him right in the balls, understand!"

She nodded. Bannon leaned down, grabbed Lansky

by the hair. Charred ash came loose in his hand. He cursed and grasped an ear and yanked Lansky to a crooked half-upright position until their faces were only inches apart.

"Sure as hell you ain't no Israeli," he said, his voice angry and snakelike. "Zoboa is Egyptian, and if there's one thing I know about you ragheads you'd rather be dead than castrated. Like a woman. Allah would spit you out like poison. So I'm telling you. You so much as twitch and the lady makes you a soprano."

He threw Lansky back to the concrete and stood. "Marty—that workstand. Help me roll it over here. Leave the toolbox on the stand where it is." They ran to the T-28 and rolled the workstand back to the B-25. "Right in front of the left engine. That's it. Right there. Wait here for me."

He ran back to beneath the airplane, hauled Lansky to his feet, and shoved and pushed him up the workstand stairs. More airplanes thundered overhead and Bannon shouted to be heard. "Get me that roll of steel tape." He shoved Lansky against the big propeller hub of the left engine.

"There are two things a raghead can't take," Bannon said harshly. "One is to become a girl because he can't go to heaven when he dies, and the other is to become a mad dog." He grabbed Lansky beneath the throat and crotch and lifted him bodily into the air, shoving him back until he was seated precariously atop the propeller hub. "And we're going to do both to our Arab hero here. Give me a hand, Marty."

Bannon forced Lansky's head back against a wide propeller blade jutting straight up. "Okay. Hold him like that." He unwound a long strip of steel tape, peeling off the backing to expose the strong adhesive beneath. Steel tape would stay in place in a wind of four hundred miles an hour. It would do just fine for what he had in mind. He wrapped the tape around the back of the propeller blade, winding it across the front of Lansky's throat to pin him like a fly. Lansky tried to twist free and the tape cut deeply into his skin. "Go ahead," Bannon taunted him. "It won't kill you but it'll sure as hell tear up your throat." Lansky stared at him with wild eyes. Bannon ran more tape around Lansky's waist, securing him again to the propeller blade. His arms were now pressed painfully between his back and the steel blade.

They spread his legs apart to place them against the other two blades, securing him with several strips of steel tape. Lansky was now a giant bug taped to the propeller. Bannon leaned close to his prisoner. "The gun won't make you talk. I know that now. But I want you to hear me good. *We're not going to kill you, understand?* I want you alive and conscious to know what I'm going to do to you. And you can kiss your balls and your brains goodbye, sweetheart. You tell us where that bomb is or we'll ship you back to Cairo in a strait-jacket." He smiled coldly. "I promise you . . . you *won't* die." His hand reached out to slap Lansky gently against his cheek. "Stay awake. I don't want you losing interest."

He turned to Marty. "Okay. Let's get down and roll this stand back out of the way." On the ground he pointed a finger at Charley. "Don't waste time talking or answering questions. Bring your Jetranger here as fast as you can." White-faced, Charley nodded and took off at a run.

Bannon jabbed a finger at Marty. "Get back in the cockpit. Get in the left seat. Be sure the brakes are locked and then start the right engine. *The right engine.* Got it? I want plenty of generator power on the line. Move it, kid."

"Got it." Marty disappeared up the ladder and a few moments later Bannon saw him settling in the pilot seat. He moved switches and controls, looked about him, shouted, "Clear right!" and hit the fuel pump, booster, and starter. The big propeller spun about, jerked fit-fully, and broke into a roar of thunder. A cloud of smoke whipped back and disappeared in the propeller blast. Marty ran the engine high for a moment and then brought it back to idle. He leaned his head through the left window.

"Okay! Generator's on the line! What next?"

Bannon cupped his hands together for Marty to hear

him as he shouted. "Left engine throttle full back, mixture off, fuel flow off, mags off!"

Marty turned back inside the cockpit, reappeared seconds later. "All set!" he called.

"Okay, kid. Just hang in a moment." He turned to Lansky, trapped helplessly against the propeller. "You know what I'm going to do, raghead?"

Lansky twisted and squirmed, steel tape slicing skin. But he could barely move. "I'll kill you!" he screamed.

"I'm going to fuck up your brains, mister!" Bannon shouted. "You're going to be crazier than a goat left out in the sun for a week without water! And if that don't work, I'm going to twist your balls into gravy. Lansky, you're going to be a whore of Islam unless you sing like a fucking canary and tell us where you've got that bomb!"

Lansky spat bloody dribble at him. Bannon shrugged and wiped his face with his sleeve. "Marty! Give this fucker three times around with the starter!"

The huge prop began to turn with a great metallic groaning sound, an animal moan of death as it spun one, two and three times around. Lansky spun crazily, trapped to the steel blades. Bannon signalled with his hand for Marty to come off the starter. The propeller jerked to a stop with Lansky at a painful angle. Centrifugal force had rammed blood into his head and face. Pain twisted his features and crimson flowed from his mouth and nose.

"How about it?" Bannon yelled to him.

Lansky cursed and spat at him again. Bannon looked up at Marty. "He says he likes it!" he shouted. "Give him five this time!"

Lansky spun up to a blur before the blades jerked him to a stop. He was screaming in Arabic, bloody everywhere, running from his ears now. Blood dripped onto the concrete beneath him. Behind them they heard the whistling roar of the Jetranger's exhaust and the blatting of its rotor blades. Everything flashed to garish white as Charley settled to the ground, the landing light turning the scene into stark contrasts to highlight the horror.

Charley ran up, shocked and aghast with what she saw. "What in God's name are you doing?" she screamed.

"I'm just getting started," Bannon said grimly. He shoved the workstand closer to Lansky and the propeller and climbed up the steps. "Got anything to tell me?" he asked.

Lansky tried to spit. Blood sprayed from him, choking him as he fought to speak. He made sounds like a kitten being gutted.

"Guess not," Bannon said. He withdrew a knife from his pocket, snapped the blade open, and stepped forward. He heard Charley stifle a scream as the blade flashed in the landing light toward Lansky's stomach. Bannon didn't cut the man. He sliced open his belt and pants and cut away his undershorts. The clothing sagged against the steel tape. Lansky was naked from his waist to his knees. He quivered and writhed helplessly. Bannon reached down to the toolbox, came up with a roll of wire and a heavy wrench. He pulled free a length of wire and wrapped it about the wrench, then leaned forward, grabbed Lansky's testicles, and pulled them forward. He wrapped the wire about the scrotum just beneath the base of Lansky's penis. He didn't bother to ask Lansky any questions, but dropped the wrench. It pulled tightly against the wire and the wire snugged tighter into Lansky's scrotum. He gasped.

Bannon went down the steps and pulled the workstand back.

He saw Charley with both hands held to her face, tears on her cheeks. "Bannon, you—"

"Shut up," he snapped.

He looked up at Marty. "Again!" he shouted.

Marty hit the starter, the propeller whirled, the scene garish white from the helicopter landing light, the crimson spray growing as the huge propeller whirled around. A thin, terrible scream rose above all other sounds from the turning blades. Charley moved to the side and was suddenly splashed with blood and vomit, dripping along her face and clothes. Bannon gave the hand signal to Marty and the propeller stopped.

Lansky hung upside down, a multi-colored horror of

blood and vomit. Bannon signalled Marty to kill the right engine. The vibration and roar died away. Bannon went up to Lansky, blood pouring from his nose, mouth, and ears, and along his body where steel tape had sliced deeply into flesh. His crotch was a terrifying mess of torn skin, blood, and hanging shreds of flesh. The scrotum had been torn open by the pulling weight of the wrench at the end of the wire.

Bannon looked up at Lansky's face hanging upside down. "Did you know that the inside of your scrotum looks like a lot of white worms?" he taunted him. "I guess they look like your brains by now." Lansky retched bloody bile, gagging. Bannon yanked him by the hair to pull his face to the side. More charred hair and skin came away.

Behind him he heard Charley screaming, again and again. Lansky was more hamburger than human. His entire head and face had swollen horribly from centrifugal force, splotching the skin and bursting blood vessels everywhere from the vicious swing of the propeller.

His torn scrotum showed his testicular tubing as a mass of obscene white worms. Charley couldn't take any more.

"Stop it!" she screamed. *"Stop it! I hate you! I—"*

Bannon turned on her like a devil from hell. "If that mother fucker doesn't talk then a hundred thousand people are going to burn alive! Do you understand *that*, goddamnit! Thousands of children who are going to die a death a thousand times worse than *this!* And if you can't handle that, then get the hell out of here!"

He had the knife in his hand again, moving closer and closer to Lansky. The blade moved like a snake of steel before horrified, mad eyes. "First I cut out your right nut. Then the left. Then I shove them in your mouth and we sew your lips together. And *then* we send you home to your momma. She'll enjoy that."

Marty ran up to stand alongside Bannon. He shouted at Lansky. "Goddamnit, you stupid bastard, *he'll do it!* I know him, man, he'll do it *and he won't let you die!*"

Lansky's lips quivered. Bile and blood dribbled from his torn face. He gagged. "Pull the prop," Bannon ordered. He and Marty grabbed a blade and pulled with all their strength, moving Lansky to a position where his body was now horizontal instead of hanging upside down. He struggled to breathe.

"Jesus," Marty swore quietly, "he's trying to talk."

"F . . . Fa . . . Fa . . ."

Bannon wiped away the blood and vomit from his lips. "Talk!" he snarled.

"Uh . . . Fa . . . Fa . . . tal, uh, fa-tal . . ."

"He's crazy as a bedbug," Marty groaned. "What the hell is fa-tal?"

Bannon's eyes widened. He gripped Marty's shoulders with both hands, shaking him as he would a rag doll.

"It's Fat Al!" He turned, shouting. "Charley! *It's Fat Albert! The bomb is in the blimp right over the Cape!*"

Charley gaped. She straightened with tremendous effort with strength flowing back into her limbs. "I'll try the radio!" she called as she ran for the helicopter. Bannon ran after her, standing outside the cabin door as Charley's hands beat futilely against the radios. Tears burst from her eyes. A terrible squeal stabbed at her from the speakers by her ears.

"It's no use," Bannon told her. "They're jamming everything. We can't get through!"

"My God," Charley said, "then they've started the final countdown!"

"Move over," Bannon snapped. Charley slid to the next seat as Bannon pushed his way into the cabin and took the controls. Marty ran up to them.

"There's only one chance, kid. We're going straight in. We'll try to hover right over the shuttle. They can't launch with us up there and even if they can't hear us they sure as hell will *see* us!"

Marty banged a hand against his shoulder. "Go for it! I'll take off as fast as I can and try to run interference for you!" He turned and ran back toward his T-28.

Bannon yanked the door shut, went to full power, and took off like a crazy man. He lifted up above the hangars, held his altitude for several moments as a flock of airplanes lifted from the runway and passed directly overhead. Then they were free and with the engine screaming Bannon went to maximum speed, heading for the launch area where a fleet of airplanes and helicopters waited to destroy any intruders.

Marty clambered up the wing of the big T-28. He paused a moment as Magnum barked furiously at him from the back seat. He'd forgotten about the dog. Marty looked into the back cockpit. Hell, Magnum was secured in his harness. Marty climbed into the front seat, secured his harness, decided to leave both canopies open. His hands flew among the controls and the engine ground slowly, choked, backfired, and exploded into life. Marty didn't wait to read his engine gauges. No time; no time. He popped his brakes, slammed the throttle forward to jump his wheels over his chocks. Rocking madly, the T-28 shot ahead, skidded in a wild turn around the end of the row of T hangars. He had a glimpse of the Jetranger racing to the east, then concentrated on the taxiway before him. Two dozen planes waited in line for takeoff, the tower releasing them with green light signals. Marty cursed. He couldn't get around the other planes and he couldn't wait. He had to take off *now*.

He swerved sharply, racing through the parking ramp, dodging wings and cars and scattering people in all directions. He hit the grass between the runway and the taxiway and rammed the throttle forward to full power. He knew he *must* fly. Bannon might not make it. He could have engine trouble. Those crazy bastards could gun him down and if anything like that happened the only person who could stop the launch was himself in *this* airplane.

He hit the switch for takeoff flaps, stood on the brakes, kept the throttle full forward until the T-28 shook madly. He popped the brakes, stick forward briefly, then easing it back as the T-28 accelerated, pounding and slamming across the uneven ground. He cursed and begged his machine to fly, the wings to grasp at air. Before him a concrete culvert loomed and Marty held his airplane down until the last possible instant and horsed the stick back and the T-28 leaped into the air. He shoved the nose down for precious airspeed and brought up the gear and then his flaps. Behind him, sensing the stark tension, his dog barked wildly, unheard over the roar of engine and wind. He had the speed he needed now and Marty banged the stick over hard and tramped rudder and went hellbent for leather for the launch complex.

Before him the sky swarmed with airplanes. He stared at a thousand flashing strobes and beacons. Fighters and bombers circled the launch complex like maddened Indians racing about covered wagons. Beyond the warbirds he knew so well he saw the deadly helicopter gunships protecting the shuttle itself. And far beyond them, flashes of reflected sunlight betrayed the presence of supersonic fighters "at the ready."

Below them, but still much higher than his own altitude, higher than any of the Shiloh warbirds, he saw the glimpse of shiny metal as the still-hidden sun reflected from the metal containers suspended by cables beneath the swaying blimp.

In the radar antenna compartment was the single bomb with its hellish energy of four hundred thousand tons of high explosives. The end of the world for all those people beneath the warbirds and his friends.

He'd made it in time.

In time for what?

His own thought startled him. It was then he realized he didn't know how in God's name he was going to stop that launch now only unknown minutes away.

✦ 23 ✦

DEATH DAWN

They went after the Jetranger like sharks boring in
for the kill. Marty stared in helpless despair as the
Cobra gunships clawed around from both sides of the
helicopter with his sister and Bannon in the cabin.
They'd made it, he realized. Two Cobras hovered to one
side of the Jetranger, their Gatling guns locked onto the
Jetranger. A single burst would tear Charley and Bannon
to bloody pulp and shred their helicopter to splintered
wreckage. But they wouldn't do that so long as Bannon
kept the Jetranger in a hover above the shuttle. He was
having a tough time doing that. A strong wind blew
from the west and Bannon needed some forward airspeed, pointing into the west, to hold his position. Much
worse was the wild eddying and turbulence of the military helicopters, hurling violent and choppy air from
their rotors as they held position with or moved about
the Jetranger. A huge Jolly Green Giant moved in, its
cabin doors slid open, men holding automatic weapons
at the ready against the Jetranger.

And no one could talk! Not with every radio frequency a shriek of ear-stabbing jamming. Marty knew
they could see the helicopters and aircraft from the
launch control center alongside the VAB, but that was
miles away and the launch team couldn't even talk to

their own security forces in the air. In the chaotic scene they would draw one conclusion only, that the Jetranger was part of the terrorist move to attack the shuttle.

Marty's T-28 under full power felt to him as if it were flying through mud. Time dragged to a horribly slow crawl. He pounded his fist in frustration against the side of his cockpit. He couldn't do anything to help, he was still too far out, and then he saw the Jolly Green make its move, the huge helicopter pulling up to the side of the Jetranger and lifting its nose as it went to full power. Enormous jet engines turned that massive rotor and a hurricane smashed outward from the rotor blades, each as big as an airplane wing. Not even the Jetranger could hover in that violence—

Damn; the blimp! He looked at it again, sick with his helplessness. But everything should be under control! *Shouldn't it?* he demanded of himself. *After all, they're jamming all the radio frequencies, aren't they? There's no way they can transmit a signal to detonate that thing, right?*

With a sickening realization the word *Wrong!* leaped into his mind and he understood what Lansky had set up so brilliantly days before this moment.

Bannon fought wildly to retain control of the Jetranger as the fierce winds smashed with avalanche-like force against the side of the helicopter. The Jolly Green Giant hung to their side, hurling massive blasts of turbulent air at them. The Jetranger swung wildly and heeled over to one side, physically hurled away from the shuttle toward the beach line. Bannon worked his controls to storm back into position over the shuttle, but he'd lost that brief and precious advantage. A Cobra came in like a barracuda in a three-quarter frontal move. Brilliant orange light sparkled from beneath the Cobra and a tornado of bullets smashed through the aft cabin. Charley screamed from reflex, throwing up her arm to shield her eyes from the plexiglas exploding about them.

"Can't they see we're trying to help!" she cried, her voice agonized.

Bannon didn't look at her; he had no time even for a

glance. "They can't know that!" he shouted above the maelstrom of noise. "To them we're the enemy and—" His voice stopped as tracers flashed before their nose. It didn't matter. They'd taken a hit somewhere in the engine compartment. Red warning lights flashed on the panel, he saw the oil pressure gauge falling and smelled smoke. The Jetranger shuddered violently and he knew he was on the edge of losing control. He had a glimpse of the big chopper nearby, two men standing in the closest doorway, guns aimed at them, one man pointing down in an unmistakable signal. Either they landed *now* or they'd be blown from the sky.

"We've had it, babe!" Bannon shouted to Charley. The Jetranger lurched, almost out of control, and Bannon dropped the nose to gain speed and keep what limited control he had left. "The next burst will kill us or hit the tanks and—damn!" He had no time to talk as the ground rushed up and he fought to save their lives.

Charley stared straight ahead, numb, uncaring about what happened to them now. "We're too late, we're too late . . ." Then, in a desperate attempt to do something, *anything*, to salvage the moment, she called out to him. "The flare gun! We could fire off red flares! They can't mistake *that!*"

He had time to yell, "Try it!" and then he was wrestling the helicopter to the ground. They hit hard, smoke wreathing the cockpit. Bannon killed the switches, kicked open the door. "Bail out of this thing, Charley! It's liable to blow!"

She didn't move and he stood outside, smoke choking him, trying to see. Out of nowhere powerful arms grabbed his neck, his arms and legs, holding him helplessly. He had a glimpse of Charley being dragged from the other side of the helicopter by security guards. *We almost made it*, he told himself, *we*— Then he knew they hadn't. The flare gun container lay on the seat where Charley had sat. It was empty. It had been empty the whole time.

Marty hung the T-28 on its wing, arcing up and over in a tight turn, looking down from his open cockpit. He had a glimpse of the Jetranger on the ground, smoke pouring from the engine compartment, security teams and troops rushing the machine. He started again to yell, knew his words weren't even ghostly whispers in the streaming wind. *Forget them*, he told himself. *They're on the ground, safe. But they've got only minutes to live* . . .

His own thoughts mocked him. So close, so close! And so helpless. And it was all so clear now. All the brilliant thinking, all the massive effort to search for that last bomb, *it had been a huge joke!* Even that enormous effort to jam every radio frequency there had turned out to be a final gasp of ironic humor.

The Zoboa terrorists had never planned to use radio. *They weren't going to use it now! It was all so clever and it was all so obvious!* He couldn't help shouting at the wind, the world, at God and anything and everything as his frustration roared through his head.

"Don't you understand!" he screamed with his helpless rage. "They're not using radio! *They're not using radio!"*

The whole thing was maddening. The bloated blimp swayed in that strong westerly wind, much stronger at its altitude than at ground level, tugged like a living thing at its tether, the mass killer in its belly unknown to the victims-to-be on the ground. But they needn't be! They needed only to release the damned cable and, freed of its weight of four thousand feet or more of cable, the blimp would leap skyward, rammed by the wind to the east, soaring up and away like a nightmare to some distant land. And there was no way he could tell anyone, there was no way he could talk to anyone.

He circled tightly, the g-forces ramming him down in his seat. He didn't feel the pressure, he knew only the blimp and the bomb and that long cable and that time was rushing away into a future that would never be. He knew the terrorists weren't using radio, but he still didn't understand how Lansky's killers could set off the bomb at the precise moment they wanted, when there was no signal transmitted to the bomb. If everything he'd been told by Bannon and the others was true, then the terrorists had to detonate the bomb six to ten seconds after the shuttle climbed away from its launch pad, and that meant a signal transmitted on *their* timing. And with the radios jammed, without the terrorists even using radio . . .

"You bastards! You crazy bastards!" he shouted, but his only audience was the howling wind and the big dog strapped in behind him, who could not know or understand what he was shouting, or even hear his maddened cries. Marty rolled out of the turn, staring at the blimp again, and he felt his blood run cold. All this time they'd all suffered from brainlock. . . . *They'd been so stupid!* There it was, right before his eyes. How they would explode the bomb exactly on their own schedule.

He rammed the throttle full forward, banged the prop control to maximum rpm for full power, going for all the speed he could squeeze from his plane. Fourteen hundred horsepower howled and accelerated the heavy fighter-bomber. Again he stared at the blimp.

Not the blimp. The cable! The cable that ran from the ground to the blimp. The cable that carried power lines as well. The cable that sent radio signals through wires. The cable that tethered Fat Albert . . . its electronics equipment serviced by Charter, by the outfit that Abe Lansky, or whatever the hell his name was, had the contract to service. *The radar equipment to which they had full security access.*

All this time, from the very first day the jet fighters had forced down that Air Force transport, *the bomb had been safely suspended from the blimp, its radio homer disconnected.* Only Lansky and his electronics crews touched the radar equipment. Only they could possibly know *the bomb had been suspended the whole time directly over the space center!*

All this time they had been one step ahead of everybody searching for the bomb, trying to figure out where it was, how it would be delivered. It had *always* been delivered . . . and they knew *there was only one way* to be certain the bomb would explode when *Antares* was six seconds in the air from its launch pad.

At that moment a raging star would leap into blinding existence and the light of a billion suns would flash

421

and the awesome mountain that was the shock wave would tear at the earth and—

Marty felt sick. He bit his lip in a desperate attempt to keep his self-control. He swung into another turn, still climbing under full power, and looked down toward the launch pad. He could barely make out the brilliant white plume of supercold gases venting from the sides of *Antares*. As he watched, he blinked. When he looked again the white plumes were gone.

Holy Jesus . . . it's only three minutes to liftoff.

He knew what he must do. He turned to the southeast and the T-28 raced over the launch pad. Other planes were still flying about far beneath him, but the pilots had been warned and none flew within five hundred feet of the shuttle itself.

He saw the jet fighters coming with tremendous speed at him. One jet pulled up in a howling climb before him, a clear signal for Marty to break away. The other slid into tight formation, dive brake down to stay tight with the T-28, the pilot signalling by hand for Marty to turn to the west. Marty felt the fine madness returning to him, dispelling the fear, banishing all uncertainty. He felt his lips open in a smile, felt the wind against his teeth. The sense of life in him was strong and wonderful. Fat Albert was closer, larger now in his vision, that enormous cable glistening in the new sun. His whole world was that cable. Glowing coals flashed before his eyes, arcing away through space. *Tracers!* The bastards were firing tracers in a final warning and then they'd aim to kill.

Mad Marty laughed aloud, a crazy grin on his face. He felt terrific. He glanced in his mirror that showed him the rear cockpit.

Magnum! He'd almost forgotten about his beloved animal . . .

"Old friend," he called aloud, knowing that only he would hear his words, but that somehow the great mountain dog would *know*, "its been great, pup . . ."

He rolled the T-28 smoothly on its back and for the moment he held inverted flight. In the mirror he saw the great Swiss dog scrambling to remain in the cockpit as his body fell heavily against the harness. Marty slammed the stick forward, still inverted, and the violent pitching movement snapped the safety clips and hurled the animal away from the plane, almost straight down. Then he rolled level, pounding the throttle for speed as the jet fighters came around for the kill.

He was close now, and for extra speed he put the nose down and he had better than four hundred miles an hour when a burst of gunfire smashed into his left wing. The T-28 shuddered violently and flame whipped back from the torn metal. But he still had control and he kept flying, and he was laughing when a jet fighter raced past him off the burning wing, and Mad Marty held his hand high, middle finger extended.

Bannon and Charley stood by the side of the smoking Jetranger under a ring of automatic weapons leveled at them. They ignored the angry men and their guns. Bannon held Charley as they looked into the sky. She couldn't hold back her tears as they watched the T-28 roll onto its back and the dark form fall away from the plane.

"No . . . oh, God . . . Marty, NO!"

Someone shouted. "There's a chute!"

"It isn't Marty!" Bannon yelled. "It's . . . it's the dog! It's Magnum!"

They saw the jet fighters race in, heard the staccato sound of firing cannon and then the flash of fire from the left wing. Bannon gripped Charley.

"He's still flying it . . ." His voice caught in his throat. He knew what was happening but he couldn't say it, couldn't bring the words forth.

The flames gushed back now, chewing along the wing. "Bail out!" Charley screamed. "*For God's sake, Marty, BAIL OUT!*"

Bannon didn't know if he'd spoken aloud, but the words pounded through his head. *He doesn't have a chute . . .*

Marty couldn't fight the flames. He was almost to the cable when the left wing tore away from the T-28. An invisible hand smashed at the airplane, the terrible forces of his tremendous speed, snapping his neck. The T-28 whirled violently into the cable, the whirling propeller blades slicing like enormous flailing knives into the tether. For a long moment everything blotted from sight as the fuel tanks of the T-28 exploded in an arcing fireball. The wreckage tore onward, falling, shedding metal and flames and debris, a grisly meteor display starting back to earth.

But the blimp was shooting skyward. Relieved suddenly of the ponderous weight and drag of thousands of pounds of cabling, it lunged upward with tremendous speed, pushed eastward as it soared by the winds from the west, over the ocean.

"They're going to launch!" a voice called out from the group about them. Charley and Bannon turned to look toward *Antares*. Cables were dropping away from the orbiter and the boosters. Long swingarms began to pivot.

"The bomb! Where the hell's the bomb?" Bannon shouted to no one and to the whole world.

The launch tracking team stood frozen before the radar display console. A flashing light indicated the blimp. Digital readouts flashed. "Same damn thing happened when we lost *Challenger*," the team leader said. "Do we look like a problem?"

The console operator shook his head. "No, sir. It's going up fast and those winds at altitude are really strong."

"Call out altitude and range."

"Six thousand feet and climbing fast. It's just over four miles now and still accelerating."

The team leader keyed his mike. "Control, radar here. No danger to the vehicle from the blimp. You're clear." He paused only a moment to confirm the increasing distance vertically and horizontally of the blimp. "Range Safety, you are go for launch," he added.

Bannon and Charley watched the blimp, only a dot now, rushing upward beneath a layer of thick clouds well out over the ocean. Behind them they heard a deep rumble and then a strange roar, like that of a waterfall. They turned again to look at the launch pad. It *was* a waterfall, the powerful water deluge system hurling thousands of gallons of cooling water into the flame buckets before the shuttle engines would ignite.

Bannon turned and looked into the sky just in time to see the blimp swallowed up by clouds.

He had no way of knowing that words spoken at that moment would have brought enormous relief to him. It was the console operator in radar tracking, announcing calmly to the men about him: "Altitude seven thousand four hundred feet. Slant range now six miles. Separating very fast now."

He turned again to look with Charley at *Antares*. The last swingarms were out of the way, the last cables dangling, and they saw the brilliant flame before the sound reached them as the orbiter engines fired. *Antares* lunged forward, stopped, and slammed back as the engines built to full power, and before he knew it was happening the solid boosters ignited. Instinctively they reeled back from eye-stabbing flame and world-ripping thunder. *Antares* went up and up, cleared the launch tower, roaring like a billion dragons. Bannon felt the heat from the boosters washing over them and the shock wave from the rockets hammered their bodies.

Bannon shoved Charley to the ground. "Cover your eyes!" he yelled over the titanic roar battering them. All about them the guards and troops did the same or knelt with their backs to the climbing shuttle. From this close up the booster flame was far too bright for the eyes to endure. Bannon brought his arm up to shield his eyes, looking away and down from the shuttle.

The atomic bomb exploded.

A thousand suns obliterated the new dawn, turned the fiery rockets to pale insignificance, washed over the world, stunned and terrified the hundreds of thousands of onlookers along the beaches and in the towns and on the roads beyond the spaceport. Hearts stopped as they believed they were witnessing once again the terrible moment of *Challenger* exploding. Screams and heartbreaking cries sounded through the entire county.

Yet they had received but a small fraction of the savage light from the exploding bomb. It was more than three miles high, several miles out to sea, and within a bank of thick rain clouds when the sky was torn by naked nuclear fire at the point of detonation.

Yet there could be no mistaking the burning line that arced down from the heavens. Bannon had rolled over, lifted on one elbow, Charley's stunned eyes watching with him. "It's the shock wave," Bannon said aloud.

"The shuttle—" Charley said and got no further. *Antares* punched through the shock wave. It was designed to take such forces when it slammed back into the atmosphere from orbit at eighteen thousand miles an hour. The shock wave when it struck *Antares* was perfectly positioned; the shuttle went through the burning arc like a spear through a diaphragm.

The boom struck them, thunder rolling from everywhere on earth. It banged and crashed and roared through homes and buildings along the coast and some windows cracked, but the thunder continued, and only then did the awed onlookers with their eyes frozen to the heavens realize they were hearing the great spasms of sound of the shuttle rockets mixing with the final gasp of the bomb, a mushroom born in the heavens and reaching upward with maniacal speed, but invisible beyond the clouds.

Thunder lessened and the sound of loudspeakers in the launch area came audibly to them now. No audience was ever more imprisoned and enraptured by what they heard from mission control.

"*. . . we have Antares coming up on solid booster separation in five seconds. That's three, two, one, sep, and ah, the pilot reports a beautiful breakaway of the solids and a flight that's right on the money. All systems are go. . . .*"

A new sound came to them. A sound heard across the space center and down the beaches and along the roads and outside the homes.

The sound of a million people crying and cheering.

✝ 24 ✝

EPILOGUE

They gathered in the upstairs pilot lounge at Morgan Aviation, the nightmare behind them, but its effects burned into their souls. They kept their distance from Charley as she stood before the wide picture window overlooking the Shiloh flight line and the runways beyond. Beyond her they saw warbirds letting down in their patterns, others taxiing, the sound of the great engines somehow softer to them now, a gentler song of power. The wall speakers provided a muted running conversation between the pilots still airborne and the tower. It was incredibly calm, the powerful machines great winged steeds obeying their masters.

Mitch Bannon and Bernie Hudoff stood by themselves by a far wall. Hudoff held his flask upside down, shaking it. He made a sour face at the empty flask and replaced it within his jacket. He sighed and looked at Bannon.

"Well, what the hell do we say? We're all here, alive, safe, able to count on our tomorrows, because of that kid . . ."

"It was too close," Bannon said, unsmiling.

"It's always too close, Ace. Always." Hudoff lit a cigar. "By the way, in case you're interested, Lansky—he *is* Sadad Jabal, I should add—is still alive."

427

"I'm sorry to hear that."

"Don't be. Dead, he's just another corpse. Alive, well, he's sprouted feathers. In fact, he's turned into a canary. Through all his bandages, of course. I don't *want* to know just what you did to him, Ace, but he's singing his heart out. We've already picked up twenty people and we're going to nail some more. It's a hell of an operation they were running."

Bannon nodded and showed interest. "How come you're missing all the fun?"

"I promised Galenko he could have his turn. He and Joe Horvath are as thick as thieves at this moment. Galenko had some leads that are helping."

Bannon smiled thinly with the thought. Abruptly he changed the subject. "Your people figured out how the bomb worked?"

"Well, once we knew what was going on, sure; then it was simple. The countdown went through the cable to the blimp where Lansky—damnit; I mean Jabal—and his people hid the bomb. They'd set it for liftoff plus ten seconds. And if *that* didn't work, they had a timer rigged to fire the thing about a minute and a half later."

"They'd miss the shuttle but they might get everyone on the ground."

"You got it."

"Bernie, you're not going to like this question."

Hudoff lifted thick brows and waited.

"How the hell could you risk the lives of four thousand of the world's top leaders the way you did today? I saw those stands. They were packed. That was the dumbest—"

"We didn't risk anyone in those bleachers."

"You what?"

"Hey, beach bum, we knew what was at stake. As fast as those VIP's arrived we shoved them into buses and drove them off to mouseland."

"You're telling me that—"

Hudoff couldn't resist the huge smile as he broke in. "We took them all to Disneyworld and Epcot. What's more normal than an international convention in those places?"

"Who the hell would be stupid enough to fill those bleachers?"

"Dummies, of course."

"I'll *say*."

Hudoff shook his head. "No, you still don't get it. I mean *real* dummies. Manikins. Talk about a job and a half! You got any idea what it's like to collect manikins from just about every damned department and clothing store in this whole state? And get them onto those bleachers? We had a thousand volunteers who worked all night long. But they did it. Four thousand dummies, Bannon." Hudoff had a sly smile on his face. "And not one of them complained.

"You were too busy last night and this morning," he went on, "to realize just how many accidents there were on the roads last night leading this way. *Bad* accidents. Cars banged up, bunch of them on their sides, burning. Lot of big trucks jackknifed and went over on their sides, too. It was a miracle that nobody got hurt. But it sure blocked all those cars from getting any closer to the center."

"That's enough, boss," Bannon said with a weary sigh. "I don't think I want to know any more. Not right now, anyway." He looked about the room at the pilots, at *his* friends. His only real family. "We got a lot of pieces to put back together here." He glanced at Charley. She'd been joined by Sherri Taylor and they were talking quietly. "You going back to work now, Bernie?"

"Shit, Ace, the details never end. I'll be filling out forms for a month." He gestured toward Charley. "That is a very great lady you have there, Bannon." He hesitated. "Anything we can do? She going to be okay?"

"Bernie, I think she's tougher than you or me."

"I can't argue that," Hudoff said. He slapped Bannon's shoulder gently. "Tell these people something for me. Tell them we owe them. We *all* owe them. So long, Ace."

He watched Hudoff leave, and then Bannon went to join Charley. He put his arm about her shoulder and drew her close. They stood quietly, not talking. Through the window they saw Karl von Strasser walking heavily toward the building. The big dog padded silently by his side. The German pilot disappeared from view. Moments later he came through the door. Magnum moved quickly to Charley and laid down by her feet. Von Strasser nodded to Bannon and then stood before Charley.

"I would very much like to be the one who brings Marty home," he said heavily. "They have recovered his body. And he was . . . my very, very good friend."

Charley tried to speak but the words choked in her throat. She touched von Strasser's arm and nodded. He moved closer, hugged her briefly, and left.

"I'll . . . I'll tell the pilots they can go on home," Bannon said after a while. He looked out the window at the warbirds. "We won't be needing them any more today."

A shudder went through Charley, an awakening that seemed to bring strength to her. She wiped away her tears. "There'll be no more of those," she said. She looked out at a gleaming Mustang fighter turning on the ramp, a great Merlin singing with subdued power. She looked at Bannon, and he knew his girl was home again.

"The hell we won't need them. *We have a show to fly.*" She shoved a finger against his chest. "Two o'clock, *Mister* Bannon. And I expect everybody to be on time, and that includes *you*."

She walked past him, the dog following immediately across the room and through the door to the stairway. Sherri Taylor moved closer to Bannon and they looked through the window as she walked along the flight line.

The Mustang fighter was still now, the great propeller unmoving. A young pilot stood up in the cockpit, removing his crash helmet with both hands. He saw Charley and a broad smile appeared as he waved.

"Hey! Hi, Charley!"

She looked up at the young man, so filled with life. She smiled, a dazzling smile, and waved her hand high.

Charley and her dog went down the line to be with the great machines of old.

That's where Mad Marty lived now.

Sign up today. Complete the coupon below and get ready for the biggest and brightest in science fiction and fantasy.

Yes, I wish to take advantage of the Baen Book Club Advance Plan. I understand that I will receive new science fiction and fantasy titles published in paperback by Baen Books every two months (6 to 8 new books). I will be charged only one-half the cover price for books shipped, with no additional postage or handling charges. Charges will be billed to my credit card account. I may opt to receive hardcover as well as paperback releases by checking the box below. I may cancel at any time.

If you wish to receive hardcover releases as well as paperback books, please check here: [ ]

Name   (Please Print)

Address

City

State   Zip Code

Signature

VISA/MasterCard Number   Expiration Date

MAIL TO:

Baen Book Club
260 Fifth Avenue, Suite 3-S
New York, NY 10001

Please allow three to six weeks for your first order.

WE PARTICULARLY
RECOMMEND . . .

ALDISS, BRIAN W.
Starswarm

Man has spread throughout the galaxy, but the time-less struggle for conquest continues. The first complete U.S. edition of this classic, written by an acknowledged master of the field.　　**55999-0 $2.95**

ANDERSON, POUL
Fire Time

Once every thousand years the Deathstar orbits close enough to burn the surface of the planet Ishtar. This is known as the Fire Time, and it is then that the barbarians flee the scorched lands, bringing havoc to the civilized South.　　**55900-1 $2.95**

The Game of Empire

A *new* novel in Anderson's Polesotechnic League/Terran Empire series! Diana Crowfeather, daughter of Dominic Flandry, proves she is well capable of following in his adventurous footsteps.　　**55959-1 $3.50**

BAEN, JIM & POURNELLE, JERRY (Editors)

Far Frontiers — Volume V

Aerospace expert G. Harry Stine writing on government regulations regarding private space launches; Charles Sheffield on beanstalks and other space transportation devices; a new "Retief" novella by Keith Laumer; and other fiction by David Drake, John Dalmas, Edward A. Byers, more.　　**65572-8 $2.95**

CAIDIN, MARTIN
Killer Station

Earth's first space station *Pleiades* is a scientific boon—until one brief moment of sabotage changes it into a terrible Sword of Damocles. The station is de-orbiting, and falling relentlessly to Earth, where it will strike New York City with the force of a hydrogen bomb. The author of *Cyborg* and *Marooned*, Caidin tells a story that is right out of tomorrow's headlines, with the hard reality and human drama that are his trademarks.   **55996-6 $3.50**

The Messiah Stone

What "Raiders of the Lost Ark" should have been! Doug Stavers is an old pro at the mercenary game. Retired now, he is surprised to find representatives of a powerful syndicate coming after him with death in their hands. He deals it right back, fast and easy, and then discovers that it was all a test to see if he is tough enough to go after the Messiah Stone—the most valuable object in existence. The last man to own it was Hitler. The next will rule the world . . .
                                                65562-0 $3.95

CHALKER, JACK
The Identity Matrix

While backpacking in Alaska, a 35-year-old college professor finds himself transferred into the body of a 13-year-old Indian girl. From there, he undergoes change after change, eventually learning that this is all a part of a battle for Earth by two highly advanced alien races. And that's just the beginning of this mind-bending novel by the author of the world-famous *Well of Souls* series.   **65547-7 $2.95**

DICKSON, GORDON R.

Hour of the Horde

The Silver Horde threatens—and the galaxy's only hope is its elite army, composed of one warrior from each planet. Earth's warrior turns out to possess skills and courage that he never suspected . . .

55905-2 $2.95

Wolfling

The first human expedition to Centauri III discovers that humanity is about to become just another race ruled by the alien "High Born". But super-genius James Keil has a few things to teach the aliens about this new breed of "Wolfling." **55962-1 $2.95**

DRAKE, DAVID

At Any Price

Hammer's Slammers are back—and Baen Books has them! Now the 23rd-century armored division faces its deadliest enemies ever: aliens who *teleport* into combat. **55978-8 $3.50**

Ranks of Bronze

Disguised alien traders bought captured Roman soldiers on the slave market because they needed troops who could win battles without high-tech weaponry. The legionaires provided victories, smashing barbarian armies with the swords, javelins, and discipline that had won a world. But the worlds on which they now fought were strange ones, and the spoils of victory did not include freedom. If the legionaires went home, it would be through the use of the beam weapons and force screens of their ruthless alien owners. It's been 2000 years—and now they want to go home.

65568-X $3.50

FORWARD, ROBERT L.
The Flight of the Dragonfly

Set against the rich background of the double planet Rocheworld, this is the story of Mankind's first contact with alien beings, and the friendship the aliens offer.   55937-0 $3.50

KOTANI, ERIC, & JOHN MADDOX ROBERTS
Act of God

In 1889 a mysterious explosion in Siberia destroyed all life for a hundred miles in every direction. A century later the Soviets figure out what had happened —and how to duplicate the deadly effect. Their target: the United States.   55979-6 $2.95

LAUMER, KEITH
Dinosaur Beach

"Keith Laumer is one of science fiction's most adept creators of time travel stories ... A war against robots, trick double identities, and suspenseful action makes this story a first-rate thriller."—*Savannah News-Press*. "Proves again that Laumer is a master."—*Seattle Times*. By the author of the popular "Retief" series.
65581-7 $2.95

The Return of Retief

Laumer's two-fisted intergalactic diplomat is back— and better than ever. In this latest of the Retief series, the CDT diplomat must face not only a deadly alien threat, but also the greatest menace of all—the foolish machinations of his human comrades. More Retief coming soon from Baen!   55902-8 $2.95

Rogue Bolo

A new chronicle from the annals of the Dinochrome Brigade. Learn what happens when sentient fighting machines, capable of destroying continents, decide to follow their programming to the letter, and do what's "best" for their human masters.   **65545-0 $2.95**

BEYOND *THIEVES' WORLD*

MORRIS, JANET
Beyond Sanctuary

This three-novel series stars Tempus, the most popular character in all the "Thieves' World" fantasy universe. Warrior-servant of the god of storm and war, he is a hero cursed ... for anyone he loves must loathe him, and anyone who loves him soon dies of it. In this opening adventure, Tempus leads his Sacred Band of mercenaries north to war against the evil Mygdonian Alliance. *Hardcover*.

55957-5 $15.95

Beyond the Veil

Book II in the first full-length novel series ever written about "Thieves' World," the meanest, toughest fantasy universe ever created. The war against the Mygdonians continues—and not even the immortal Tempus can guarantee victory against Cime the Mage Killer, Askelon, Lord of Dreams, and the Nisibisi witch Roxane. *Hardcover*.   **55984-2 $15.95**

Beyond Wizardwall

The gripping conclusion to the trilogy. Tempus's best friend Niko resigns from the Stepsons and flees for his life. Roxane, the witch who is Tempus's sworn enemy, and Askelon, Lord of Dreams, are both after Niko's soul. Niko has been offered one chance for safety ... but it's a suicide mission, and only Tempus can save Niko now. *Hardcover*.

65544-2 $15.95

MORRIS, JANET & CHRIS
The 40-Minute War

Washington, D.C. is vaporized by a nuclear surface blast, perpetrated by Islamic Jihad terrorists, and the President initiates a nuclear exchange with Russia. In the aftermath, American foreign service agent Marc Beck finds himself flying anticancer serum from Israel to the Houston White House, a secret mission that is filled with treachery and terror. This is just the beginning of a suspense-filled tale of desperation and heroism—a tale that is at once stunning and chilling in its realism.   **55986-9 $3.50**

MEDUSA

From the Sea of Japan a single missile rises, and the future of America's entire space-based defense program hangs in the balance. . . . A hotline communique from Moscow insists that the Russians are doing everything they can to abort the "test" flight. If the U.S. chooses to intercept and destroy the missile, the attempt must not end in failure . . . its collision course is with America's manned space lab. Only one U.S. anti-satellite weapon can foil what *might* be the opening gambit of a Soviet first strike—and only Amy Brecker and her "hot stick" pilot have enough of the Right Stuff to use MEDUSA.   **65573-6 $3.50**

HEROES IN HELL®—THE GREATEST
BRAIDED MEGANOVEL OF ALL TIME!
MORRIS, JANET, & GREGORY BENFORD, C.J. CHERRYH, DAVID DRAKE
Heroes in Hell®

Volume I in the greatest shared universe of All Times! The greatest heroes of history meet the greatest names of science fiction—and each other!—in the most original milieu since a Connecticut Yankee visited King Arthur's Court. Alexander of Macedon, Caesar and Cleopatra, Che Guevara, Yuri Andropov, and the Devil Himself face off . . . and only the collaborators of HEROES IN HELL know where it will end.

65555-8 $3.50

CHERRYH, C.J. AND MORRIS, JANET
The Gates of Hell

The first full-length spinoff novel set in the Heroes in Hell® shared universe! Alexander the Great teams up with Julius Caesar and Achilles to refight the Trojan War using 20th-century armaments. Machiavelli is their intelligence officer and Cleopatra is in charge of R&R ... co-created by two of the finest, most imaginative talents writing today. *Hardcover*.

65561-2 $14.95

MORRIS, JANET & MARTIN CAIDIN, C.J. CHERRYH, DAVID DRAKE, ROBERT SILVERBERG
Rebels in Hell

Robert Silverberg's Gilgamesh the King joins Alexander the Great, Julius Caesar, Attila the Hun, and the Devil himself in the newest installment of the "Heroes in Hell" meganovel. Other demonic contributors include Martin Caidin, C.J. Cherryh, David Drake, and Janet Morris. **65577-9 $3.50**

SABERHAGEN, FRED
The Frankenstein Papers

At last—the truth about the sinister Dr. Frankenstein and his monster with a heart of gold, based on a history written by the monster himself! Find out what really happened when the mad Doctor brought his creation to life, and why the monster has no scars. "In the tour-de-force ending, rationality triumphs by means of a neat science-fiction twist."—*Publishers Weekly* **65550-7 $3.50**

VINGE, VERNOR
The Peace War

Paul Hoehler has discovered the "Bobble Effect"—a scientific phenomenon that has been used to destroy every military installation on Earth. Concerned scientists steal Hoehler's invention—and implement a dictatorship which drives Earth toward primitivism. It is up to Hoehler to stop the tyrants.

55965-6 $3.50